Satsang with Baba
Questions and answers with Swami
Muktananda

January 3-April 24, 1972

Volume Two

LCCN 76-1384
ISBN 0-914602-31-4

Copyright © 1976 Gurudev Siddha Peeth, Ganeshpuri, India
All rights reserved.
published by S.Y.D.A. Foundation, P.O. Box 11071, Oakland, California 94611

Printed in United States of America

Bhagawan Sri Nityananda

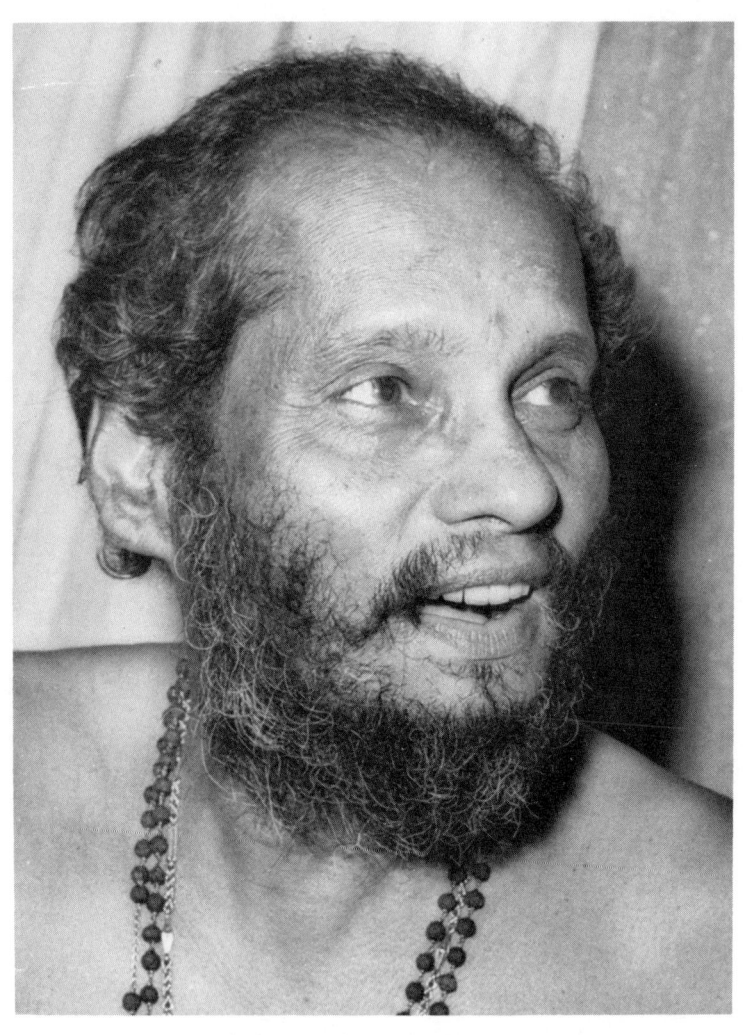

Baba Muktananda

INTRODUCTION

"I welcome you all with all my heart."

This is what Baba Muktananda always says whenever people gather around him. In the case of this second volume of Satsang With Baba, it's not just a welcome to a book, but to an experience—being with Baba in his Ashram in Ganeshpuri from January through April, 1972.

As with Volume One, this book is drawn from the Question and Answer sessions that took place during the period between Baba's first and second World Tours. It was a unique time in Ashram history. Westerners were coming to Ganeshpuri in large numbers, and Baba responded to the new situation in his characteristic way by giving more and more of himself.

The needs of the growing Western population in the Ashram were reflected not only in these satsangs, but in every area of Ashram life. Baba's genius is not restricted to just one facet of life, but runs rampant; it oozes out of every pore, flavours every gesture, resonates in every word. No matter what he turns his attention to, it receives a kind of magic touch that makes it blossom, grow and flourish.

These Satsangs With Baba are a modern scripture in the traditional Indian sense—that is, they are the expression of one who is permanently established in the highest truth. Only what makes these books so unique and exciting is that the gaze of this divine consciousness is focused on problems that arose out of the concrete and tangible situations and events of the everyday life of the people with Baba in 1972. And Baba's answers, both individually and collectively, reveal that consciousness. They give us a glimpse of his state.

These pages contain a wealth of knowledge on a wide variety of subjects. The context of spiritual life is life itself. Baba makes us realise that there is no separation between worldly and spiritual life. In fact, what happens is that one's whole life becomes spiritual the minute he looks at it with right understanding. According to Baba, it is God who has become the world. It is God who has become us. So to find God what we have to do is find our Self.

Although as a Siddha Baba is part of an ancient tradition of India, he is not bound to any rituals, cult, sect or religion. At the same time, he uses the tools of his tradition that he has tried and tested himself. Therefore, his advice is extremely practical, even when it seems to be most sublime. When he says, "See God in each other. God dwells within you as you," he is not asking us to believe in some high-sounding philosophy or concepts. He means for us to actually go about learning how to see God in each other and ourselves.

Gurus are saints. They are a boon to all mankind. They are aware of the purpose of life and they bring others to that awareness. They benefit all who come into their sphere of activity. And they love seekers. That is what comes across most in Baba's answers: his deep love.

So, this is really just a big hunk of Baba's love which has taken the form of a book so that it can get around in the world. The love that was shared by Baba and his devotees in these sessions is offered to you. Have some. Enjoy.

—Uma Berliner

January 3, 1972

Ram: *Could you please explain the attitude that is necessary to perform Guruseva properly?*
Baba: To perform Guruseva you need to identify yourself with the Guru, you need devotion for him. Identification with the Guru, Gurubhava, is possible only when you become aware of the true nature of the Guru. Only when one begins to understand that the Guru encompasses all gods and goddesses, all holy places, all duties, all rituals and actions, would he be in a position to acquire Gurubhava. If we take the example of the greatest saints of Maharashtra, who were also great writers and poets, such as Jnaneshwar and Eknath Maharaj, we find that they attained their high state only because of their ideal Gurubhava. The Guru has been given a most important place in all the books dealing with spiritual philosophy, and in epics such as the *Mahabharata* we find Gurubhava considered to be very important in many different contexts. Even in daily life, for the learning of trivial ordinary skills, you have to treat your teachers with great respect and honour. Many people come here telling me that they learned a particular skill from a particular teacher and they speak of him with warm admiration. Then how great and deep should our feeling of devotion to the Guru be? But we cannot develop such a feeling if our mentality is vicious, if it is low. Only when we rise to the level of the Guru would we be able to entertain true devotion for him. The purer we become, the greater the inner transformation that we undergo, the more sattvic our minds become, the more our attitude towards the Guru also changes, and we discover new depths in him, new greatness in him, new dimensions in him. Our devotion and faith also increase.

There is a very significant story relating to the Guru-disciple relationship between Govinda Singh and Nanak Dev. Govinda Singh would always ask Nanak Dev, "Please say something about the importance of the Guru, about his state, about his role, about his ways."

And Nanak Dev would always say, "As you move

towards the ideal of discipleship you will come to understand the glory of the Guru yourself. I don't have to talk on the subject."

One day, to drive the point home, Nanak Dev took out a jewel from his pocket and gave it to Govinda Singh and asked him to go into the market and approach every dealer, from the smallest to the biggest, and find out how much each was willing to pay for it and come back and tell him about it. It was a jewelled bracelet. First he went to a vegetable seller and asked him what he would pay for it. He said, "I'll give you two bundles of this vegetable." These days it costs about ten paise, but those days it couldn't have cost more than one.

Then he went to a flower seller and asked him, "What will you pay for it?" He said, "I'll give you one garland in return for it." That garland could not have been worth more than Rs. 1/25.

Then he went to a fruit vendor and said, "What would you give for it?" He said, "Three apples."

Then he went to an ordinary grocer who offered to pay two pounds of rice in return for it. Then to a petty goldsmith, who priced it at Rs. 100/-, then to a better jeweller, and he said that he would pay Rs. 1,000/-. Then he went to a still better jeweller, who offered to pay Rs. 20,000/-. Then he went to the biggest jeweller of the town and he said, "Look, it's invaluable, it's impossible to pay its price. You shouldn't sell it. What would you gain by selling it?"

All these different people were not really evaluating the ornament, but were evaluating their own worth. Therefore, to be able to serve the Guru properly, first be a true disciple; then alone will you know what it means to serve the Guru properly, and what it means to be devoted to him. If you wish to understand it fully, then you should look up Jnaneshwar, particularly Jnaneshwar's comment on the phrase 'Acharyopasanam', service to the Guru, or worship of the Guru, occurring in the 13th chapter of *Jnaneshwari*, his commentary on the *Gita*. Just as we are sensitive to climate or weather, when it goes bad we react to it, similarly we should be sensitive to our Guru. This is what is meant by Gurubhava. Just as we identify ourselves with our senses, with our body, with our minds, similarly we should identify ourselves with the Guru, feeling that he is as essential for us as the mind, the vital forces, and the senses.

Barry: *Will you speak about our duty and debt to our parents? What should my course of action be when living in my parents' home for an extended period, if certain spiritual practices learned here are prohibited by their religion, at least on the surface, and rational explanations do not help?*
Baba: Not only according to Indian culture, but according to the ideals of humanity, it is everyone's prime duty to take good care of his parents, to behave in a way that would be acceptable to them, and in their old age, to make them happy. A child's duty is to give financial security to his parents. Once that has been done, he should not be affected at all by their attitude to his spiritual practices.

It is not at all good for one's family to be unsympathetic to one's spiritual leanings. They are doing no good to one of their own. If the head of a family tries to keep his children away from God, devotion, good conduct and character, away from divine virtues, then he is sure to bring about a downfall of the family. If your family cannot help you advance on the path, then of what use is a family? Does a family exist just for its members to work more and more for its sake, and rot like that? That is the reason why more and more families are breaking up, why antipathy towards family life is on the increase. Even if our family has no sympathy for our spiritual life, we must not give up our spiritual pursuits. It's not the family who is responsible for your spiritual growth, it is you yourself who are responsible for it.

It is sometimes seen that parents go off their rockers in their old age and they do not understand what you are doing. When it is time for you to meditate they would want you to sit and have a nonsensical chat with them. So you are not obliged to fulfil that sort of desire of theirs. There are quite a few children who come here whose parents are addicted to alcohol. Not only are they addicted, but they would also like their children to start drinking. Obviously in this situation the parents are being stupid and the child is fully justified in not obeying his parents' wishes. But that doesn't mean that the child should be negative towards them or that he should withdraw financial security from his parents. But in such matters he has every right not to obey them. There are other parents of children who come here who are addicted to a frivolous life and they would like their children to follow in their illustrious footsteps. Such children are justified in living apart from their parents.

A child's duty is to extend protection and financial help to his parents. Beyond that, he is under no obligation to follow their religious practices or their ideas of religion. In fact, if anyone tries to obstruct your contemplation of God, your meditation on the inner Self, or any other spiritual practices, then you should consider him to be your worst enemy, whatever his relationship to you may be.

Mira belonged to a royal family and in those days kings thought that they were the Almighty Himself, and they did not understand spiritual practices. They thought it was below their dignity to practise devotion, and they began to torment her. They did not let her sing or chant, they did not let her meet any saints or go to any temples. When she found herself in such a situation, she wrote to Tulsidas and asked his advice. She wrote, "I am in a fix. On the one hand there is the demand of my duty to my husband, and on the other hand, there is this inner spiritual longing. Which should I prefer?" Tulsidas wrote back in a song that consists of seven couplets. He says, "If anyone tries to obstruct your meditation on the inner Self, your devotion to the Lord or your other spiritual practices, you should discard him as your worst enemy, even if he happens to be your best friend, your most beloved relation." Prahlada, when he found that his father was opposed to his devotion to the Lord, gave up his father. Bharat gave up his mother when she opposed his devotion to Rama. Bali gave up his teacher when he interfered with his devotion to God, and Vibhishan gave up his brother.

Therefore, do not let anyone interfere with your spiritual disciplines. If they do not help you, at least don't let them hinder you. If they try to stop you, you may tell them, "I can see what your beliefs and way of life have brought you and I have no desire to make the same mistakes."

Larry: *What should the attitude of the Ashramites be*

toward the crowds that come here and the subsequent confusion? Should we remind them of the discipline or should we just mind our own business?

Baba: There is no harm in reminding people of the discipline that prevails here. Generally people are not very disciplined and this is perhaps the only place where people behave in a disciplined manner. If you were to go anywhere else, you would find them behaving in a most disorderly fashion. There is no harm in your telling people to be quiet and to behave themselves here. They know what purpose they have come here for. If the occasion demands, then you can even tell them in a stern tone to be quiet and well-disciplined. But usually your tone should be polite and gentle. Quite frequently you will have to receive terms of abuse in return, but you should bear with them, too. A month ago a certain family came here. They quarrelled with practically everyone here, and yesterday I pulled a fast one on them. I asked somebody to take them for lunch. Then I went and stood right in front of them and told two servers, "Serve only them, because these people are addicted to being taken a notice of everywhere, and if they are not taken a notice of they make a hell of a lot of noise and disturb others' peace. Don't mind about whether others are served or not, you take care of only them." After finishing their meal, they came to me and begged forgiveness. Then I asked them, "Why did you behave so foolishly the other day? Would you permit every passerby in Bombay to come into your house? What makes you think that we would permit all sorts of people to come here and move about freely in our Ashram which is full of so many valuable things? This Ashram must not be treated like the Hanging Gardens in Bombay."

They said, "We shall never behave like that again," and I said, "I, too, will never speak like that again."

The Ashram has to be run in a very skillful manner. There should be a combination of tact, good humour, and also sternness. All kinds of people with all sorts of motives visit the Ashram. First you have genuine seekers who come here for meditation and spiritual growth. Then there is a class of people who know that we serve a very good lunch here, and that is what brings them to this place. And then there are people who would like to take advantage of the crowds and pick pockets. The last class consists of burglars who would like to find entry into the dorms and rooms and rummage through the boxes. In Marathi there are four rhyming terms which are used to describe these four classes of people.

Yesterday at least 5,000-6,000 people must have come to visit me, and I wonder how many of them came out of devotion and love, or for meditation. They must be rare. The day before, a person dressed as a gentleman tried to deceive Desai, and introduced himself as the Assistant Charity Commissioner. He was being quite clever. He knew that the Charity Commissioner would be treated with utmost respect in the Ashram, because the Ashram is a public trust. So Desai immediately gave him a very good suite. But he would not come near me. I asked Desai again and again to call him, because I wanted to have a look at him, but he would not oblige. The next day, I myself went to his room and I could see that he was a ruffian.

Then I told Desai that I suspected that he was a fake and he should go and find out what the fact was. Mr. Wankhede, Yande's boss, holds the Charity portfolio, so Yande knows all the Charity Commissioners working under him. Then Yande went there and took out his stick, telling him, "You rogue, you dare to cheat such a big important Ashram?" Then we came to learn that while traveling by public bus he told the driver that he was one of the bus inspectors and didn't pay for his ticket.

We should not keep our eyes closed or remain blind to these characters, because the Ashram is so large; we have to be very wide awake and alert. If you happen to find any strange character prowling around, stop him and ask him what he's doing. Because it is fear that makes people behave themselves. You should not be misled or misguided by what the textbooks tell you—that you should be full of forgiveness and love and all that stuff. If we extended forgiveness and love to all these characters, none of you would be here, you would all have been kidnapped by this time, including me. If you were to go to the Samadhi in town and make inquiries you would find that many pockets were picked and many purses were stolen and many people were ill-treated. But you won't get any such reports about this place. There was a time when some of the old devotees would come and complain to me that the people on duty at the gate would not let them in, in spite of the fact that they told them they were old devotees. I had given strict instructions to the people on duty: "You should not at all listen to any such pleas that 'I am an old devotee'. You should insist on discipline in their case like you would insist on it in any other case." Therefore, if you find anyone mishandling any Ashram property, or behaving in a frivolous manner, or treating the place without any respect, you can turn him out. I am quite aware of the fact that there are people who come here only for frolic and are not interested in what an ashram is. We are a community which is disciplined and self-controlled and we live a very regular and very orderly life, so nobody from the outside has the right to disturb the quiet and order which prevails here. Such people should stay out. We don't need such characters. Even if you find some such characters among the new devotees, who have no respect for the Ashram discipline, who move around in a most irresponsible manner, who come here only to fill our septic tanks with their stinking shit, but who are not prepared to abide by our rules and discipline, and have no respect for our ways, you can tell them to behave themselves, because we do not need all these characters here. There are so many people living in the Ashram and all of them work so hard to keep the Ashram neat and clean and pure, and if there are people who claim to be devotees, but who don't show any respect for the work, they are not needed here. Everyone should come here to learn something, not to spoil the beauty of the place. All the visitors should know how to sit and how to stand, and how to carry themselves, and they should help the Ashramites keep the place neat and clean, not increase the burden of their work. In the Ashram we have seekers who are very intelligent, who are well educated, who come from decent families, and who are cultured, and who work very hard to keep the place so pure and clean. If there are visitors who have no respect for this, who do not show any consciousness of the value of the work of the Ashramites, then they have no business here. They have absolutely no worth in my eyes. Everyone should treat the Ashram as a very sacred and pure place and treat the

Ashram things with great love and reverence. What's the point of utterly stupid and irrational conduct in an Ashram like this which is full of Shakti and which is saturated with spiritual particles? What's the point of sitting anywhere in any frivolous manner, mishandling Ashram things, breaking Ashram property or giving other examples of your lack of consideration?

Uma: *No matter how wide awake I may be when I sit down to recite Guru Gita, by the time I have sung three verses my head droops and the book slips from my hand, and I go out. Is this sleep, or the state of dhyan? Sometimes it happens in Vishnu Sahasranam too. What should I do about it?*
Baba: This happens when the mind becomes perfectly one-pointed. When the mind becomes one-pointed it's difficult to keep it focused on the book, and it passes either into the state of sleep or the state of tandra. What happens is very good, but at the same time you should try to pull yourself out of it immediately. That state which may appear to be like sleep or tandra, that state of one-pointedness is a samadhi state, but you should not forget that you are getting that state from swadhyaya, so you should not neglect swadhyaya. That state will come of its own accord so you should not neglect swadhyaya and prefer that state. You should continue the swadhyaya and that samadhi state will follow you. Therefore, continue to recite the *Vishnu Sahasranam* or *Guru Gita* until the very end, with great reverence. What happens in this state to your mind is known as shravana samadhi—samadhi which comes through listening or through reading of holy texts. While you are reciting holy texts you are likely to pass into this state.

Ramesh Agrawal: *Even if you have found the Sadguru who is Lord Shiva Himself, and you are living in an Ashram which is full of the flames of the fire of yoga and yet you are not able to meditate, how can you explain this? And what should one do about it so that one may be able to meditate?*
Baba: If you have found the Sadguru you should become a disciple, a true disciple. There was somebody who asked,

"Even if you were to have just one dip in the holy Narmada you would get liberation. Then how come this rock which has been lying here for hundreds of years has not gotten liberation?"

If your heart happens to be dull and impervious, how can you lay it on the Ashram? There is no reason for despair. Try to put fresh vigour into your heart, for the Ashram is good, the Guru is good, but if you yourself are not good, what can the Ashram or Guru do about it? However, you should not worry. Continue to do japa intensely and continue to sit for meditation. Meditation will come in due course.

Kedarnath: *Does the Shakti received from the Guru through his grace begin to guide the disciple from within of its own accord, and if so, how should one make sure that a particular demand coming from within is coming from the Guru or Shakti received from him, and not the voice of a supressed craving or the voice of a latent illusion?*
Baba: Yes, the Shakti does guide the seeker from within. It's a delusion to consider the urging of the inner Shakti as an illusion. If the urging of the inner Shakti is an illusion, then the Guru, too, is an illusion, and you, too, are an illusion. If you begin to doubt the inner Shakti then the Shakti can also turn against you. However, you should see whether the commands from within are proper or not, and then you can always approach the Guru and find out from him which commands should be obeyed, and which should not be. This question should not come from a person who is living in the Ashram. It is all right if someone living away from the Ashram were to put this question, because if you are in any difficult situation I am available all the time and you can come to me and ask me what you should do; you don't have to turn to the inner voice to find out what you should do. Whether the commands which you receive from within are valid depends on how pure you are, how much faith and devotion you have. If you are false then the commands that you receive from within would also be false. If you are true, they too will be true. But if you are a cheat, the inner voice will also cheat you. Those are the voices which would only lead you astray. You should continue to meditate and culti-

vate witness-consciousness and you should not worry about those inner commands.

January 5, 1972

Jyoshi: *My body is that of a brahmin. From my student days right up to my present age, I have been living on alms received from others. Being a brahmin, people make gifts of food, clothing and even money to me, and for this reason I am in debt to society. Please let me know how I can clear myself of this debt to society.*
Baba: You can be free of this debt through tapasya, and you should do something for society in return. You should also change your attitude now. Previously you might have thought that people belonging to a certain caste were brahmin, but after coming here you should think that the world which has come from God is divine, and everyone because he comes from Brahman is a brahmin. However, there is no harm in accepting gifts from friends, relations, and others who make them of their own accord, without your begging for them. You should keep only as much with you as you need. The rest you should give away as you have received. When one is able to rise above body-consciousness through meditation and knowledge, one becomes free from everything including debt.

Hari Prasad: *My financial position is not good and I am also under heavy debts, due to which I have not been able to make any advances in the yoga of meditation. I have not been able to progress either in the field of spirituality or in worldly life. Please tell me what I should do.*
Baba: If you are under debt to people, it would be very difficult for you to attain God-realisation or to meditate. It is for this reason that our ancient seers emphasized renun-

ciation so much. Their renunciation was so great that they ate only a handful of food—just for bare survival. If you are a man with a family, with wife and children, it is much better to take a job somewhere, work and pay off your debts. You should realise that you are in your present condition of poverty because of your past bad karma, and if you persist in the same sort of karma now, what will happen to your future? One can take any job and earn enough to meet one's needs. Take my case: even during the period of my sadhana I never liked to receive food in charity. I always worked for it. I carried earth, did dishes, swept floors, picked up dung but I did not sell any spiritual Shakti just for a handful of food. If you meditate and chant the Name of the Lord for a little time, and run into debt to others for that, you will lose its benefit. I am reminded of a verse in this connection. The seers say that the tongue gets burnt by eating charity, by not working for food. It cannot then acquire any power from japa, swadhyaya and asceticism. One's hands can acquire tremendous spiritual powers through tapasya. Take the case of my Guru. Even if he gave a stone to somebody, that would work miracles. But those hands that are always accepting gifts, always begging alms, get consumed. Similarly, the heart gets consumed through continuous thinking about worldly problems, about the petty things of everyday life. How can you then obtain peace or liberation or bliss? Whatever way that is suitable for you, you must work for your own bread, and if you keep working with perseverence, God, too, will help you, sooner or later.

Malou: *Once Baba gave the example of Lakshman's obedience to Rama in leaving Sita in a forest, even though he didn't think it was the right thing to do. On the other hand, last week Baba said that it may happen that one may have to disobey his parents, and even his Guru. Is it possible with a Sadguru? Can he test the disciples' discrimination in giving orders?*
Baba: If a teacher takes you away from your Self and God, puts you on a wrong path, and leaves you anywhere dry and empty, you must discard him. Bali discarded his Guru. Anyone who tries to deprive you of your faith in your Self, who condemns the science of the Self, who compels you to give

up your duty to your Self, who takes you away from inner peace, you have every right to discard, whether he is your father, mother, brother, friend or Guru. If there are any obligations that obstruct your spiritual practices, those, too must be discarded. But, we must remember that Bali's teacher was a demoniacal teacher, and he had certain impurities, and that was why he had to be given up. One will never be compelled to give up a real Guru. In fact, it is the disciple's supreme duty to have faith in the Guru and obey him.

The Guru tests the disciple quite frequently. When he puts a test, the disciple should make sure that he gets through that. The disciple must pass the test; it does not matter whether he obeys or disobeys the Guru on a particular occasion. If you spend a long time in the Guru's abode, you must be able to gain perfect understanding of the Guru's words, of what exactly he has said. There was a Guru who had a large number of disciples and one day he called two of them, handed an apple to each of them and said, "Go and eat this apple in a corner where there is nobody to watch you. If you are able to do this, I will honour you with a high title and make you a Guru, and authorise you to have your own disciples."

One went eastward, and the other westward in search of a corner where nobody would see him. They went here, they went there. Finally one landed in a deserted forest. He looked around to see if anybody was watching him. He then devoured his apple hastily because he wanted to be the first to go back. He was afraid that the other one would return before him and get the Guru's throne. If you become a disciple just for honour and not for Guruhood, you lose discrimination. This specimen rushed back to the Guru in the hope that he would immediately succeed him. He said to the Guru, "Sir, let me be your successor. I ate the fruit where nobody was watching." But the other one came back after a long time with the uneaten apple, and placed it before the Guru. He said, "I thought it over and pondered this question very deeply, and I went to so many places, yet I could not find a corner where nobody would see me. According to the knowledge received from you, wherever I went I found myself surrounded by the elements of earth, air, water, fire and ether and if none of these was present, at least I was present, consciousness was present, and I could not find any place which was without consciousness, which was pure void. That is why I have come back with the apple."

The Guru said, "You deserve to be my successor."

The other who had eaten the apple had only received an apple, whereas he received Guruhood. Therefore, the tests prescribed by the Guru are sometimes very strange, and it's very difficult to pass them. Even if you are prostrating yourself to him all the time and showing him the utmost reverence, it doesn't mean that you have become a true disciple, who only obeys his Guru's command. Usually the Guru will ask you to do something that is good for you and you should obey him. However, if there is a command from the Guru which seems to go against the scriptures, which would alienate you from your own Self, you have to pause and think very deeply whether you should obey it or not.

Kalyani: *There are many teachers who prescribe exercises and other external practices to arouse the Kundalini. What could be the result of such an awakening, if it were to occur without the guidance of a perfected Master?*

Baba: There are some people who by means of Hatha Yogic processes, particularly mudras and the three bandhas (locks), try to arouse the Kundalini. Even if the Kundalini were awakened, it would be very difficult for one to lead it upwards, because that is not so easy. If the Kundalini were not to rise in a proper manner then it may prove to be harmful. Besides, in such a case a seeker, right from the moment his Kundalini is awakened, up to the moment when it finally merges in the sahasrar, has to depend on exercises all the time, has to depend on others. But when Kundalini awakening takes place through grace, it is most natural and spontaneous. Moreover, She works of Her own accord in those centres where Her work is necessary. And She stops Her activity at the right time. So there is absolutely no danger. Besides, the seeker now becomes Shakti's responsibility. Sometimes your Kundalini may get aroused by external means, but the important question is whether this awakening is going to last, or whether it's just a brief episode.

There are many seekers coming here from different teachers who tell me, "Babaji, I have come to a dead end. I cannot meditate, I am not making any progress. Kriyas have stopped. My inner state is not yet worthwhile. I don't feel enthusiasm for anything." Therefore it is always better to have the Kundalini aroused by one who has already achieved perfection. If the Kundalini is aroused by a lesser teacher it may not be so rewarding. In this case, one gets stuck, unable to reach the final goal.

Girija: *Upon reflection I came to the conclusion that all my insecurity, fear, defensiveness and feelings of inferiority are due to a sense of being unloved. Is this correct? Is this just an impurity of my own heart, or does it mean that my parents were not sufficiently loving? Would you please speak about what love is?*
Baba: It's a very good question. I thank you for that. This is a question that is very close to my heart, because independence is very dear to me, freedom from dependence on others is what I cherish the most.

There was a certain companion of mine who used to study Vedanta with me, and he also later became a swami, his name is Swami Satchidananda Saraswati. Whenever we talked about our parents, I would talk about my parents with great pride, telling him how wonderfully they had taken care of me, and the different presents they had given me, and with what love they fed me. And when he would hear that he would flare up, because he was full of hatred for his parents, and was always complaining that his parents had done nothing for him, had given him nothing. If his parents were present before him at that moment, he would even hit them with rocks. I got so fed up with his tirade against his parents that I stopped talking about my parents. One day I asked him, "How much land did you have, how large was your house and family?"

He said, "Well, we had no land, and my father is dead, and my mother used to do some petty menial work and would get a few pennies for that and she would give me something to eat with great difficulty. In fact, I had to be looked after by some other family."

I said, "Look, aren't you stupid. You have been blaming

your parents for not giving you what they did not have. I talk about my parents with such pride because my parents were very wealthy, they had everything, and they could give me so much because they had so much. You abuse your parents for nothing"'

Satchidananda realised his mistake and said, "What you say is true. I will not talk against them from now on."

Similarly, most parents do not have love. They also long for love. What they do not have they cannot give to you. They may give you cakes, clothes, or a bottle of cream in the name of love, but if they have no love in their hearts, how can they give love to you?

You ask for love from your parents because of the weakness of your own heart. You never cared to discover the treasure of love hidden within your own being and enjoy it. For this reason you want it from others. I am telling everyone all the time that if one is weak and helpless, he always wants things from others and suffers.

Now we have so many Ashramites here and all of them are contributing work, doing the various Ashram chores. But there was a time when there were only three of us here, Venkappa, one other person and myself. At that time only the three of us would do all the Ashram work right from washing the toilets to washing clothes and dishes, gardening, and agriculture. We did not depend on others. There are certain devotees who have known me for the past thirty or forty years, and I can challenge anyone to say that I ever complained that "He never gave me anything. He never served me with food or drink. He never brought any offerings." I would not complain like this even when I get annoyed with somebody. If there is anyone who could say that I did complain, I will give him a special reward. Now so many people come to this Ashram. I never think that anything given by others could help me in any way.

Therefore look for contentment within yourself. This is certain: if you want happiness from others you will receive misery, but if you look for it within yourself you will always be full of bliss. Joy lies within your own soul, and you are looking for it outside. How can you find it outside when it doesn't exist there? It's just like my friend complaining that his mother never gave him anything, when the fact was the poor thing had nothing to give. There is a vast ocean of bliss surging inside. In fact it is more than enough for your needs. No one should expect or beg love from other people; everyone should find it within himself. Everyone should start loving himself, his senses, his body, his mind and his inner spirit. I am reminded of a verse from the *Mahabharata* which occurs in a dialogue between Krishna and Duryodhana. The Lord tried every possible way to persuade Duryodhana to give up his evil course, to give up his stubbornness. He said that if he did not want to return the entire kingdom to Yudhisthira, then he should give half of it, if not half of it, then a quarter, if not a quarter, then even less. And then He also painted a very grim picture of the consequences that would follow his stubborn refusal: he would be destroyed, his entire family would be destroyed, all his friends would be killed, nothing would survive. The Lord tried to frighten him in every possible way, but it did not have any effect on Duryodhana. After he had heard all that the Lord had said, Duryodhana began to speak. He said, "Lord, You say that this course of action will bring me misery, or this person will bring me happiness, and that person will cause me misery. But that is entirely wrong, because nobody can give me either happiness or misery. Man reaps the consequences of his own actions."

Everyone reaps the fruits of his own karma. Therefore you should begin to love your own Self, love your own body, love your own face, love your own mind, love your own inner Self. You should honour yourself. You should sit in a solitary corner and look at your body. Say to it, "How beautiful this body is; it is endowed with such wonderful capabilities. It has eyes which can see things in such a beautiful manner. God Himself dwells in it. Prana and apana flow in it. It has a mind which can think. It is the seat of bliss and gladness. How blessed I am. What more could I need? Is there anything that I could want when I have such a perfect system?" This is the best kind of love.

Ramesh Agrawal: *I have been told that it is possible to attain knowledge and meditation through one's own effort, but for devotion one has to turn to divine grace, devotion can be received only through Guru's grace. Is that correct?*

Baba: The Guru's grace is essential for everything. For devotion, for knowledge, for yoga and meditation as well. You do not seem to have understood this fully; you have grasped only a little bit of it. The scriptures say that for knowledge one should approach a Sadguru, and get initiation from him. That applies to devotion also. It comes by the grace of a realised saint, says Narada. One needs Guru's grace for everything. But then the Guru also needs grace—the disciple's grace.

Jorgon: As far as I know, two factors decide how long one is going to live. One is prarabdha, and the other is an allotted number of breaths. Does this mean that the number of breaths are a part of prarabdha? Is it possible to extend life through pranayama?

Baba: The yoga texts and yogis say that if you consume less pranic Shakti through pranayama you can prolong your life. But you do not find even a single great saint or great yogi who would do that in order to live for a long time. I am talking about the very greatest ones. Take the case of Jnaneshwar Maharaj, whose greatness cannot be described in words. He left his body when he was just a boy, and that is what happened with Shankaracharya, Hasta Malaka, Ram Tirth, Vivekananda and others. From this one is forced to conclude that though pranayama may enable you to consume less pranashakti and make your prana strong, steady, as far as the span of your life is concerned, it depends entirely on prarabdha, not on any allotted number of breaths. Kabir says in this connection that on the sixth day after the birth of a child, when a special rite is performed, God Himself comes down and decides the destiny of the child, and that cannot be altered. So the allotted span of your life can neither be increased nor decreased. Tulsidas also says that whatever had to be allotted has already been allotted. Therefore, you should live free from anxiety.

Besides, for a great yogi a long life does not have any special charm. Only unintelligent, undiscerning fools go after a long life, and scream and cry and suffer the miseries of this world for a longer period. If you were to think about it deeply, you would find that there is really nothing in life that would tempt a genuine yogi to prolong his life. To eat the same food day after day, to use all kinds of devices to digest that food, to excrete it, to wash oneself and to eat again, to suffer from indigestion on eating too much, to put more into the belly if one has eaten less, to take pills on catching cold, to take pills on suffering from heat, to take pills if the head aches—to take pills on every pretext, to wrap a blanket around oneself when it gets chilly, to eat ice cream when it gets hot—this way just to manage to survive, somehow or other—which yogi would cling to such a troublesome life? However, this is true: pranayama purifies the prana and makes it even, and when the prana becomes pure the entire body becomes pure and one enjoys a perfect sense of well being.

January 7, 1972

Asha Bhagavat: *My second daughter, 18 years old, is always complaining of lack of love from me. She doesn't want to stay at home, she has no regard for her parents, in spite of the fact that she is given enough money and facilities, and the atmosphere at home is very pure and disciplined. What should I do?*

Baba: Your daughter seems to be lacking in love, and if there is a girl who has no love for her parents, she will have no love for her home, and if she has no love for her home, she will have no love for her near and dear ones, and if she has no love for her near and dear ones she would not even care about her duty. Ask her, "In what way would you like me to behave? It may be true that I have no love for you, but at least let me have some love from you. If the daughter doesn't get any love from the mother, let the mother get some love from the daughter." It shows that her understanding is defective and that is why she is behaving the way she is. In course of time she will change.

Dr. R. Rai: *If you are not able to meditate even after doing japa, what should you do?*
Baba: This is a very concise question and is worthy of being given a prize. People ask such long questions and one wonders what they are asking. He has stated his question very concisely and in answer to this I can speak for two hours. This question is very properly phrased. Most people are fond of giving lectures on the pretext of putting questions.

It does not matter if you are not able to meditate or pass into the state of tandra, or if you are not able to achieve concentration. What matters is japa. Continue to do japa, because japa has great divine power. When Lord Shiva was asked a question about the importance of japa He said, "Dear beautiful-faced One, by japa, realisation; by japa, realisation; by japa, realisation." It's neither necessary nor proper for one who is practising japa to complain that such and such experiences have not come, that this has not happened or that has not happened. All these considerations are neither relevant nor respected by the scriptures. I can assure you that japa does not go to waste. However, it does not bear fruit immediately; it takes time. But when it begins to bear fruit it will fulfil you. Therefore, persist with japa. If you were to look at it from a subtler viewpoint, then you would realise that even if the mind were to become completely still as a result of japa, how would that matter? While if you were to practise a lot of japa that would certainly be of great advantage to you. I will give you an analogy to explain this. Take the case of a man who is cutting the same branch on which he is sitting, and seems to be deluded that he is secure. But when the time to fall comes, it will not take him even a moment to drop down. Similarly, one who is practising japa may feel all the while that nothing is happening, but when it begins to bear fruit it will not take more than a moment. Kings such as Janaka and seers such as Vyasa attained the highest realisations through japa. Why should you worry so much about your mind? Why do you chase it so much? Continue to do japa. One who is really interested in japa or nam, who is a japa yogi, or a nam yogi, is not at all interested in emptying the mind of all thoughts, because if he were to empty his mind he would not be able to do japa any longer, and it is japa which is his very life. Leave the mind alone. If the mind were to cease working completely, how would you do japa?

Dr. Kapur: *A few days after I received Shaktipat I found that my eyesight had begun to improve and I could read without glasses, and I could even see distant objects, but now again, I need glasses as before. Does this deterioration show that something has gone wrong with my meditation?*
Baba: It's quite in order that your eyesight remain the same as it was before you received Shaktipat. Your eyesight will not become weaker. Even now if you were able to meditate deeply enough, it might be possible for you to see without glasses. But why should you want to do that? Why not see with your glasses? You shouldn't spend the sacred Shakti acquired through meditation on just seeing trees and leaves. It is enough that the Shakti has demonstrated Her power to you once. You may be able to discard your glasses, but then that is not necessary, and your eyesight will not deteriorate further; it will stay at the same point at which it was before you received Shaktipat. Continue to meditate deeply and use Shakti for something else. If you used that divine power just to get rid of your glasses, then you wouldn't be able to have other realisations.

Uma: *How can I be rid of the desire to listen to good music, to see ballets, and hear operas? It has been a habit since early childhood.*
Baba: All habits are rooted in childhood. All people crave the pleasures of the five senses. You are no exception. Through ballets you receive the pleasure of form, and through music you receive the pleasure of sound. I am reminded of a verse in which the poet says, "Take the case of an elephant: an elephant is a slave to the sense of touch, and he even loses his life because of clinging to the pleasure of touch. The deer is a slave to the sense of smell, and for smell he lays down his life. A serpent is a slave to music, to the sense of sound, and he loses his life for the pleasure of sound. A fish is a slave to the sense of taste, and a moth to the sense of sight, and they lay down their lives for the pleasures of taste and sight." The poet says that each of

these creatures lost his life because he was a slave to only one sense pleasure. "How pitiful your plight is, O man, because you are addicted to all five different forms of pleasure. How can you ever save yourself?"

This is nothing special in your case; everybody is addicted to one sense pleasure or another. You should try to overcome this desire and try to listen to the inner music in meditation. Ordinary music is without any real delight, without any real taste, while the chant of *Hari Ram* is full of sweetness and nectar. Therefore, you should exercise firm control over yourself. Look at this deerskin. We have it here because the deer was a slave and was irresistibly drawn towards music and was killed. Before he was killed, the deer said to the hunter, "It doesn't matter if you kill me, but at least sit on my skin when you have killed me, so that I can hear you play your instrument."

Randy: *Do Westerners who do not understand Sanskrit or Hindi derive as much benefit from the chanting and recitation of the Guru Gita as those who understand the words that they are chanting?*
Baba: What makes you think that while Indians understand the *Guru Gita* the Westerners do not. The *Guru Gita* is in Sanskrit. Very few Indians know Sanskrit. Here there are only two women who understand Sanskrit; one is the dark Amma and the other is the fair Amma. The third person is Vyas, the brahmin who recites the Vedic verses. Still we all recite it. We recite the *Guru Gita* in honour of the Guru, and if the Guru understands it, there is no need for us to understand it. Our inner Self understands it in any case. I am reminded of a conversation between Ram Tirth and a mendicant. In a certain place a fakir was praying to the Lord in Sanskrit verses. Ram Tirth asked him, "Do you understand what you are saying?"

He said, "Look, I don't need to understand what I am saying. Only God needs to understand what I am saying. All that I need is to pray and it is for Him to understand."

The *Guru Gita* must bear its fruit whether you understand it or not. Therefore, you must recite the *Guru Gita*. Just today we have started reciting the *Guru Gita* in the morning. For some time we chanted the *Bhagavad Gita* in the morning and everyone learned to read it well. And after that we recited the *Vishnu Sahasranam* for some time, and that way everyone could learn that, too. Now we have taken up the *Guru Gita*. The *Guru Gita* is the foremost among all the *Gitas*. It bestows all powers and realisations. For some time we will continue to recite the *Guru Gita* every morning. The Guru holds a high place in the world, and only a true disciple can understand his significance. The Guru's significance cannot be understood by one who is not a disciple. The Guru's greatness defies all words. If you continue to sing of the glories of the Guru you achieve Gurubhava or identity with the Guru. The *Guru Gita* says that Gurubhava is the holiest water. We bathe in holy waters to purify ourselves. For purification, we practise yoga, meditation and prayer. Gurubhava is the best of all these. It completely purifies the inner being at once. The name of this Ashram is Shree Gurudev Ashram, it is dedicated to the Guru, and every day we perform arati to the Guru and we chant the *Guru Gita* and our mantra is *Guru Om*, because the Guru is our supreme deity.

The other day Marie asked me to narrate a story about the Guru, and that day, because it was late I said that I would narrate it next time. Once upon a time all the great saints of Maharashtra got together and decided to go on a pilgrimage together. They all went to Eknath Maharaj. They asked him to accompany them, assuring him that they would have very good satsang on the way, and that after a dip in the holy Ganges at Hardwar they would come back. Eknath said that he would ask his Guru about it. His Guru's name was Janardan Swami, and he was a great warrior, and also a great yogi, a warrior yogi. Eknath said that if his Guru agreed to come, then he, too, would join them. So Eknath went to his Guru and asked him, "Sir, would you accompany all the saints who are going to Hardwar for a holy dip?"

The Guru said, "It's the atman itself which is the highest, purest centre of pilgrimage. Now that I am old I do not feel like going anywhere. I would much prefer to remain here and meditate on the inner Self. If you like you can go and join the group."

Eknath told the group of saints that since his Guru was

not going, he would not go either. Such was the devotion of Eknath to his Guru. He gave a penny to the group of saints, and requested them to offer it on his behalf to the holy Ganges, telling her that Eknath could not come because he was engaged in service to his Guru, and she should accept his little offering graciously.

Eknath Maharaj is considered to be one of the most distinguished among the saints of Maharashtra, because the Lord Himself used to draw water for him. In the time of Eknath there were two tanks which had to be filled with water each day, and there was a boy called Shrikhand who used to fill them. People said that the boy was the Lord Himself. On Ekadasi day millions of people gather there. That place is not very far from here and maybe one day we shall undertake a pilgrimage to that place. There is a large tank still existing there, and all the pilgrims try to fill that tank, each pouring his share into it. No matter how hard they try, the tank remains half empty. Then all of them begin to sing with great vigour and chant *Jaya Jaya Rama Krishna Hari Hari* with great abandon, and begin to dance ecstatically, and then all of a sudden the tank is filled. People believe that the tank is filled by the Lord. Though Shrikhand is no more, the half-empty tank becomes full all of a sudden. The tank is as large as the inner court here. I stayed there for a long time, and about two years ago I made a visit to that place.

The group left the place with the penny given by Eknath. On the way they visited different places including Kashi, and finally they reached Hardwar. That group contained some of the greatest saints, who were Siddhas, such as Tukaram, the potter Gora, the maid Kanupatra, the barber Sena, the gardener Sauta. They came from all classes. The Ganges at Hardwar is particularly beautiful, particularly the portion called Hara ki Pedhi. It is a series of steps where you get into a different state all together for a while, and all the devotees go there and make their offerings of coins and flowers to the mother Ganges. All the saints stood on the bank and all of a sudden they remembered that the penny given by Eknath had to be offered, and they went down to the river to offer it. As the coin was about to be dropped, two hands appeared from below the water to catch it. Here the story ends. Such is the effect of devotion to the Guru. So deep was the devotion of Eknath to his Guru that the Lord felt indebted to Eknath for his devotion to the Guru and in return for that he began to draw water for him.

So, therefore, today is a day of special significance because this morning we started reciting the *Guru Gita*. I hope that by tomorrow morning everybody will be reciting the *Guru Gita* with great feeling and reverence.

Rajmohini: *What is the difference between the Sadguru and the formless Supreme Being?*
Baba: Though the two appear to be different, they are one. Though the Sadguru appears to have a form, he is really formless. The body of a Sadguru is not made of flesh; it is divine, being one with Brahman. You discover the glory of the Guru only when you get beyond the Blue Pearl. The Guru's body is fashioned by pure blue light, the light of consciousness. Therefore, there is no difference between the personal form of the Sadguru and the Formless Being. The Formless is the form and the form is the Formless.

Amrita: *What is the length and breadth of the inner Self? You find the Self on the one hand in an elephant, and on the other in an ant.*
Baba: You will have to measure it with a tape to find out how wide and long it is. The truth is that the atman is larger than the largest and smaller than the smallest. So how can you ever measure it? The atman is supremely subtle, supremely refined, and it pervades everything. It is so subtle that its subtlety cannot be grasped by even the most subtle use of the language. If you wish to describe the subtlety of the Self, then you have to discard language all together and become silent. It is so vast that it stretches from east to west and from north to south and above and below. It also lies beyond. It is both immanent and transcendent.

Larry: *What is meant by one's duty to oneself and society?*
Baba: Whatever man does for himself, follows for his own sake and considers worthy for himself, to do exactly the same for society is his duty to society. It is necessary to

follow all the social ideals of the religion of man. One should find out what is good and applicable for oneself, and that one can find out from the examples of great beings. What you think is good for yourself is also good for others; what you want to do for yourself you should do for others also. If there is a conflict between your duty to yourself and your duty to society, that means that you have become involved in self-deception. You want comforts and pleasures for yourself and all the good things for your children and you want to live in a very neat and beautiful place. To want the same for others and help them to get these is your duty to society. You should think that you are the society and society is you. You should live and act in society following the footsteps of great men.

Kailash Amma: *Why is madhur bhava considered to be the best form of devotion? (Madhur bhava is the love of the Gopis, the love which the wife has for her husband.)*
Baba: Madhur bhava is the state of true love, in which there is no cheating or deception. You find many so-called devotees coming to the Ashram and they always pester Desai about various things. They would go to him complaining that the lavatories are not clean, and should be cleaned immediately, or they haven't got proper accomodations, and should be accomodated in a proper suite. In spite of being looked after so well in the Ashram, if Desai happens to ask them to bring something, they come to me and complain that they are being forced to bring things for the Ashram. One should not try to cheat in the name of devotion. Desai should realise that those who come and stay here for a few days and fill our septic tanks with their stinking shit have done all that was necessary for them to do for the Ashram, and he should not ask them to do anything more.

Why should he ask such a cheat for anything which would make him conscious that he is a cheat? You want your room to be clean and if Desai happens to ask you for some soap powder to clean the room, why should you cry about it? And why should you later on talk secretly and ill-humouredly about it? You want the toilets to be clean, and if he asks for Fenol, why should you begin to complain? Such behaviour shows a very low mentality. This is not true devotion; this is only pretense of devotion. Such a one is only trying to cheat the Guru. In madhur bhava such an attitude would be utterly out of place, because madhur bhava is pure love. One who has madhur bhava would have pure love for the Guru, and he would not behave like the so-called devotees who want all kinds of favours for nothing.

Take the case of one who comes and complains about having to wait before he can get accomodations here, and he comes with a complaint about Desai, without realising that the poor fellow is already hard-worked, that he has to get up at three in the morning and go to sleep at ten at night, while the visitors fill their tummies to the utmost capacity and sleep their entire time away: they have the cheek to come with all kinds of complaints. When Desai asks you to bring something, it is not Desai who is asking, it is in fact Muktananda Swami himself who is asking you to bring something. What Desai says is, "Baba, a certain devotee wants five bedsheets." I say, "Well, you can give him five bedsheets, but tell him next time he comes to bring ten." Why should one react in such a deplorable fashion, particularly when he has been given five sheets for his own personal use, and he is asked to bring ten sheets just once in a long while? Would you call it devotion to the Guru, or just a fraud? Somebody suggested that malpuras be cooked in pure ghee. I said, "Your suggestion is excellent, but one kilo costs Rs. 20/-. When are you leaving?" He said, "Tomorrow." I said, "See me before you leave." He came to meet me when he was to leave, and then I said, "Look, when you return, bring a tin of pure ghee." He gave a gasp, it seemed to break his heart. I said, "Look, that won't do." Then I fired him right and left and said, "Look, you want us to cook malpuras in pure ghee, and yet you do not want to bring any ghee yourself. Do you think that your father is supplying all the things here? You should not behave in this way."

It is only those people who make demands on whom demands are made. The Ashram will not make any demands on those who come without any demands.

Then there are the specimens who want to have a good house. I say, "Well, all right, give some money to the Ashram so that we may build a good house for you and furnish it very well." At the mention of money they gasp.

As long as they don't have to pay a single penny for any facilities, they are content to use them, but the moment that they are asked for a single penny they become disturbed.

One day a person came along with four friends and asked Desai for accomodations. They were provided with them. Next time he came with twelve friends and he began to make all kinds of demands. His friends had absolutely no sense, and they were using the Ashram facilities in an improper manner. Then the third time he came and said to Desai, "Look, next time I am coming along with fifteen of my friends, but none of them likes to take hot things." So that meant that Desai had to cook special food for them. I said to Desai, "Look, I'll tell you, you don't yet know all the tricks, I'll tell you one trick. Ask him to contribute Rs. 200/- to the Ashram, and all his friends will disappear." This device is resorted to, to keep certain people away. After that fellow was asked to contribute Rs. 200/-, he has disappeared; nor have any of his friends come back. The Ashram doesn't need money from him. This device was being used by Muktananda Swami, not Desai, to keep out these fake characters. If there is anyone coming to this Ashram complaining that he was asked to contribute something, then you should immediately think that that person is some kind of cheat. And on the other hand you have these girls from the West who wanted to give me all of their money, and I had to pursuade them to keep some for their own use.

Madhura bhava is very good, and it is the opposite of this bhava I have spoken about, which is bitter bhava.

January 10, 1972

Elona: *How does one face a society that has no respect for spiritual incentive?*
Baba: We should not let the attitude of our society affect our mode of life, our ways, or our spiritual viewpoint. There

can be only two reasons for the lack of respect for spirituality—stupidity and egoism. If others are not willing to give up their egoism or stupidity, why should we give up our spiritual seeking? One should not let one's spiritual values be affected by the attitude of society towards them. One should behave like a true spiritual seeker towards the members of even an antagonistic society, treating them all with honour and love, considering them to be divine. One's social conduct should be guided by right principles. One may or may not accept it, but our spiritual practices influence society a great deal. Take the case of Mahatma Gandhi of our country. Mahatma Gandhi had made it a rule to hold his prayer meeting every evening and when the time for the prayer meeting approached, even the Legislative Assembly in Delhi would be suspended for a while. The members of the Assembly would also participate silently in the prayer. Thus, if a spiritual seeker persists in his seeking with courage, self-control and steadfastness, it is bound to have its effect on others also. Such is the power of the pursuit of truth.

Malou: *What is suffering? Is it an unavoidable means for evolution? Why has the blissful Lord given this strange boon to mankind?*
Baba: According to me, suffering is a manifestation of the grace of the Lord in its purest form, because it is suffering which compels us to seek all good things. It is suffering which has made man human, which compels him to live a disciplined and self-controlled life, and prevents him from behaving wildly like creatures of the air, water, like animals living in forests and other parts of the earth. Suffering impels one to seek God. It is only when we suffer that we begin to seek happiness, and visualise what it would be like. When suffering comes, man begins to think about why he is suffering, what exactly has caused his suffering. He finds that it is lack of discipline, lack of self-control, lack of good principles which have brought all this suffering. Then he makes an effort to change himself and get rid of suffering through self-control and righteousness. Generally you find people avoiding or shunning evil actions out of fear of suffering. Therefore, suffering is a great blessing. In the *Maha-*

bharata I am reminded of a prayer made by one of the most important characters, Kunti, the mother of the Pandavas. She says, "O Lord, whenever I was surrounded by misery or hardship I remembered Thee and longed to take refuge in Thee very intensely. But when I had overcome that hardship and misery, I tended to forget Thee."

Suffering is essential because it is that which impels us to seek total happiness. When a man has to suffer again and again, when he falls into the grip of suffering hopelessly, then he begins to find out how he can get away from it, if there is any means which could bring about total cessation of suffering. Suffering is experienced on account of identification with the inner psychic instrument (antahkarana), when our external senses and inner mind come together. While explaining this to Arjuna, Lord Krishna says in the *Gita* that experiences of pain and pleasure, heat and cold come as a result of the contact of the mind with external objects through the senses. But when the mind rises above this sense world and gets into the state which is beyond, where the world appears no longer, he becomes centred in the state which is free from joy and sorrow, the state of supreme bliss. The Lord adds that joy and sorrow, pain and pleasure arise and subside. They are temporary. He says therefore they should be risen above. A wise person values neither of them. He says, "O Arjuna, conquer both pleasure and pain by self-control and even get beyond them." Just as night leads to day, suffering leads to bliss. We should be grateful to suffering.

Amrita: *The Guru Gita says that even sages and seers do not know the proper manner in which to serve the Guru. What is the proper manner to serve the Guru?*
Baba: I am in the same class, the class of sages and seers. That means that I, too, do not know it. So what shall I say?

By sages and seers are here meant ascetics, those who practise austerities such as sitting around 'five fires', who do japa and worship, who go on pilgrimages, and follow other similar disciplines. There are so many different methods and if one were to give an elaborate discourse on a difficult method, people would rush to adopt that method. But if one tells them only, "Find a genuine Guru and live with him, serve him," people begin to wonder what is there in that. They do not know that all that one may gain from japa, austerities, pilgrimages, and Hatha Yoga is also gained by service to the Guru; but people from the West get easily drawn toward difficult practices. To them the words 'Guru', 'Guru's house', 'Guru as the supreme deity' and 'Guruhood' must sound quite strange and unfamiliar. But that is not so in India, because for Indians, the Guru is the highest and greatest being. The Guru is the highest deity because he has the power of granting the fruits of even the most rigourous austere disciplines. Scriptures, sages and seers only point toward the Lord, but the Guru makes his disciple himself divine. Just as in the West great importance is attached to big gadgets, bridges, jet planes and fashions, here in India importance is attached to the Guru, the Lord and centres of pilgrimage. There is a very great centre of pilgrimage in Maharashtra State, called Pandharpur; and we are in Maharashtra State. A great bhakta called Namdev used to live there. It is said that the formless, the attributeless Supreme Being would assume a form and attributes for his sake and appear to him in a personal form, and treat him with love like a companion. No one should think that it is just a mere flight of imagination. It's quite possible for a devotee. The other day somebody who had driven his wife away out of sheer anger asked me whether there was any particular mantra or tantra that he could use to deal with the situation. He said that even though the wife had been driven away, at night he would hear her knocking at the door. Then he would complain that the figure of his wife would appear and she would sometimes sit at the head of the bed, or on his pillow, or sometimes at the foot of the bed, or sometimes she would shake him out of sleep, but when he got up there was no one there. He was being tormented by this figure and he wanted me to suggest a way out of it. I said to him, "Take some sacred ash from the temple and before going to sleep, place it on your forehead and you will surely get some relief." Now I'll get the report when he returns here next week.

You can see how vulnerable, how impressionable the mind is, and when you do not practise any special form of devotion, and yet get so attached to a mere woman that she begins to haunt you like that, then what is so surprising if a saint like Namdev were to be haunted and even actually visited by the Lord whom he had worshipped very intensely for a very long time?

And since the Lord had become almost his pal, Namdev used to take great pride in it, and used to behave in a very conceited manner about it. At that time there were saints coming from different classes who were Namdev's contemporaries, particularly from the lower strata of society, cobblers, peasants, maids, sweepers and barbers and so on. At that time there lived saints such as Janabai who was a maid-servant, Gora who was a potter, Sena who was a barber, Sauta who was a peasant and the cobbler Devidas. Yet they were all God-realised. They saw Him everywhere. Their most distinctive quality was that they were all householders; while one wove clothes, another cobbled. On the Ekadasi day in the month of September and October a great fair was held there, and all these saints would gather in Pandharpur on that occasion and they would sing the Names of the Lord and dance in great abandon. Namdev was quite proud of the fact that the Lord was his constant companion, that He used to play with him. However, the Lord was aware of this weakness of Namdev and He wanted to root it out of his system. He knew that Namdev was a victim of pride and pride is a hellish defect, and it must be completely eradicated. So to teach him a lesson the Lord suggested that he go to Pandharpur and meet all the saints and that would be of a great help to everybody, and because he was such a great devotee they would all be able to get inspiration from his example. Namdev agreed. Everybody suffers from his own particular mental trip. If somebody begins to meditate and just begins to jerk his neck in meditation, he begins to look upon himself as a very great seeker, and his chest swells with pride. And that is what happened with Namdev. Namdev thought that he was a very great devotee, and so the moment he appeared in Pandharpur, all the people would stand up and receive him with great honour; they would garland him and show the utmost reverence for him. But the poor fellow was not aware of the fact that the Lord was present within each of those saints in a different form. For Namdev the Lord seemed to have only one form, while for all the rest the Lord had countless forms; He was all-pervasive.

So all the saints congregated there. Whenever there is such a congregation you usually have question and answer sessions like the present session. So questions were being asked and answers being given. Namdev reached there, but unfortunately nobody took any notice of him. All of them were absorbed in what they were doing. Namdev had expected that the moment he reached there people would stand up and ask him to sit down, that they would recognise his greatness, they would show respect for the fact the Lord was his constant companion. But nothing of the sort happened and Namdev was completely ignored. He felt very small and he even had to be content with sitting anonymously in a corner. The oldest of these saints was the potter Gora. Jnaneshwar Maharaj knew whatever was transpiring in the heart of everyone present, and so when Namdev sat down, Jnaneshwar whispered in the ear of Gora, "Uncle, look, here is a new pot, and you must tap it to see whether it is baked or not." In our country the custom is to tap a pot to see whether it is fully baked or not. So Gora tapped Namdev on the head. Namdev was greatly insulted and flew into a rage. "What the hell are you doing? What do you take me for? The Lord is such a great pal of mine, He constantly plays with me, and He never deserts me, and what do you take me for?"

Gora said, "Well, here is an unbaked pot. He hasn't yet been purified through the fire. Who is your Guru?"

Namdev said, "What do I need a Guru for? The Lord is my constant companion."

The other saints asked him to get out. He went back and felt greatly humiliated. On the way, he was wondering that in spite of the fact that the supreme Lord was constantly with him, that these chappies from the lower classes, such as a potter and a gardener, had treated him in such a shabby manner. So he went back and met the Lord and said, "I didn't find anything praiseworthy in those saints."

The Lord said, "No, you are mistaken, they are very great, genuine saints. They are absolutely dependable authorities on religious and spiritual matters." Then He said, "What happened?"

"I was completely ignored. Nobody bothered to take any notice of me, much less treat me with any reverence."

The Lord said, "Aren't you being stupid? How could anybody else's honouring you be of any use to you? Why shouldn't you start honouring yourself?" It is for this reason that I repeat again and again: worship your own being, honour your own Self, meditate on your own spirit. And if Namdev had learned that lesson he would have been so much the better for it.

Then the Lord said, "What else happened?"

And he said, "Then those present said that I was an unbaked pot and I was without a Guru."

The Lord said, "Did they call you unbaked and without a Guru? What they said is absolutely right; the saints know the truth, they cannot tell a lie."

Namdev said, "Lord, even You consider me to be unbaked?"

The Lord said, "Yes."

Namdev said, "Am I without a Guru?"

The Lord said, "Yes, where is your Guru?"

Namdev said, "Well, You, the Lord, are my friend."

The Lord said, "I am the friend of all creatures, I dwell in the heart of everyone. There is nothing special about your friendship with Me. But one without a Guru is not respected anywhere."

"What should I do now?"

"Go and find a teacher."

"Very good, but who should I accept as my Guru?"

At that time, in the town of Alandi, where the Samadhi shrine of Jnaneshwar is situated, there lived a great Siddha named Visoba Kechar. Then the Lord said, "Go to him, get instruction from him. Only then will people consider you to be a baked pot, one who has a Guru. Then go and meet those saints and after that come back and see Me."

So Namdev went to the town of Alandi to Visoba Kechar and he asked the people, "It is said that a saint called Visoba Kechar lives here. Where does he live?"

Somebody said, "He dwells in the temple of Mahadeva." (We haven't visited the temple. Next time we will visit the temple.) When he reached the temple, he asked, "Where does Visoba live?"

The people said, "He must be inside the temple."

Inside the temple there was a small lingam of Shiva. He found a strange creature with his legs outstretched, and his feet planted in a most irreverent fashion on the lingam, snoring away. Namdev was amazed. He had already been insulted once, and now he was wondering why he had been sent to this strange, outlandish fellow. "What could he teach me, this fellow who doesn't even know how to treat a symbol of the Lord? He has the temerity to put his feet right on the lingam," he thought to himself. He looked at him for a while, saying to himself, "Well, he can't be my Guru, but all the same I will wake him up and certainly insist on his moving his feet from the lingam. Then I will bow to the image and leave."

He went near and he clapped his hands and shouted, "Who is snoring here?"

That man was very old and he said, "It's me, I am Visoba, who are you?"

"I am Namdev."

"What brings you here?"

"That I'll answer later, but now you explain to me your strange behaviour. "

"What have I done?"

"You don't even have the good sense not to put your feet on the head of the Lord. Is that the limit of your knowledge?"

Visoba said, "Look, Namdev, I have become very old and also very feeble, so much so that I cannot even move my feet from one position to another. I would be extremely grateful to you if you would kindly move my feet from the idol and put them away, and bow to the idol and leave."

Namdev agreed to oblige him. Then a most amazing miracle happened. As Namdev lifted Visoba's feet and put them in a different spot, another lingam immediately appeared. When he lifted them from there, a third appeared. Wherever he put Visoba's feet, a lingam appeared under them. Namdev immediately realised that the fellow was not an old fool. He realised that he was a great Master and that the Lord had sent him to the right being. Then he said to him, "Look, I am Namdev, and I have come in search of a Guru. You are my Guru, please instruct me."

Visoba instructed him in a verse that consisted of five stanzas. Visoba addressed him as Nam, not as Namdev. To address somebody by the first name does not show that you are being polite towards him. So the Guru treats him in a familiar manner and then says, "Nam, you should not suffer from the illusion that God exists here but not there. Nam, show me a spot that is without the Lord. You must completely overcome the delusion that the Lord exists in that corner, that the universe exists in this corner, and that good lies in that corner, and that evil lies in this corner. Just as a painter paints different figures, those of men and animals on the same canvas, with the same brush and colours, so this varied universe, which consists of different forms, different creatures, is made by the same Lord, and the question of high and low cannot arise. It is only the Lord who can become such a vast varied universe. Nobody else could ever become the universe. When you become aware only of the one Lord, the one all-pervading Supreme Being, and when you are completely rid of the notion of multiplicity or diversity or duality, only then can you be considered to be realised and beyond the distinction of bondage and liberation. Know that the same Lord whom you consider to be dwelling in a particular place dwells in the heart of every creature as its innermost Self."

This way the Guru instructed the disciple and Namdev was enlightened. From there he went to Pandharpur which was close by. He found the same congregation of saints. He greeted everyone and everyone called him and asked him to join them. Everyone said, "Now you are with a Guru. You are a baked pot. Now you have realised the truth. One who sees the Lord only outside, not within his own heart, is like one who sees only the universe and not the Lord. Even if he has had a vision of the Lord that doesn't mean very much."

You find sages and seers suggesting different methods and techniques. They will turn you to japa, tapasya, almsgiving, pilgrimages, pranayama, and asanas and the like. But it is only the Guru who has the power of revealing the Lord who is present in your own heart. Take the case of all the creatures created by the Lord: you find them being pushed around, being swept around from hell to heaven, from good to evil, and they are tormented by the flames of suffering. But the seeker who has been remoulded and transformed by the Guru becomes the Guru himself, and begins to dwell constantly in supreme bliss.

The best manner of serving the Guru is to submit yourself completely to him, to surrender yourself to him totally. To identify yourself completely with the Guru, in joy and in sorrow, that is what true service to the Guru is. Namely it is obedience to the Guru's commands which matters. "I shall do thy bidding," as Arjuna said to Lord Krishna. If you are able to cleanse your heart by the words of the Guru, then you have served him in the most proper manner.

Larry: *Should a person remain calm even when he sees his ego making disturbances for him and those around him? I usually feel disappointed with myself, and also that as a disciple I am letting you down.*

Baba: Egoism is the worst enemy of everyone, but unfortunately people consider the ego to be their best friend. Isn't is a great irony that the ego, which is the most dreadful enemy of the entire world, which surely leads everyone to the most hellish suffering, is hugged most affectionately? The great poet-saint Sunderdas says in his verse that it is because of the ego that one remains bound. When the ego has melted, one discovers that he is the Lord Himself. You shouldn't feel disappointed. The ego will dissolve itself in due course. The stronger one's ego is now, the greater the love that one will radiate later. When your egoism is transformed into love you will give as much love to the world as you were giving ego before. Your ego may be very strong at this time, but in the future you will remain with the same strength in this awareness: "I am Brahman." Don't worry. When your ego makes too much noise, remain calm. Keep working with joy. Remember that the ego turns peace into peacelessness.

January 12, 1972

Penny: *Every morning I feel very weak and tired and don't even have the energy to chant. Do you think I should eat breakfast?*

Baba: If you need breakfast, take it, but the feeling of fatigue or weakness is not due to your not taking breakfast. It is due to the change of climate, food, routine and place.

Chandra: *Are cheese, ice cream and garlic good food for meditators?*

Baba: Yes, whatever contains milk or sugar is good for meditators. Ginger is very good, because it removes gas from the system. So are garlic and onions. They destroy germs. They have great medicinal value, but they must be taken in a small quantity.

Sumitra: *While meditating I cannot keep my head from nodding. How can I maintain a correct posture for meditation?*

Baba: When you sit for meditation, sit in a correct posture, but after you have begun to meditate, if certain movements begin to take place, you shouldn't worry about the posture; don't try to resist or check those movements. If your head nods during meditation, it's very good. That movement indicates that the chakra in the throat, which is very important, is being opened. And then sometimes it happens that the breath is retained in the upper chakras and the head begins to sway gently. It should not be confused with nodding. It happens even with great saints. That slight movement will continue even after you have completed your sadhana, and that is an indication that you are constantly dwelling in the sahasrar.

Sylvia Newman: *How can we benefit most from a short stay in the Ashram?*

Baba: If you have only a short time to spend in the Ashram, stay in a meditative state all the time, because meditation is the chief purpose of this Ashram. Every morning and every evening you should sit in the meditation room, whether your mind cooperates with you or not. What matters is that you go there and sit, and repeat your mantra until you get into meditation. One should learn to spend more and more time inside the meditation room. The vibrations prevailing there will catch you very soon. You should repeat the mantra more and more. While in the Ashram you should identify yourself with the Ashram. If an object arouses strong feelings of love and delight in us, we open up. Likewise, if you can feel great love for the Ashram, you will get utmost benefit from your short stay. However, I quite appreciate that it is quite trying here for people coming from abroad, particularly for the first few days, because everything here is so very different: our ways are different, the climate is different, the food is different. Yet you should talk to your mind and turn it toward meditation. If you could understand the importance of the inner realms, it would be very helpful for you. It is not right to think that God dwells far away and if we pray to Him and are able to please Him, He will send a gracious message from His distant abode. The Lord dwells right within us. He is very close to us, the closest in fact. This understanding will benefit us greatly. If one is unable to sleep, and yet if he lies down and keeps thinking about sleep, he will get into the sleep state after half an hour or one hour. Similarly, if your mind doesn't become one-pointed, you should keep on trying to focus it and in the process dive deep within yourself. This way, you will attain the divine state. You will find yourself to be a completely new person. The moment you become aware of the greatness and purity and sublimity of the Ashram, particularly of the meditation room here, your heart will be opened and it will absorb greatness, and your reward will be most satisfying. Thank you, it's a very good question. It's the question of an earnest seeker.

Herbert Kruckman: *If I have a harmonious and good life, why do I need a Guru?*
Baba: If your life is happy and harmonious, you do not need a Guru. However, it shows that you have already been blessed by the Guru. We need the Guru to fill our life with joy and happiness, not to form a new faith or creed. If your life is already full of happiness, it means that you already have a Guru. However, your happiness should be arising spontaneously within. It should be pure and independent of all external factors. This happiness should not be confused with the trivial and momentary feeling of pleasure which arises from good food or a cup of ice cream, or from good clothes. It should not depend on any outer factor. The scriptures define joy as that bliss which transcends the senses and their objects, which wells up by itself, and which once attained never vanishes. If you have such joy, that is very good. It means that you have been blessed by the grace of God and the Guru. Anyone who experiences such joy is worthy of great honour. I salute you for that.

Selma Kruckman: *Why do the sadhakas in the Ashram practise celibacy?*
Baba: Celibacy is a high austerity. If there is anything in the world which you should earn, it is not dollars, not machines, not political opinion or anything else: it is brahmacharya. We generally find that you learn a particular skill or art readily during childhood, because when you are a child you are a celibate. Later on, when you begin to use your seminal fluid, it becomes difficult for you to absorb any fresh learning. Unfortunately, man does not seem to be aware of the great importance of seminal fluid. It is unintelligent fools who think themselves to be very lucky if they are able to use it. Wise people are happy to save it. You can realise its importance from the fact that one drop of seminal fluid gives rise to a human being. So what makes you think that such a precious drop is so worthless that you could throw it away in a bathroom or anywhere else? The influence of celibacy can be seen among animals. Certain elephants and serpents, who are celibates, have most precious jewels in their foreheads. When the seminal flow of such an elephant or serpent is directed upwards, this jewel is

formed. And when such an elephant dies, his head is cut and that pearl is taken out. It is extremely precious; its price runs into millions. If this elephant weren't a celibate he might have produced two or three calves that couldn't have fetched more than Rs. 2,000/- each. All our Ashramites, whether foreign or Indian, are able to meditate here so well and so intensely because they practise celibacy. For the same reason, they are clean and pure, calm, radiant and full of love. All the bodily fluids are generated from that vital fluid. If semen is lost, strength, radiance, beauty and joy are also lost. Therefore, the seminal fluid is valued very highly. For this reason we impose a very strict discipline on our boys and girls, at least until they get married. Some of the modern Indian boys and girls consider this restriction to be like a prison. They are foolish. Whoever has had repeated experiences of sensual pleasure can find out from his own experience how he was as long as he practised celibacy, what the condition of his body was, the condition of his inner organs, what glow his skin had, how well his digestive system was functioning and how vigourous and energetic his gait was, how he slept, and what has happened to all these things after he started indulging. When you are possessed by the desire to discard your seminal fluid, for that length of time at least, you lose your sharpness and clarity and you become absolutely incapable of learning anything or reading and writing. As long as one is a celibate one doesn't have to take refuge in a doctor; it is only after you start losing your seminal fluid that you have to depend more and more on doctors. In our Ashram you will find that the celibates need very little medicine. There is one Ayurvedic physician who says in verse, "If you discard semen, you fall into misery, and if you hold feces you fall into misery, so you should hold onto semen and discard feces." Therefore, one must conserve the seminal fluid within the body. If you lose your seminal fluid, your body will start stinking and it will lose all its charm. Your loveliness is due to the seminal fluid and meditation.

Morty Newman: *Our religion does not accept reincarnation and karma. Please explain these concepts.*
Baba: I have studied the Jewish religion as it is followed in

India, and many Indian Jews come to visit me. Generally speaking, we find a very great similarity between our modes of life and modes of conduct. They have their own separate temples, they don't go to the church; and we have their holy texts in our library also. If the Jews do not accept reincarnation and karma, what is it that they accept? Are they not in favour of good actions? (Yes.) Don't they oppose evil actions? (Yes.) Well, that is what we also do; we support good actions and denounce bad actions, and that is what the theory of karma is. And we certainly accept reincarnation. If there is no rebirth, if your present actions do not form your future karma, if actions are without consequences, one can live any way he likes. What is the need of sticking to good actions alone? By recommending good actions, your scriptures in fact support rebirth. One performs good deeds only beacuse good deeds bring good fruits. One avoids evil deeds, because evil deeds bring evil consequences. There is no escape from the consequences of actions. The Jews may not accept reincarnation, but do they perform any funeral rites? There are quite a few religions which do not accept reincarnation. However, we do. Good deeds are performed so that one may reap the good fruits of those deeds. He who has had a direct experience of the truth must also have visited all the different worlds. Just as there is a world on the moon, similarly there is a world called the world of ancestors, the world of our forefathers, and you can read about it in my book, *Guru*. Reincarnation is also a fact. Then the Ten Commandments or rules of conduct prescribed by the Jewish faith are the same as the ten rules prescribed by the Hindu faith.

Pratibha: *Even though Namdev suffered from pride, he had still attained God. Here also we find that those people who are said to be meditating very well suffer from anger, jealousy and egoism. How do you explain this condition?*
Baba: It is true that Namdev attained God; but at the same time he also received a kick from the potter Gora. But the nature of Namdev's pride was entirely different. He was proud of the fact that he had attained the Lord, he didn't suffer from pride of the flesh, he didn't identify himself with the body. He did not suffer from the pride which is born of

attachment and aversion, which you experience in your everyday life. Namdev was proud because he knew that he was very worthy, as the Lord Himself was his constant companion. But even the companionship of the Lord could not save him from the kick of the potter Gora. Therefore, ego should be completely overcome. Namdev was a very great saint, and he did not suffer from low pride. His pride was of a much higher nature. Those who are living in the Ashram should find out what it is that makes them feel proud. Is it our learning, our education, our family, beauty, our dress or our body that makes us proud, or something else? It is absolutely true that the moment the ego leaves one, he feels he himself is the pure Supreme Being.

Amrita: *Take the case of a seeker who has already wasted many years of his life, and whose mind is very impure, and yet who possesses a couple of qualities by the grace of the Lord, by means of which he can serve the Guru. Wouldn't the Guru like to do a special favour to that seeker so that he may be able to serve the Guru earnestly and make rapid advance on the spiritual path?*
Baba: Anyone can be redeemed by service to the Guru. However stupid or impure one may be, he can conquer bondage just by service to the Guru. One may not have even one good quality, may not know any skill, yet if he serves the Guru without wavering, he will be saved.

One should know that he has been reduced to his present wretched condition because he had been guilty of partiality in birth after birth. Why should he expect the Guru also to become partial and lose his sense of equality? A Guru does not need to do that. Why should a Guru be partial to one, why not to all? Even if someone is unintelligent, he should engage himself in serving the Guru. For that you do not require learning or study of philosophy. Service to the Guru, service to the Lord, removes all defects, including dullness. However, one should realise that he has lived a very bad life so far. It is now high time to turn over a new leaf.

The Maharashtrian poet, Krishnasuta, says in one of his poems that even one who is wicked, not to speak of a dull-witted one, becomes pure the moment he turns to the Lord and gives up his evil conduct. A seeker who is serving the Guru does not need any special favours or compassion from the Guru. Service to the Guru has such power in it that it will certainly redeem him.

Kalyani: *Babaji, how can I develop an attitude of forbearance towards pain so that I can accept whatever comes to me graciously?*
Baba: If through meditation you can learn to dwell all the time in the causal body, or in Tandraloka, then forbearance would come to you itself. When you are in a state of deep sleep, somebody may be using the foulest terms of abuse for you, or hurling the worst insults at you, yet that doesn't affect you, because in the state of sleep you are not conscious. The forbearance that we are talking about should be combined with awareness, and it is through meditation that we can get into a state in which forbearance comes to us easily. Though we are aware of the outside world we are not at all affected by what happens there. As you meditate more and more, right discrimination, right thought begins to arise from within, and helps you to cultivate forbearance. Forbearance comes naturally to one who through meditation becomes anchored in an inner state and acquires true discrimination.

Suneel: *Is it true that man acquires knowledge about God through reasoning?*
Baba: God is beyond reasoning. By reasoning, one can never know God. Reasoning is valid only in the sphere of relative knowledge. Ordinary intellect cannot know God. All of us possess intelligence and yet we do not know God. You are such an intelligent fellow, but do you know God?

However, there is another kind of intellect, which the Lord talks about in the *Gita*. He says, "He who worships Me, who meditates on Me, who thinks of Me constantly, acquires a refined intellect by which he can know Me." In the *Shivasutras* this pure intellect is called shuddha vidya, pure intuition or pure knowledge. It is only when such knowledge arises through meditation that one knows God. By pure knowledge one becomes the Lord of all cosmic powers.

January 14, 1972

Uma: *What is the correct way to repeat the mantra Guru Om?*
Baba: The best way of repeating a mantra is to combine it with the breath, repeating it once while inhaling and once while exhaling. This is the correct technique. Once your breath becomes accustomed to the mantra—and that happens in a short time—you will not be able to breathe in or out without the mantra. If the mantra repetition ceases, the breath will also cease. You should find out how much joy there is in it.

As the prana enters and merges inside, you should follow the prana with the mantra, becoming one with it. This is a most excellent technique because it affects all seven constituents of the body. This combination exerts a powerful influence on the inner and outer worlds, on the sense organs and on the physical, subtle, causal and supracausal bodies. It has even greater importance than meditation or Hatha Yoga or pranayama or knowledge. In the end it raises you to Guruhood, the state of pure Being. And this is also called ajapa japa. Most saints have practised this form of japa. The greatest Siddhas of Maharashtra, Kabir and Surdas and others, obtained the supreme state only through ajapa japa. Kabir sings in his poetry, "If you practise ajapa japa you get beyond sin and virtue." It involves spontaneous pranayama, it awakens the Kundalini in a spontaneous manner, and it purifies the body most naturally. It also brings the grace of the Guru and enables you to become stabilised in the sahasrar.

The mantra has great power. It is called mantra because by repeating it one is redeemed. To understand how powerful the mantric sound can be, one doesn't have to turn to the authority of sacred history or myth. One can understand it from a very simple illustration. If somebody happens to use a term of abuse for you, you flare up immediately, it changes your mood, your blood begins to boil, your limbs begin to tremble and you begin to stammer and even forget what you were going to say. So when a simple term of abuse has such a powerful influence, there is no reason to believe that a sublime mantra like *Guru Om* would not exert its influence. It is bound to stabilise you in the sahasrar, in the supreme state.

Besides, this mantra is worthy of great honour. *Om* has been sanctioned by the *Vedas*, the *Puranas*, the *Tantras* and the yogic texts. Some people repeat *Hari Om*, while others repeat *Shiva Om*, and we repeat *Guru Om*.

Barry: *Is just the first serving at each meal, exclusive of sweets and rice, sufficient enough food to maintain my sadhana, or should I take anything else?*
Baba: You are already very thin; you need rice very badly. For sadhana a certain amount of sugar or sweets is essential, because sugar turns to semen. Certain seekers become emaciated when they meditate very intensely and I recommend milk and sugar to them. In our country, there is a custom to offer special prasad to the Lord or to a great saint who happens to visit us, and one of the essential things in that prasad is a payasam, a sweet milk rice pudding. And we are going to prepare that pudding next Thursday. However, you must eat only as much as you can digest. You must take a little rice; in any case we don't serve much rice here. Rice contains sugar, and it is very easy to digest. Different foods take different lengths of time to be completely assimilated. Some foods can be digested in about half an hour, others take one hour, two hours, four hours, six hours, or even nine hours. Rice is a very light food, and it can be digested in about one hour.

Pratibha: *Which is stronger, prarabdha or Shaktipat?*
Baba: It depends. Both are equally strong in their own spheres. Prarabdha is strong in its sphere, Shaktipat is strong in its sphere. Prarabdha always precedes the formation of the body, and so when you are going to receive Shaktipat is determined by prarabdha. There is a poet-saint whose one statement is very well known in our country. He says that whatever is written by destiny on the sixth day after your birth can never be blotted out. Shaktipat follows the writ of prarabdha. Yet Shaktipat is stronger than prarabdha. Prarabdha has dominion only over the body which

is the product of your past karma, while in Shaktipat it is the divine Shakti which comes into operation. Prarabdha is nothing but the force generated by your past karma, and that is not free, while Shakti is absolutely free. Prarabdha follows the law of karma, while Shakti transcends all law. Therefore, Shaktipat is stronger than prarabdha.

During the tenure of Dr. Rajendra Prasad as the President of this country, a very interesting event occurred. There were two persons who were convicted in a court of law and the death sentence was given. They appealed to higher courts, they went even to the Supreme Court, yet they could not be exonerated. Now the whole world wanted those two convicts released, wanted them to escape punishment somehow or other, but the law wasn't on their side. Then a petition was made to the President on behalf of the accused. Then the President ruled that even if the law did not favour their release, he, as the President of the country, by his special power, would acquit them.

Prarabdha has dominion only over your physical body, which is the result of your past karma, while the Shakti involved in Shaktipat is the absolutely free independent power of the Lord. Once one has received Shaktipat he should not look to prarabdha any longer; he should only look to Shakti. If even after receiving Shaktipat you are worried about your prarabdha, it shows that you don't have any discernment. He is just like that stupid guest in a royal household, who is dear to the king and yet seeks protection from an ordinary policeman.

Herbert Kruckman: *From reading Guru and from everything I have seen at the Ashram I see that you worshipped Baba Nityananda as God Himself. This is most difficult for me to understand and accept. Would you please explain how a man can be God?*
Baba: How man becomes God is the greatest mystery of life. I repeat over and over that man first considers himself a poor, pathetic sinning specimen, inferior and very insecure. Then he claims this thought as his exclusive trademark and even gets it registered. He never shows willingness to rectify his wrong understanding of himself. He looks upon

others also from the same standpoint. The world is as you see it. We find that people in the world by and large have the attitude which would be illustrated by the story that I am going to narrate. One day a great fair was taking place somewhere in honour of a great saint, and thousands of people were going to participate in that fair. One of them was a great Siddha. On the way, since it was quite hot, he sat in the cool shade of a tree, and as he reclined against the trunk, he looked as though he had had a little too much alcohol. A great Siddha would quite often look drunk. There were many people passing by and one of them was a ganja addict. When he looked at this Siddha in an intoxicated condition, he thought he had met a most interesting companion, that he was of the same flock. So he went and sat next to him against the same tree. Since all kinds of people go to see such fairs, soon other characters also came and joined them. One was an alcoholic addicted to toddy, which is a local liquor. One was a thief, one a learned fellow, and one a pandit. Now four characters were looking at the great saint, each from his individual viewpoint. The toddy addict is looking at him and says to himself, "Look, he must have cracked at least one bottle, but it has affected him much too strongly. I take two bottles every day, and nothing of the sort happens in my case." The ganja addict says to himself, "Well, this fellow must have smoked ganja, he must have had one deep puff too many, which knocked him out." But the wise man says, "This man is a very great saint; he is enjoying the supreme state after having become centred in the sahasrar. All of you are just projecting your own stupidity onto him. "

After some time the saint returned to his normal state, and he looked quite normal. But the four people who had been watching were each projecting their own image. The saint was what he was, regardless of what a particular spectator was thinking of him. You find different people being limited by their own limited knowledge, and nobody seems to know what the whole truth is. A lawyer looks upon truth from his legal angle, a doctor looks upon it from his medical angle, an engineer would look upon it from his engineer's angle. But one wonders whether any of these guys has been able to get at the truth in its fullness. Now a thief was looking upon him as a thief, a drunkard was looking upon him as a drunkard, the ganja addict had looked upon him as a ganja addict. And the wise man looked upon him according to his wisdom.

Similarly, a disciple who as a result of following the path shown by the Guru has been able to realise the divinity dwelling within his own heart, would be bound to look upon the Guru as a direct manifestation of God; he can't consider him as anything else, because he has realised God within himself after having surrendered himself completely to the Guru. If a disciple cannot worship his Guru as God, then he is not a disciple, he is a deluded fool. A disciple can realise the divinity of his Guru only after he has risen to a certain state as a result of his grace. Everyone is limited by his knowledge and ignorance. Normally we find that a person identifies himself with a role that he happens to play at a given moment. If he is driving a car, he thinks that he is a driver. If he is running a shop he thinks he is a shopkeeper. If he's lecturing to a class he thinks he is a lecturer. But has he ever tried to see what his true nature is, minus all these roles? If after following a certain true Guru you are able to realise your own divinity by his grace, it is only then that you would understand that the Guru is God Himself. It's not only the Guru himself who is God, you are also God. Man is not just a body; he must not be confused with the nature of his physical covering, his physical body, or with an acting mechanism, or with his degrees or with his status. He realises this when he begins to meditate and experience the inner realm through meditation. His understanding of himself also begins to change and so does his attitude towards the Guru. As long as he considers himself to be inferior or sinful, he will consider others to be inferior and sinful. But when he realises that he is divine, he is Shiva Himself, he also worships the Guru as God. The Guru is indeed God. If you were to do sadhana, you would also realise this truth. Your question is very good, and it must have done a lot of good to many people here. It is a very good question. If you were to do sadhana you would be able to realise God within your own heart. I am very happy with your question, because it concerns what you have directly observed, it's not an academic or theoretical question.

Shyama: *It is said that one should live at the Ashram of a Siddha with vigilance. What exactly is the nature of this vigilance?*
Baba: You should follow the rules of the Ashram most faithfully. Here everything happens punctually. There are some women from Delhi who seem to have made it a rule to come to the *Gita* five minutes late. That doesn't show vigilance, that is a crime. That does not indicate respect for the ways of the abode of a Siddha. It only shows that one is treating the Ashram like one's own kitchen, lighting a fire whenever she likes. One should be punctual for every little thing which happens in the Ashram. You should enter the meditation room very softly so that you do not disturb the meditation of others by your shuffling feet and rustling clothes. When you sit to meditate you should not spoil the cushion on which you are sitting. Every morning I go for inspection and with my flashlight I see the quality of the meditation of a particular seeker, and in what manner he is sitting. You should be aware that the cushions provided for backrests should be used for backrests; they shouldn't be used to sit on. Now that you are here for a short while, it would be much better if you observed all the rules of the Ashram. Otherwise, if you go back as blank as you came here, would it not have been better if you had never come? You should come to the Ashram with the purpose of meditating here or chanting here, or helping the Ashramites to keep the Ashram clean and learning to get up early, not for a frivolous end. No purpose would be served if your coming were simply because you had a quarrel with your father or husband, or wife or your son, and are using it as a place where you can shed tears safely. You won't gain anything if you come here with that attitude.

    I am quite often invited to inaugurate the reading of the *Shrimad Bhagavat Purana*. When I go to speak on such occasions I find that there are many women in the gathering who come with basketsful of different grains of wheat or rice or lentils. They come from their homes to listen to the discourses on the *Bhagavat*, but their real motive is to get away from their mothers-in-law, or to get away from their noisy children. Then you find others coming with wool, and while the discourses are being held, you find them either cleaning grains or knitting. Is that a way to make your mind one-pointed? Is that the proper way to act at an ashram This shows that you are coming to the Ashram with an obsession. The consequences of that are not good for the persons concerned. You should live in an ashram most vigilantly. As far as possible, you should be truthful, silent and pure, and entertain clean thoughts. The scriptures say that if in the course of your ordinary life in a town or city you happen to commit certain wrongs, certain bad deeds, then you go to a holy place to expiate them. But what is going to happen if you persist in the same sinful deeds in a holy place also? If you happen to commit certain bad deeds in a holy place, you go to an ashram to get rid of their evil consequences. But if you persist in the same kind of deeds, even in an ashram, then who can possibly save you? Therefore, while you are in an ashram, as far as possible follow all the ashram ways.

Whatever there is in the Ashram, all the little things that you see around you, I do not look upon them as my personal possessions, or as personal wealth. To me they are gifts of love. Every little thing is the heart of the devotee who has offered it to me, and I honour it as such, and I treat it with great love. Take for instance this clock. I didn't go to the market to buy it; it has been offered to me by a French devotee. But I do not look upon it as a watch. I have kept it here with great love. To me it is nothing but pure love, religion in its purest form. We should not look upon the different items of furniture or other articles in the Ashram as we would look upon similar things in a guest house. We must be fully aware all the time that these things are donated by devotees out of pure love, and they are embodiments of dharma itself. We should be very careful that our speech does not disturb or upset others. Otherwise the Ashram will prove to be our worst enemy.

There are many people who raise this question: "How is it that even after staying for such a long period in the Ashram that person degenerated?" Well, my answer to that is if you stay in an ashram without following the Ashram rules, without following the Ashram discipline, you are bound to degenerate. Even if somebody presents a little piece of chocolate to me I take care that it is added to the fruit salad, so that it may reach everyone. Because I value it as dharma and I do not like it at all if the cook happens to help himself to a part of it while making the fruit salad. Then that fruit salad which could have been pure dharma becomes vitiated. You should realise that whatever you may eat, however delicious it may be, will finally be turned into shit, so why should you violate the principles of dharma, the rules of the Ashram, just for the palate? Once my Guru for certain reasons asked me to stop eating mangos. I stopped eating mangos, and for twelve years he did not refer to the subject. And I didn't ask him again whether I should begin to eat mangos. It so happened that I practised my sadhana under a mango tree and I had all the finest experiences under that mango tree. You see, here also I have planted so many different varieties of mangos and all those trees get heavily laden with fruit.

You should look upon all the things in the Ashram as embodiments of dharma, as purity in its purest form, and use them accordingly. Every little thing, every little object is a living body of dharma. Every morning and every evening you find girls sweeping the paths and Ashram floors most diligently, and if some foolish character who was passing by were to blow his nose there or spit, well that would send me into a rage immediately, because I cannot tolerate a person that could be so stupid that he would make the place filthy, and show no respect for the work which seekers are doing out of pure love. So, if you were to live in an ashram with such awareness, then you would be justifying your stay in the Ashram. If your attitude to the Ashram is not proper, your stay here will not yield any results.

January 17, 1972

Selma Kruckman: *Is it possible to be a disciple of a Guru and still live in the world?*
Baba: If anyone thinks that the spiritual relationship be-

tween the Guru and the disciple goes against worldly life, he is entirely wrong; such an idea is totally improper and he should get rid of it. The Guru-disciple relationship has meaning only if you are living a worldly life. If you are not living in the world what is the need of such a relationship? In fact, we do not understand what constitutes a worldly life or exactly what spiritual life is. 999 out of 1000 people who come to me tell me when I speak about God that it is very difficult for those who are living in the world to turn to spiritual life. But what exactly is it that is meant by 'spiritual life'? And what is a worldly life? Does it mean spending days working and nights sleeping; the husband-wife relationship; having children; maintaining a home? What is the difference in the life of a renunciate and a so-called worldly person? Who is free from worldly needs? Even a renunciate needs food and shelter. You may live in a bigger house, but he, too, needs at least a hut to live in. He also needs a little bit of money to meet his various needs.

Spiritual discipline has meaning only when you are living your life in the world. Both the Guru and the disciple live in the world, and it is in the world that you must attain liberation. Your various worldly possessions such as cars, planes and clothes, and activities such as playing tennis or seeing movies and other things do not disturb you. You look upon these activities and possessions in a very friendly way. You do not frown upon doctors, lawyers, engineers or architects. You welcome advice from all of them. Then why do you frown upon the Guru alone? Why can't you make the Guru as much a part of your life in the world as those others? Everyone else can become a part of your life, so why should you exclude the Guru?

It's quite easy—in fact, it's quite natural to have a Guru and live your life in the world. No sensible Guru would ever make his disciples turn away from worldly life, because life in the world does not go against spirituality. On the contrary, it is of great help. The objective world has as much importance and significance in the spiritual field as it has in everyday life. So why should a Guru turn against the world? Every wise Guru would like you to pursue a spiritual discipline while living your normal life. That is how my Guru functioned. His teaching always was that you should live in your home, do your normal work and attend to your normal duties, and at the same time remember the Lord.

Pratibha: *Can a Siddha student attain higher states of meditation without having kriyas?*
Baba: It is not possible without kriyas (yogic movements). However, outer physical kriyas do not take place in all cases; but inner kriyas will certainly always occur. Until you have perfected yourself you will undergo any of the three types of kriyas—either one or two or all of them—that is, physical kriyas, subtle kriyas and kriyas which are still subtler, say, causal kriyas. Some seekers undergo more physical kriyas, others less. But most seekers will have some kriyas on the physical level. A seeker who has already practised Hatha Yoga—say surya namaskar—and kept his body clean and pure by its means, would have fewer kriyas. Though before receiving the grace of my Guru I had practised Hatha Yoga very thoroughly, I passed through an intense phase of physical kriyas.

Subtle kriyas are essential for the subtle body and subtle kriyas will last for a long time. Kundalini Shakti in fact, likes play very much. She is very fond of manifesting Herself on the visible level. She is full of bliss and is always intoxicated. No matter whom She awakes, She manifests Her sport in his nerves, romping and leaping, and this causes kriyas. As kriyas become more and more subtle, your joy, your delight, your bliss will also become more and more refined and absorbing. You will pass from one wonderful inner state into another. Kriyas are essential. However, kriyas may not necessarily take place on the physical level, but inner subtle kriyas are indispensible.

Kalyani: *What should we do with feelings of anger that rise up from within for no apparent reason and yet seem to demand a target for expression?*
Baba: When a strong feeling of anger arises, begin to talk to that feeling. "You big fool, who could be more stupid than you?" Don't let it express itself on an outer level. Tackle it within yourself.

Let your anger become its own victim, instead of making somebody else its target. If your anger falls on an innocent person you are being unfair to him, but if it turns on itself, then it is reaping the fruits of its own karma, which is quite fair. Instead of afflicting others, it should afflict itself. That would be the best way of teaching a lesson to your anger.

Irrational anger is due to some impurity and a seeker should not be subject to such fits. If there is a certain reason to make you angry it can be understood, but if anger arises within for no reason, it obviously shows that your heart is tainted. The Lord says in the *Gita* that anger destroys discrimination. Anger is self-destructive. It will not depart leaving you feeling blessed and happy; nor will it help you to live a longer life. It erupts only to vitiate your mind, to destroy your capacity for reason and to swallow your joy and bliss; then it departs.

It is anger which is the cause of all the different kinds of mental imbalances and degrees of lunacy, neurosis or psychosis, whether it be fits of neurosis lasting for a week, a fortnight or a month, or whether it makes one 25%, 50% or 75% crazy. In all these cases, the imbalance arises from anger. Anger is a terrible fire which burns up the capacity of right reason. You will find that all the insomniacs and people who have become slaves to drugs are people who are particularly great friends to anger.

There are many boys and girls who come here and tell me that they don't feel like studying, and they ask me what to do. I ask them if they flare up often even on small pretexts, and the answer is almost always in the positive. Then I tell them that it is anger which is destroying their capacity for absorbing anything. Therefore, discard your anger, because anger is one's worst enemy.

Noni: *What should I do so that the mantra may go on within me throughout sleep?*
Baba: You watch me sleep every day because you remain awake while I am sleeping. I sleep in the corpse posture with my head on the pillow. I put my legs and feet together, cross my hands on my chest, or stretch them out by my sides. Then I close my eyes and begin to do my mantra. And if I lie in this posture, I fall asleep at once and wake up only at 3:00 or 3:15, after enjoying a very deep, sound and peace-

ful sleep. Besides, sadhana also goes on during such sleep. And if you do not get time for sadhana during the day, it takes place automatically during sleep. You shouldn't move your body too much while trying to go to sleep, because then it is difficult to fall asleep. The best thing to do is to lie absolutely still, stretched straight like a log, and stop tossing about. Close your eyes and focus your mind on your spiritual goal. Take up your mantra. Combine it with your breath. Repeat it once with the incoming breath and once with the outgoing breath. This way you will fall asleep quickly. This way you combine sleep with meditation. Japa will continue even during sleep. If you don't get time for meditation during the day, you will get both sleep and meditation during the night by following this method. Don't think of anything else but the mantra. You can resume your thoughts after waking up. What do you think about even during sleep? What's the value of your thoughts? By thinking and thinking constantly, you only court madness. Empty your mind of all thoughts and then go to sleep. You will get most enjoyable sleep, and when you wake up you will find that your mind is calm and fresh. You will feel the call of nature immediately upon getting up, and your bowels will move without any difficulty, without any pills. Your blood will circulate freely. After I wake up I have a drink of water, and then I pace up and down a couple of times and then my bowels get clear at once. You may ask about my morning routine from any of my attendants. Such is the result of good sleep. All the food inside is thoroughly assimilated and the bowels are ready to deliver their contents. This is the result of sleeping in one posture. I will not be late even by five minutes for the toilet. You can ask Noni how I sleep and what happens after I wake up. I lie absolutely still. If your body is moving too much then your sleep will be disturbed.

In fact, it is through thinking endlessly, through thinking unnecessarily one causes the greatest harm to oneself, one ruins one's life, body and tapasya. And you think while eating and drinking, you think while coming and going, you think even while sleeping. Why do you think so much? It's a terrible disease—to think endlessly. It surprises me how you contract it. If you could think less, you would enter into direct contact with the divine world, and receive a telepathic message from the Lord Himself.

Kedarnath: *What should I do if I find, while I am meditating, that my neighbours are happily snoring away? Should I disturb their deep samadhi or not?*
Baba: Usually it's not good to disturb them. For people who can't resist falling into such a state, they should not sit where a group is meditating. They should find a corner place for meditation. Everyone should have proper respect for meditation, for the place of meditation, and for the state of meditation, otherwise you commit a sin against meditation. Sleep is said to be so important that even the judges have held that you should be punished with three months' imprisonment if you disturb someone's deep sleep. No true hunter, who is really interested in hunting, who comes from a family of hunters, not phony characters, no courageous character will ever shoot an animal or bird when it is asleep. He will wait for the animal to wake up, and then he will shoot him. When sleep is so important, you can understand how much more meditation is. So everybody should show respect when another is meditating. As far as possible, you should learn to meditate without making the least noise. However, when you can't help it, you can't do anything about it. Then there is a state which resembles sleep, but which isn't ordinary sleep, and which you pass into during meditation. It is a very high state. My Guru always dwelled in that state. He would make this gutteral snoring-like sound, but he was wide awake all the time. The moment anyone entered he would immediately ask, "Who's that?" This gutteral sound, which may resemble snoring, indicates a very high state; it is the typical sound of the sushumna; it shows that the mind has been completely emptied. If, while hearing such a sound, or seeing a person in such a deep state, if you could also glide into a very deep state then you would not hear that sound. But, if there is somebody who habitually snores, he should be careful, and he should realise that he has no right to disturb others. If he can't help it, he should seek another spot for meditation. The Ashram is quite large, and you can find any solitary corner for meditation. Besides, the cave is meant only for those people who

meditate quietly, and those who can't meditate quietly should not meditate in the cave; they should sit upstairs. However, when the sushumna becomes active then a sound resembling snoring would emanate from a seeker. Sometimes when I sit out, I find Gauri making such a sound and then I ask her to get up and go inside.

Camille: *After lunch I would like to meditate or do japa, but as soon as I sit I fall into a deep sleep which lasts at least two hours. If I try to sit up I feel that my body has lost its strength and I am obliged to lie down again. If I try to open my eyes they lock closed themselves. I have tried many ways to resist sleep, like reading and walking, but as soon as I stop these activities sleep comes back. What should I do?*
Baba: Does this sleep come only after lunch or other times? (After lunch.) This indicates that either you are eating too much or too little; you are not eating the right quantity of food. Take just as much as you need; neither overeat or undereat. Generally we find that one who eats less than he needs is seized by this kind of sleep. If I want to sleep less, or if I have to go for a lecture anywhere, I overeat; that is my way of overcoming sleep. Besides, if after a spell of hard work you take food that is fresh and hot, during the process of digestion some alcohol is released inside which is quite intoxicating; that indicates very good health. I am sure that you must be working very hard in the morning, and you must be eating in a strictly measured quantity, and that is why you get overpowered by sleep after lunch. After lunch have a stroll in the garden. In the morning I don't have any breakfast, and then after lunch, I, too, find myself falling into this sort of sleep, and it is for this reason that I go to meet Swami Vijayananda and stay with him for about half an hour after lunch. If you like you may read a book. However, if you were to have a stroll that would reduce your sleepiness.

Shaun: *In the book, Dhyan Yoga and Kundalini Yoga by Amma, it is stated that in meditation there are three areas of concentration. The heart, the head, and the spot between the eyes. Please explain the significance of each, and which is better to work with.*

Baba: Let your mind remain wherever it focuses by itself. Those three centres are of equal importance, and they are all equally holy. They are equally strong seats of God's power. Wherever your mind focuses itself spontaneously, let it remain in that centre. Do not struggle with your mind to concentrate it on any particular spot. Let it function naturally. The heart, the ajna chakra and the sahasrar are holy centres that are far holier than the outer holy centres. The divine light is blazing in all three. If your attention gets focused on the heart, it is very good, because the Lord dwells there in the shape of a thumb-sized light. The same divine Being dwells as the Guru in bhrikuti, and if your attention is focused there, that, too, is very good, because you meditate on the Guru. In the sahasrar, the same pure attributeless formless Being dwells in the midst of countless beams of light, and that is the culminating point. If your mind can remain focused there, then there is no higher place it can go, for that represents the end of the journey. That is Kailas. All three centres are each A-1, not A-2, A-3 or A-4.

Randy: *Will you tell us the origin, history and meaning of the Shivalingam?*
Baba: The scriptures do not speak of the rise or setting of the Shivalingam. Shivalingam is self-begotten; it is without a beginning. It is a pure mass of light according to the scriptures. Just as out of pure love we have made a statue of Baba's form to keep him alive in our memory, and we worship it, similarly, devotees of Shiva made an image of the lingam shape which they call lingam, and it is worshipped as Shiva. It is self-existent, and that is without any beginning. Shaivites worship it as Shiva and Shakti. The lower part is considered to be Shakti, and the upper part Shiva. The two together represent the oneness of Shiva and Shakti. In fact, Shiva is not different from the lingam. He is the Supreme Being who is pure light and pure consciousness. The lingam is nothing but an image to worship the Lord. Take, for instance, the day of Shivaratri. On that day, many devotees must have been blessed with the vision of Lord Shiva, and that is why it has come to have a special significance. It is like our Republic Day which falls on Jan-

uary 26th. The lingam is also called atma lingam, an image of the Self. Its inner meaning is pure consciousness; the outer form is a mere symbol. Take for instance, another symbol called the swastika, which is considered to be very highly auspicious, and worshipped for that reason. If a great man worshipping a certain image with a strong feeling receives some power from that as a result of that worship, others also accept his deity of worship as their own. While worshipping the Shivalingam, a true devotee would identify the lingam with the entire universe. That is the true attitude.

I also believe that this entire universe which stretches itself on all sides is pervaded by the Lord, not only the lingam. The entire universe is His visible body. Take, for instance, the mode of meditation which I practised. I have attained a certain state through that, and as a result you will find many people practising this mode of meditation for many ages to come. I am sure the first worshipper must have gathered some clay into a small mound, and he must have begun to look upon it as the Lord Himself, and that is how its worship originated, and he must have offered flowers to it, and realised God through it. Only later some artist gave it a definite shape and other materials began to be used to make it.

What matters is your own attitude. You can worship anything as God. There are so many different images such as Shivalingam, or Shaligram which is considered to be sacred to Vishnu, and rudraksha beads. There lived a great queen in our country whose name was Ahalya Bai, and she was also an ardent worshipper of Shiva, and she would always hold a Shivalingam in her palm. Even today you will find many Shaivites wearing Shivalingams around their necks as you wear rudraksha beads.

Pratibha: *How should we feel thankful to those sorrows and sufferings which plunge us into despair and which makes us inactive?*
Baba: For that you have to learn a new language in which you could thank those sorrows. How to thank sorrows? Well, you will have to learn to do that.

January 19, 1972

Ekbal Shankar Chaudhary: *It's not possible to be absolutely celibate if you are married. Does that mean that one's meditation would be obstructed? What is the effect of Shaktipat on a married person? Should he receive Shaktipat initiation or not?*
Baba: Even if one is married, the wife cannot prevent him from contemplating God, observing vows, practising austerities and following his faith. A wife should in fact help her husband to completely fulfil his vows. In any case, she should not obstruct his spiritual path. If you read the *Puranas* you will find many examples of men and women who were married and who helped each other in fulfilling their pledges relating to complete abstinence for a given period of time. Women observed complete abstinence for four, eight or nine months, and so did men. Husbands and wives did not obstruct but helped each other to keep their pledge. Women are by and large very discriminating, and a wife should always be ready to help her husband to keep his vow.

If higher kriyas have started taking place, or if one has taken some sacred vow, it is necessary for him even if he is married to observe complete celibacy for a certain length of time. However, if you read the *Karma Kanda* you will find a section on 'Ritu gam', the correct time for mating between men and women, and according to that a man should have physical contact with his wife only once a month. Such a person would be regarded as a celibate. And this, too, is allowed if you are young, and you don't have any children yet. So, for the sake of getting a child you are allowed to have contact with your wife.

Generally, if you have already passed half your life you should take every care to conserve your seminal strength. It is by the force of semen that a seeker pursues sadhana with great enthusiasm. Quite frequently I recommend that all the seekers who have received Shaktipat take milk and sugar or sweets, because sugar helps in the generation of more seminal fluid. It is for this reason that here we serve sweets every day. For the different kriyas taking place as a result of Shaktipat, plentiful seminal fluid is required.

Gunnil: *How can we best work for you when we are back in Sweden?*
Baba: First you should see what exactly you can do, and what kind of skill you have. Do only worthwhile work. If, after having meditated here successfully for a length of time, and gained inner contentment, steadiness, equanimity and peace in a certain measure, you go back to your country and talk to people about this path of peace, you will be doing them a lot of good. In every country life is in terrible shape. Everywhere people seek peace and yet they don't find it. Their condition is like that of a butterfly who wonders where he will fly, where he shall settle. Like the butterfly, they keep flitting from one flower to another. They go after money, after movies, after dances and various other modes of sense-gratification only to regret and repent later. If you can create in them an interest in meditation, you will be doing them a very good turn. You can serve people by spreading meditation.

Larry: *How can the mind be kept calm and withdrawn during insult, degradation and dishonour?*
Baba: Honour and dishonour are equally misleading illusions for man. It is very hard for me to understand what satisfaction one can derive from being honoured by others. If somebody happens to honour you very highly, what inner satisfaction will arise as a result of that? The recent war has ended and many of the soldiers have been awarded special awards and honours for their gallantry; to some these honours have come posthumously. That amuses me very much. I wonder what purpose those honours serve, particularly for the people who are now no more. If you could rise to any worthwhile state through being honoured then I would honour you very highly right now.

When you gain nothing from being honoured, what can you lose by being dishonoured? Why should you attach any importance to dishonour? I am reminded of a verse from one of the Maharashtra poet-saints called Krishnasuta. He says, "O seekers, make the Lord your own through the force of your devotion. Do not pay any attention to what others may say. Your only concern should be in strengthening the tie of love between you and the Lord. Do only those things which strengthen that tie. Just as you throw away mucous from the nose, throw away both praise and blame; don't attach any importance to them because they are equally worthless. Completely get rid of the notion of 'I and mine' and only work for strengthening that knot of love. O man, if you really wish to reach somewhere, if you really wish to gain a worthwhile state, then completely eliminate selfish desires; purge your devotion of all selfishness and make it completely selfless. Only then can you really love the Lord. You should realise that birth in a human form is extremely rare and after having been born in this form you should realise its value with your power of discrimination. Your only concern should be with serving your Guru, not with praise or blame, honour or ignominy."

Praise or blame are things which arise from ego and lack of discrimination. They are absolutely irrelevant to worship of the Lord. Kabir also sings a song on this subject. He says that you should be absorbed in your pursuit like an elephant. An elephant while walking does not pay attention to anything else; he is intoxicated by his own gait, by the movement of his own body. Dogs may be barking at him but he couldn't care less. Likewise, you should be absorbed in remembering the Lord; you shouldn't care at all about what others are doing or saying about you. Only fools try to insult or dishonour you, blaming you unnecessarily. The person who is insulting you may be interested in insulting you, but if you are wise and discriminating you won't pay attention to that. Once a certain fellow began to abuse Lord Buddha. He kept on abusing him for about an hour, but Lord Buddha was not ruffled in the least, in fact, he kept smiling. There was another person there who asked the Lord, "Why did you not answer him back?"

Lord Buddha replied, "That fellow was interested in abusing; he was enjoying the nectar of abuse. But I was not at all interested in that, so the abuse did not affect me."

Therefore, let others pursue their interests. Don't take any interest in that. Pursue what interests you and just remain calm.

Durga: *What is the origin and meaning of the song to Durga that you sing on Tuesday and Friday nights? Is there a*

translation available? Also, why are there three devis that are worshipped in the Vajreshwari temple?
Baba: It might have been translated by the Ramakrishna Mission. If you were to get hold of a translation you would get to know from the introduction how this hymn originated. The name of this hymn is *Durga Sapta Shati*, and it is a great hymn composed by an ancient seer. In this hymn, one seer speaks to another. As it is the creation of a seer, it is true. It is believed that if you recite this hymn with faith and devotion then the Goddess Durga is pleased, and this is absolutely true. If you read the *Puranas* you will find that certain seers got into a certain difficult situation and then they began to call upon Durga singing this hymn to Her, and She was pleased and removed their obstacles. After She helped them, She declared that in the Kali Yuga, whoever recites this hymn will be blessed by Her in the same manner.

Though the Shakti is one, you find three devis at the Vajreshwari temple, but three in one is a product of the human mind. In the neighbouring temple, the temple next to the main Ashram building, there was once a very shabby idol of the Goddess Durga being worshipped by the local folk and that continued for a long time. Then I decided to replace it with a different statue, a more artistic one. That is how the present statue came to be installed there. There are people who said that the older one should not be thrown away, so the older one, which is just a head, is also still there. Someone may ask who those two devis are. Those who do not know will be hard put to answer this question, but I know what the fact is. So Goddess Vajra is only one. The proper manner of Her worship is to worship Her as one in all her three facets: Maha Kali, Maha Lakshmi, and Maha Saraswati. According to one tradition, Shakti is worshipped in the form of three goddesses. Hence the three statues. But we should only be concerned with the one Shakti.

Nathalie: *Should you repeat your mantra even when listening to something else, for instance when somebody is talking to you, or when listening to the arati music, or is it wrong to listen to different things at the same time?*

Baba: When the arati is being recited, you should recite the arati; you can't do the arati and your mantra at the same time. But during the first ten minutes when various instruments are sounded you can keep doing your mantra. The different sounds that are produced before the recitation help the mind to become one-pointed. They purge the atmosphere of all impurities. If you keep listening to these sounds regularly, even if your mind happens to be weak, it will acquire strength in course of time because those sounds are very good for the mind. While listening to those sounds all the vicious living germs present within are destroyed. However, if one's mind is weak through constant anxiety, through constant brooding, he may even feel giddy. While those sounds last you should keep repeating your mantra and then afterwards join the arati.

If somebody asks you something you should pay attention to him to answer him. But you should answer him in the fewest possible words. Anyone who is fond of japa should stay away from unnecessary conversation, particularly from gossip. Chatting is a crime. Anyone who is a chatterbox, who is constantly talking, cannot gain any realisations through japa. I told you the other day that Kali Yuga appeared holding his tongue in one hand and his sex organ with the other. That shows that it's essential to exercise restraint in speech. Only one who hardly talks can really repeat the Lord's Name. You will find quite a few Sunday visitors who are chatterboxes, and will put all kinds of questions to you—irrelevent questions, because they don't know anything else. Questions like "Where did you buy this saree?" or "How does your husband treat you? Does he take you to the movies?" and so on. It would be much better to keep away from them. Since these persons know nothing else besides what they think is the pleasure of married life, they may begin to ask you, "Why are you wasting your life here, why don't you get married?" Because they think that everything that is worthwhile in this world can come only from a husband or a wife. Their imagination may stretch to include a couple of children, and perhaps their children, also. If any of such characters try to engage you in conversation, don't pay any attention. You may answer a polite "yes", but you shouldn't take any interest in what they are saying. Their knowledge of life is restricted only to a husband, a couple of kids, a house, a car, their clothes, pet dogs and cats, and that is what they think is the be-all and end-all of life. And that is the limit of their interest. So you should talk less with such characters.

George: *Would Baba please explain the full symbolism and proper use and care of one's rudraksha beads, and why the rudraksha plant is used for the beads?*
Baba: The answer to this question could fill a large volume. It would be enough to say that rudraksha beads stand for Rudra and Rudra is Shiva. According to the scriptures, one who wears rudraksha becomes like Rudra. These beads are very pure. Each object has its own characteristics. I'll give you one example. According to the Vaishnavites, a Vaishnavite should inhale the fragrance of tulsi every day, and he should wear tulsi beads all the time, and he should sip water from a tulsi leaf and before starting to eat he should touch his lips with a tulsi leaf, and he should take a stroll in the tulsi garden. When I studied Ayurveda I discovered that tulsi was a great medicinal herb and it had so many wonderful properties. Tulsi destroys the germs of different diseases. It is a wonderful remedy for all fevers and for skin eruptions, and it kindles the digestive fire. If I sometimes catch a chill then I take a drink made from tulsi and bel leaves. Thus besides being holy, tulsi is very useful. Similarly, rudraksha beads also have numerous virtues. They destroy all the impurities of the blood and brain and they keep the system entirely pure. While talking about His glories, the Lord says, "It is true that I pervade everything, yet there are certain things that manifest My glory more than others." Lord Vishnu says that He dwells in tulsi, and Lord Shiva says that He dwells in rudraksha. All the devotees of Shiva wear rudraksha beads considering them to be Shiva.

Marie: *You said on Monday, that in order to be able to accept suffering with gratitude it was necessary to learn a new language. Would you please tell us how to learn this language?*
Baba: This new language arises when you suffer again and again in your life. To accept suffering as something good, to

bear it with courage and steadfastness, that is the new language. To realise that one's suffering is well deserved, to accept it cheerfully and endure it with fortitude, that's the new language. Generally people begin to cry even when visited by the slightest suffering and they begin to invoke the blessings of the Lord, of time, of destiny, every force in the universe. They think everything has gone wrong in their life. But, the attitude of a wise man is entirely different. He welcomes suffering with great love, because he is aware that if he is able to bear his present suffering gracefully he will get free from certain bad karmas and pass into a phase of joy and happiness. It's like one who has been sentenced to three months' imprisonment, accepting his imprisonment decently, being fully aware that after having borne this with courage he will be completely free from the crime that he has committed. To realise that suffering comes to us for our own good, our own benefit, to remain calm and unruffled, that is the new language.

Chandra: *What are subtle kriyas?*
Baba: Subtle kriyas occur within and are countless. Subtle kriyas are the kriyas which happen in the subtle body and they can't be described just in answer to a question. They take place in the inner nerve channels and inside the red and white and black and blue lights. I will give you examples. Sometimes the movement of prana is suspended on the gross plane, but inside it remains active. The body becomes extremely light, and filled with a new consciousness, a new inspiration. It's not a subject which can be talked about. One should find out through one's own experience. Various visions, visits to different worlds, spontaneous throbbing of nerves and prana within, all these are subtle kriyas. For this, you should read *Guru*. You may find the book called *The Science of the Soul* written by Vyas Dev somewhat helpful. Peace, contentment and bliss bubbling up from within, tears of love flowing profusely, talking to oneself in sheer rapture, swaying in joy, these are other examples of subtle kriyas.

Pratibha: *Should we try to control the yogic kriyas that are*

happening to us? If so, in what circumstances and how can our effort be successful in this direction?
Baba: You should not resist the yogic kriyas; but then you must find a place which is proper for these kriyas. If you are sitting in a crowd, or if you are in a situation where kriyas would be out of place then you should start praying to the Lord if kriyas begin to take place, and that way you can control them. Then the kriyas won't bother you either; they would listen to the Lord. Normally you should not restrain them, but if on a certain occasion control becomes necessary, then exercise it. All the same, you should honour these kriyas, because these kriyas deserve love and respect.

January 21, 1972

Ekbal: Is it true to say that so long as the disciples haven't obtained liberation the Guru does not merge into pure Being?
Baba: This is a statement which has no logic, and which is without any basis, which is without any scriptural authority behind it; it seems to be the creation of somebody's unbridled imagination. This is a statement which only a fool would make, not realised seers. No experienced beings or sages or scriptural writers would ever subscribe to it. What, after all, do you understand by the term Guru, and when does one become the Guru? Can he become the Guru when still in bondage? Or does one become a Guru only after he has attained total liberation? It doesn't make any sense to say that the Guru must also be bound like a disciple, and that the two will work together for their liberation. This is just like saying that if a student has failed, his teacher has failed. This doesn't make any sense. One attains Guruhood only after becoming totally liberated and the question of any further liberation does not arise. One becomes a Guru only after he has become one with his Guru, and there is no

question of his being in bondage. He cannot fall or sink. If the Guru is bound, he can never liberate his disciples. It is only when the Guru himself is liberated that he can liberate his disciples. If a disciple is in bondage that doesn't matter, because by the grace of his Guru he will be able to win liberation some day or another. This question seems to imply that if a devotee does not win liberation, the deity is no longer divine.

Pushpa: *Should one go for darshan and satsang with other saints, and if he does, should he accept prasad from him or not? And if he accepts prasad, with what feeling should the prasad be accepted?*
Baba: There is no harm in attending a satsang where no demands are made on you; but you should not get lost while attending any such satsang. There is absolutely no harm in accepting prasad as long as it is pure, but if the prasad happens to be impure, then don't accept it anywhere. A saint will always distribute pure prasad; he will never be willing to distribute any prasad which is impure. But he who distributes what is left over of his food after he has eaten it, or he who encourages people to take the water from his feet is not a true saint, and such a one should not be encouraged. It is good to go to satsang with different saints, but you should make sure that you don't become confused or deluded. If ever I wanted to attend any meeting somewhere then Baba would say, "Well, what's the point of going there? Whatever you will hear there comes from the mind. Why don't you think with your own mind?" He was fond of using one word, that was mitti—"dust". Sub mitti—"It's all dust". He would use it in every context. You must attend a satsang which is beneficial, without any strings attached, and which may help you in your sadhana. There is, however, no need of attending any meeting which is likely to create confusion in your mind, or which is likely to implant any fresh doubts and thus cause your downfall.

Jon: *You often encourage people to meditate, but around the Ashram and in Amma's article, I hear that one should not worry about meditation, it's Guruseva that counts.*

Please explain. Also, please explain what Guruseva is after the devotee has left the Ashram.
Baba: If you want your meditation to be really fruitful, if you want it to be consummated, then you must put in service to the Guru. Otherwise you will be sitting with closed eyes for any length of time but nothing much will happen. Guruseva does not only mean that you put in a little physical work in the Ashram. Guruseva implies that you obey all the instructions of the Guru most faithfully. If you are meditating without Guruseva then you will have to make a very strong effort, but if you are putting in Guruseva then meditation will come to you automatically. Your attitude to Guruseva must be the right one. You must not look upon Guruseva as a task or chore which you have to do, as if you were working in a factory or an office. If your attitude is such, then Guruseva will not yield any fruit. It will be just like any ordinary work. What matters along with action is the feeling behind it. If the attitude with which a particular action is undertaken is not a right one, it takes a very long time for that action to bear fruit.

There are some boys and girls here who are hardly allowed time for meditation, and it is for this reason that meditation chases them. I ask some people to meditate more because I know that they are not meditating very well. You may be sitting for two hours, but how much of that time has been spent in actual meditation? Meditation is like an atom bomb and has to be handled with great care. You should be able to bear the heat of meditation. If you don't have much fat on you and you still insist on meditating for a long time, in a short while you will become emaciated and your body will lose all its radiance. That is why I ask some people not to meditate at all and they shouldn't meditate then. If they do, the Shakti will eat up all their vigour and make them useless.

The reason I insist on celibacy in the Ashram is so that you will have enough seminal fluid in your body to be able to bear the heat of meditation. I ask good meditators to drink milk and take other foods that generate more semen for the same reason. For meditation you need all the strength and vigour you have. To provide you with a sweet every day we have to spend so much money every month.

The sweets are provided to make your meditation better, to enable you to have more semen in your system, not to gratify your palates. (If I say that sweets generate more semen in the body that doesn't mean that you should begin to take sweets three or four times a day and thus spoil whatever little health you have.) The fire of meditation is generated from ojas (vigour or strength) which comes from seminal fluid. So anyone who is experiencing a high state of meditation should not meditate too long. I ask only those who are not meditating well to meditate for longer periods. But if you want to rise to the high state of the pure imageless Being in meditation, if you want to tap all the inner treasures, then it's Guruseva which will afford you immeasurable help.

After leaving the Ashram, meditation and rememberance of the Guru constitute Guruseva. The best Guruseva would be to live according to the dictates of the Guru, obeying him in both the spirit and the letter.

Lotte: *When I was in America, people who found out that I was going to an Ashram in India always asked me why I was running away from the world. They said I should stay there and help others. What should you tell people like those?*
Baba: When I was going abroad somebody asked me, "Why are you going abroad? First you should try to set things right in your own country."

I said, "Look, it's your limited vision that looks upon this country as my country and the other places as foreign places. For God the whole universe is one."

It's not right to split the world into fragments and name them India or America or Paris or London. Those who are intelligent and perceptive would not worry whether you are in America or India or elsewhere as long as you are being helpful or useful.

Going to the Ashram does not mean that you are stopping helping people. The question arises: what sort of help are you going to render to others? If you have wealth you can help people with your wealth; if you have a skill or art you can help people with that; or if you have something else you may help them with that. But if you have nothing, how will you help people? There is no point in being satisfied with using the word "help" which has a certain romantic glamour about it. By your stay in the Ashram you will acquire enough strength to come back and really help others.

And what makes people think that the Ashram is not part of the world? It is as much a part of the world as any other place. You will be helping people as much in the Ashram as anywhere else.

What people say is an outcome of their own limited vision. Take the case of a tenant in a large building. He considers the particular apartment that he is living in to be his own and he doesn't concern himself about the rest of the building. But the owner of the building regards the entire building as his own. For God, the distinction between east and west or native and foreign is not valid at all. As far as He is concerned, you may live anywhere and still help people.

Kailash Amma: *What exactly is meant by total surrender to the Guru?*
Baba: You would understand the meaning when you have made this total surrender to the Guru. If somebody holding a mango in his hand were to ask me, "What would happen if I gave it to somebody else?" I would say, "Give it to somebody else and find out what happens. Don't raise a question as long as it is in your hand." If the disciple is able to make a total surrender then he becomes one with the Guru. In this connection Mira said, "You give yourself and get Hari, the Lord, in return." Mira sings in one of her beautiful bhajans, "I have chased God, I have even weighed gold in a balance and purchased the whole of Him." If you want to buy, say, a kilo of apples from the market, you have to pay a certain amount, so one may ask, if you have purchased the Lord, what would you give for that? And Mira says, "I gave Mira and got the Lord in return." She gave herself. This is what total surrender is: to give yourself completely to the Guru and to get the whole of him in return is what constitutes surrender. Jnaneshwar Maharaj says in his commentary most expressively, "He who takes refuge in the Lord gets up after having become one with Him."

Nathalie: *After lunch I often feel like sitting for meditation, but I have been told that it might be harmful. Is that true? Is there any proper time for meditation?*
Baba: How many chapatis do you eat? (1). Do you take rice (Yes). Then you can sit. Do you fill your tummy? You are told not to sit immediately after a meal because your stomach is full, and for meditation your stomach should be empty. If you are eating less you can sit after a meal. However, it is better to wait for half an hour or forty-five minutes after a meal and then meditate. If you are able to pass into meditation, then meditation will help you to digest your food very quickly. You should take one and a half chapatis for lunch.

Larry A.: *Should one meditate when he is ill?*
Baba: It's good to meditate during illness, because meditation will help you get over it quickly. If you meditate calmly either in the sitting or lying position, meditation will help you overcome the illness. Or if there is pain in any part of the body, meditation will drive it away. However, if you are ill, you should not practise asanas or pranayama, particularly bastrika. But meditation can be practised in all conditions. It will help you to overcome your illness very quickly.

Uma: *Does the pujari recite mantras while he is waving the lights to Bhagawan Nityananda? What mantras?*
Baba: Yes, there are certain specific mantras for this purpose mentioned in the *Vedas* and *Puranas*. There are mantras of various kinds, and there are certain mantras which are meant for this particular purpose, and which embody the true feeling and attitude of worship. But then even if you do not know these mantras it is enough to wave lights while chanting *Guru Om* or *Om namah Shivaya*. There are certain mantras which help you to remember the different parts of the deity's body while you are waving lights to Him. For instance, you will be made aware that you are now waving lights to the head, now the neck, shoulders, arms, and so on. And then there are certain mantras which contain the higher aspects of such a ritual, and that is the aspect of knowledge. The meaning of the first verse of the

arati that we sing every day is, "Oh Master, please grant discrimination and knowledge to all your devotees, and make our minds happy and fill them with joy." The second line means, "Please help me overcome the dualistic notion of thine and mine, and establish me in the state of equality-consciousness, in the state of perfect identity." The third line means, "I am waving lights to you because you encompass all gods, you are Hari, you are Shiva, you are Vishnu, and all other deities are embodied in you." The last verse says, "Muktananda says, 'You are the father and mother of the whole universe, and you are also my father and mother, and that is why I am waving lights to you'."

There are certain mantras that you can recite while waving lights but if you don't know any mantras, it's enough to recite *Guru Om* and wave lights to different parts of the Guru, his head, neck, shoulders and feet, and so on.

Shyama: *If there is a relation of yours to whom the stars and planets are unfavourable, can you help him by practising certain austerities and japa? If so, which austerities and mantras should you practise?*
Baba: The best austerity is to recite the *Guru Gita*. Recite the *Guru Gita* twice or thrice every day and all troubles will go. *Guru Om* is the prince of mantras. Keep on reciting it. If you recite this mantra, you don't have to recite any other mantra. It destroys all sins and all forms of poverty. It destroys all calamities. It frees you from the evil influence of evil spirits, ghosts and demons.

It's good to sit on a mat while reciting this mantra. For your particular purpose you should sit on a blanket, facing east or north. After performing the arati to the Guru, you should say to the Guru, "I am reciting the *Guru Gita* now in order to deliver my relatives, to free them from certain difficulties." The *Guru Gita* has great power. The *Vishnu Sahasranam* is equally powerful, and so is the Chandi hymn. All these different texts have equal power, but the *Guru Gita* is very simple and you all know it.

Kalyani: *What are the major obstacles for a student on the path of Siddha Yoga?*
Baba: Do you have any particular difficulty in mind? Talk

to other people and find out from them. Everyone is faced with one obstacle or another, but if you are sufficiently intelligent you can be free of all these obstacles. Who is free of obstacles? Take the case of an ordinary student. Is he free from difficulties? Take the case of married life, is that free from difficulties and obstacles? Or take your factories and offices and again you are faced with different hardships and different problems. There is no field in life which is free of hardships or difficulties. But those who are self-disciplined will not be unnerved by these obstacles and difficulties, while those who don't have any strength will be unnerved by even the slightest difficulty. I can at the present moment mention only one obstacle, and that is the pull of pleasure.

There is no such thing as a difficulty or an obstacle. There may be obstacles on other paths, and there may be reasons for that, but in the field of meditation for a Siddha student there are no obstacles, because this is the easiest of all paths, and you can pursue it with great ease. If you don't get time during the day you can meditate while sleeping. What's so difficult about that? If you hang around with people who are hostile to it, obstacles may arise, but for the students there are no difficulties. For everyone there is only one obstacle, and that is outer activity and the play of the sense organs and unbridled thoughts and useless fantasies. There are no other obstacles for a student of Siddha Yoga, and if there are particular obstacles that you have in mind, bring them up. It is, however, very difficult to receive Siddha Yoga. It is difficult to become a student of Siddha Yoga. But all difficulties vanish once you follow Siddha Yoga. You fall only before accepting Siddha Yoga. Love of independence, individual freedom, wanting to do whatever you feel is good for you, and difficulty in surrendering yourself to a Master are such obstacles. But after you have accepted Siddha Yoga, after you have accepted a Master, then there are no difficulties. The more you efface yourself in relation to Siddha Yoga and the Guru, the more you grow. To humble yourself before the Guru does not mean self-humiliation and self-belittling, but to be free from pride and to accept divine virtues. It is only stupid fools, not wise, discriminating people who think that humility or surrender to the Guru or the practice of the divine virtues implies slavery and dependence. In fact, the greater you are, the more divine qualities will you have.

Elizabeth: *How does one know whether one has received Shaktipat or not? Does the Kundalini start to rise when one has received it?*
Baba: What else is Shaktipat if not the rising of Kundalini? Shaktipat means the awakening of Elizabeth. Are you asleep or meditating? When the inner Shakti is awakened the person concerned will get to know himself. Different and new processes will begin to take place inside which indicate that something new has happened.

Don Sharpe: *What are dreams?*
Baba: The scriptures haven't laid down any laws relating to the subject. All that can be said is that dreams are subtle movements that take place in the subtle body during the state of sleep. Your dreams are composed of various ingredients, some of which are purely imaginary, while others are related to your life. Some relate to what you are doing, while others may have nothing to do with that. Some dreams are worthwhile while others are worthless. However, dreams always have an element of truth in them. Some dreams are prophetic, and they turn out to be true later. Some devotees in Bombay sometimes have a dream that they are receiving a fruit from Baba, and when they come here, it so happens that I have a fruit lying by my side and I give it to them, and their dream comes true. The world that you experience during dreams is a purely mental creation, and as you become more and more absorbed in meditation then dreams become less frequent. Generally speaking it is the outer world which is reflected in dreams. But at the same time you can not completely reject dreams as something totally unreal because during certain dreams Siddha purushas can come from Siddhaloka and initiate you. Dreams should not be taken too seriously or too lightly. I quite often see impending disasters in dreams, approaching floods, or an approaching war or approaching accidents, while at other times I don't see them. There is no point in making any definite statement about dreams. Dreams are

things which pertain to the subtle body. In dreams you experience your own mind in different forms. You experience dreams only as long as you are in the subtle body, but once you have gotten beyond the subtle body and start experiencing the causal body you will not return to the subtle body and you will not experience dreams any longer. Dreams do not exist in the deep sleep state, and after you have enjoyed sound slumber you get up and say, "Well, I had such wonderful sleep, that I didn't even dream." Dreams have nothing to do with the causal body. Different books would give different interpretations, but they are all inconclusive. Dreams are creations of your mind and imagination. All kinds of dreams keep arising and vanishing on the screen of the mind. But one who is able to see dreams like a witness is very advanced. This world is considered to be a dream by many, but it is the one through which you are able to get to the final truth. Dreams indicate something beyond them. You sleep and dream, and on getting up you know that you have dreamt: that proves that there was somebody who was watching the dreams, who was not asleep while you were dreaming. Dreams do indicate that there is some higher reality, and that is what their value is. Dreams are an inner phenomenon, the support of which is the inner Self. The dream world is based on the inner Self. Dreams continue to appear for a very long time, even to a seeker.

January 26, 1972

Nathalie: *How does a true disciple spend his day with a true Guru?*
Baba: I always remember the different questions put by different people to me. I don't know whether those who take notes remember which questions have been put by which people or not, but I certainly do, and I have observed that

Nathalie's questions are in fact only different forms of the same question which concerns the relationship between the Guru and disciple. That shows that she has the quality of ideal discipleship. It's a very good question.

A true disciple should spend his day with his Guru by feeling completely one with him, merging his separate identity in him; he should not feel different from him in even the slightest measure. The most important thing is that the disciple should be willing to obey the bidding of the Guru, and this is what Arjuna told Krishna, "I shall do Thy bidding." For a true disciple this much is enough: obedience to the command of the Guru.

This science of the relationship between Guru and disciple is a very important, very noble science. People should, in fact, look at this question very carefully; they should give deep thought to it. Not only foolish, ignorant people come for instruction, people who are very intelligent, very educated people come to him, even the educators come to him for instruction. One can understand a poor destitute fellow coming to the Guru, because he would be interested in some material gain, but people who already have enough also come to the Guru. What on earth could they be getting from him? Not only the weak approach him, but even the strong approach him, even those who are holding the reigns of the government, who are wielding great authority and power.

Nathalie is always putting one question, and I always remember the questions put by different people, because the question put by a certain seeker shows his quality.

A disciple should always behave in a manner that is in perfect accord with the Guru's wishes, and obey his commands all the time. You will find a large number of self-styled disciples who interpret the Guru's commands in their own way, and who like to serve the Guru in the light of their own interpretations of his commands. They will be raising doubts and reasoning all the time. There was a seeker with Kabir who was always putting one question, and that was, "What should a disciple be like?" He would put this question on every occasion that he happened to be there. Once it was on Ekadasi day. (Ekadasi day is considered to be very sacred in our country. On that day many people do not take full meals, they do not take any cereal, they take only fruit.)

It being a sacred day, a large number of people had gathered in order to hear Kabir talk about spiritual matters. This seeker was also present there and he was sitting in the front row. He put the same question to Kabir, "What should a disciple be like?" He said, "Today in particular you should talk on this subject because it is such a sacred day."

Kabir looked here and there and then he called one of his disciples whose name was Kamal. Kabir commanded Kamal to bring some mava (solidified condensed milk) for prasad, and he said that he should flavour it with salt, adding that since such a large number of disciples had gathered on such a sacred day, prasad should be distributed to all of them. Kamal got a certain quantity of mava and added quite a bit of salt to it. And he brought the prasad and put it by the side of Kabir. Then he asked the seeker who had put the question to Kabir to distribute the prasad to everyone. He said, "You also partake of it and then sit quietly."

Then Kabir began to work at his loom, and while he was working, the shuttle happened to fall down. Kabir said to Kamal, "Look, Kamal, one of the shuttles has fallen down, please bring a big lamp so we can find it."

Kamal lighted a lamp and came with it. He said, "Try to find it."

Kamal, during broad daylight, was using a lamp to find the shuttle that had fallen. He found it and gave it to Kabir. There were many clever ones in the audience who were highly educated, and they were wondering what had happened to those two characters; they thought that both of them had gone nuts. It could be understood in the case of Kabir, because he was an old man, but it was absolutely ununderstandable in Kamal who was a young fellow and who seemed quite clever. Here was a Guru asking the disciple to bring mava mixed with salt, and then to find a shuttle with the help of a lamp when it was broad daylight. And the disciple obeyed the Guru. So there must be something wrong with both of them.

Kabir got busy with his weaving again, while the seeker who had put the question was waiting all the time to hear Kabir, because he was a true seeker and was very much interested in that subject. Then, pointing to Kamal, Kabir said, "Haven't you realised what a disciple should be like?

A disciple should be like Kamal. What makes you think that Kamal is so unintelligent that he doesn't know that you never add salt to mava, you only add sugar. But because I asked him to mix salt with it he obeyed me. And who would think that you would need the light of a lamp to find a shuttle when it's such a bright day?"

This is how a true disciple should spend his day with a true Guru. He should continue to obey whatever the Guru says. Jnaneshwar Maharaj says that a true disciple would not let his mind interfere with the commands given by the Guru, he would obey them absolutely. A disciple should always behave in a manner that is in perfect accord with the Guru's wishes, and obey his commands all the time.

Rajendra Pandit: *Does total surrender mean that we should bear whatever happens in life, or should we pray to the Guru to remove the obstacles, trust in his help and pray for the same?*
Baba: If a seeker is only interested in having the Guru remove whatever obstacles or difficulties come in his path, then he is behaving like a businessman. There was a time when businessmen in Bombay used to employ tough characters to keep the ruffians away. Those people who go to the Guru only to have the obstacles removed are using the Guru like a businessman; they are using the Guru as a means. The Guru is, after all, not like a lawyer employed by a wealthy man for the purpose of fighting all his cases; or like a doctor who is employed for treating him whenever he falls sick; or like an engineer who looks after all the technical matters. The Guru is certainly not like any of those employees, whose specialty is removing all obstacles and troubles. This should not be one's attitude to the Guru. As far as worldly advantages are concerned, they are purely transitory. Wealth comes and goes, success comes and goes. So should one use the precious wealth of the Guru's Shakti to acquire these petty advantages?

I never approached my Guru for anything. I never described to him how I was at any given time, whether I was in a good or bad condition. The Guru is there to promote your highest welfare, to bring the highest good within your reach. So why expect him to help you overcome petty problems and insignificant disorders? One does not go to the Guru, worship him or serve him only to overcome trivial physical ailments. You do not worship the Guru to get rid of a bad cold. Because if you get rid of a bad cold, it is quite likely that you may begin to suffer from heat, and then you would want the Guru to remove that trouble. Then after he has freed you of the heat, it may be an excess of phlegm that may attack you, and then you want the Guru to solve that problem. But all these disorders will keep following you, one after the other. The Guru is not meant to help you overcome these petty things. He is there to enable you to get rid of the bondage of birth and death.

Tukaram Maharaj says that one should not pray to the Lord for the removal of small, insignificant difficulties. After all, pleasure and pain are purely transitory. Pain is followed by pleasure and pleasure is followed by pain. Pain did not exist before it came and it will not exist after a while. Similarly, pleasure did not exist before it came and will not exist after a while. So why pray to the Lord for things which are purely shortlived? It would be as stupid as approaching the Commander-in-Chief of the Army to help you pull out a thorn from your foot when it could be removed with the help of a needle.

A few days before Lord Krishna was about to leave His body, He called Arjuna and they went for a walk in a vast forest. They had covered quite some distance when Krishna said, "Arjuna, I am feeling very thirsty. Please find me some water to drink."

Arjuna looked for water in all directions but he could not find any. Finally he climbed a tree and looked around. He saw a trail of smoke rising so he went in that direction. He thought that since there was smoke, there must be some human being there who would know where water was. He walked until he came to a cottage in which a very old lady was sitting. She was wearing only a small piece of cloth around her waist and the rest of her body was bare. She was worshipping Krishna. A picture of Krishna was in front of her. She had applied kum-kum on it and decorated it with beautiful flowers. In front was a new cushion decorated also. On both sides of the picture, however, there was a naked sword hanging on the wall. As Arjuna looked in he was amazed. Such an old woman was sitting with closed eyes repeating the name of Krishna on her beads, obviously deeply absorbed in japa, yet there were two shiny swords hanging on the wall. He could not understand why the swords were there.

While he was standing there wondering, the old woman opened her eyes and saw him. Arjuna came in and bowed to her. "What brings you into this thick forest?" she asked.

"I have come in search of water," Arjuna replied.

The woman said, "You will find water over there. Help yourself."

"O mother," said Arjuna, "may I ask one question of you?"

"Certainly," she said.

"Mother, I am greatly bewildered. I see that you are a great devotee of Lord Krishna, and your heart is saturated with love for Him. I see a picture of Krishna and beside it a cushion that hasn't been used by anyone. You obviously get deeply absorbed in japa. But I wonder what those two naked swords are for. What are they doing here? You are so old, you surely cannot use them. And you are filled with such love and the atmosphere is so pure. In such an atmosphere, why could you possibly need the swords?"

The old woman said, "The sword on the left is meant for Draupadi and the one on the right is meant for Arjuna."

"What is their crime that you have kept swords ready for them? What have they done?"

She flared up and said, "You say Arjuna has committed no crime? For the sake of power, for the sake of the throne, for the sake of merely ephemeral, fleeting power, Arjuna troubled and pestered the Lord so much—the throne, which after you have enjoyed for a while is bound to pass from your hands—the throne which can be seized by any robber, by any unworthy man who happens to have some power—for the sake of that throne, for the sake of political power, Arjuna compelled the Lord to wash his horses and do his other tasks for him, making all sorts of demands on Him all the time. Arjuna thinks that he is a great devotee, but I think that he is a rogue, a villain, and the moment I see him I will cut off his head."

As Arjuna heard this he shrank back in fear. Then he

said, "What was Draupadi's crime?"

At this question the woman became furious. She said, "Draupadi was the worst sinner. She harrassed the Lord so much. While she was being stripped in court she began to call upon Him in sheer distress and the Lord had to run to help her. He had to change Himself into a roll of cloth to cover her and save her honour. Why was she so particular about it? If she had let her sari go when it was being pulled, no harm would have come to her. After all, the body is a corpse and after it dies you do not care whether it is kept covered or not. And on every slight occasion she was calling upon Krishna, wanting Him to save her honour even though she had not given Him any devotion. If I happen to see her, I am going to cut off her head too, and I wouldn't think a minute before doing it."

"What is the cushion meant for?" Arjuna asked meekly.

"This cushion is for true devotees such as Uddhava and the Gopis, who loved the Lord selflessly, who did not make the least demands on Him in return for their devotion and love."

Therefore, why should you want to use divine power for gaining petty material advantages which are not going to last in any case? Why shouldn't such great power be used for spiritual growth and enlightenment? One's devotion should be utterly selfless and it should not be accompanied by any petty or trivial desires. Pleasure and pain come and go; and all misfortunes and fortunes do not last. Spiritual power should not be used for material advantages. It should be used only for spiritual growth. True devotion is free from selfish desire. Selfless love is just another name for true devotion. Those whose devotion is tainted by desire are not real devotees. They are only shrewd businessmen.

Chandrakant Sheth: *When will I get Gurukrupa so that I can advance on the path of mukti?*
Baba: You will receive it the moment you are worthy of it. If somebody were to ask me, "When will I be able to sleep?" I would say, "The moment you lay down." It has nothing to do with time. Similarly, if somebody were to ask me, "When will my hunger be satisfied?" I would say, "The moment you take food." For that I don't have to make any prophecy. You

will be blessed with Gurukrupa the moment you make yourself worthy of it; and once you are blessed by the Guru's grace everything comes to you.

Draupadi: *Should an aspirant depend on others for his personal tasks like washing his clothes, cleaning his room, making his bed and so forth? Isn't it better for a sadhak to wash his own clothes than have them done by the village dhobi? Is it necessary for a meditator to wash his own clothes, or can they be sent to a dhobi?*

Baba: A seeker does not have to get his daily wear washed by a dhobi. However, under certain circumstances, there is no objection to your using the service of a dhobi. For example, if you are living in a city and there isn't much water available, and you don't have much time to wash your clothes; then instead of wearing dirty filthy clothes, it's better to have them washed by a dhobi. I am always telling you that you should not change your place of meditation, you should stick to the same spot, and I also tell you to have a special set of clothes for meditation, and you should not use them for anything else. The clothes that you wear should be very neat and pure. I have visited the ghat where the dhobis wash clothes and where they live; some of you might also have visited it. If you were to visit such a place you would find the clothes of so many different people with different mentalities all mixed together. The clothes of people carry their vibrations, and your vibrations are pure and they get mixed with impure vibrations. Your healthy germs get mixed up with the morbid germs of other people. Would you like that? That is why I have got different rooms for seekers and we ask the visitors to put up separately. Would a dhobi ever be concerned about the purity and neatness of your clothes?

As far as possible you should do your own personal chores, you should make your own bed. As far as washing of clothes is concerned, it's better for you to wash your own clothes, or friends can help each other, but if that is not possible then you should at least set aside a set of clothes for meditation, because a dhobi mixes up clothes with different vibrations, and you should give a thought to that. And if you were to wash your own clothes it would only mean a half an hour of work. If you really care for purity then you would not have your clothes washed by a dhobi. During my sadhana I would not change my underwear, the special type of underwear that I used for meditation, I would not change it even for six years. I did not mind it getting old; my concern was with the particles of Shakti with which it would get saturated in course of time. Such underwear becomes so saturated with power that it used to happen in the olden days that when a woman was about to deliver a baby, if there was no nurse or doctor available in the neighbourhood then it was enough to soak that underwear in water and sprinkle a few drops of water from it on the woman's private parts, and she would have the delivery with no difficulty. The residents of Kokamthan would bear testimony to what I am saying. You shouldn't be washing your clothes in soap every day. In fact I become very angry with Noni or Sudhaka if they wash my clothes in soap every day. You do not need it every day; occasionally you may use a simple soap. From now on you should approach the dhobi after giving careful thought to what I have said. If you can't do without his services then I will give him special instructions that he should wash your clothes in special water. A variety of smallpox has broken out in the town and the germs were brought here through clothes you have given to the dhobi. Here smallpox could not break out; our food is so pure. You should think about it.

Kalyani: *Where is the sound emanating from inside us when we are chanting? Sometimes I feel that it is coming from my heart, and I have trouble chanting, and other times it seems to come from a deeper point. Is this so?*
Baba: The sound when you chant arises from the heart in every case, and, in fact, no one should have any trouble while chanting. If you have trouble that shows that you are suffering from some gastric disorder; a lot of gas must have accumulated in your stomach. If you are not suffering from any disorder you would not have any trouble chanting; even now you couldn't be having any trouble during the morning chant. If there is any trouble it must be coming during the afternoon or evening chanting. (Yes).

In fact, there are four levels of sound present within a

human being which are called Vaikheri, Madhyama, Pashyanti and Para. Most people confuse speech with its grossest level only, the level that is uttered by the tongue. It is not the tongue which speaks; it's a subtler level in the throat from which the gross sound arises. Underneath this subtle level there is a still deeper level called Pashyanti, the causal level which is present in the heart. But that does not represent the origin of sound, either. The origin lies still deeper in the transcendental level, the centre of which is situated in the navel. That is called the Para level.

Through chanting one should be able to get to the deepest level, the transcendental, the Para level. So far you have experienced only the third level, the level which is in the heart. If you were to experience the deepest level, your speech would become absolutely purified, and you would have no trouble. When the sound begins to emanate from the navel centre, it will sound very sweet and melodious.

My Guru was no singer by any standards, yet he was quite fond of humming what appeared to be a very funny tune, and whenever he hummed it people would rush to hear it because it would always sound so sweet and melodious. When you begin to chant from the deepest level then your voice acquires extraordinary sweetness and whatever you utter will come true. Whatever arises from this fourth level is arising, in fact, from Shakti Herself, not from any particular individual, whether it is you or me. In the course of chanting, just as you are able to penetrate to the heart level, if you are able to penetrate to the navel level, you would come to have divine realisation. Chanting has great importance, and it affords you access to the deepest level, to the transcendental level.

January 28, 1972

Selma Kruckman: *What is meditation and what is its function?*

Baba: In ordinary parlance meditation means concentration—that is, when the mind remains focused on what it happens to be engaged with at a given moment. There are many different kinds of concentration. For instance, even before certain people get up from their beds they begin to meditate on their morning cup of tea. And their meditation is so intense that if the morning cup of tea weren't given to them they would feel that the life was passing out of them. Their longing is extremely overpowering. Similarly, in the evening, one begins to pursue whatever one is interested in. For instance, an alcoholic would rush to liquor, a cricket player would like to have a game of cricket and a drug addict would like to have a shot of drugs. So, meditation means becoming absorbed in the object of your particular pursuit. But this is meditation on an outer object.

In the same manner, meditation in its highest form is the complete merging of the mind in the inner Self, the complete identification of the mind with its source. Meditation is that state of total inner bliss and peace in which the mind becomes completely absorbed in the inner Self and no other thought or image flits across it. This total inner stillness is the goal. Whatever processes help to bring about this state are also included in meditation.

The mind is in the habit of depending on an object. It must engage itself with something, whether an outer object or inner feeling. Sometimes it is overcome by anger and it focuses on anger. Sometimes it is overcome with love and its attention remains focused on love. When it is overcome by desire or lust then it stays focused on that for some time. But in deep meditation the mind is drawn away from all those emotions, feelings and objects, and is directed towards the inner Self. Therefore, when you meditate, try to pull your mind back from roaming around among different objects and turn its attention towards the inner heart. When the mind begins to experience the peace, joy and bliss which surround the Spirit, then it is in a state of meditation.

Meditation serves very important functions and its results are not trivial or insignificant. Through meditation a complete universe is brought into being. The *Upanishads* say that the earth is held in position by meditation. The ancient sages and seers found out how to govern society, how to insure that it functioned and ran smoothly through meditation, and it was through meditation that they discovered various laws. Those sages accomplished great tasks through meditation.

If you are able to meditate well, in the right manner, then through meditation your body will be able to get whatever it needs. It is in meditation that the inner Shakti is awakened. As the mind becomes purified through meditation, as inner bliss begins to trickle through, and the mind begins to sip it, then all the particles of blood which are generally hot and boiling become cool and experience that peace. The movement of prana also becomes even and regulated. In our present condition when our mind is disturbed and distracted the movement of prana is not smooth, it is jerky and disturbed, as a result of which we suffer from different ailments and we suffer from peacelessness. Through meditation the body is brought into a state of perfect balance, perfect equipoise and all its deficiencies are made up and excesses corrected. For instance, if there is a particular part of the body which is not receiving enough blood, then the blood supply of that part will be increased. If there is a part of the body which is receiving too much blood, then the blood supply to that part will be decreased. Meditation also promotes longevity and oxygen will be evenly distributed to all the parts of the body, and thus the needs of all the parts of the body begin to be attended to by the Kundalini Shakti Herself. In the course of time through proper meditation you will overcome all wickedness, passions of jealousy, hate and hostility to others. Meditation transforms you into a veritable abode of love and peace and bliss. Not only this—meditation makes you aware of the divine inner power. Due to ignorance of this power we consider ourselves to be small and insecure. Through meditation we become aware of our inherent divinity.

Meditation is not meant only for monks, nuns or renunciates. Meditation is meant for everyone. Only this afternoon we received a letter which said that a boy of seven or eight was meditating very well; he was having extraordinary experiences. So even children can meditate. The distinction of child and adult does not hold as far as meditation is concerned, because only the body is young or old. The inner Shakti is neither old nor young; She is ever in the same state.

If you were to exclude meditation from life, what would be left? It is meditation which makes us aware of the essence of life, its inner meaning, which makes us feel that we are really living for something, that our life has some significance, some purpose. Otherwise life is reduced to a mere hideous mockery. Thus meditation initiates significant inner processes and keeps them going, and in the end it makes us realise our inherent divinity, our Godhood. If you wish to understand it more fully, you should read *Chitshakti Vilas (Guru)*.

Lowell: *What constitutes the inner relationship between the Guru and disciple, and how important is the external relationship compared to this?*
Baba: If the Guru is the Guru of the disciple, and if the disciple is the disciple of the Guru, then the question of the inner and outer doesn't arise. The disciple and Guru are neither one with each other, nor separate from each other. As long as one does not become a perfect disciple one is bothered by such a question, but the moment that one becomes a perfect disciple, one also becomes the Guru. As long as a Guru has not become a perfect Guru he is bothered by this question, and the moment he becomes a perfect Guru he also is a perfect disciple. There are many people who claim, "Well I have become a disciple," and then after some time you find them complaining, "Well, I am afraid I haven't yet received anything." If you have really become a disciple, the question of any desire, even the desire for attainment, would not arise.

In this connection I will narrate a story. There was a millionaire who had two sons, but he wanted many more, so he put an advertisement in the paper saying that he was willing to adopt any number of children. Then he adopted about a dozen or more, and he came to have a large number of sons. All the adopted children would tell him again and again, "You are more than a real father to us." This is how days were passing. All the adopted children were making merry and enjoying comforts and luxuries that their father's wealth had provided them.

Now each of them started worrying that they had not really received anything from the father. They started whispering among themselves, saying, "Look, even though we consider him to be our real father, he hasn't yet apportioned any of his wealth to us." And they were also able to get a number of people to sympathize with them. Then they complained to their accomplices, "Look, we have been loving him more than a father for such a long time, but he hasn't given us anything, in spite of the fact that he is such a wealthy person." Then they got together and held a meeting one day and they decided to approach their father through a spokesman with a letter. They wrote a letter saying that they had been loving him for such a long time and yet they hadn't received anything. Their lawyer was present and there also was a professor there.

When the father received this letter and read it he felt very happy about it. He called all the sons and said, "Look, I am very happy with the step that you have taken. I am delighted with it. In fact, I hadn't thought about it. I was always under the impression that since you are my children all my wealth is bound to come to you. But now that each one of you wants his share, I have appointed a committee consisting of two lawyers and two professors, and they will discuss the matter with you. Please let the committee know what exactly your demands are, each one of you."

Now the different sons expressed their demands. One of them said, "Well, I would like to have the Mercedes car."

The second said, "I would like to have the Turiya Mandir."

The third demanded the meditation room, and the fourth demanded the kitchen. There was only one among them who said that he really didn't want anything. The committee asked him, "Why is it that you haven't asked anything of him?"

He said, "Look, I am his son, and he is my father, and everything that belongs to him also belongs to me. How can the question of expressing any demands arise?"

Now the document was presented to the father. The father went through the contents and then he said to all the children who had expressed demands, "Look, all of you should leave after having a delicious meal, and all my wealth will go to this child."

So, for a true disciple the question of receiving anything from the Guru or not receiving anything from the Guru would never arise, because the Guru is his, in fact entirely his; he belongs to the Guru, and the Guru belongs to him. The question of an outer relationship opposed to an inner relationship, or inner opposed to outer, would be entirely irrelevant. For one who has totally taken refuge in the Guru, who has totally surrendered to him, there is neither internal nor external relationship. He becomes one with the Guru. He becomes the Guru's and the Guru becomes his. The difference between Guru and disciple vanishes completely. So for a true disciple the distinction between the inner and outer is not at all valid. To him the Guru pervades the inner and outer. The Guru is above, the Guru is below, the Guru is all around, and the disciple enjoys intimate oneness with him all the time.

However, this distinction between inner and outer can be considered to be valid only in one sense, and that is that even though the Guru and disciple are one, yet for the purpose of devotion, the disciple looks upon himself as being different from the Guru; the Guru is his deity and he is the worshipper. Otherwise the Guru and disciple are one. Tukaram Maharaj says in one of his verses, "Tuka lies prostrate at the feet of one who worships a deity by himself becoming the deity." Viththale can be worshipped only by becoming Viththale, not by remaining ignorant. Don't think that these saints were fools, that they didn't know the secret of worship. They all say that the ideal way to worship the Lord is to become the Lord yourself. Similarly Muktananda says, "He who worships the Guru, himself becoming the Guru, is worshipped by all." This is the secret of non-dual devotion. This is not worship of form, nor is it a sectarian ritual, nor is it any secret variety of Hinduism. This is the highest mode of expressing one's love. This is how love for the Lord, or love for the Guru, finds expression. So you worship the Guru by becoming the Guru yourself. The secret of the Guru-disciple relationship is that the disciple loves and worships his Guru, himself becoming the Guru.

Kedarnath: *Baba, you told us not to meditate for more than* *one hour and forty-five minutes. Does this apply to chanting, japa and swadhyaya also? Or can these be practised throughout the day? If there is a seeker who gets into a state of meditation spontaneously which lasts for more than two hours, would that also prove harmful?*

Baba: As far as you are concerned, you should meditate only for an hour, not even for one hour and forty-five minutes, because to be able to meditate for that long you must have a tremendous reserve of seminal strength in you. Through meditation that vigour is consumed, and by meditating too much, the body will become completely emaciated. Someone asked me the other day why celibacy is practised in the Ashram, and in this connection I would like to make it clear that the Ashram is not a nightclub. In the Ashram it is not dollars which count; it's the seminal fluid that counts. For meditation what you need is not dollars, not eggs, not sweets, nor chocolates or cakes, what you need is this strength, this seminal vigour. Therefore I insist on total celibacy as long as you are staying in the Ashram. It is meant only for meditation and no other purpose. After you have left the Ashram and go back home, you can revert to your earlier ways, if you want to—whatever suits you. It is for this reason that we serve a sweet dish every day in the kitchen, because it is necessary to have some sugar to be able to generate more seminal fluid, and that is why I ask people to take milk. And it is for this reason that I had a fruit store opened next to the Ashram. If the body is full of this fluid, then the Shakti will be able to do its work with utmost vigour; otherwise the Shakti does not have any basis to work upon. It's only people who have a lot of fat who should meditate for one hour and forty-five minutes, but a boy like Kedarnath or Rama, that is Bonnie, who is so thin, should not meditate even for that period. You should meditate just for an hour. Do more japa.

As far as other things are concerned, japa or chanting, or swadhyaya, this reservation does not apply. If I ask you to eat less it doesn't mean that you should reduce your food too much all of a sudden, because you need a certain amount of food to generate more of that fluid. For meditation a person must have a certain amount of physical vigour. As far as japa is concerned, you can practise it at all times, and there doesn't have to be any break or interruption. That will not consume vigour; on the contrary, it will increase it. As far as chanting or swadhyaya are concerned, follow the Ashram routine. One should not meditate too long, otherwise all the physical vigour will be lost. If you meditate too long you lose peace of mind and you start suffering from inner vacuity. You should go about any practice in a gradual, graded manner. You also suffer from the disease of talking too much. Reduce that also.

Jyoshi: *If a seeker is not living with his Guru, how would he know that he is making steady progress in his meditation? And what exactly is the nature of the meditation which one is supposed to practise for no more than one hour and forty-five minutes?*
Baba: If a seeker has discrimination and understanding, for him there would be no place where the Guru is not. If the seeker lacks discrimination, lacks understanding, even if the Guru were to live with him for twenty-four hours a day, it would not do him any good. What else is the inner Shakti dwelling within the seeker if not the Guru? What else is the mantra, if not the Guru? Or the various kriyas which take place inside—what are they if not the Guru himself? If one hasn't understood this it means that one hasn't understood who the Guru is, and he is behaving like a person who believes Rama dwells only in the stone image that he is worshipping, and he remains totally ignorant of the Rama dwelling in his own heart.

It is only by being conscious of the fact that the Guru is present within you all the time in the mantra that you are practising, that the mantra begins to work fully inside of you. It is only by regarding the inner kriyas as the Guru that they become more effective.

Meditation is the state in which the mind is free from any change, free from thoughts. In meditation all thoughts and feelings should cease and the mind should become merged in the heart, and one should be able to dwell in the causal body. Even after you have finished what people call meditation and you come back to the outer world and your eyes are open, you should not be subject to any sense of duality. Your state should be such that even if certain sounds are falling on your ears you should not hear them. If you find others doing kriyas, that shouldn't disturb your meditation. Even while there are things around for you to see, you shouldn't take note of them—so deep should be your meditation.

Carol: When we first become conscious of an attachment, what should our attitude be towards it? How can we best surrender it to you?
Baba: The question is whether you have begun to surrender or not, whether so far you have surrendered any part of yourself to the Guru or not. If you have begun to surrender certain things to him, you should surrender attachments also in the same manner. Generally speaking, the mind should not get caught up in an attachment; you should keep talking to the mind again and again. If there is a particular object to which you are feeling excessively attached, then the first step would be to surrender that object to the Guru. Have you heard the story of Swami Ram Tirth and his apple? You should read it. Ram Tirth was awfully attached to apples and even when he laid down to sleep he would have two apples under his pillow. It's a long story. You should try to overcome attachment through discrimination, through the right kind of thoughts. If you can not do that, then you should surrender the attachment along with yourself.

* * * *

All of you should be meditating properly, meditating on the inner Self, considering yourself to be noble and sublime. You should be meditating and worshipping a deity by yourself becoming that deity. You should be worshipping the Guru by yourself becoming the Guru, and take a dip in a holy place by yourself becoming that holy place. You should become your mantra and then repeat it. Do not become oblivious to your own divinity while performing any action. While giving become God, while taking become a mendicant. The scriptures say that a sacrifice is the Lord Himself. But then it requires a great deal of money to perform a yajna. We will perform a yajna and all of you will witness it. The giver is also the Lord. A yajna is a good deed, a noble deed. Alms are distributed to the poor most generously. The poor are also the Lord.

January 31, 1972

Everard Peters: *Would you please explain the way that mantras differ, in particular those of Om namo Narayanaya and Om namah Shivaya, and also the importance attached to the Guru himself giving a mantra, as opposed to an individual himself simply adopting one?*
Baba: There is no difference between the mantras. There may be a million different mantras, but the goal of all of them is the same: that is the Lord. Both *Om namah Shivaya* and *Om namo Narayanaya* refer to the same deity, and there is not the slightest difference between the two. There may be a large number of mantras, but as far as the deity of the different mantras is concerned, it is one deity; there aren't different deities. Shiva is He who is benevolent, who is the inner Self of all, who bestows liberation, and who promotes everyone's welfare. In the scriptures an important question is asked, and that is, "Who is the Shiva we refer to when we repeat *Om namah Shivaya?*" And the answer that is given is that Shiva is the One who is all pervading, the author of all, the illuminator of all, the support of all, who is supremely tranquil and perfect. It is Him I remember intensely within myself with the utmost intensity. *Om namo Narayanaya* refers to the Lord Narayan, and Narayan is the being who becomes the world that we see. He is the Self of all animate and inanimate creatures, who is present within and without, who is consciousness, the Self behind the thinking mind. He is within me. I remember Him—that is the meaning of *Om namo Narayanaya*. Only the words are different. The meaning is the same.

Take for instance the different words for the substance water in different languages. In French it is *eau*, in English it is water, in Hindi it is *pani*. Though the words are different, the thing denoted by them is the same. So the goal of all mantras is the one Being.

Seers have divided mantras into two classes: one is the class of inert mantras, lifeless mantras; the others are the mantras that are endowed with consciousness. Even if you were to receive a mantra from a teacher, from a teacher who hasn't himself practised the mantra and realised the full potential of the mantra, who hasn't envisioned the goal of the mantra, who has not been able to realise the conscious force within the mantra, it will take a very long time for the mantra to bear fruit, and even then it will do so with great difficulty. But the mantra which comes down through a line of Gurus is of an entirely different kind, because it is endowed with life force, and it passes from one Guru to another, each one of whom has realised its full value, its full potential. So when you receive that mantra from a Guru who has himself realised its full potential, then the mantra, being full of God's grace, serves as a great blessing, and it will bring you the same divine state which the Guru himself is in, and protect you and your descendants. If you receive a mantra from a great teacher, that is from a Self-realised Master, then his own power, his own inner Self, enters into you through the mantra. If you select a mantra from a book on your own, then nobody's power is coming into you. A mantra which comes through a succession of Gurus has divine authority behind it. To understand it, one can take an example from ordinary life. Take the case of a police constable—he has the authority of the government behind him. If he were to come with a legal document, an insignificant looking document containing the expulsion order of a foreigner from the Ashram or an Indian from the Ashram, he can, on the basis of that letter, drive that character away. But if there is on the other hand a person, however rich he may be, who doesn't have the authority of the government behind him, he can't turn anybody out of the Ashram even if he comes with ten supporters.

The difference between adopting a mantra on your own and receiving it from a great Guru is that while in the former case it would take a very long time to bear fruit, in the other case, it would work very quickly. If you receive a mantra from one whose inner power is awakened, then it means that the mantra will bear conscious force.

Sumitra: *What is the first step towards controlling one's diet? How do we make our efforts lasting?*
Baba: Here you will find many people taking the pledge that they will eat only at certain times, and that could be the first step towards the control of diet. Many of you unfortunately seem to be under the impression that if you were to eat at all hours then your health would improve. Eating all the time is only a result of a certain habit—a sheer addiction. That's why you are driven to eat again and again. Otherwise, as far as the amount of food that is consumed is concerned, whether you eat once or a number of times would not make any difference.

In our country there are many people who eat only once a day and at one time they eat only as much as they need. There are people who would eat as many as eleven chapatis at one time, and if the same person were to eat four times he would not eat more than eleven chapatis; he would eat the same number. So the quantity of food that goes in remains the same, whether you eat once or twice or four times. When Amma was teaching at a college she used to have tea at least fifteen times a day. But now she has given it up; it hasn't made any difference. Eating again and again is nothing but an addiction. However, you must eat enough to survive, and to have good health. It is always good to have a long interval between meals. Have a light breakfast just once in the morning, and then let a long interval elapse. You should feel hungry at lunch time. You can eat your fill at lunch. Then let your lunch be completely digested by not eating anything until supper.

People keep on eating at all times, but that is not good. In fact, the more hungry you are, the more will you enjoy your food. In our country many people fast, and they reduce their diet that way. There are women who observe partial fasts on Monday. They don't eat anything during the day, but have something light at night. Many women observe a complete fast on Ekadasi day, which comes once in a fortnight. They eat the next day. These fasts give self-control in eating. You should eat if you are very intensely hungry. If you were to eat less, it would be good for meditation, but at the same time you must not emaciate your body in the name of meditation. Today, when I asked a girl how much she eats, I found that she was eating too little. There are quite a few here like her. This is the other extreme.

Amrita: *There is a verse in the Guru Gita which reads, "Mannathah srijagannatho, madgurus trijagadguruh." How exactly should one understand this particular verse?*
Baba: The meaning of this verse from the *Guru Gita* is, "My Lord, or my Master, the Master of my inner Self, is the Master of the entire universe. My Guru is the Guru of the whole world, and he is my inner Self." Here the disciple is depicting the glory of his Guru. The disciple does not consider his Guru to be small; he considers him to be the Guru of the entire universe. The greater we think our Guru to be, the more fervent our contemplation of his vastness, the more we know and remember his glory, the more we understand his divinity, the greater will be our progress. Adoration of the Guru is the secret of spiritual progress. "I bow to the Guru, to my Guru who is the Guru of the whole world."

There were a number of people around my Guru who were followers of the head of the Saraswati sect. Whenever he came they left Baba for as long as their teacher chose to stay. Sometimes Baba would ask them, "You haven't been here for a long time, where were you?" And they would say, "We had gone to our Master, the head of the Kashi Math, who was here, so we could not come."

This doesn't show absolute fidelity to one Guru, and this kind of attitude is not at all conducive to devotion to the Guru. One's devotion to the Guru should be single-minded, it should be unpromiscuous. If, for instance, tomorrow a Jagad Guru were to come here, that is one whose title is 'the Guru of the whole world', and if some of you, thinking that he is a great teacher, were to turn to him, well that would not show that you are good disciples. It is not good to think that one who is the master of an ashram extending over only ten or fifteen acres is smaller than a teacher who is the teacher of the entire world, which is so vast. For a true disciple, his own Guru, however small his ashram may be, is the Guru of the whole world. In the same manner, one should not belittle one's own inner Self. Here the seeker who is devoted to the Guru says, "My own Self is the Self of all, the Self of the entire cosmos. " That is Shiva and that is Narayan. "As my own inner Self is the Self of all, so is my Guru the Guru of all." One's devotion to the Guru should be accompanied by this attitude.

Jon: To what extent should I rely on inner impulses for starting and ending meditation?
Baba: Generally speaking, one should follow a strict schedule for meditation. Once you have begun to follow such a schedule, you will be able to meditate at any time. As far as inner impulses are concerned, one has to see whether it's true inner inspiration or not. You should not meditate for more than an hour or an hour and a half. For the remaining period you should repeat your mantra in your inner mind. It's always better to go about meditation in a graded, systematic manner. Don't try to jump or leap. If we sometimes have a heavy sleep, which is not at all necessary, then after waking up we feel very tired, and for at least one hour we feel as though the last ounce of energy or strength had been squeezed out of our body. In the same way, if you were to meditate more than you could bear, it would dry up your body for some time. One should meditate in a systematic manner, being fully aware of how much his physical body can bear. You should follow, as we said earlier, a strict schedule. You should fix a certain length of time for which you are going to meditate, and also from which hour to which hour. In fact, the still posture which you adopt for meditation is even more important than meditation, because it has a great soothing effect on your nerves. Even if you are able to meditate for a short while just once a day, that state will last throughout the day. You should not strain yourself to sit long in a meditative posture; let your posture be easy and comfortable. If you strain, your nerves will be adversely affected.

M. Sagal: Why do we meditate in the dark? If we meditate in the bright light, does the Shakti work less intensely?

What are the advantages of meditating in the dark?
Baba: What happens is that most of you are accustomed to looking at other people all the time, noticing what they are wearing, what they are doing, what colour somebody's sari is, what style she wears her hair, etc. If you start to meditate in the light, that's what you will be doing all the time. But if you are sitting in the dark, you won't be able to see what other people are wearing or doing, so you will be able to turn your attention to your own Self. Besides, it is the inner light which really matters, not the external light. If you wish to have a vision of the inner light, it is much better to sit in a dark room. It is for this reason that you are able to see the inner light at night much more clearly than during the day. The light of the sun eclipses the inner light. You will also be able to hear the inner music at night more clearly than during the day.

Bill: *What are the panchabhavas (mentioned by Ramakrishna)?*
Baba: Did you read the *Gospel of Sri Ramakrishna* fully? You should read the whole of it for the description of the five bhavas. The term bhava indicates the descent of the Lord into your own body while you are worshipping or remembering Him. Gurubhava is the state in which while worshipping the Guru, while remembering the Guru, you begin to feel that you yourself are the Guru; you identify yourself completely with him. There are so many different kinds of bhava, but the best—you will find different scriptural authorities indulging in hair-splitting on this matter, making distinctions where distinctions don't exist—the best bhava is the tanmaya bhava, that is the state of deep absorption. Gurubhava is the state in which you merge yourself completely in the Guru, and you are no longer aware whether you are the Guru, or whether the Guru is you. The other five bhavas: the relationship with the Lord as a friend, husband, son, etc. are very ordinary states which any seeker would experience during the course of his sadhana. I'll describe the mahabhava, the highest state: that is the state in which you lose yourself completely in the Guru or in the Lord. There is a verse relating to this state, it is composed by Nagaridas. Through calling upon Krishna continuously,

Radha herself became Krishna, and then she began to ask her friends, "Where has Radha disappeared?" This is the supreme bhava, mahabhava. All other bhavas are ordinary states. It is the mahabhava which one should be able to attain. In the course of meditation you should completely overcome the sense of difference between yourself and the Guru.

Pratibha: *These days it seems that the seekers here are having more and more intense yogic kriyas. Is this due to the upcoming Shivaratri celebration?*
Baba: This afternoon Amma read out a letter. There is a certain devotee who is not a very advanced meditator—his wife meditates far better than he—and she gave birth to a child the other day. A fifty-year-old man from the Punjab went to that man's office looking for me. This is what the letter that I received today says. "I asked this devotee, 'When will Baba come to Delhi, because I want to learn to meditate from him'. The devotee said, 'Come along with me to my house, because Baba dwells there'. So he took me home and made me sit in the meditation room. Then he applied the sacred ash to my forehead, and made me sit in front of a picture of you and asked me to repeat *Guru Om, Guru Om*. Then I began to experience intense spontaneous kriyas." He was so amazed that he has written today about it. Here is an ordinary householder who meditates in a certain room every day, as a result of which Shakti accumulates there. In spite of the fact that he has children, in spite of the fact that he has so many other things to do, he was able to get at least one person into meditation.

Then you can very well imagine how much more powerful the Ashram would be. Here every day we hold so many different chanting sessions. So many of us chant the *Guru Gita* and the *Vishnu Sahasranam*, and *arati* thrice a day, and we live such a pure life, a life of discipline, and we think pure thoughts. So how much more saturated, how much more intense should the atmosphere of this place be? It should not be at all surprising that more and more seekers should have more and more intense kriyas. In fact, in course of time, if one were to just remember the Ashram anywhere, whether in India or abroad, he would pass into meditation. You would only have to say "Shree Gurudev Ashram," or "Ganeshpuri." Whoever comes to visit the Ashram will be absolutely swept off his feet at the beauty of the place and he will feel extremely happy and wonder how the Ashram has grown into what it is. Here, like the ancient seers, we are practising intense tapasya, we are not wasting a single moment of our time. It is true that our tapasya has taken a different form. Only an unintelligent person will not understand it. Come to think of it, you can see how busy, how intense our daily routine is. Right from the moment you get up until the moment that you go to sleep something or other is taking place in the Ashram, and all the time you are being exposed to divine vibrations. And if more and more people get caught in such an atmosphere, it is no surprise. This is in spite of the fact that our temple has not completed even one year as yet; it is only a few months old. We are going to hold a one-week continuous chant on the occasion of Shivaratri, and then there will be other occasions on which we will hold similar chants so the atmosphere will become more and more powerful. In fact, in the future, people will be caught even while they are on their way to the Ashram. Many people may even feel scared to enter the Ashram, because something strange might happen.

All the seekers here are performing such intense tapasya: they chant the *Guru Gita*, the *Vishnu Sahasranam*, *Shiva Mahimnah Stotra*, *arati* and dhuns with such feeling, such purity and such devotion. Then they are working hard, putting in so much service to the Guru. Some people are working in the garden, others sweeping the floors, still others are working in the office; yet others are doing some writing work. But that doesn't mean that one kind of work is superior to another. Whether you are writing or sweeping the floor, all your work is the same. What matters is the spirit behind it.

So as time goes by, the Ashram atmosphere becomes more and more powerful and the seekers also become purer and purer. The seekers coming from abroad or coming from outside the Ashram, by living here for a certain period of time, begin to experience inner transformation. Here a sadhaka undergoes a complete change in the way he thinks, in the way he looks at different things, and he becomes divinised, as it were.

February 2, 1972

Bruno (the elder): *Four years ago after finishing meditation, I was in a state between sleep and waking when all of a sudden I saw a dreadful figure above me in the air, and it looked like a vampire. Then instead of shouting for help I began to repeat So'ham japa with intense faith and after a few minutes the figure disappeared. It was not a vision, but it appeared to be a real being. Can such a being do some harm to a seeker? From which world do such beings come? In case we should have the same experience in the future, what can we do to protect ourselves?*

Baba: Anyone who is a student of Siddha Yoga would naturally have countless experiences, and to regard any of these experiences as obstructions or harmful shows wrong understanding. I have told you many times, on previous occasions also, that there are countless worlds and these worlds are inhabited by different orders of beings, such as celestials, Gandharvas and Kinnaras. Beings from these different worlds appear to a student of Siddha Yoga at one time or another, in one state or another, either while he is in meditation or while he is in the dream state. Such an experience can never be an obstruction. On the contrary, the student should feel happy about it because it shows that he has been blessed, that such a being of some other order has appeared to him; and this also indicates that he is progressing. Not only this, to some advanced seekers, these beings from different worlds also provide guidance. In our country there are thousands of stories relating to such visions. Therefore, you should consider it to be a blessing. That experience betokens well for you. He who practises Siddha Yoga, who is repeating *So'ham* with intense faith, and who is devoted to his Guru, can not be harmed by any power in this universe. There was a yogini called Bahinabai and she says in one of her verses, "All the beings of the three worlds become friendly to a yogi." And none of them can cause any obstruction on the path of a yogi. It is only due to wrong understanding that we could consider these beings harmful.

Kedarnath: *If one receives a mantra from a Sadguru or a Siddha Purusha, without having accepted him as his Guru, or without feeling absolute devotion for him, how much will the mantra fructify?*
Baba: How much fruit the mantra is going to bear depends on the qualification of the one who receives it. The fact is that without the knowledge of the true nature of the supreme Lord, the deity of the mantra, the mantra, and the one you receive the mantra from, a mantra won't do much for you. In fact, if you undertake any practice without proper knowledge, it will not do you much good; it will not have much significance for you, and it will not bring you any experiences either. There was a great poet-saint called Purundardas, whose poetry I have read in my mother tongue, Kannada. He says, "While an enlightened person would feel happy even when enveloped by complete darkness, an ignorant person would be utterly miserable even when surrounded by bright light."

Therefore, we should know the true nature of the mantra. And we should also have knowledge of the nature of the Guru from whom we receive the mantra. There is a verse in Hindi which goes like this, "The mantra is true, and the Guru is true, provided that the seeker is true."

All the same, one should keep on repeating the mantra because the mantra has inherent power. The only difference that it would make is that the mantra would take much longer to bear fruit. In fact, words bear fruit immediately if you understand them. For instance, I am speaking now and these words are striking certain chords within you because you are able to understand them. Without understanding, the mantra would not bear much fruit. Therefore one should acquire the knowledge of the nature of the mantra, the nature of the Guru from whom the mantra is being received, and of one's own nature. And that's not very difficult, either.

Durga: *Often my kriyas are very spastic and uncomfortable—an unexpected jerking of the limbs, itching on the skin, feeling like insects biting, frequent pain in different nerve endings, energy shooting intensely to parts of the head, and locked head positions that are sometimes very painful. Are these normal, or does it indicate that the flow of Shakti is being obstructed? Can I help the situation somehow?*

Baba: These yogic movements or kriyas do not take place to impress those who may be watching; they are not deliberately artistic movements which are meant to please spectators. These kriyas take place so that your body may get what it needs; they are uniquely suited to your particular organism. Furthermore, the Shakti is not acting to give you pleasure; the Shakti acts to purify your system, to purify all those parts of the body which need to be purified. In your case the flow of the Shakti is not being obstructed because the Shakti is shooting up into the head. You shouldn't have the least worry about it. All you should do is continue to meditate. The pain that you are feeling is just a temporary phase.

Kalyani: *What attitude should be upheld by a seeker who is wearing saffron clothes without having taken the sacred vow of sannyas?*

Baba: You already have the right attitude, namely the awareness that you are wearing saffron clothes but you have not taken the vow of sannyas. The best attitude would be to regard saffron clothes as a symbol of great inner purity and holiness. When you have a vision of the Lord in meditation you will find that the Lord is surrounded by a saffron halo; and it is the colour of that halo which is used for the garments worn by a sannyasi. You should therefore regard saffron as a divine colour.

Take the case of an ordinary person who happens to be wearing a constable's uniform. The moment he wears that uniform he begins to feel that he is a constable. Similarly, when you wear saffron clothes you should begin to feel that you are a soldier in the divine army of liberation. The saffron colour is worthy of great reverence and that is how you should look upon it.

Bill: *How do we strengthen our will to right discrimination and right action, and to surrender?*
Baba: Through right understanding. You can stabilise right discrimination and other things through right understanding, and through single-minded loyalty. It is discrimination which is at the root. Steadiness is gained through discrimination. Find out what is making you unsteady and try to overcome that.

Carol: *Since I have begun to meditate I have felt a new sense of ignorance about my body, so I have hesitated to continue the asanas I have been doing for some time, and to take the vitamins and minerals I am used to taking. Please tell me what is best in each case.*
Baba: Discontinuing the asanas that you were practising would not make any difference, but you should continue to take vitamins and minerals. You must take good care of your body. Ask yourself, "What is the instrument through which I will achieve perfection in meditation?" Your spiritual journey will be consummated only with the help of the body. Therefore, you should keep your body pure and strong. If you have to go to a far away place like Delhi, if you do not take care of your horse or car, it may not be able to carry you to the destination. You may get stuck on the way. A meditator or an Ashramite or a seeker should not neglect his body. That isn't right. Until your meditation is consummated, your body is as important as meditation itself. You can see light only with the help of these eyes. So if you were to neglect your eyes you wouldn't be able to see any light. Similarly, you would receive a message from the Lord through the ears, and if you were to neglect the ears what's the point of meditation?

If in certain contexts the scriptures condemn the body, you should not let it rest there, you should go further and see what else the scriptures say about it. If you really wish to taste the divine nectar, divine bliss, you will be able to taste it with an inner sense organ which, too, is a part of the body. Therefore, you should know your body. Your body is a sacred temple; it is as sacred as the temple to Baba in the hall, and you must have seen how neat and pure and beautiful that temple is kept.

In Yeola, where I spent several years, there is a large number of silk weavers. This happened long ago, about twenty-five years ago. One day many of the weavers wove special silk pieces for me. They offered them to me, and I put all of them on. I tied one on my head and put others on other parts of my body and I was sitting inside my room. It so happened that at the same time a certain naked ascetic came there. His entire body was besmeared with sacred ash and he was shouting "Hara Hara Hara Mahadev." Then he said, "What sort of saint are you, wearing such expensive and luxurious garments?" "Look," I snapped back, "I am not a stupid fool like you. I know that my body is an abode of the Lord. Should I then besmear it with mere ash, shouldn't I adorn it with the best garments?" Therefore, look after your body.

Nala: *When I first came to the Ashram I accepted everyone with love and benevolence; then followed a period of negativity and anger. Now I am either indifferent or scornful. What would you say about this?*
Baba: This is due to the fact that your mind is vitiated. As far as the Ashram is concerned, it is the same, it doesn't change; only your mind keeps changing. Your mind is basically sick. You should not be that fickle, you should not change that quickly. The root cause of such fluctuation is that you are here with some selfish motive. Take my case; I don't have any selfish motive and that is why my love neither decreases or increases, it remains the same all the time. I neither get attached to anyone, nor do I become averse to anyone. I am always communicating the same kind and same degree of love to everyone. If your love arises from desire and selfishness, then it will turn into hatred when your desire and selfishness are opposed. You should learn to become selfless. You should be able to overcome your desire regardless of where you are staying or living. There are sixteen centres of disturbances of different kinds. There are centres of love, anger, enmity, and so forth and the mind keeps on moving from one centre to another. Sometimes it begins to love, and then you feel more and more love. Sometimes it gets angry. Sometimes it begins to doubt. It's always thinking. I would suggest that from to-

morrow on you forget all about the Ashram. Concern yourself with what you are here for, what exactly it is that you want. Become calm. Have neither attachment nor aversion to the Ashramites. Ups and downs are caused by selfish desire, and if you could rid your mind of selfishness, you wouldn't have such a problem. If I expect love from people, and if that love is not forthcoming, then I would begin to feel frustrated. That frustration would cause anger and that shows that the root cause of my anger is my own desire, not these people. Therefore, whatever you desire you should desire from your own Self. Do not direct your desire to other people. As far as the mind is concerned, it is inconstant. If you were to look at your mind—right from your birth until now—you would find that you have not loved consistently for a year or even for a month.

There was a great king in our country called Akbar, and I was very fond of reading stories about him in my childhood. He was a great emperor and his reign extended over the entire country, not merely one province. He writes in his life story that right from the time of his birth to the time of his death he felt love for three and a half minutes. Such is the nature of the mind. The mind will keep fluctuating constantly. It will be constantly wandering, constantly seeing bad in good, good in bad, low in high and high in low, favourable in unfavourable, unfavourable in favourable. I am reminded of a verse in this context and this verse is from the great poet Sunderdas. Sunder says that it is the nature of the mind to keep fluctuating constantly; it swings between high and low, love and hate. It loves a person at one moment, and the next moment turns against him. This inconstancy is inherent in the mind, so it should be accepted. It's this wicked mind which makes the sublime spirit think that it is abject and low, and makes it weep all the time. Eknath Maharaj says that the mind is so deplorable that it has reduced what was Narayan the supreme Lord, the free Being, to a chained, petty individual.

Therefore, do not attach any importance to the fluctuations of the mind. Whatever passes through the mind is purely temporary. You should continue to increase your love without expecting anything from anyone. You should change your attitude to other people, to the Ashram and to other things. In the Jain sect the sadhus are not allowed to stay in any place for more than three days, and it must be this awareness of the nature of the mind that brought about this restriction. Because if you live for more than three days in one place you will get caught up in aversion and attachment, you will begin to love some and hate others. Therefore, you should not be carried off your feet by your mind. You should insure that you remain pure and noble and untainted.

Loman: *How is it possible to forget a clear realisation or lose an attainment?*
Baba: You can make a realisation permanent only through persevering, steadfast practice. It is a strange irony that there are certain seekers who after having their inner Shakti awakened by the Guru, begin to neglect the Ashram, the Guru and their sadhana. And the result of all that is that the Shakti will begin to neglect them. Sometimes, after a little realisation or a few experiences, a person begins to think that he has become perfect. But he forgets that one has to work diligently for a long period of time to stabilise what he has attained. Therefore, continue to practise steadfastly for a prolonged period, and that way attainment will become permanent.

George: *At the time that I received Shaktipat, which was seven weeks ago, the force was so overwhelmingly strong as it rose upward in the sushumna. Since then it has remained in a quiet, steady, but not so strong, glow in my head and face. However, I never felt it anywhere else but in the head and face, that is, in none of the body chakras or nerves or even in the sushumna nadi. It just appears in my head. Would you please give an explanation?*
Baba: You shouldn't worry about it. Only seven weeks have passed and you will have more experiences in course of time. When Shakti begins to work in the subtle body, sometimes it's difficult for the seeker to perceive its subtle activity. Once you have received Shaktipat you shouldn't have the least apprehension. The Shakti will certainly make you perfect; it will not leave you imperfect if your devotion to the Guru remains steady. One should not begin to look for

the chariot from heaven on the third day after having received Shaktipat. Don't think perfection will come so soon. It takes a long time to arrive at the destination.

I once read a story relating to a marriage, and one who has received Shaktipat should not behave like the couple in this story. Two young people were married. The marriage was performed by a great sage. After the ceremony was finished, the sage blessed the couple saying, "May you have a son." After all the guests left, the bride and bridegroom began to look all around the place for a son. Some people asked them, "What on earth are you looking for? You have just gotten married. Have you lost something?"

The couple said, "The sage has blessed us saying, 'May you bring forth a son', and we are looking for the son. Where is he?"

Then the people said, "Look, you haven't even taken off the marital robes. The blessing will certainly come true, but it will take time."

So you should remain calm, being fully aware that all the experiences will not come to you at once. They will come gradually over a long period of time.

Shyama: *On behalf of all the devotees, what can we do that you may live a very long life?*
Baba: When there is no death for me, how can such a question arise? If you were to achieve agelessness and immortality through meditation, my life would be automatically prolonged. It's you who are subject to death, and that makes you think that I, too, will die. You are projecting your mortality on me.

February 4, 1972

Rana: *Guroraradhanam karyam, swajivitvam nivedayet (One should offer the Guru one's life as a gift); karmana manasa vacha nitya maradhyed Gurum (serve the Guru* *with all your heart, speech and actions). How are these verses of the Guru Gita relevant to the attainment of samadhi?*

Baba: These two verses relate to sadhana not to samadhi. You should continue to do sadhana. One should spend one's entire life in the worship and service of the Guru. One should constantly worship and serve the Guru with mind, speech and action. Attainment of samadhi is worth just a farthing compared to service to the Guru. Millions of experiences of samadhi float in the waters of the Guru. They come and go continually.

What do you understand by samadhi? What exactly does it indicate to you? There are some people who think samadhi means to become motionless like a piece of wood, to lose consciousness of the world and remain in that state for a long period of time. They don't understand it at all. How is this kind of samadhi different from the samadhi induced by chloroform during an operation? Can you consider that a yogic realisation? The highest samadhi is the state in which the intellect gets established in equality, free from ups and downs. For a wise person no other samadhi has any value. He who has no direct personal experience of samadhi, and who has only read lyrical descriptions of it in the scriptures becomes very eager for this experience. He would like to experience it at least once. It is just the elder brother of sleep or dreams. Just as in sleep you move in an inner world, just as in dreams you have the categories of the seer, the seen and the act of seeing, knower, known, and knowledge, similarly in the state of samadhi you move in the realm of equanimity or equality-consciousness. Sleep is just one state, samadhi another. Therefore, you should continue to serve the Guru calmly and also meditate, and through meditation you will be able to get into samadhi. In fact, you should experience samadhi even while attending to your ordinary duties. Yoga should be reflected in our practical life. I have met many yogis and jnanis and devotees and practicioners of Hatha Yoga and many holy men who begin to rest on their laurels after a while, who are not free from anxiety, who cannot even make a livelihood, who do not possess any skill. Through meditation one should attain the true state of the inner Self, which is even beyond samadhi. That state attained through meditation remains unchanged whether you are awake, moving in the external world and having outer experiences, or dreaming or asleep. A person who is building a house feels that his task is complete after he has installed the kalas, the top dome. The state of equality-consciousness attained through meditation is the true realisation of samadhi. The author of the *Guru Gita* first attained the state of equality and then he wrote about service to the Guru. He is not talking without experience.

Carol: *During chanting I often feel strongly drawn into meditation. If I meditate then I don't continue to chant. Should I meditate during the chants? Why do the inner Self and the outer Guru sometimes seem to be in conflict? How does one please both?*
Baba: Meditation doesn't have much value as compared to chanting. In fact, meditation is the reward of chanting. Tukaram Maharaj says in one of his short verses, that he keeps on chanting even during sleep and the Lord Himself descends and stands before him. Such is the glory of chanting. Each action must bring its fruit. No action can go without giving you its fruit. Therefore, when you are chanting you should chant, and later when it's time for meditation, you will be able to meditate deeply. Do not attach much importance to meditation during chanting. The divine Name has enormous importance. I started chanting the divine Name from a very young age. Right from my early life I have been fond of holding week-long chants and singing the divine Name. As a result my ferry reached the other shore, while I saw the boats of many great Vedantins getting sunk midway. I am going to hold a continuous chant on the occasion of Shivaratri, and that chant will not bring us any material gain. The gains we will get from chanting for that time will be much more valuable.

Tukaram Maharaj talks about chanting with great truth. He declares, "The power of my chanting is so glorious that by means of it I will make the mouth of one who pours out philosophy water, just as one's mouth waters on seeing another person eat rasgulla. By chanting Rama Krishna Hari, I'll bring yogis out of samadhi and make them dance to the tune of my chant. By the power of the Name, I'll turn this very world into a most glorious heaven compared even to which Vaikuntha and Mt. Kailas will fade into insignificance. So glorious is the power of chanting." While chanting, you should consider meditation to be secondary. If you are chanting in right earnest then meditation will come after you. Why should you go after it? Meditation is the reward of bhajan and swadhyaya.

Whenever you find that there is a conflict between the inner Self and the outer Guru, you should think that what you are hearing is not the voice of the inner Self, it is just an echo of the mind. It is nothing but the mind playing a trick on you. The mind is sometimes friendly and other times antagonistic, sometimes pleased, at other times displeased. There are sixteen kinds of feelings that pass through the mind constantly. You should not attach any importance to the inner voice, as long as your mind is subject to these feelings; your inner voice will not always be free. It is only after you have had perfect realisation that your inner voice becomes completely dependable. Until one has seen the blue light in his sahasrar and his deity within that light, the inner voice must not be relied upon. Until then it is tainted with different gunas, sometimes with tamo, sometimes with rajo and sometimes with sattva guna, and all these gunas keep changing. So you should not attach much importance to it. During the period of sadhana you should always listen to one who has initiated sadhana. During this period you should not depend very much on your inner inspiration. However, once your sadhana is consummated then you can rely totally on the inner inspiration. The Lord also says in the *Gita* that whatever thoughts arise in the mind, whether favourable or unfavourable, are the products of the interplay of the three gunas: "Oh, Arjuna, transcend the three gunas, becoming free from them."

Nala: *What is the reason that we transmit either love or strength or intelligence, but rarely two or three at once?*
Baba: Only one of the three will be manifested at any given time. All three will not manifest simultaneously. Discerning saints consider these as three different aspects of the one Self. The same Self considering itself to be impure and un-

clean, gets involved in false reasoning. God Himself becomes the world and all its objects that are subject to all the gunas. The Lord Himself becomes the impure or tainted mind. It is for the purification of the mind, for washing and cleansing it, that we have all the different spiritual disciplines, such as Jnana, Bhakti, Yoga, and Vedanta. The mind will not remain focused on one thought. When it is possessed by greed, it expresses greed, when it is possessed by anger it expresses anger. When possessed by ignorance it behaves ignorantly. From hostility it will shift to love. When it is filled with love it begins to expand, and this way it keeps on fluctuating from one emotion, from one thought to another constantly. When the mind is engaged in the study of the scriptures then it will become possessed by scriptural truths, or scriptural knowledge, and when it begins to meditate then it will be absorbed in meditation. When it begins to sing the divine Name, it will be filled with the ecstasy of the Divine. Therefore, you should try to withdraw your mind from everything else and fill it with love. And to fill it with love you should chant the divine Name as intensely as you can. At a given time it is only one of these three things which will be experienced, not all the three together.

Pratibha: *Is it proper to introduce those people to the Sadguru who are caught up in minor, petty troubles and who want to be blessed by the grace of the Guru?*
Baba: It is quite proper to introduce them. If you can impress them with an account of what you have attained from the Guru, and thus turn their attention towards what is really significant, then you will be doing them a lot of good. We can create the same degree of interest in others with which we pursue a particular path. In fact, everyone should become devoted to the Lord, to the Guru; everyone should become aware of the existence and the glory of the inner Self. This consciousness should not remain confined to just one or two or even a dozen. If you haven't experienced the inner Self, how can you ever be happy? One finds that most of the people in the world, millions and billions, are caught up in sheer misery. However, if you have been able to experience some joy, some inner happiness, there is no

harm in your trying to enable others also to find the same kind of happiness within themselves. But, you must be careful that in the process your own happiness is not lost; that is what I am against. First one should reform oneself. Only after that should one try to reform others. Once a certain Health Minister came to see me. His neck was bandaged and he had a bandage around his waist. As I looked at him I was greatly amused. Here was the State Minister of Health who was one of the most unhealthy fellows in the entire state. His concern was to promote the health of other people, while he himself was suffering from all kinds of weaknesses. This should not be the case with you. Generally speaking however, it is very good to help others.

Pratibha: *When we repeat a mantra mentally, where does that silent sound arise from?*
Baba: It is you who experience a certain sound arising within you, and you are putting the question to me. I should be asking you, "Where does that sound arise from?" I shall narrate a story to you in this connection. Once Ram Tirth was sailing to America. He was a great lover of beauty, of nature and in the evening he was sitting on deck. There were a few other people around, also enjoying the beauty of the blue sky and the blue waters of the ocean. He was swaying with joy. Two people had fallen asleep, and all of a sudden one of them started shouting, "Save me. Save me." He got up in sheer fright and looked around. Then he looked at the swami seated in a chair and he asked him, "Look, there was a tiger with three horns here a few minutes ago. Where has he disappeared?"

Ram Tirth said, "What on earth are you talking about? I have never heard that a tiger has three horns, and I have been sitting here for a long time, and I haven't seen any such tiger here. My dear fellow, you must realise that we are in a ship moving on the surface of the water and how could a tiger come here?"

He said, "No, I saw the tiger in a dream."

"Well, you saw the tiger in a dream. You were in the dream state, and I was in the waking state, so how could I answer a question relating to your dream?"

The question is very good, but it is you who are repeating the mantra mentally and hearing the reverberation of the mantra; but you are asking me about it. It's just like the fellow asking, "Where has the tiger disappeared?" You must be repeating the mantra on the Pashyanti level of speech. The Pashyanti level is the third level, the subtlest level of speech from which the sound arises when you repeat the mantra mentally, and the best thing to do is repeat the mantra mentally and hear it within yourself.

If one does not listen to the mantra while he is repeating it mentally, the mantra will not bear fruit very quickly. Mantra japa is the most important of all disciplines. If you were to use an ordinary term of abuse for somebody, it would have an immediate effect on him. All seven fluids of the body would be in a state of turmoil. Then it should be no surprise that the Name of God has such enormous power. The sages say that the Lord manifested Himself originally as sound.

One should repeat the mantra in the privacy of one's heart and hear it himself. The mantra should pass from the gross level of speech to the subtle, from the subtle to the subtler. From the tongue it should penetrate to the throat and from the throat to the heart, and from the heart to the navel. It is only when the mantra begins to arise from the navel that you realise what it means to do japa. The repetition of the divine Name is the most important spiritual technique in the world. If you keep listening to this inner sound then the mind becomes one-pointed. Get into the state of what is called mantra samadhi. In that state all seven constituents of the body are transformed.

In the course of my life I met one saint whose shoes also reverberated with the sound of the mantra he practised. If you were to hold his shoe against your ear you could hear the sound of the Name coming from the shoe. All seekers should be repeating the mantra continually because mantra repetition is a very important method. During mental repetition you will hear a sound arising from the subtlest level of speech.

Shyama: *Can one overcome the tendency to self-praise by the attitude of self-deploration or self-condemnation, so that one's ego may be annihilated?*

Baba: Self-praise and the tendency to self-praise is not at all good, and those who are given to it get caught up in all sorts of snares. They will pretend that they are practising certain disciplines only for praise. Whenever you begin to depend on others for anything, whether it is praise or something else, you are a beggar and you can never become a truly wealthy person. One should have no desire for praise from others. One should be contented with one's own being, and satisfied with one's own Self. One who has a craving for praise, who becomes a disciple to get praise, or becomes a teacher for vainglory is bound to fall at one time or another. Such disciples are severely tested by the Guru. Therefore, praise should be of no use to you.

But at the same time you should not condemn yourself. I had certain disciples. Some of them had true experiences, while others were mimicking them and showing off. Some of them were Indians, while others were foreign. They would tell me again and again that they had seen the Blue Pearl, and not only seen the Blue Pearl, but they had seen me within the Blue Pearl and had surrendered fully to me.

There may be a certain person who comes and claims that he had a vision of Lord Rama, but that claim doesn't mean anything. There are people who try to impress me by indulging in fake kriyas. They sway their waists while others begin to shed tears, and others fake other kriyas. Even though I am aware of these, I will not let on that I know they are fake because I am neither pleased nor offended by these exhibitions. There was a certain so-called disciple in California whom I asked, "Have you seen the Blue Pearl?" And he said, "Yes, I saw it this very morning. It's because I have completely surrendered myself to you." I said, "Look, you had better be very careful about this, because anyone who has seen the Blue Pearl achieves total humility; and anyone who has seen the Blue Pearl will never claim to have seen it; he would not make a show of it like this. You are saying that you have seen the Blue Pearl because you want to be complimented, because you want to soothe your vanity. It is only when you are put through a test that you will realise how much you have really attained."

Take the case of a musician who is addicted to his music.

You will find such a vocalist humming or singing even when nobody is there to hear him, even when there is no tabla player there to accompany him. He is singing because he has become a victim of it. There are certain teachers who become such pitiful victims of the role which they have assumed that they keep on making all kinds of claims all the time that they have had this or that experience, they have seen the Blue Pearl and the Blue Person and what not, and they are not even bothered about whether their audience is taking them seriously or not, whether people are believing what they are saying or not. They are only addicted to making tall claims. You must have seen that there are certain businessmen who are utterly dishonest and who have no qualms of conscience about cheating anyone; they go on cheating people one after another. This is what happens with those so-called spiritual preceptors also; they become so blinded by their spiritual profession that they are not able to see what is obvious even to a fool. Finally they are caught in their own trap and in course of cheating others they get cheated themselves.

I narrated a story to that disciple. There was a certain ashram which was headed by a saint whose fame was widespread. That saint was a being of very great realisation. There was a person who used to visit his ashram clad in an impeccable suit. He walked with a swinging and proud gait, making a lot of noise with his shoes. One day he was on his way to the ashram. An ashram girl was sweeping. He shouted from a distance, "Stop, stop for a moment." The poor girl stood aside. The Guru was watching him from a distance. He said, "Please, sir, come here. What brings you here?" 'He said, "I have come to get initiation."

The Guru said, "Look, you haven't learned anything so far, nor will you learn anything now. You still suffer from a bad disease. Nothing will enter within you now."

He went back thinking about why he had been treated in such a manner by the Guru. After a few months he came again, but this time he wasn't wearing such smart clothes. He had put on very simple clothes. He came at about the same time, the time at which that girl was sweeping. The Guru instructed the girl to sweep the dust so that it would fly into his face. This time he did not shout at the girl telling her, "Don't you realise who I am?" He went around her. He kept silent, but he still felt insulted. Then he met the Guru.

The Guru asked, "Why have you come here?"

"To be initiated by you."

"You are very impure, and at present you are not ready to receive anything. Come back after you purify yourself."

And after going back he started practising humility in different ways. He also assumed much simpler ways. He started wearing simpler clothes and shoes and talking more politely. He started to pay more attention to what others were saying. The next time that fellow came to the ashram, the Guru saw him coming from a distance. He must have been sitting on a platform like I sit on here where he could see everyone coming from a distance. This time he instructed the girl to fill her basket with rubbish and to bash into the fellow as he came near the ashram so that the rubbish would fall on him. She dropped the basket of rubbish right on his head so all his spotless white clothes were soiled. But this time he did not react. He only shook the dust off and went inside. He went to the Guru, "Sir, I have come again."

"Aren't you the one who has already come here a number of times? You still aren't ready. Go back and return when you are truly ready."

He returned after four months. This time the Guru posted an old woman to sweep in front of the ashram and instructed her that the moment the fellow reached there she should strike him with her broom. As the fellow came walking in the middle of the road where the woman was sweeping, she hit him with the broom and shouted, "Look, you don't have any sense. Can't you see that I am sweeping here?" She was not involved in it. She was only obeying the order of the Guru.

This time he apologised to her, saying, "Mother, please forgive me. I should have been more careful." Then he went to the Guru.

This is how a disciple is tested. As long as everything goes well, and you have no challenge coming from the side of the teacher, and you respect and revere him, it doesn't mean very much. It's only when you are tested by him, when you are insulted by him, whether you are truly loyal to him will be shown.

After having received the blow from the old woman and bowing to her, he went to the teacher and then the teacher said, "Now you are ready, I will certainly instruct you."

Both praise and self-condemnation are of no consequence. What matters is faith in the Self, devotion to the Self. If you receive praise from people about your great devotion and surrender, that has no meaning. Your actions should live up to your words. Otherwise, what happens is that even when the Guru pretends to flare up at a certain student, even slightly, he throws away his loincloth and runs away. There is a certain Marathi verse which narrates a story. There was a very generous-hearted person who fed a beggar for twelve years with milk. One day this beggar needed some buttermilk, so he went to his benefactor and asked him for buttermilk. It so happened that there wasn't any buttermilk in the house and the rich man said, "We don't have any."

The beggar immediately flared up and began to shout at his benefactor, "Look, you are such a mean, miserly fellow. You have so much wealth, so many cows and you have so much milk in the house. In fact a river of milk flows in your house, and I come for a small quantity of buttermilk and you refuse me."

This fellow was provided with milk for twelve years and just one little refusal evoked such a sharp reaction. He was so low.

In the same manner, the disciple from California turned away from his Guru. He began to grumble and complain only because he was not given honour on a certain occasion. And what does praise matter after all? It is ephemeral, particularly for a disciple who has been nourished with Shakti, with knowledge, with everything for such a long time by the Guru. What a worthless disciple. What a worthless human being. The truth is that such a fellow is not at all interested in the Guru-disciple relationship, he is not at all interested in spiritual progress, he is only interested in business. Until now he had earned a lot through a worldly trade, and now after realising that spiritual goods have started selling in the market, he turns to the spiritual path and begins to sell spiritual goods. His interest is not Kundalini Yoga, his interest is not any inner enlightenment. His interest is only in self-glory. He is a trader, a fake, a cheat.

February 15, 1972

Barry: *Milk and sweets are aids to meditation, and I have been told that lemons hinder or destroy semen and detract from meditation. Is this true? Are there other foods which detract or aid meditation?*
Baba: We don't usually prepare any dish here which would be an obstacle to meditation. Lemon isn't that good. It should be used only rarely. It may be used once or twice a week, particularly in the hot season, and then, too, one shouldn't take more than half a piece. You can squeeze the juice of a piece into water and take that. Milk, however, is very essential. Onions and garlic are not that useful. Your food should always be the sort which would help meditation.

If you were to look at the true nature of meditation, you would find that meditation is a process which renews one's body. In other words, one builds up a new inner body. Meditation is such a glorious process, that in course of time, through it a completely new body is prepared inside. A seeker only knows that things are happening within him. Sometimes his body moves one way, other times another way. The senses and the prana undergo kriyas also. Blood circulates more freely through the veins. Then suddenly he becomes still. There is more to them than just physical or physiological movements. These kriyas have enormous importance, and what is happening through these kriyas is that they create an entirely new body within this body.

It is only after you have achieved perfection through sadhana that you realise exactly what this yoga means. In the Ayurvedic system, when medicine is given to a sick person, two things are kept in view. One is to overcome the sickness, and the other is to make up for the loss suffered due to the sickness. Similarly, meditation, or Siddha Yoga, on the one hand is removing all the impurities from the old body, and on the other bringing a new body into being. Many of you must have had this experience: that after you have had a very deep meditation, you get sour eructations. If you were to take lemon on top of that, who would call you wise? So much acid is already being generated through meditation. It is for this reason that Brahmadeva says, "It is very necessary to know the true importance of Siddha Yoga through meditation, but it is difficult to know it." Meditation is not exactly Hatha Yoga, pranayama or Vedantic contemplation or devotion. You know that through Karma Yoga you overcome inner impurities, and through pranayama, you get rid of certain imbalances, and through bhakti your faith becomes stronger, or through Vedanta your conviction about the Self becomes stronger. But Siddha Yoga is very different from all these. It prepares an entire beautiful new body, which is in perfect accordance with all the yogic criteria of what a body should be like. This body cannot be seen from the outside. Kundalini makes the body conscious. Sometimes a meditator gets a vision of this purified inner body as though it were outside. It is so beautiful, and so pure and so radiant, and so glowing that he falls in love with it. His outer body may be in any condition, but this inner body remains every bright.

Milk is essential, and also a little sugar. But you should eat only as much as you can digest quickly and easily.

Durga: *What is the proper way of using a mala?*
Baba: The only proper way of using a mala is to pass continually from one bead to another. The purpose is to help you remember the Lord and do your mantra without stopping. When one is unable to repeat one's mantra all the time, a mala is quite useful.

The sages have said that rudraksha beads are like Rudra or Shiva. Rudra is the one who destroys all miseries, all pains, dreams and all mental fluctuations. Rudraksha beads also accomplish all that if you have pure feeling towards them, and use them regarding them as Shiva. They steady the mind, putting an end to its wanderings. While wearing them you should feel that you are wearing Lord Rudra Himself around your neck. That is the right attitude to one's mala. It is with this attitude that one should be doing japa with the mala. The proper way of using it is to hold it between your fingers and keep on passing from one bead to another while doing your mantra. But even more effective than this is to keep repeating the Name with the tongue and not let a single moment pass without repetition of the Name. That is the best mala. That is the inner mala. There are people with whom using a mala is a mere ritual, and the members of that sect use it as a means of business. With one hand they tell the beads while with the other they direct very worldly affairs. This is a mere mockery. This is the corruption of the mala. This has no meaning. Kabir also talks against such a use of the mala. There are so-called devotees who keep wandering from one sacred place to another, who wear all the external symbols of devotion, the sacred mark called tilak, and mudras, and who dance and sing and even cry, and yet they are completely ignorant of their inner home. They do not know what they gain from these practices. They gain nothing.

Dharam Yash Dev: *Can one worship more than one Guru or seek light from more than one Siddha purusha?*
Baba: You can, if you are addicted to it. Otherwise there is no need. There are people who get addicted to tea or going to restaurants. Similarly, if one is addicted to going from one Guru to another, one can do it. When each true Guru is perfect, what is the point of going to several Gurus? If your Guru happens to be a perfected Master, then the seed which he implants in you in the form of Shaktipat will be a perfect seed; that seed is bound to bear full fruit. You do not need another Guru. However, out of sheer respect for holy people, you can honour great saints. No matter whose disciple you are, you can attend their satsangs. However, if another Guru proves to be an obstacle in your own sadhana, this is not good. There was a devotee in Delhi who received intense Shaktipat. Two years ago a certain sadhu had come to Delhi, though he didn't meet me, and that devotee went to attend his lecture. During the course of the lecture that

devotee began to perform violent kriyas. That sadhu asked my devotee to come meet him privately later on. When he met him privately, the sadhu said, "All this is very dangerous. This will seriously impair your brain. I am a leader of all sadhus. I have been practising pranayama and other yogic techniques for the last twenty-five years and I have been practising other disciplines, but my inner Shakti has not been aroused. This arousal could not have occurred in you either."

But this devotee was very clever, and he said to the Guru, "Look, I don't mind if my brain gets affected in the future, but yours seems to be affected right now. Your Shakti has not been awakened in spite of your twenty-five years of sadhana. But I received Shaktipat not very long ago and the inner Shakti was fully awakened and all these wonderful kriyas began. You have not gained anything. It seems that something is seriously wrong with your head."

It is good to be in the company of Siddha purushas, but one must ascertain whether they are Siddha purushas or not. Their company must not impede or interrupt your sadhana. It must not create any doubt in your mind. It is all right if you are blessed by many Siddha purushas, but one is enough. If you have received the grace of one, you have received the grace of all.

Then every Guru has his own mode of worship. One may be a devotee of the Goddess Kali, like Ramakrishna, another may be devoted to Narayana, the third to Shiva, and a fourth to the Guru. A true Guru transmits the same mantra to his disciple by means of which he himself has attained perfection. Once you have received Shaktipat from one perfect Master, by the power of this Shaktipat, by the power of the mantra received from him, you will see Narayan and Chandi and also Ganapati. To have a vision of Ganapati you won't have to use a Ganapati mantra, or to have a vision of the Devi you won't have to use the Devi mantra. To have a vision of the Guru you won't have to repeat *"Namah Gurave."* If you have received the grace of one Siddha, then all the Siddhas dwelling in Siddhaloka will shower their love and affection on you.

One should not spend time with a fake Kundalini yogi.

You must make sure that you are having satsang with a genuine Kundalini yogi. Some people practise Kundalini Yoga and even arouse their Shakti, but the consequences are very strange. One's mind gets agitated or intellect vitiated. These Gurus read all kinds of books and give all kinds of advice. What is the point of going to them? If you were to look at Kundalini, what is it that She is not? Kundalini not only activates yoga but enables you to handle any situation in your daily life effectively. Once a doctor came to me and said, "I have dissected so many bodies, and I haven't seen a single chakra."

I asked him, "Which of your instruments can pierce a chakra? Tell me."

One's concept of Kundalini will reflect his own understanding and field of interest and will be based on his approach to his subject and on the way he has practised Kundalini Yoga. There are plenty of these yogis in India. Can they be called yogis? I had a friend who was an electrical engineer. He renounced the world and began to practise sadhana in cremation grounds. He also studied Vedanta, but he did not forget what he had studied as an electrical engineer. For purusha and prakriti, he used the terms 'negative' and 'positive'. Votaries of science try to have Kundalini experiences without the grace of a perfect Guru. Siddhaloka does not exist according to their science. Devaloka does not exist, Pitruloka does not exist. Heaven and hell are missing from their science. So is the Blue Pearl. They only know how to mix different chemicals. How can they see Kundalini? What is the use of their brand of yoga?

Only the authority of that Kundalini yogi is acceptable who has practised Kundalini Yoga systematically under the guidance of a perfect Master, according to scriptural injunctions, and who has achieved final perfection. To practise Kundalini Yoga according to one's own private notions, to awaken Shakti in all sorts of ways and to say all kinds of things—can these be the characteristics of a Kundalini yogi? The other day I happened to meet one such Kundalini yogi who said that he had not visited any of the worlds that I had talked about. Then I asked him, "Have you seen me before today?"

He said, "No."

"Does it mean that I did not exist then? Have I come into existence just now? I have seen these worlds. I have seen them because I practised Kundalini Yoga under the guidance of my Guru, and in a systematic manner. Anyone who practises Kundalini Yoga under a Guru and in a systematic manner will see everything gradually; but those who practise Kundalini Yoga in an unsystematic manner, without being guided by a Guru will not have the experiences which the Kundalini awakening could bring to them.

How much of the inner realms we are able to explore, or what kind of visions come to us will depend on our depth of devotion, the intensity of reverence with which we are practising our sadhana. You may move in the company of many Gurus, but you can worship and be devoted to only one.

Dharam Yash Dev: *Until a few months back I never thought of Gurus or seeking one, until I had the good fortune of meeting Babaji. Since then he is my Guru. Whether he has accepted me as his disciple, I can't say, or if I am worthy of it either. Since meeting Babaji, my interest in spiritual matters is increasing. Then I read the life stories of some yogis and Siddha purushas, and I felt I was not being fully loyal or faithful to my Guru. This is the point I want to make.*
Baba: There is nothing wrong with reading the life stories of great saints, as long as this does not interfere with your single-minded loyalty to your Guru. It is not at all necessary that a Guru accept somebody as his disciple. What is necessary is that a seeker accept a great Master as his Guru. A seeker should not even bother or worry whether or not he will be accepted as a disciple by the Master concerned. He should, however, accept him as his Master. Take the case of Dronacharya and Eklavya. Dronacharya looked down upon Eklavya because he was an uncivilised tribal boy, but Eklavya accepted him as his Master.

One should not really worry whether the Guru is going to accept him as his disciple or not, because the Guru will certainly accept him. It is like asking the sun whether or not he will give light. It is the nature of the sun to give light, that is all that he has to give. It is the disciple who should accept a Master as his Guru. I receive letters from many foreign seekers whom I don't even know who say that they have accepted me as their Guru, and as a result of that acceptance, they even get Shaktipat. I come to know about it only later after receiving their letters.

Bess: *In one's worldly life, one can set aside a specified twenty minutes or half hour to meditate, but how is it possible to achieve inner peace? Is it necessary to chant every day? If a Guru is essential to attain this peace, how can one communicate with him when a great distance is between them?*
Baba: Everyone must meditate for at least an hour every day. The more you meditate, the less sleep you need. You do not need sleep as much as you need meditation. If you are able to meditate deeply for half an hour, that will give you as much rest as a thousand hours of sound sleep. You should not look upon meditation as an ordinary religious duty which should be performed in a half-hearted manner. Just as it is necessary in life to eat food regularly, and to use utensils, wear jewellery and clothes the right way, so it is necessary to meditate. You should chant all the time, not only every day. You become like what your mind continually dwells upon. If you think of sex, you become possessed by sex. If you think of greed, you become possessed by greed. If your mind turns to anger, it becomes possessed by anger, and if your mind turns to hatred it would be possessed by hatred. Similarly, if it turns to God, it will be possessed by pure love. Then why shouldn't you be chanting all the time? Why must you specify a period of time for it? There is nothing like remembering Him continually.

For attaining inner peace, the Guru is absolutely essential, and it is good that you seem to have realised this truth. But the contact with the Guru has nothing to do with physical distance. No matter how far the disciple is from the Guru, never consider the Guru to be far away; he is not far. It is only the Guru's physical body which may be away from you, but as far as the Guru's inner body is concerned, it is all-pervading. It encompasses the entire cosmos, and also transcends it. I can give you one very simple example. Someone presented a tiny radio set to me the other day. By keeping the dial set at a certain point I could be tuned to Delhi, but by turning the dial just a quarter of an inch I could be tuned into America. On one plane America is thousands of miles away from India, but on another plane America is only a quarter of an inch away from India. The Guru is as pervasive as the Self. Therefore, the Guru is within you, and he will also keep on guiding in matters relating to your sadhana. He works within you as grace. You may not understand this subtle truth at present, but the fact is that when a Guru transmits his mantra to a disciple, he himself enters into the disciple in the form of the mantra. That means that he takes seat within your heart, and wherever you go he will be within you, he will always be traveling with you.

In the *Shiva Purana* I read a short story. Two pilgrims set out on a pilgrimage and they had to pass through a large forest. One said to the other, "Look, this is a very dense forest; it is very difficult to traverse; it is quite dark, and I am scared. How should we go? What will help us? What should we do?" The other was discerning, and he said, "Look, I don't worry about it at all, because I know that my protector is with me, my Lord, my Guru is with me."

The first said, "Where is he?"

"*Namah Shivaya, namah Shivaya*, that is my Guru. That is my Lord. That is with me."

If your perception were subtle enough, you would be able to see that the Guru lives within you in the form of the mantra. If you confuse the Guru with his physical body, and think that if you are away from the physical body, you are away from the Guru, you will not get very much from the Guru no matter how much love or affection you may show for the Guru. Whatever devotion you profess for the Guru, you fail as a disciple. The only disciple who is a true disciple is one who believes that the Guru is present within him, that he is very close, very intimate with him, that he is within him in the form of the mantra; and he worships him with devotion, with this understanding.

February 16, 1972

Vishnudas: *Are the awakening of the Kundalini and the rising of prana one and the same phenomenon or is there a difference between the two?*
Baba: The prana rises upwards as a result of the Kundalini awakening. As the Kundalini is stirred awake, the prana begins to rise upwards. Kundalini is the divine consciousness behind prana. Kundalini is also called Chiti or Shakti. It is Chiti Kundalini Herself who turns into prana. Therefore, the prana begins to rise upwards when the Kundalini is awakened. As long as the prana and apana do not become even and balanced, one cannot attain the vision of equality regardless of how much he has been practising yoga, how much Vedanta he has studied, or how long he has stayed in the state of samadhi through the control of prana. A seeker may be able to remain in samadhi by controlling his prana for as long as months, or even three years, but he would not be able to attain equanimity as long as his prana and apana are not balanced or are uneven. Lord Shiva also says that it is only when the prana and apana, that is the incoming and outgoing breaths, become equalized, that the true sense of equality arises from within spontaneously. You do not have to make any special effort to achieve equanimity. Once the Kundalini is awakened within, in course of time the movement of prana becomes even itself.

Vishnudas: *How long does it take for a seeker to achieve total liberation or moksha after the awakening of Kundalini? For how long does this course run? How many days or years?*
Baba: After the awakening of Kundalini it may take a seeker any length of time to achieve moksha—3, 6, 9, 12, 15, or 18 years. Many have to be reborn. Even one whose practice is very intense and who has absolute devotion to the Guru would take at least three years to achieve moksha. How fast your progress is and how intense your sadhana is after the Kundalini awakening depends on how intense your devotion to the Guru is. Those seekers who come to have the highest kind of sublime devotion to the Guru, who begin to

feel tremendous reverence for him, would take from three to five years to have the final beatific vision. Otherwise it would take much longer. There are different degrees of faith. I am talking about the deepest faith in the truth of the Guru, a faith which is as strong as faith in anything which you can perceive with the senses. In fact, there is no time limit to this course. Nor does it depend on how long you meditate. It depends on the quality of your inner faith in the Guru. If your faith in him is absolute, if it is untinged by doubt, then the inner Shakti becomes more and more intense and one goes towards the final goal by leaps and bounds. But if your faith is mingled with doubt, then the pace of your progress would be slowed down. It is solely your devotion and faith which will determine how fast you are moving towards the destination. The only means for accelerating the pace of the Kundalini is a great feeling of devotion for the Guru. If your devotion is mixed with doubt it would take you a long time to achieve the higher visions and you would not be able to attain the final beatific vision.

I do not belong to the school of idol worshippers. In fact I have always been opposed to it. But such was the influence of my devotion to my Guru that I myself have installed a statue of him and I hold arati to him thrice a day. Not only this, as a result of my deep devotion and intense reverence for him, I was able to see him within the Blue Pearl.

Once you have received Shaktipat, it will not go in vain. It is bound to bear fruit, if not in this lifetime, then in your next birth. You have heard about yogis who are born Siddhas, who are born great yogis. They are yogis who attained a high state in their past birth. When you die after achieving a certain state in sadhana, in your next birth you start from that same point. Such yogis achieve perfection in a short time and leave a blazing trail of glory behind and do a lot of good for mankind. The Shakti stands behind you with the same force and intensity. So the pace of your progress depends on you—on the depth of your devotion to your Guru. The deeper it is, the faster you go.

Dhiraj: *Is there any such thing as a proper or fit time for Shaktipat, at which time Shakti is transmitted?*
Baba: The Shakti is supreme. She is free from the limita-

tions of time and space and rules of any kind, or laws foreign to Her being. She depends on two factors only: one is the intense aspiration of the seeker for liberation, and the other is the strength and depth of his faith in his Master. As far as Shakti is concerned, every human being is worthy of it; nobody is excluded from Her boon. It is, however, true that some people may receive it very quickly while others may take time. It does happen that some people receive it sooner, while others receive it quite late.

Visitor: *Is one's daily practice of meditation affected by the quality of time by whether the hour is auspicious or inauspicious?*
Baba: After Shaktipat has taken place, the quality of the hour of meditation cannot affect your sadhana. In fact, all the planets and stars begin to help you. However, if your attention is distracted by contemporary incidents or events, say, like a war or political movement, that may affect your sadhana. But as far as planetary movements are concerned, that has nothing to do with it. Chiti is the supreme power, and all other forces are subsidiary to Her. So planets and time are powerless before Chiti. However, depending on the condition of our body or the state of our mind, Chiti can accelerate Her pace or slow it down; but that depends on Her own sweet will.

Dharam Yash Dev: *Until such time as a devotee gets his diksha or special mantra from his Guru, what mantra should he use for his daily prayers and peace of mind?*
Baba: A seeker can repeat any one of the divine Names. There are infinite Names of God. You people go to different discourses and sankirtan and you must have heard many divine Names. Whichever Names of God you happen to like, continue to repeat.

Carol: *How can one become a perfect instrument of the Guru?*
Baba: That disciple who has become conscious of the true nature of the Guru, and who has offered his entire life at his feet, and who has resolved to follow his instruction faithfully, will become his perfect instrument. That seeker becomes

a perfect instrument of the Guru, who submits himself to him in body, mind, and speech. With his body he serves the Guru, with speech he glorifies him, and in his mind he continuously thinks of him. And thus he becomes the Guru's completely. This is a very good question.

Kathy and Robert: *In one of your books you are quoted as saying, "Let the world remain as it is, try to forget it, and turn your mind inwards." Please explain.*
Baba: It is a very good question. Everybody who is living in the world is surrounded by problems. Some people have more problems—more possessions, bigger offices, households, etc., more people to look after — and others less. Yet when you want to go to sleep, what is it that you do? You do not renounce your wife, your children, your husband, your office or your car. You do not renounce any other possession. You let all those things stay wherever they are and you only forget them for a while, gliding into the world of sleep. You haven't destroyed any of them. You haven't turned against any of them, you haven't discarded any of them. You are only turning your mind away from them for a while. After a sound sleep, when you wake up, you are a new person.

Similarly, it should be possible for you to meditate while surrounded by your possessions and family. There are many people who wonder how they can meditate when they are married and have family responsibilities. Do you think that you have to renounce your worldly life in order to meditate? What makes you think that God is a creature who is full of jealousy and who would not be able to bear to let you have the little pleasure which you may have in your worldly life? Therefore, I tell you, do not disturb the world around you. Let it remain as it is. Just turn your mind inward and meditate on your own Self.

Raul: *Gurubhakti emphasises worship of the Guru's external form as a means to stimulate devotion to the inner Self. If one is adverse to all kinds of external rituals, what should be done to overcome this apparent obstacle?*
Baba: I would like to know what it is that you are interested in. If you are adverse to all kinds of external rituals, what

exactly is it that you are not adverse to, or that you favour? If you are interested in the inner Self, how can you be adverse to the Guru's external form? The external form is nothing but a reflection of the soul, the inner Self.

Do you feel any affection for your own body, for your own external form? Do you feel any attachment for your own head, your own eyes, ears and other senses? (Yes.) Are you being reasonable? When you say that you have attachment for your own form and you don't have any attachment for the Guru's form, what you are saying is only a cover for a certain kind of insensitivity. If a person loves his own body but is adverse to the body of the Guru, can you call him sensible? Or can you call him fair? Doesn't it show that he is being absolutely selfish and insensitive? He loves his own body but he feels adverse to the Guru's. As far as you yourself are concerned, you are attached to the physical form, but when you turn to the Guru, you suddenly shift to the impersonal. Who teaches that? This is not a fair teaching—this is a teaching of jealousy, selfishness and narrowness.

It's very difficult to know the inner Self. When the body is being honoured, worshipped or fed with different kinds of foods, or when attention is being paid to the body in different ways, who exactly is it that is being honoured? (The atman.) In that case your question doesn't make any sense. It appears as though you wrote it while you were drowsy. Aren't you contradicting yourself? When you are worshipping the Guru's external form you are really worshipping his inner Self. You are not worshipping his flesh. Whatever you offer to the Guru in the course of your worship, you are offering to his inner Spirit, not to his flesh.

I, too, am a worshipper of the impersonal, and I am surely aware of the fact that the inner Self is beyond form, that the inner Self is pure Being, pure wisdom. And I do not impel anyone to worship a particular physical form.

We also should not be led by what is written in different books, or by an inadequate understanding of them. We should try to understand from our own experience, from our own lives, how valid what we read is. There were some people who believed in the existence of the world of ancestors and there were others who did not. One day a debate was held. The fathers of both the debaters were dead. One learned man said that Pitruloka, the world of ancestors, did not exist. The other said, "I have seen it and I know that it does exist. But you do not believe in its reality, so that means that your father was an eater of dogs." (He had in fact used a much fouler term of abuse, but I am not reproducing it for fear that it may be taped, and it may shock the tender sensibilities of the women here.)

Now the other one rolled up his sleeves and was getting ready for a fight. He said, "Look, you have the cheek to abuse my father even after he has died."

The man replied, "Please forgive me for asking you this impertinent question, but what makes you think that your father is still around to hear this term of abuse?"

So there is no point in becoming fanatical in following any particular school, or in taking up a certain academic position. It is generally seen that most people forget all about their loyalty to the impersonal and all their ideas of the attributeless and formless Being when they are caught in concrete situations. The Guru's body is like your body; the Guru's Self is like your Self, and you shouldn't get involved in this controversy about the personal and the impersonal. Those people who raise such a controversy are utterly ignorant. Everyone has a personal form and everyone is beyond form. You may be meditating on the personal, but when your mind becomes absolutely still you will attain the impersonal. This controversy is the creation of those so-called religious people who have vested interests in their precepts. A seeker should have no use for it. Continue to meditate and when your meditation is consummated you will have attained the impersonal.

February 21, 1972

Girija: *During the Saptah my mind became clear and controlled and even seemed to enter a higher level of conscious-*

ness. But one day after the chant ended, it became very rajasic—more so than for several months. I also noticed an increase in tamas and had strange and unpleasant dreams. I have read that whenever a higher level is reached, there is a corresponding descent to a deeper level of impurities. Is this correct, and does it account for this experience?

Baba: Participating in a Saptah is living in a veritable Vaikuntha, and to understand the full value of a Saptah you have to rise to a higher level still; you are not yet worthy of it. You take part in a Saptah because we hold it here. During my life I have held so many Saptahs, particularly during my sadhana. I used to hold very frequent Saptahs in Yeola, and in Kokamthan where I spent a long period of time. I organised great Saptahs which were attended by thousands of people. They were also treated to a feast and they sang the divine Name in great ecstasy. Participation in a Saptah is a nectarean experience. When the Saptah ends, it is like moving from one country to another. A Saptah is the most fruitful, the most beneficial of all the different modes of sadhana. It is far superior to yajnas and other sacrificial rituals, and it is better than any individual japa or austerities. It is better than any other spiritual practices, and it makes the greatest contribution to the general good. There is nothing which is more beneficial for all people than a Saptah.

When the Kali Yuga was about to begin, it so happened that King Parikshit was cursed by a great sage. It happens quite often that one who is in a high place is possessed by the pride of his status, and it is very difficult for him to remain humble, however intelligent, however good, however noble he may be. It is for this reason that Mira says, "Rama belongs to the meek who don't have any pride of power; those who are intoxicated by power cannot find Rama." Parikshit was an emperor; he enjoyed sovereignty over a very large domain, and it began to seem quite natural to him that whoever he passed should get up, as a sign of respect for him. One day King Parikshit went into a forest, and there was a sadhu, an ascetic who was sitting there absorbed in meditation, and he did not get up. Parikshit got annoyed and put a dead snake around the sadhu's neck. That sadhu had a disciple. When he saw the dead snake on his Guru's neck he flared up and lost all control and immediately pronounced a curse, "Whoever is guilty of this foul deed will be bitten by a snake in seven days."

After the King returned to his capital, he realised what he had done and began to feel sorry. He began to feel remorse about his foul deed, because an intelligent person will always think about what he has done, and if he has done anything wrong, he would be full of repentance, and he would never repeat the same wrong twice. The king kept thinking that he should have put a garland of flowers around the sadhu's neck. In the meantime, that ascetic came out of his samadhi, and when he came to learn that his disciple had lost his discrimination because of anger and pronounced a dreadful curse on the emperor of the land, he began to feel sorry for the emperor, and concerned for the subjects, because a noble king like Parikshit is very essential for a kingdom; his presence insures the welfare of so many people. Now that the curse had been uttered nothing could be done about it. The sadhu however, felt that the king should at least be informed about the curse, so he sent a message saying that a young boy had done something which was very improper and that he should think about it. While the king was still thinking about what he had done, he received word that a curse had been pronounced that he would die of snakebite within a week, and he should take some steps to save his life. The king was highly intelligent and discerning; he belonged to the dynasty of the Pandavas. But, sometimes it so happens that when a bad time comes, however wise and enlightened one may be, for that period of time, his intellect becomes clouded. King Parikshit was the same person who had been saved by the Lord Himself in the Mahabharata war. The enemies had tried their best to kill him while he was still in the womb of his mother. They were shooting missiles at the womb all the time, and yet the baby could not be killed because he was under the protection of the Lord. That very child had grown up to be King Parikshit, and he belonged to a very noble family and was a favourite of the Lord; yet he had committed such a foul deed. Such is the influence of evil time.

But the king did not get perturbed on hearing this news. He said to himself, "It is good. I richly deserve the curse. In any case I have to die one day, and it doesn't matter if I die in a week." But, being the wise person that he was, he decided to renounce the throne at once and retire into the forest. He sent his crier around proclaiming that all sages and seers, all enlightened beings, all the learned priests and scholars of the kingdom should gather in the forest where the king had retired, and they should all try to get him liberated within a week, as he was fated to die shortly. He had extended protection to all the followers and leaders of different religious sects of his time all his life, and now during his last seven days, they should extend their protection to him and save him. As the king was in such a severe crisis all saints and great-souled beings belonging to different sects gathered in the forest from all directions. This gathering included such ancient sages and seers whose matted locks were as long as a hundred feet, and their nails were ten feet long. Some of them were 500 years old, others were 1,000 years old.

The king prayed to all the holy men who had gathered there. "I am fated to be bitten by a snake in a week. One day has already passed; only six days are left. If there are any here who can insure me salvation during such a brief period, I would welcome their teaching. I would not like to die if my soul is not saved."

Some of the holy beings were amused by the king's excessive eagerness, and they said, "The king is an infant as far as these spiritual things are concerned, because he has absolutely no idea of what salvation is, and how long it takes for one to achieve salvation." One said it had taken him six hundred years to attain salvation. One said it had taken him eight hundred, and another nine hundred. There are eight limbs of yoga, and it took at least thirty to thirty-five years to perfect just one aspect. There were fifteen stages of devotion. There were four sets of qualities required for the study of Vedanta and fifteen steps in Vedantic reflection, so how could the king achieve salvation in six days? What made him think that salvation was so easy, so cheap, that they could award it to a being just with a flick of the wrist? The king had spent all his life wielding the sceptre. How could he attain moksha without thoroughly purifying himself?

The king fell into despair, and in the meantime there appeared at a distance from the assembly a young boy called Shuka. Somebody approached Shukamuni and said, "Sir, the king is having a crisis. He has only six days more to live, and he is in search of someone who can grant him liberation within six days. He has been asking everyone for help. The saints and sages who have gathered here have told him that it can't be done, that moksha is not so cheap. If you can save him, please go and instruct him."

Shuka was a nice lad, just sixteen years old. He was the son of the great sage Vyas. He was wearing only a loincloth, and he was so young that there was not a single hair on his face. He moved towards the king, and the sages and saints who had gathered there all rose up out of sheer reverence for this young boy, and they hailed him. The king was amazed to see that a mere lad should be so honoured by all these stalwarts who were hundreds of years old, and who had such long matted locks. The king asked some of the wise old courtiers, "Who is that boy for whom even very ancient sages and seers have stood up out of respect?"

They said, "Your Majesty, it is true that we have practised japa and austerities for a much longer period than him, but as far as the direct knowledge of God is concerned, he knows much more than us. It is he who knows all the secrets of moksha and God. That is why all of us revere him so much. He is called Shukamuni."

After everyone had made obescence to him, Shuka sat on the high seat offered him by the king, and all the high beings who had gathered there also sat down. The king prayed to Shuka saying, "Sir, I am fated to die in a week of a snakebite because I am guilty of a foul deed. Please grant me total liberation in these six days."

Shuka said, "Look, you have six days, that is a long time. I can grant you liberation in an instant. Listen to me, Your Majesty. Kali Yuga has so many serious defects. He is extremely strange and weak, but he has one great quality —only in this age, just by chanting the Name of the Lord, by chanting *Hare Rama, Hare Krishna*, one can attain Vaikuntha or inner peace."

Such is the great value of a Saptah. It bestows liberation instantly. It was natural for you to get into a higher state of consciousness during the Saptah. After the Saptah ended, you returned to your normal state. During the Saptah you had gotten to a different place, a different area within yourself. During the Saptah you were hearing the name of Rama and Krishna every moment, no matter where you were. How far away from the prayer hall were you? It was broadcast through the speakers. All the time you only heard "Krishna, Krishna". There is great power in the divine Name. It was quite natural for you to get into a higher state of consciousness. This summer we are going to hold a fourteen-day chant. We will hold it with great love, and in an orderly manner. Preparations have already begun.

Shuka asked the king to say the divine Name, and the king began to sing. And this is how the remaining six days passed. The king got so rapt in the ecstasy of the divine Name, that when a snake came and actually bit him, he wasn't even conscious that he was bitten by a snake.

It was then that the tradition of the Saptah was born, and it is still alive. Take the case of the greatest yogis of Maharashtra. All of them finally turned to the divine Name and all of them sang the divine Name, and sang of the divine Name in their works. And I, too, have great love for the divine Name. In fact, the divine Name is the Lord Himself in living form.

In the yoga of meditation, it is quite natural for you to have strange, even unpleasant dreams, but those dreams will bear good fruit, so you don't have to worry about them. Even now, though the Saptah has ended, you should continue to chant the divine Name inwardly, with great love all the time, because that facilitates meditation very much. It is entirely true that one rises to a higher level of awareness during a Saptah. And it was Parikshit who proved the glory of the Kali Yuga, the glory of the divine Name.

Kedarnath: *Some Gurus hold that if you remain a witness while satisfying a desire you can transcend it. Does this imply that sense mastery or self-discipline is not necessary?*
Baba: If you continue to indulge your cravings although remaining a witness to them, you will never be able to overcome them. On the contrary, you will fall deeper and deeper into the mire of cravings, and your mind and heart will be

permeated by the evil influence of cravings. And one day you are bound to sink to the depths of degradation. I know of many alcoholics who were so addicted to drinking to such a degree, that the amount they consumed increased day by day until it got to the point where they were not only drinking alcohol, they were bathing in it. And I compelled them to stop drinking.

Some of you are quite addicted to tea and coffee, and you indulge that desire every day. Have you been able to overcome craving by indulging in it? Those who are always angry and jealous and giving expression to those passions—have you been able to overcome them by indulging them? I have yet to see a person who has overcome a craving by indulging it. Who has achieved contentment through self-indulgence and then got rid of his craving? To me it appears that the gurus who make this kind of claim are themselves helpless victims of their own lusts, and it is in the interest of the gratification of their own passions that they mislead people, they spread this kind of teaching. They misguide people, they give wrong teaching only to indulge their own wrong cravings. Such a guru is not one who could lead his students to God, who could free them from lusts. On the contrary, he is the type who would only make his students worse, more helpless victims of their own lusts. He is spreading a wrong kind of teaching, strengthening passions and lusts and not making any headway in delivering people from the clutches of those horrible passions and lusts. The great sage Vyas says that you cannot overcome a desire by indulging it. You cannot overcome a passion by trying to satisfy it. You can only overcome it by renouncing it. And that is what the experience of all seekers has been.

Shyama: *Sometimes we serve the Guru because through serving him our desires are fulfilled, and our hearts are filled with delight. Is pure service different from this kind of service? Please speak about the nature of pure service.*
Baba: That service is pure which is without any desire behind it. It is only that person who is completely free from attachment and aversion, who is not even conscious of whether others are pure or impure, who can render pure service to the Guru. Take the case of the ideal bhaktas

mentioned in the scriptures, such as the *Shrimad Bhagavat Purana*. They never made any demands on the Lord in return for their devotion. They only offered devotion; devotion was their sole concern, the means as well as the end. The *Shrimad Bhagavat* says that such great saints are completely free from dependence on any outer things; they have equality-consciousness, their minds are tranquil, and they have achieved total self-mastery. They serve the Lord for the sake of serving Him. They have absolutely no desire or motive behind their service.

A poet in his poetry makes a very clear distinction between selfish and selfless service. And when I say 'poet', I don't mean an ordinary poet, a person who works with his mind. When I use the term 'poet', I mean poet-saint, one who is seized with divine inspiration, and who composes his poems by divine grace. He says that he who served the Lord without any desire, without any motive, got the city of gold in return, while he who served him with selfish desire only got fetters around his feet. This refers to Sudama who was an ideal servant to the Lord. He served Him ceaselessly without asking Him for anything, and as a result of that the Lord was so pleased that He rewarded him with a city of gold.

Take the case of Vasudeva and Devaki, Krishna's parents, on the other hand. They, too had served the Lord. It was only on one occasion that they expressed the desire that the Lord be born to them, and as a result of that desire, they were thrown in the prison by Kamsa, and their feet put in fetters. It is for this reason that the poet says that, "He who has no desire becomes the master of the entire wealth of the Lord. While he who has a selfish desire gets only what he desires."

A pure servant is not even conscious of the fact that he is putting in selfless service, because if he is conscious of it, then it means that his heart is still impure, and a pure servant has absolutely no craving, no desire.

Shankar: *Baba discourages intellectual questions. Can these ever have value? Should curiosity about how everything fits together be stifled? Is reading the writings of other Siddhas who discuss such questions, like Sri Aurobindo,*

being promiscuous or a bad thing to do?
Baba: It's not that I don't like intellectual questions, but at the same time, I am fully aware for what purpose a particular session is held, and I am also aware of what is proper at a given time. During the question and answer sessions, nothing else is important. We hold these question and answer sessions, and all of us get together here only for one purpose—the various obstacles or problems that we come up against in our sadhana should be taken up, and we should be able to benefit from each other's questions, and from the answers to the different questions. I would not allow any distractions during such a session.

But this question, whether you should read the works of Siddhas who have intellectualised yoga, is not an intellectual question, and you can certainly read those works provided that they do not interfere with your mode of sadhana. If these works tend to draw your mind away from your sadhana, you should become vigilant immediately. I have told you many times that all kinds of impressions, good and bad, are embedded in the sushumna, and they arise and subside there like clouds in the sky. They are not of much importance. All that you need is to remain a witness to all these. For this you need not read fat volumes. However, if you are interested in them, you may read them.

The books that we have kept in the library can be read by anyone here, and you don't have to ask me for that, because we are keeping the right sort of books there. We wouldn't keep books that are not proper in the library. The world is as you see it, and it is the nature of the outgoing Kundalini to keep throwing up all kinds of thoughts and feelings, all kinds of impressions from inside. It is here that remaining a witness to whatever is happening inside would have some value.

February 23, 1972

Elizabeth: When my mind wanders from my mantra during meditation, I fall asleep. This happens many times. Is there anything I can do about it apart from trying to concentrate harder?

Baba: Mantra japa is the very soul, the very prana of meditation. If your mind is really saturated with the mantra, it will never wander away from it. It is only when the mind is not saturated with the mantra that it wanders. However, sleep is a good sign, and it indicates that the mind has become one-pointed. The state of sleep is quite close to the state of intense concentration, and there is no harm in having a nap in the sitting position during meditation. Sometimes you should try to shake yourself out of sleep and turn your mind to mantra japa and meditation. The sleep that you get during meditation fills your mind with peace and new enthusiasm. Is that your experience or not? During the meditational sleep the body, the nerves and the mind get complete rest, and they get renewed.

Janaki: I often strongly feel that I am not doing enough, but I am not sure what more I should do, if anything, what more I am capable of doing, and how much I should demand of myself above and beyond the regular Ashram routine. Or perhaps this feeling is just another trick of a proud ego. How can I understand and resolve this feeling honestly?

Baba: The feeling that you are not doing enough is the right sort of feeling; you have done enough only when your mind completely merges in the Blue Pearl. Until then this feeling will chase you. While following the Ashram routine you should not neglect the inner discipline—that is constant inner recollectedness; constant inner japa of the mantra that you feel attracted towards, whether it is *Om namah Shivaya, Guru Om,* or *Shivo'ham.* You don't have to change your mantra. Continue to do the one that you have been doing before. Let this mantra become your greatest friend, your very prana, your highest deity. If you identify yourself with one mantra, in course of time it will bear rich fruit. If you repeat a mantra with single-minded devotion for a prolonged period, it shows wonderful results—you come to realise that only later. There is a small room within the room where you meditate, and in that room I practised mantra japa for a long period of time. Now I keep it locked. Don't think that that is my treasury; don't think that it contains any dollars. All the dollars are under the custody of Venkappa. Once a very high official visited me, and we were discussing this question of the mantra. I said to him, "Look, I don't have to give you a mantra. Go into my meditation room and put your ear against the wall, and you will be able to hear the mantra that I have been practising there."

Then I made him sit inside, and bolted the door from the outside, and he believed my word, and he actually heard the mantra sound coming from the wall. Later he admitted that he had had the most wonderful experience. I said, "Look, it's not enough for you to admit it orally, you must give it to me in writing."

The feeling that you should do more than what you are doing is a good feeling. It's not your ego masquerading in a different form, and even if it is ego, it's a very healthy form of ego. We must have great respect and reverence for the mantra. I had as much reverence for the mantra that I received from my Guru as I had for my Guru himself, and it is only when you begin to respect the mantra as much as the Guru, that the mantra will begin to work inside you as much as the Guru himself would. Mantra japa is a most mysterious process and it's not easy to comprehend its full significance. A mantra is so called because it redeems the one who practises it.

Don't try to overcome this feeling; it is the right sort of feeling. I am certain that you must be meditating very well. In fact, after I have had my bath and go out to bow in the direction of Baba's Samadhi, I make a round of the meditation room, and look at every face, with the help of my flashlight. I have looked at you many times, and I feel that you are meditating very well. Sometimes I even twirl my flashlight and you make a certain gesture. Perhaps you are not conscious who is waving the flashlight.

Larry A.: *I have been experiencing a drilling sensation in* *my spine at about the level of the heart, and also sometimes between the eyes. Usually it occurs during chanting, work and sometimes meditation. Does this indicate awakened Kundalini, or just purification of the chakras? How can I keep from hindering its progress?*

Baba: This is a very good experience, and it is a sign of awakened Kundalini. It doesn't just show that your Kundalini is about to be awakened, it shows that it has been awakened. When the Kundalini works on different chakras, trying to open them, you have this kind of sensation between the eyes, and sometimes your eyes will even start spinning; that experience is called piercing the bindu. It is a very highly significant experience. You don't have to resort to any special practices to maintain your experiences. Continue to do whatever you have been doing. You should also continue to pray to Gurudeva. Whatever is happening to you is very good. However, you should keep your mind free from distracting thoughts, you should not let your mind wander amidst irrelevant thoughts. Keep yourself aware of the great power of the Kundalini, and keep your mind in a state of constant recollectedness.

Carol: *You have said that we should meditate on the Guru's form, and on the mantra. Sometimes in meditation my breathing becomes very irregular, or bhastrika occurs, or the breath is suspended. How do I use the mantra with these? How do I put my attention on the mantra, and the internal sensations at once?*

Baba: Meditation on the Guru's form, on the mantra, or on the inner Self is one and the same thing. It's not three different forms of meditation. It's not difficult to keep the mind fastened on the Guru's form. A meditator should be aware of three things. If he is not aware of these three things he will not make good progress. He should be fully aware of the exact nature of the Guru, the mantra, and the inner Self. The Guru is the same being whom we call Shiva, and Shiva is Guru. Guru is Shiva and Shiva is Guru. Guru and Shiva are one. And the disciple is the same as the Guru and Shiva. *Om namah Shivaya* is nothing but a concrete embodiment of the Guru and Shiva. One should be constantly aware that one's own Self, the Guru and Shiva are absolutely one. There is not the least difference between these three. The Guru is one who injects the mantric fluid into the seeker. In fact, it is he himself who enters the disciple through the mantra. So it is necessary to look upon the Guru and the mantra as one and the same.

When bhastrika occurs there is no need to repeat the mantra. When bhastrika takes place, attend fully to that process; when the breath becomes suspended, mantra repetition is unnecessary. In fact, suspension of breath is the fruit of the mantra repetition. It is, as it were, the remuneration paid to you for the task of mantra repetition. Kumbhak or suspension of breath is a most significant event, and quite often it is the result of bhastrika. When that takes place one should not try to divert one's mind to anything else, to concentrate on any form or to mantra repetition. Let the mind be fully occupied with the kumbhak. It is not necessary that mantra repetition go on constantly during meditation. It is the state of complete inner stillness, complete inner silence, the state of complete inner detachment which is the goal. Mantra repetition is the means to attain that inner state of pure silence, the state which is totally free from anxiety. Kumbhak has the greatest significance, it is the most significant realisation. There are different varieties of kumbhak. Sometimes it is suspended inside, sometimes outside, sometimes above and sometimes below. Sometimes the breath will be held in the heart region and other times in the muladhar, and yet other times outside. So wherever kumbhak may take place it has great value. Kumbhak has a very great place in yoga. It purifies the mind, removing all taints, it purifies the body, it purifies the prana. One who experiences kumbhak again and again should be awarded the Nobel Prize.

Olivier: *Sometimes I feel a great force in my body, particularly in my eyes, legs, shoulders and arms. It seems to overcome an obstacle and pervade my body. During this time I cannot touch anybody and cannot bear to be touched by anybody. Sometimes I am afraid because I believe that I am going to be a fool. What is it and what to do?*
Baba: This is a very significant experience; sometimes you do experience Shakti pervading the entire body. In fact, this

experience should be constant. You should feel Shakti saturating the body all the time. Through frequent repetition of this experience you finally become established in the state in which you experience Shakti all the time in you. You begin to feel that you are nothing but Shakti. This experience will not make you a fool. On the contrary, this experience will lead you to the supremely effulgent, glorious divine Being. It leads you from darkness to light, it doesn't lead you into stupidity.

It's also very good that you can't bear to touch anyone, or that you can't bear to be touched by anyone. There is no compulsion for you to touch anyone. It is very good to remain pure, not to touch anyone or to be touched by anyone. It is for this reason that sadhus in our country are so very particular about their purity, about being touched. It is for this reason that I flare up when I find certain people touching my feet. However, if you begin to feel Shakti in the touch of another person, then you will no longer be adverse to it. You should intensify your sadhana even more so that you may be able to repeatedly experience the great vibrations of Shakti.

Shaun: *In your book, Guru, you speak about your method of meditation, that is touching every part of your body saying Guru Om, and thus installing your Guru in your body. Should we use Guru Om, or the mantra you have given us for this purpose? Also how often should this method be used?*
Baba: All the mantras are alike. The Guru mantra is the mantra which you have received from the Guru, and it is always better to repeat the mantra that you have received from the Guru. Is it mentioned anywhere in that book how often this method should be used? It's enough to touch a part once and chant your mantra once. (How should we use that method when having kriyas?) This method is not meant to be used when you are having kriyas. This method should be used when you are not having kriyas. When a kriya is taking place, you should not let your mind be distracted by anything else. You should only remain a witness to what is happening. That is your highest duty at that time.

You should keep watching whatever is happening, and not try to interfere with the kriyas or do anything else. If you have the inclination, then while remaining a witness to the processes which are taking place, you should continue to chant the mantra with great devotion. When you are touching the body to the accompaniment of the mantra received from the Guru, you mentally identify yourself with the Guru.

Jon: *What is the place of rational thought and/or giving up rational thought in sadhana?*
Baba: Only if you are addicted to rational thought can you continue to indulge in it during the period of sadhana, otherwise, it is unnecessary. What is the need of thinking about everything? Why not let your mind remain fastened on the subject of meditation? Did you read *Guru*? There is a kind of rational thinking in *Guru*: that is, to let your intellect be occupied with the Guru all the time. In many places I have described the nature of the Goddess, the Mother, Kundalini. Did you pay attention to that? Wouldn't it be good to let the rational part of your mind be occupied with Chiti, with thinking about how glorious, how wonderful this divine force is which manifests Herself in so many different forms, which though one becomes many and which begins to regard Her own manifestations as being different from one another, and puts them in separate categories? If you are very addicted to rational inquiry, then direct it towards the wonderful workmanship of God. Take this body, for instance. It has definite form but it has emerged from the formless. Think about how this miracle can be possible. Then think about the glories of your own body. Look at, for instance, your own eyes, which have the power of perceiving countless different objects. Think about them. Think about the tongue which can formulate so many different words, which can speak in so many different languages. Or about the central nerve, the sushumna, in which different gods and goddesses are situated. Try to find out why God has created this system. It has been created. Now what should you do with it? What is its purpose? Let your intellect be occupied with finding out the answer to this question,

"How is it that God, after having created this wonderful system we call the body, and after having equipped it with different kinds of gadgets, Himself took seat in it, and though He has manifested Himself in the heart, yet He is not perceived by anyone? What art is He using to conceal Himself?" Let these be the subjects for rational thought. If your mind is directed towards these questions, it will have a place in your sadhana.

Nala: *What is the relationship between the love that is human, warm, coming from the heart, which can make you cry, and the love which is only concerned with the development of consciousness?*
Baba: There is no basic difference between these two forms of love, because both these forms spring from the same consciousness. The only difference between the two is that whereas for the first kind of love you need somebody else, you need to embrace somebody else in order to cry together, in the other kind of love there is no one to cry with you.

Kalyani: *You have mentioned that we should be practising continual recollectedness. Would you please explain this more fully?*
Baba: What more is there to explain? Have you read a story which is included in a work on Ramakrishna's life? Every year his devotees used to gather on the occasion of Dassera and they would ask him, "What should we do?" And Ramakrishna would say, "Continue to contemplate."

The next year the same question was repeated, and the same answer was given, and the third year also the same question was repeated, and Ramakrishna repeated the same answer. Then some of the devotees complained, "During the course of three years you have said only one thing." Ramakrishna then said, "Look, I have got only one thing in my shop; I have nothing else, so what else can I do?"

Therefore I repeat also that you should be continually thinking about the Lord. This continual recollectedness or contemplation is the best thing to do. It should not be practised haphazardly.

Your mind should not be engaged only with the gross body. The mind should be able to penetrate to the causal body. Just as you repeat with your tongue, *Guru Om, Guru Om*, similarly the vibration of this mantra should be occurring automatically in the navel. The navel should be vibrating with this mantra without any effort on your part. Your mantra japa should pass deeper than the tongue. If it remains confined to the tongue, then it doesn't bear much fruit, no matter how long you have practised it. Then you begin to complain that you have practised *Hari Ram* for such a long time, yet you haven't gained much as a result of it. The mantra japa should become more and more subtle, more and more refined. If your mantra repetition is only on the gross level, then it will sometimes cease, but if it has gone deeper, it will go on continuously. There are, in fact, four levels of speech, one deeper than the other: the tongue, the throat, the heart and the navel. After repeating the mantra for a prolonged period of time with the tongue, japa descends to the throat region. That means you have achieved the next higher stage. When it descends to the heart from the throat, you rise still higher. Unfortunately many of us are not able to go deeper than the tongue and our mantra remains confined only to the gross level. Therefore, one should talk only as much as is strictly necessary, and devote the rest of the time to japa. Otherwise, one's most precious time is wasted. You have come all the way to the Ashram for devotion, for spiritual evolution, and if even in the Ashram you continue with idle gossip then your coming here will have absolutely no effect. If you want the japa to descend to the navel region, if you really want to realise the deepest level of Shakti, you should talk very little.

I read a poem where the poet says, "I lost everything through conversation." Most of us waste our time in conversation. Therefore, let your japa descend to the deeper levels of your body. For that it is necessary to repeat the mantra with your tongue and keep the mind focused there. If your japa is pursued with one-pointed attention, in a very short period of time you will gain full control of your mind. If I go around inspecting at different hours of the day, say early in the morning, at noon, or night, at all sorts of odd hours, it is only to see whether you are spending your time in silent mantra repetition or wasting it in foolish conversation. In fact, this excessive fondness for conversation is not a good quality. On the contrary, it is a terrible sickness, and it doesn't do anyone good, whoever he may be. Those who are fond of talking incessantly, whose tongues never like to take rest, begin to suffer from sleeplessness. They cannot fall asleep on time, they cannot wake up on time, they cannot finish their work on time, and when they are not able to finish their work on time, they get disturbed and try to find all sorts of excuses. And they begin to pity themselves if they are not able to enjoy good sleep.

At the junction of Dwapara Yuga and Kali Yuga, at the time of transition, King Parikshit was very worried about what was going to happen in the Kali Yuga, because all of the priests and seers had made the most dreadful predictions. He had called all the learned men of the kingdom, and all of them were concerned with this question. While they were discussing this question, a horrible dark figure appeared in the court, absolutely naked, holding his tongue with one hand, and his sex organ with the other. He appeared to be in a state of intoxication; he was dancing wildly in that posture. The king, as he looked at him, was horrified. He said, "Who is this dreadful creature if not Kali Yuga? Only Kali Yuga would have the temerity to appear in such a dreadful form before a king like me."

The king immediately drew his sword from its sheath, and asked his men to grab this dreadful person, because he was ready to behead him there and then. He had no business to come in that terrible condition before a king, and it was not for the king to forgive such a horrible lapse. A saint might forgive him, but it is absolutely out of place for anyone to appear in such a way in the court of a king. That shows that one has absolutely no respect for royal authority or decorum.

The creature was grabbed and brought before the king. As the king was about to cut his head off, the creature implored him to pause. He said, "Please don't kill me. At least listen to what I have to say. Why are you taking such an improper step? Why do you want to cut my head off?"

"Haven't you understood why I want to cut your head off? By your most indecent behaviour you have proved that you have absolutely no respect for the authority of the king, you have no respect for the learned, no respect for courtly decorum, and no respect for the gentlemen and ladies that are gathered here. In my court I would not permit a person even to dress immodestly, and the question of appearing naked here would not arise. Since you are guilty of this most indecent, indecorous behaviour, I am not going to let you live even a moment more."

Then the creature began to say, "Your Majesty, you are a great saintly king, and you belong to the family of the Pandavas." (Parikshit was the grandson of Arjuna.) "You belong to that family which had a most intimate friendly relationship with the Lord Himself, so please give thought to what I am about to tell you." He said, "Weren't you all engaged with the question about how the world could be redeemed during the Kali Yuga? You were terribly worried that the Dwapara Yuga was waning, and the Kali Yuga coming, and how people could be saved in Kali Yuga. And here I am with the answer to that query. I am presenting the answer in a most concrete form. I am the very embodiment of the Kali Yuga. Those who hold their tongue in check in Kali Yuga, who do not indulge in idle gossip, who force their tongues to repeat the divine Name ceaselessly, and who exercise full control over their sex organ, will not suffer from any ill effects of Kali Yuga. In fact, they will always live in Sat Yuga. I would never exist for them. But those who let their tongues and their sex organs behave in an unrestrained and undisciplined wild manner will be my most easy victims."

You want me to explain more fully this theme of recollectedness: I would say that just as you are filled with disgust when you have to taste something which is rotten, which is unsavoury, similarly the moment your mind, which is engaged in japa happens to hear a single word which is distracting, which is irrelevant to your japa, it should be filled with loathing and disgust. If you only play-act, if you only show off that you are doing japa, and yet are engaging in ceaseless chatter, you are only bringing disgrace to japa. You are not practising it honestly.

February 25, 1972

Uma: *What is the place of self-effort in sadhana if you have surrendered everything to the Guru?*
Baba: Surrender has the highest place. Indeed, there is nothing higher than surrender. Yoga, japa, austerities, and even meditation and Shaktipat are inferior to surrender. Surrender leads to the highest, imperishable state. Surrender is, in fact, the culmination of one's self-effort. But the kind of surrender that the scriptures talk about is very difficult to achieve. One may be very good and very noble, yet surrender is still very difficult. Surrender does not come easily and naturally due to the impurities in one's own heart, and though one may say that he has surrendered everything to the Guru, the fact is that there is a lot which has been held back.

It is not enough to say, "I have surrendered myself" over and over. Surrender should be real. One should have actually achieved it. Otherwise, one would be in the same class as the parrot who belonged to a Vaishnava. The Vaishnava had taught his bird to say to every visitor, "In the time of crises take refuge in the Lord. Take refuge in Rama and He will certainly protect you." The parrot would say that to every visitor who came along. One day, it so happened that after feeding the parrot the Vaishnava had forgotten to close the cage properly, and had gone away. After he had gone, a cat appeared on the scene. The parrot was in trouble. Now that he was in a crisis, he forgot that he had been telling everyone to take refuge in Lord Rama at such a time and began to scream wildly. So surrender should not be confined only to the verbal level.

Lord Krishna gives surrender the highest importance in the *Gita*. He says in Chapter 18, "Give up all your duties, all your actions and take refuge in Me." If one has really achieved this highest state of surrender, which is the highest tapasya, he will receive from the Guru whatever the Guru has to give in its fullness.

King Janaka was the disciple of the seer Yajnavalkya, who lived outside the capital in a forest. All the seekers used to gather there every day to have satsang with Yajnavalkya. One day, one of the seekers said to Yajnavalkya, "Please show us a true example of surrender."

Yajnavalkya said, "Okay, I will show you in course of time."

The next day an old brahmin came to the satsang with his two young sons. He said to the king, "Your Majesty, I am a poor brahmin and I have to perform the sacred thread ceremony for my two sons. But I have no money. I have come to you for a gift of money so that I may perform this ceremony. You are the king and it is your duty to protect all your subjects. I am one of your subjects belonging to the brahmin caste, and I deserve to be protected by you. Please give me a little money so that I will be able to perform the ceremony."

But the king just kept silent.

Then the brahmin said to the king again, "Your Majesty, it is getting late. I have to perform the sacred thread ceremony for my two sons."

(In our country the sacred thread ceremony is considered to be very important. All the saints hold this ceremony for poor children. I also hold it occasionally when there are worthy recipients.)

The brahmin begged the king once again for some money. The king was still silent and this began to enrage the brahmin and he became angry and said to the king, "I have asked you two or three times, but you don't seem to be paying any attention to me. You are obviously showing disrespect for me, and that goes against your duty as a king. Once again I ask you to grant me a little wealth so that I may perform the sacred thread ceremony for my sons."

But the king just kept quiet.

Now the brahmin thought that since the king wasn't paying attention to his tone of love, he would use a different tone, a tone of anger. He became so angry that he began to shout and abuse the king saying, "O you wicked king, you have absolutely no heart. You have no sense of duty. You are one of the most villainous persons I have ever met. My sad plight has no effect on you. You have no mercy, no kindness, no heart."

The brahmin got so worked up that he even tried to attack the king. The king made no move to defend himself, but his guards grabbed the brahmin and took him away. The satsang then continued as if nothing had happened.

Afterwards some of the seekers approached the king and said, "Your Majesty, you have immense wealth. You could have easily given that poor brahmin some money for his sacred thread ceremony. You have done the same for countless others. Why didn't you? And why did you remain unmoved even when he abused you and attacked you? You have such power, you could have easily given him at least two slaps. But you didn't even do that. Why?"

The king said, "Yesterday I surrendered everything—all my wealth—to my Guru, Yajnavalkya. So when the brahmin asked me for money I couldn't give him any. I have also surrendered my body and mind to him, and to have struck the brahmin I would have needed to use the body. But since it is no longer mine, I didn't. That's why I just sat there."

If you have surrendered everything to the Guru there is nothing else to do. That is the supreme effort. But what usually happens is that you say you have surrendered but the next day you complain that you haven't made any progress. If you have really surrendered everything to the Guru there is no question of such a comment arising. That is not surrender, that is just a mockery of surrender. Once you have really taken refuge in the Lord, the question of measuring your progress does not arise. You should not keep a sort of meter with you by means of which you continually judge how much distance you have covered. You would not even have the craving for any realisation or attainment if you had surrendered.

Jnaneshwar's comment on the theme of surrender is most significant, and that comment springs from Jnaneshwar's own personal experience. He says, "If you take complete refuge in another person, you become completely one with him; you undergo total transformation. You are not like you were before. You do not hold anything back, you merge completely." Jnaneshwar says that if an ordinary girl is embraced by the king, she becomes the queen. Such is the miracle of surrender. Once you have surrendered everything to the Guru, you become the Guru. Surrender is the greatest achievement of self-effort.

Bill: *I was in an accident last March. Since then there has been a constant high vibrational sound in my right ear, occasionally changing in pitch, tone and volume, sometimes single in note, sometimes multiple, but rarely, and then only vaguely musical in quality. Is it nada? Is that the same as the Omkar? Would focusing attention on it be in conjunction with or in place of my mantra repetition? What is its meaning?*

Baba: Sometimes accidents are the worst misfortunes, but at other times they prove to be the greatest of blessings, and I keep wondering about this matter. Here you have a student of engineering who got involved in a serious accident. Before the accident took place he had identified himself completely with his engineering studies, and he considered his studies to be his God. But after the accident, he has become so intensely interested in the Lord that even a so-called sannyasi who has given up the world, who has renounced everything cannot compare with him as far as this devotional intensity or quality is concerned. So that accident has turned out to be an enormous blessing for him.

The sound that you hear is nada. It is, however, true that nada appears in countless forms, though the scriptures talk only about ten major forms. That doesn't mean that this exhausts the varieties of nada. Whatever the quality or pitch of a particular sound that you hear in meditation, or inside, is originating from *Om*, so it should be considered to be one with *Om*. In any case, it will finally lead you to the primal sound which is *Om*.

It is wrong to say that nada doesn't have any musical quality, or that this particular form you hear doesn't have any musical quality, because nada is the inner music. What happens is that you do not experience its musical quality or sweetness if you listen to it only for a moment or a short while. It is only after you have listened to nada for a prolonged period of time that the breathing is held above in the sahasrar, and when that takes place, nectar begins to drip. Only after that great event does one begin to discover the musical quality, the great sweetness of nada. If one who is able to hear nada could combine his mantra with the nada, he would derive the utmost benefit from it. You should practise listening to this nada all the time. Sit or lie calmly and keep on listening to it. Whatever form it may take, nada is inner music. In fact, nada itself is the highest mantra; there is no mantra which could be higher. It is the greatest blessing of the Lord. According to Jnaneshwar Maharaj, nada originates from the abode of the Lord. So by listening to nada one could reach the divine abode. While listening to nada you should keep yourself aware of the fact that that inner music is arising from the abode of the Lord, which is situated in the sahasrar. You will certainly experience its sweetness, but that will take time. When you become completely absorbed listening to nada, then you will discover its musical quality.

Carol: *Lately I have felt more blessed and free from anxiety than ever before in my life, but it seems that the more I become absorbed in my inner growth, the more I crave your attention outwardly. I know that I should not need any acknowledgement of my inner growth. What should I do about my desire for your attention?*

Baba: Very good question. I am very happy to hear this, particularly from one who is living in the Ashram. It means that there are some people in the Ashram also who feel that they have never had the sort of experiences before which they are having now. There is not the least doubt that the experiences of the different seekers here are quite true, and the divine Shakti is working in all of them. Kabir, the great poet-saint has said, "The most precious divine light is present in every heart." Therefore everyone should be able to experience this inner joy. That is, in fact, the very purpose of human birth.

Now you have the craving for attention from me. Why do you look upon your inner joy as being different from me? If you were to begin to look upon your inner joy as being one with me, you would overcome your desire for attention from me. The craving and the joy which bubble up from within again and again should be identified with me, and then you will overcome the craving for outward attention from me. From one point of view, there is nothing wrong with the craving, it's a very good craving. There was a time when I, too, had an identical craving. In fact I would crave that my Guru would call me to him, talk to me, give me prasad to eat, give me some piece of cloth to wear, and pay some attention to me in various ways. Even now, sometimes, now I begin to entertain the hope that he will talk to me when I am in meditation, and sometimes he does talk to me. It was only after receiving a message from my Guru within me, that I went on my foreign tour, and it was the miracle of that message that I achieved such great success. The other day a distinguished saint came here, and he said that he had visited several countries, but before undertaking his visit, he had written to all the different yogic institutions abroad, and he had worked very hard, and it was only then after the way had been prepared for him that he could do some work. But I hadn't written to anyone, and no previous preparations were made, and I just rushed headlong, as it were, and yet I achieved success. That was the glory of obeying my Guru's command. Your desire is a very good one.

Amrita: *In Guru Gita, verse 100, it is said that the object of knowledge should be considered to be one with knowledge itself. How is that possible?*
Baba: The question of equating the object of knowledge with knowledge itself doesn't arise, because the two are already one; one has only to discover their identity. Knowledge and the object of knowledge are not different from each other. There is a short treatise by Jnaneshwar Maharaj called *Changdev Pasashthi*, which deals with this particular theme. That work deals with the seer, the act of perception, and the seen—particularly with the seer and the seen. In that work the seer and the seen are shown to be one with each other. The one who sees is called the perceiver, and that which is seen is the perceived. Take for example, what is happening here. Now I am seeing you, so that means that I am the perceiver, and you are the perceived, and you are seeing me, and that means that you are the perceiver and I am the perceived. The *Guru Gita* says that the highest means is to perceive the identity of the seer and the seen, to perceive the unity of all objects of perception.

Damayanti: *I feel as if I would like to serve you with all my*

heart. *How can I become increasingly grateful and filled with love and reverence and compassion for all of creation?*
Baba: First fill your heart with love and reverence for your own Self. Once your heart is filled with love and reverence, that begins to flow outwards to every object and finally to entire creation.

Olivier: I like the elephant very much. Sometimes I am like him, I think. Why is an elephant important for an Ashram and you?
Baba: I am very pleased to know that you like the elephant so much, but for God's sake, please do not eat as much as the elephant, because that would not please me at all. An elephant has great importance. His importance has been described in our scriptures such as the *Vedas*, the *Puranas*, and philosophical treatises. In fact, Indian culture regards an elephant as a living form of Ganapati, Ganesha, as a living deity. In ancient times kings and emperors and other great personages, whenever they had to go some place, would ask the astrologer for the auspicious hour. But if an elephant was around, if they were able to see an elephant, they would never bother about the auspicious hour, because the elephant is auspiciousness itself. If you are going to have a very important guest to your place, then you have to prepare for a reception which will suit his status and dignity. For example, take the case of the present visit of the President to China. Chou En Lai himself received him at the airport. Similarly, to receive Lakshmi, the Goddess of wealth, you have to have somebody who will suit Her dignity. Only en elephant is suitable for that purpose.

An elephant is present in one of the six lotuses, the spiritual centres in the body. In the yoga of meditation, of course, it has enormous importance. While diving deeper and deeper into his own Self a meditator has the vision of an elephant at a certain state; he sees the elephant within the red aura. Then in meditation there is one particular elephant called Airavat, the mount of Indra, the king of heaven, who appears as the precursor of the final vision, the vision of the Blue Pearl. Airavat stands before the meditator for a long time, and he prepares for the welcome of the meditator into the world of Indra. If you have to receive a great personage, then you make various preparations, but if you have an elephant to receive him, then all other preparations are not necessary, because an elephant is considered to be the most majestic, the most dignified. I visited many places in the South, many temples and maths and ashrams, and everywhere I found I was received by an elephant and musicians. The elephant would always carry a garland in its trunk. The people look upon him as a god, as a deity.

As far as this Ashram is concerned, the elephant was presented to me, so I accepted it. The elephant is one of the many gifts which have come from the devotees. However, I have described to you the true importance of an elephant. An onlooker may have different feelings about the various things in the Ashram, but as far as Muktananda is concerned, an elephant is just another item in the Muktananda museum. Somebody offered a car, so the car was kept here. Somebody offered a gold throne, so the gold throne was kept here. An elephant was offered, so the elephant was kept here, and similarly, other gifts which come are also kept in this museum, and kept with great care. This is my way of honouring my devotees. However, the elephant is a very important being, and if you were also to become like an elephant, like Ganapati, I would be very happy about it.

February 28, 1972

Nala: *Sometimes I would like to meditate, but I feel separate from you and my heart is completely closed. At such times do you not want me to meditate or should I persevere by using force?*
Baba: A meditator, if he gets into a state of deep meditation, should ask himself who does he get united with? And who says that when one likes to meditate one gets separated from me? How did you come to feel that your Self is different from me? What makes you think that the mantra which would help you to meditate is different from me? You are

having this problem only due to wrong understanding. You cannot feel separate from me; you can only feel at one with me. Only one who looks upon the Guru as being different from himself would feel separate from him. If he were to identify the Guru with his inner Self, the question of separation would not arise. On the contrary, one would become merged in the Guru; that is what the final state achieved through meditation is. Whether you are meditating on the Guru, or on a deity, or on God, if you are conscious of the distinction between the meditator, that is you, the act of meditation and the object of meditation, that shows that you have not reached a high state in meditation; you are still at a very ordinary plane. If there is a meditator who while meditating on the Lord or on the Guru, imagines that the Lord or the Guru is standing before him in his utmost beautiful form, and even when he seems to go into ecstasy as a result of that, he is still far away from a high state. The best form of meditation is that in which there is neither the seer nor the seen; the two become one. This is what is known as the state of deep absorption. A Gopi, while singing of the subject of meditation on the Lord, says, "I am no longer aware of who I am or who He is. I become one with Him." Continue to meditate and while meditating learn to forget yourself. That is a high state of meditation, and that is also a high attainment.

Draupadi: *A sadhak should not ask anything of the Guru, but in the course of his effort to surrender to the Guru, could he pray for the grace of the Guru for total surrender, since it is not easily achieved?*
Baba: A sadhak can certainly pray for the grace of the Guru, and even if he does not pray, the grace is bound to descend upon him. Take the case of two persons who are serving a wealthy man. One has entered into an agreement with him according to which he must be paid a certain salary every month, and the wealthy man pays him accordingly. And then the other is serving him without demanding anything. Does it mean that the wealthy man will not pay him anything? What makes you think that he is that stupid or foolish? And the one who has decided to work provided that he would be given a certain salary would not get more

than that, say if he has accepted Rs. 200/- or 300/- per month, he will get only that much, but the one who is working out of love, can receive anything from the wealthy man, in his time of need he can get even Rs. 3,000/- or more. In the *Srimad Bhagavat Purana* a very interesting question was put to the Lord, and that was, "Lord, you grant people whatever they demand of You, but what do You grant to the one who doesn't make any demand of You?" The Lord replies, "Those who make specific demands have their specific demands fulfilled. If somebody begs for children, he gets children, or if one asks for money, he is granted money, if there is another that asks for something else, he gets that something else. But he who doesn't make any demand receives Me in My fullness."

A sadhak can certainly pray to the Guru for his grace, but even if he doesn't pray, that prayer is taking place automatically. That is what the essence of the verse, "Karmanyeva dhi karaste, ma phaleshu kadachana" contained in the *Gita* is. You should perform your duty without asking for its fruit, because you are bound to get its fruit whether you ask for it or not. Take the case of the wicked people who commit wicked deeds and who do not want to suffer the consequences of their wicked deeds; yet they have to suffer from the consequences of their wicked deeds. Then if there is a person who is performing noble deeds, even if he doesn't want any fruits in return, he is bound to get them.

Madhu Daga: *How can one know that the Guru has adopted one as his disciple?*
Baba: There is no need for one to know whether he has been accepted as a disciple or not. However, the disciple must feel certain within his own heart about whether he has accepted a certain teacher as his Guru or not. A Guru does not have to accept a disciple as his disciple, whereas it is absolutely essential for a disciple to accept a Guru as his Guru. The reason is quite obvious. I have said that you are bound to get the fruits of the deeds you perform. If one has accepted the Guru as his Master, with firm and full devotion, even the Guru will be powerless.

Take the case of Kabir who had accepted Ramananda as his Guru, but Ramananda had not accepted him as his disciple. In those days untouchability was at its worst, and Kabir, being a weaver, was not being accepted by Ramananda as a disciple. Kabir spent time wondering how to be accepted by his Master. He thought of a clever trick and was able to get his mantra from his Guru.

Ramananda used to go out for a walk at 3 a.m. Kabir decided to dig a pit on the path which Ramananda used to take. He dug the pit, crouched in it and covered himself with earth and rocks. Ramananda used to wear wooden sandals when he went out for a walk. As he walked on the head of Kabir, Kabir screamed and Ramananda, too, got frightened and he uttered, *"Sri Ram"*. Because Ramananda thought that he had stepped on a human being, he asked, "Who is that?"

Kabir said, "It's me, Kabir."

Then Ramananda went away. Kabir ran away from there repeating, *"Sri Ram, Sri Ram,"* because that was his Guru mantra. Kabir received divine Shaktipat a short while later, and he became a Siddha in his own right. He became a great poet and he also began to hold sankirtan and thousands of people would gather around him. At the end of such a devotional meeting he would ask people to repeat the name of his Guru, to shout out, *"Sadguru Ramananda ki jai"* and they would hail him.

Now some people went to Ramananda with the complaint that though Kabir was an untouchable he had received a mantra from him. Ramananda said, "I know nothing about it. I have never given him any mantra."

Then they went to Kabir and asked him about it. Kabir said, "Yes, the name of my Guru is Ramananda, and I have received my mantra from him."

Then a meeting was held to which both Ramananda and Kabir were called. Ramananda called Kabir to come near him. He said, "Be truthful. Tell me who your Guru is, and from whom did you receive your mantra, because people are after my life."

It was Ramananda's habit to utter *Sri Ram* before doing anything, before calling anyone. For example, it is my habit to write *Sri Gurudev* on the top of any piece of writing, whether it is good or bad. Then Ramananda said, "Again, Kabir, tell me who your Guru is, because people are harrassing me. They say that I am your Guru and you have received your mantra from me."

Kabir said, "That is absolutely true, you are certainly my Guru, and I have received my mantra from you."

This enraged Ramananda and he began to shout, *"Sri Ram, Sri Ram, Sri Ram,"* and added, "Look, you wicked fellow, I never gave you the mantra, and you are telling a lie." Then he took off his sandal and hit Kabir on the head with it.

Then Kabir said to all those who had gathered, "Look, in your very presence he has granted me the mantra. He might not have been my Guru before, but he is certainly my Guru from this moment onwards. In the presence of everyone he uttered *Sri Ram* and struck me with his wooden sandals. That means that he has initiated me."

Therefore, there is no need on the part of the Guru to accept somebody as his disciple. It is the disciple who should accept the teacher as his Guru, and he should hold onto him firmly. Then Ramananda declared, "It is only Kabir who is my true disciple, none of you are my disciples." Once the disciple has accepted a teacher as his Guru, the Guru's acceptance of him as a disciple comes automatically.

Girija: *For the past two weeks, after meditating for about forty-five minutes or less, I have a strong uncomfortable pressure in the head. There is also aching in the neck, inability to hold the neck upright and an intense desire to lie down on my side to relieve the pressure. Leaning forward does not help. After ten to fifteen minutes of lying on my side I feel better and I can sit up and resume meditation. The problem is that I feel badly about lying down in meditation. What should I do?*
Baba: You should try this posture. Press your chin against your jugular notch. If you were to sit like that how would you feel? You can hold a cushion under your chin. That pressure is very good, because that is the indication that the breath is being held upwards and that has great value. That is pressure in the sahasrar, and as a result of that you will begin to hear nada and also to see the Blue Pearl. There is nothing wrong with lying on your side for a few minutes. This process is of a very great significance, this process of

the breath being held upwards. Since you haven't practised sitting upright you are having this difficulty. It is for this reason that people practise asanas, so that they will be able to sit upright. The scriptures prescribe that one should sit upright either in the lotus, perfect or easy posture. The reason behind that is that one would not feel uncomfortable. But there are people who would sit in a chair, or in any irregular position and that is why they begin to feel uncomfortable after a short while. If you like, you can lie on your side for a few minutes, but you can be sure of one thing, that you are having very good meditation. Are you hearing any inner music? (Sometimes a sound like a mechanical instrument.) That is one of the recognised sounds; that is like the sound of the veena. It is a very significant sound. You should practise sitting upright for longer periods and then your neck will not ache. The reason why it aches at present is that you don't sit upright; you are either bending forwards or backwards. If you were to sit upright, and if your neck were to sway or swing, then you would not feel this ache. You are making very good progress.

Ram: *It has been said that when the sex act is performed with full consciousness, with deep absorption, one glides into the transcendental state; through sexual experience one thus experiences samadhi. How far is this correct?*
Baba: This can be claimed only by a stupid person who is completely off his rocker. This claim cannot be made by one who has had the actual experience of samadhi and who has attained true wisdom. If Rama could be attained through the sex experience then it is whores, the harlots who should be the first to have attained Him. They are swimming in sex all the time, so Rama should be sitting in their homes before visiting anyone else. But I have heard that they don't know Rama. The teachers who teach this should open whore houses instead of giving lectures or writing books. Then they would be helping people to attain Rama without any difficulty. There is a section in Bombay where prostitution is going on. Rama must be revealing Himself in His full glory in that area.

Such a teacher is not only misguided himself, but he is also misguiding others. If this were true, would it not be much better to be born a sparrow, because a sparrow is deeply absorbed in sexual gratification. Why be born as a human being, why practise Ashtang Yoga, if samadhi could be attained through the sexual experience? This kind of teaching will only ruin the lives of certain young people who are intoxicated by their youthful vigour but who don't have much discrimination. It certainly will not help them to move towards real inner peace or the spiritual goal.

If one were to have even the slightest experience of samadhi one would derive immense benefit from it. All seven constituents of the body would be rejuvenated and one would become more alert and clever and would acquire a certain radiance and glow. But I wonder what possible benefit one could derive from the absorbing delight of the sex act. If a person is weak, he is generally advised by doctors to abstain from sex until he regains his strength. But no one would forbid one to practise samadhi. In fact, there is not even so much delight in the sex experience. The seers who describe the nature of the bliss of samadhi say that if there were an emperor who enjoyed sovereignty over the entire earth, who enjoyed perfect youth and health, who had every possession, the kind of joy that he would experience could only be called human joy. But the joy experienced by an ancestor in Pitruloka is a million times greater than the joy of the emperor. And the joy of a minor immortal is a million times greater than the joy of a million ancestors put together. The joy of a chief immortal is a million times greater than the joy of a million minor immortals. And the joy experienced by Indra, the Lord of Heaven, is a million times greater than the joy of a million chief immortals. But the bliss enjoyed by a saint when he is absorbed in Brahman is a million times greater than the joy experienced by one Indra. So what makes you think that the sex act is as blissful as samadhi? If you were to look at the faces of those who indulge in sex you wouldn't even want to look at them again.

There are people here who have had the experience of sex samadhi and also the experience of dhyan samadhi. They can decide from their own experience which is superior. Even if you haven't had the experience of pure samadhi, you have had the experience of the one-pointed state of mind. As a result of that, joy must have flowed into you. So you will be able to judge for yourself if such a statement has any value or not. I am not against sex, because that preserves the race and anything which preserves the race must not be shunned. But one who meditates daily can find out from his own experience that if he were to indulge in sex frequently he would become weaker and weaker instead of rising higher in the field of yoga. One should discard feces but hold onto semen. If you hold onto feces you will acquire diseases, but if you hold onto semen you will acquire radiant health.

I am certain that this kind of statement cannot be made either by a yogi or by a person who is steeped in the scriptures. It is only one who has an irresistible attachment for sexual pleasure who could make this kind of statement. People are already following wrong courses. A teacher who makes this kind of statement is just showing a new wrong path. I once knew a certain sadhu belonging to the Kabir sect who use to go around preaching that it was okay to take a little toddy (a local liquor) once in a while. He said, "There's nothing wrong with it. After all, it's only the juice of a tree."

One day I caught hold of him and asked him, "Tell me the truth. How many times a day do you take toddy?"

He said, "Muktananda Swami, I confess that I take a little every evening."

I said, "You wicked fool. Simply because you want to keep on drinking toddy with a clear conscience you are teaching people that there is no harm in it."

This is the impression that I get from this statement.

Jagannath Goenka: *Can an ordinary householder make spiritual progress while living his life in the world, particularly in the atmosphere of a modern city? And if so, what are the do's and don'ts for him? What kind of vigilance should he practise in his life?*
Baba: One has to take food, sleep and perform other activities of everyday life regardless of which age one is living in, or which place one is in, regardless of what time it is or his condition. Similarly whatever one's circumstances or environment may be, one can always meditate, one can always

contemplate God. There is really not much difference between different ages. Maybe our age is inferior or has more impurities than the previous ages, and it may be a little more difficult now, but that is about all. Just as we have no difficulty in going to sleep whatever our circumstances may be, similarly, we can certainly meditate in whatever circumstances we might have been placed. However, one must have a genuine interest in it. After all, all external circumstances are outside you, and the environment only enters your heart as much as you allow it to. Kabir used to live next door to a butcher. Next door the butcher would be slaughtering animals and Kabir in his house would be chanting the Name of the Lord. As far as the outer circumstances go, they are outside of you, in any case. All that one should do is saturate one's inner heart with the Divine.

March 1, 1972

Purnama and Malou: *Baba once told a story of disciples who left the Guru stealing the golden pan, comparing them to those who want to go into solitude. Who does this story concern, power-seeking disciples, or God-seekers? Is it not normal for God-seekers to be attracted by solitude without leaving the inner Guru? Was it not the case with Baba and most saints? Is there a time for Ashram and a time for solitude and deeper silence?*
Baba: Take the case of the people who live in solitude, in remote places such as Nagaland and Kulu Valley. How many yogis do you find among them? Those people always wait for visitors from the cities so that they can get some money for their needs. If one's Shakti can be awakened while one is in the midst of people, what does he need solitude for? When I went around, I was going around for a different reason; I was looking for something else. At that time my concern was not with sadhana. Whatever sadhana I practised was practised in Yeola, Nagad and Ganeshpuri;

and none of these places could be considered to be worldly. It was only before I came to Ganeshpuri that I kept on wandering around. But after I reached here, I did not leave Ganeshpuri to go to any other place. Most people seek solitude only because they are bored with themselves, with life, and they are interested in sloth and comfort. You can go to the kitchen and ask the cook there when he is cooking, whether he is in the midst of people or in solitude. Only those people who have absolutely nothing to do are always thinking in terms of solitude. But those who are busy have no use for the distinction between solitude and society. It is only one who is unable to focus his mind on the object of meditation, who wants to go into solitude. But after he goes into solitude, there, too, his mind does not come under his control, it remains as restless as ever.

You go to Bombay sometimes for a week, and sometimes for a fortnight. And though Bombay is such a noisy and crowded city, don't you fall asleep there every night? Or do you spend the fortnight without sleeping, and get your quota of sleep only after coming to the Ashram? If you can sleep in Bombay, that means that at least in the state of sleep Bombay has ceased to exist. Similarly, those whose minds are focused on the Lord, who are in a state of meditation all the time, and who are conscious of their final goal, never worry about solitude. If the Ashram does not appear to be a solitary place to you, then it means that you haven't understood what Ashram life is.

What, after all, would you do if you were to retire into solitude? How long can you meditate? You have to eat food, and you have to sleep, and you will have to do something to get food and to get sleep. All that is possible in solitude is that you spend your time any way you feel like, whereas in an Ashram you have to conform to a strict discipline, and that is what irks people.

What really happens is that one gets attracted by what one calls freedom, which one could enjoy in solitude; and freedom is very much in the air. Every country wants to be free, even India wants to be free, and you want to do whatever you feel like, and it is really this desire which drives people to solitude.

It is true that many saints have lived in solitude, but I

do not know what they attained as a result of living in solitude. At the same time, there are many others who lived in society, and I can tell you what they attained. Kabir attained a high state while engaged in weaving, and he helped a large number of people. Take the case of Gora, who was a potter; he attained a high state while making pots, and he also told people what he had attained. Take the case of Sena who was a barber. He found the Lord right in his hair-cutting salon; he did not have to go to a cave to find him. Take the case of Sautamali, who was a farmer, and he seems to have said to the Lord, "Look, my dear Lord, I don't have time to leave my farm, so You had better come to my fields. I have no time to go to Your temple in Pandharpur." Or take the case of Janabai, who was quite advanced in age. She used to ply the grinding wheel, and while other people had to go to the temple for the darshan of the Lord, the Lord Himself used to go to her to help her in her grinding chores.

I know of the case of many seekers who found the Lord right in their homes. According to the *Upanishads* concept of solitude, solitude is entirely different than people think. According to the *Upanishads*, solitude cannot be found in forests or monasteries. Solitude is the state which one gets into after one's body consciousness has been dissolved. I'll narrate a short story that occurs in the *Shrimad Bhagavat Purana*. One day the Pandavas were being taken out in a splendid procession through a public street, and bands were playing and there were many other interesting things in the procession. At that time, an ironsmith was making a sword for Arjuna, and he had been commanded to finish it by the evening. This fellow had concentrated his mind fully on the sword. It's not easy to make a perfect sword. This ironsmith was scanning its edge, and that is a very special process. He was seeing whether it had come out properly or not. In the meantime the procession passed by his shop. After a short while two fellows came running into his shop wanting to know how far the procession had gone, so they asked the blacksmith how long since the procession had passed his place. And the blacksmith said, "When did the procession pass here? My mind was completely fastened on the edge of the sword and I wasn't at all conscious of the procession."

One gets into the purest solitude if the mind is withdrawn from body-consciousness. In the 13th chapter of the *Gita* the Lord refers to solitude through the phrase, "Aratir jana samsadi," which means "distaste for crowds." There are many people who have commented on this particular phrase, and one poet writes, "A seeker is he who goes into solitude far, far away from crowds, and who spends all his time in remembrance of the Lord." But at the end of the 18th chapter, the Lord says to Arjuna, "You have heard Me. Now you can decide what to do. " And Arjuna says, "I will do whatever You ask me to do."

    The Lord did not send Arjuna into solitude, He asked him to fight a war. It's a strange irony that the Lord should speak of solitude in the 13th chapter, but, as Jnaneshwar says, Arjuna was granted the experience of samadhi right on the battlefield. It's most natural for a seeker to be attracted towards the Guru. I am not sure whether attraction towards solitude is a sure sign of a seeker or not. What solitary place could be better than one where you are able to practise a spiritual discipline fully? It is generally seen that solitude is preferred by idle and slothful fellows, not by genuine seekers. When you can get to know the inner Self right in the midst of people, what more could you gain if you were to retire into solitude?

Mira: *For the last two days during meditation I have become aware of a burning sensation just below the navel. After some time my stomach is automatically drawn upwards and my breath is held in for some time. I completely lose consciousness of my body, but when I come out of meditation I feel very peculiar, and it is difficult to walk straight or focus my eyes and speech is nearly impossible. What's the meaning of these experiences?*
Baba: Is the burning sensation very acute, and do you feel a lot of heat inside? (Yes.) You get this burning sensation because the yogic fire becomes very active. The stomach's being drawn upwards is a most important process. In fact I keep on asking different seekers whether any such thing is happening in their case. It is not only the stomach, but all the abdominal and pelvic organs which are being drawn upwards. You probabaly don't notice what's happening fully. This is a most valuable process: the drawing up of all the

abdominal and pelvic organs. The fact that you lose consciousness of your body shows that you go very deep into the Self, and, Malou, would such a seeker need solitude? Would she have to go to Nagaland or to a cave for meditation?

After you have had an experience of deep meditation, it is quite natural for you to feel peculiar, because the world which you get into during deep meditation is entirely different from the objective world, and it is certain that you are diving into your very great depths. In the realm of inner consciousness, there is peace and bliss all around, and perfect silence prevails. Your state is the one which cannot be described; but one can say that the objective world is very different from that. The peculiar condition that you get into after meditation is again quite normal. It's like a man who wakes up suddenly from a very deep dreamless sleep, and for a while finds it difficult to come to himself. He keeps wondering why he woke up at all, and he doesn't want to notice anything; he doesn't want to talk to anyone.

The best thing for you to do would be to lie silently for about fifteen or twenty minutes after meditation; during this period you will return to the normal world, you will come back from the inner realm. Sometimes you will also feel as though a knot were being tied below the navel, and you may also begin to feel awfully hungry. But you must not eat more than your usual amount. During such a phase of sadhana you must take your food in a very strict, controlled measure; you must not take more. If you usually eat, for instance, two or three chapatis, you must not increase the number no matter how hungry you may be, whether those chapatis satisfy your appetite completely or not. If, because of hunger, you begin to eat more, then further progress is stopped. You should stick to what you usually eat. You will also find your feces becoming very hard, as hard as wood. Do not get worried and begin to drug yourself to get rid of constipation. Your sadhana is going very well.

Malti: *Is Siddha Yoga connected in any way with hypnotism or mesmerism, and if so, please let us know what kind of mesmerism or hypnotism is used in this Ashram.*

Baba: If there is a teacher who says that meditation involves mesmerism or hypnotism, he does not deserve to be called a teacher because he lacks in understanding and awareness. I would even go to the extent of calling such a person an absolutely unalloyed, pure fool, who doesn't at all understand what it means to meditate, what happens in meditation and who doesn't know anything about the nature of Shakti. Such a one does not deserve to be a Guru; he does not even deserve to be called a student of meditation. If I were personally conducting meditation sessions, if I were to ask you to meditate in my presence, ask you to gaze into my eyes, or if I were to raise my hands and ask you to do the same; or if I were to tell you, "Look, I am the Lord and you should look upon me adoringly with utmost devotion," then it might be said that I was using mesmerism and hypnotism.

But in this Ashram we do not conduct any group meditation sessions. Here each individual practises meditation on his own. People meditate morning, noon, and night, but they are all meditating spontaneously under the inspiration of the divine Shakti. At Shree Gurudev Ashram, women meditate in the hall meant for them and men meditate in the place meant for them. Then there are others who meditate in their own rooms. And Muktananda Swami does not visit any of those places. Each meditator is absorbed in meditation on his own Self, so how would the question of mesmerism or hypnotism arise here?

The first thing necessary for exercising hypnotism would be that the Guru must be physically present with his disciples. And not only that—he must forbid them to close their eyes, and he must ask them to keep on looking into his eyes, telling them, "I am sending out spiritual rays and you must receive them. You must not be careless at this time."

But when you are meditating I am sitting in my room. Here we are practising pure meditation, and hypnotism does not come into the picture at all. Here the divine Shakti enables everyone to meditate. In this Ashram while you are meditating it is not possible for you to see even your neighbour. Nobody is passing any message to anyone else and all of you are absorbed in your own meditation. You are meditating on your inner Self by the power of the divine Shakti.

Through Her divine power people are able to meditate even far away in other countries, so how could the question of hypnotism arise?

Ram: *I am currently suffering from an intense stabbing pain about two inches above the base of my spine. It is not consistent; it comes and goes suddenly, and may suddenly jolt me regardless of what I am doing. Does this have any relation to the Kundalini Shakti? Or does it have just a physical basis? Could it be related to an increase in japa and meditation and prolonged sitting in siddhasan?*

Baba: What is happening in your case doesn't show there is anything wrong with the body. On the contrary, it shows that there is nothing wrong. The centre of all the nerves spreading throughout the body lies in the muladhar, and it is the Kundalini who forms the hub of this complicated system of what are called nadis. When the Kundalini is aroused, these nadis begin to throb and if they throb you get the kind of jolt you are getting. Sometimes the pain can be very acute. I, too, used to get such pain quite often, and it has great significance. This process has a very important place in sadhana. Continue to meditate regardless of the pain. The more intense the pain is, the faster your sadhana is going, that is what that would indicate. Sometimes the pain becomes so intense that seekers begin to cry and groan. This is a very important kriya. This is one of the kriyas of Siddha Yoga. These kriyas take place under the inspiration of Kundalini and they take place only when the body needs them. When you get this pain you will find it much easier to concentrate on the Kundalini Shakti working in that particular region.

Pratibha: *Which is better, japa and meditation, or service to all creatures, including human beings?*

Baba: Japa and meditation are far, far superior to what is called service to all creatures. If service were better than japa and meditation, then japa and meditation would not have been emphasised so much by the saints. However, if service is combined with japa and meditation, there is nothing like it.

What gives meaning to any activity is japa and meditation. Japa and meditation are like the digit 1 in the number 10. If there were no 1, the number would have no value; it has value only when there is a digit in it.

It is generally seen that those who are engaged in service do not enjoy much inner peace. Whether the ones who are being served get inner peace or not is irrelevant. During my recent tour of Gujarat I came across one such social worker. He said, "Swamiji, unfortunately I am without inner peace, in spite of the fact that I have served people so earnestly and for such a long time."

I said, "I am amazed by the condition that you are in. You are without peace yourself, and you are trying to serve others. I don't understand that kind of activity at all."

Therefore, japa and meditation are primary, and service comes next.

Roderick: *You urge us to pray. I used to pray in church with people, with formal prayers, and also in my bedroom by myself, free form, and I would pray walking down the street. Now only the last seems to have a place, walking in the spirit. I want to do more concentrated prayer, however. Should I use half my meditation time, and leave off mantra repetition?*
Baba: Whatever you did in the past was very good, but then we should first decide which kind of activity is superior. The prayer of all prayers, the innermost essence of prayer, is the nirvikalpa state, which is attained through meditation. Meditation is true prayer. True prayer is absorption in the Lord, and that is what meditation is. To be able to pray with more concentration, you don't have to reduce the time of meditation. Continue to think of the Lord intensely, and that would be your prayer. Constant mantra repetition, constant recollectedness, constant remembrance of the Lord is true prayer, and when you get even beyond it, and you enter into the state of detachment, you are praying in the best possible manner. That was the mode in which Jesus prayed. Through prayer you enter into total communion with the Lord and attain perfect detachment, the state of perfect inner stillness. That is exactly what meditation is. You are only getting confused by different words.

Remember the Lord intensely. If you remember Him

intensely, you will enter into communion with Him, and that would be meditation, and also the highest form of prayer. Here we hold collective prayer thrice a day, but this is a very ordinary process; this is meant to give us a certain stable basis. But it is inner recollectedness which is true prayer.

Larry: *The more I try to increase mantra repetition, the more pressure begins to build up inside, and tends to make me irritable, stiff, not wanting to talk or be around people. It feels unnatural, but I think that the discipline is necessary for inner change. Yesterday you said that a man should take care to attain a good state for himself through self-effort, but other times you say to forget about attainment, as it is selfish to do so. Some impurity is always throwing me into confusion about these things.*

Baba: What happens is quite normal during the mantra japa phase. As you keep repeating the mantra, the mind begins to get restless, as a result of which it is quite normal for one to fly into anger on the slightest pretext. But one should exercise self-control in such moments. A seeker should be mainly concerned with himself. Why should he bother about what somebody else is doing? Kabir, in one of his very important songs, writes, "Kabir's home is situated next door to a butcher shop. Why should a seeker get disturbed by that? Because the one who is committing a sin will suffer from its consequences."

How correct is it to notice what passers-by are doing, or what the people around you are occupied with, while you are supposed to be doing your japa? Again, it is quite normal to feel that it is unnatural, but that is what happens to everyone. After a prolonged period of practice your mind will change. You get confused, not because of some impurity, but because of a wrong, incomplete, understanding. When one does not try to understand a statement in its context, one gets into all sorts of difficulties. I must have said that if you have surrendered yourself completely to the Guru, then you don't have to worry about attainment. I must have said that in the case of one who has accomplished total surrender, the concern about personal sadhana would be selfish. You should continue to do japa without any selfish motive. It's only if you pursue something with a selfish motive that it becomes bad. By being unselfish, however, I do not mean that one should not try to overcome one's impurities, and imbibe good qualities. It is not selfish to cultivate those qualities which are congenial to spiritual pursuit, and to overcome those defects which are hostile to spiritual pursuit.

March 3, 1972

Mark: *What should one do when passing through a period of dullness, depression or confusion?*
Baba: All that you should do is continue to remember the Lord with single-minded faith and not become upset about it. Surrender such a phase to the Lord. Do not waste your energy either through anxiety or by following different methods to overcome this phase.

Durga: *When in a high state of anxiety or emotion, should I force myself to sit in one place and continue to meditate, or should I get up and force myself to perform some kind of constructive action? Often in that state prayer seems to be just another form of worry.*
Baba: If you can force yourself to meditate for a while in that condition, it would be very good, because meditation will help you overcome it. If meditation doesn't help, then prayer, too, is equally good; a prayer is always accompanied with devotion, with a feeling of personal inadequacy which may cause slight distress and that cannot be equated with worry or anxiety. Prayer will certainly divert your mind. If even prayer doesn't help, engage yourself in some Ashram work, and that will certainly bring you out of your state of anxiety and emotion. If that, too, doesn't help, you can go to the upper garden, look at the sky, look at the trees, remember the Lord, have a stroll around, and it will not take long to get out of anxiety. Sometimes I go up to per-

form a specific task, and as I go up and look around, I forget what I came for, and when I reach the place where I was to go, it is difficult for me to remember exactly what it was that I came up there for. You should not let your mind dissipate its energies on thinking all kinds of things. You should keep it concentrated on the Lord, and that should be the only thing which should matter for you. Other things should fall into the background.

Kalyani: *How can we stop identifying with our past sinful actions, the very thought of which fills the heart with pain and remorse, so that we can dwell on the pure nature of the Guru?*
Baba: When you realise that identification with your past actions is wrong, undesirable and useless, your mind will take the hint and will stop. At the same time, you should resolve with all your inner strength never to repeat those actions. If you have indulged in certain behaviour because of inadequate understanding or under compulsion from others, and subsequently your understanding develops to the point where you see that those actions were wrong, then even God will not punish you severely for those actions. He will take a very kind and lenient view of what you have done.

It's not good to keep remembering past sinful actions. One should have strength enough to tell the mind to stop thinking about something and strength enough to make the mind stop thinking about it. However, sometimes it does happen that the mind begins to think repeatedly about the past undesirable actions, and then it is difficult to take its attention away. At those times you should look upon these thoughts as a play of Chiti, and then things will be all right.

The moment the mind becomes aware of the true nature of the Guru it will settle on that, and will shed all past memories. Only as long as you do not become aware of his true nature will your mind dwell on past memories. What makes you think that the mind has taken a solemn pledge to keep thinking about the past for the rest of your life?

There is a story relating to this. There was a sadhu who lived in a hut in a forest. The king of that region was his disciple. One day the king came to the forest while the sadhu was out. The sadhu's attendant asked the king to have a seat but the king wandered restlessly from one place to another, and would not take any of the boy's suggestions. When the sadhu returned, the attendant told him that the king had come and although he had been offered so many seats, he would not sit down anywhere. The sadhu said, "You must prepare a proper seat for the king. Take a pillow and cover it with a velvet spread, put soft cushions for his back and then ask him to sit there."

The king came and when he saw the seat prepared for him, he sat there and his restlessness vanished. This is exactly what happens with the mind. The mind is quite proud, like that king, and it does not like to rest in a place it doesn't like, which it doesn't find suitable. That is why it keeps wandering from one thought to another, from one occupation to another. If you let it dwell on the awareness of the true nature of the Guru, it will become so calm and still that even if you want it to attend to something else, it wouldn't like to.

Kedarnath: *The inner peace and cheerfulness of mind which result from service to the Guru, even when it is performed with a selfish motive, are not obtained even from selfless social work. Why is it so? After all, service is service, whether it is rendered to the Guru or to society.*
Baba: If your body comes into contact with the water of the Ganges, whatever your motive, it will still get cool, because the nature of the water of the Ganges is to cool whatever it comes into contact with. In the same manner, the service rendered to the Guru, whether it is selfless or done with a selfish motive, is bound to grant peace of mind and cheerfulness, because that's all that it results in. Whether you serve the Guru selflessly or selfishly, the ultimate fruit of that service is total inner contentment, because it is the Guru alone who grants inner contentment. The Guru is the only perfect deity who can bestow perfect contentment. And that is why one enjoys perfect inner peace as a result of serving the Guru.

Shankar: *What is the nature of the will? What is its relationship to the mind? What causes a weakness in the will,* *and how is it corrected? Do small acts like giving up tea, etc. strengthen the will?*

Baba: The will has the greatest significance, because it is by His will that the Divine has created this most magnificent universe in pure void. God created this world full of diversities by the primal thought which arose in His mind, namely, "Let Me become many." It was by the power of that thought alone that He created this universe. There were no engineers, architects, labourers, or masons to work for Him at that time.

In the *Upanishads*, also, the seers say again and again, "O my mind, think noble, sublime thoughts." Our will becomes weak and feeble when we let our mind think all kinds of impure, filthy, foul thoughts, when we let it engage itself in all kinds of fancies, with all kinds of ideas, whether they are necessary or not. If you live a life of discipline, if you carry out the promises that you have made, and if you practise self-restraint, the will becomes stronger. There is nothing more important than purifying your mind, and thus strengthening your will.

It is when the will or the mind becomes clean and pure and taintless, that you get into what is called samadhi, or the nirvikalpa state. This entire universe is the result of a pure thought on the part of God. If a man with a pure mind entertains a certain thought, it is bound to take concrete shape. The best way of strengthening the will is to develop more and more faith in the Lord. The purer and stronger your faith in the Lord is, the stronger will your will be. As the will becomes stronger, it is not difficult to give up petty habits such as taking tea. That is child's play.

In the *Upanishads*, thinking of sublime thoughts is given the highest place. To make your will stronger, you should make your mind think less and less or entertain fewer and fewer thoughts as the time goes by. If you must think, think good things. You must not let your mind think evil thoughts. One's thoughts should be pure, clean and wholesome, and if possible, one should try to get beyond even those thoughts into the state which is free from thoughts. This way one can acquire enormous power by means of which He can create a new world from within. Everyone should strive diligently to keep the mind still, to keep it free from thoughts. Those who keep their minds silent find that in course of time their will becomes stronger, their body becomes younger, the seven constituents of the body acquire a new force. Thinking evil thoughts about others, feeling jealous of others, greedy about what others have, taking unnecessary interest in what other people are doing —all these are signs of a weak-willed person. A person who has a strong will will never occupy himself with these undesirable tendencies.

Aumashanand: *Please say what experience it was that let you know that Nityananda was God on earth. I know that your heart and mind were as strong at that time as they are now, and you could not have accepted that the Guru was God on the basis of mere hope.*
Baba: I am not the sort of person who would accept anything on mere hearsay. I had read quite a great deal, and had met many saints, and I had been to many different places, and during my life I came into contact with many, many saints. In fact, during the time of Nityananda, there was a large number of living saints in the country. Unfortunately the number seems to have diminished now. And those saints were true genuine saints. They were not magicians. They were not ones who dabbled in cheap tricks, or that cheated people by smearing their bodies with white ash. They did not come out with all kinds of novel theories about Kundalini, or all kinds of processes for awakening it. The saints I went to and talked with were full of great praise for Nityananda. Everyone would say that he was a most exalted being, and he was Self-perfected. Thus, many great saints had praised him to me. I had great love for Zipruanna. Zipruanna was a most extraordinary being. He was a great yogi and by the power of yoga he had attained that state in which the body becomes so completely purified that it cannot be tainted by anything. Though Zipruanna used to sit on shit, his body was not at all affected or tainted. Though he was a very great yogi, and I used to visit him frequently, I could not accept him as my Master. I still have great love for him, and I revere him as a very great saint. It was he who asked me to go to Nityananda, saying that Nityananda was my Guru.

You don't seem to have studied much of the Vedantic philosophy. When you study it thoroughly, you will understand one of its major doctrines according to which a saint, in the course of his search for God, comes to realise God, he becomes one with Him, he becomes God Himself.

Take the case of a river which is seeking the ocean. After it has found the ocean and fallen into the ocean, it becomes one with the ocean—nay, it becomes the ocean itself, and in no way remains different from the ocean. Its contents are the same as those of the ocean, its nature, its activities, its properties, everything is in no way different from the ocean.

Nityananda was a knower of Brahman and he was not a passive type. He was a most active, dynamic being, and from this point of view also, he was the living God. Then he was a perfect yogi. He was, in fact, a Master of yoga, and a Master of yoga is the Lord of lords. Jnaneshwar says in his commentary on the *Gita* that a Master of yoga, a perfect yogi, is the God of gods. The Lord says, "Such a being is My inner bliss itself." Nityananda was saturated with divine bliss, and for this reason I was compelled to accept him as my Master. A disciple comes to know the Guru fully only when He attains the highest realisation and has a direct experience of the true nature of the Guru. Have you read *Guru*? From that book you will come to know when I came to understand exactly what Nityananda was, and that was only after the highest realisation had come. I was certainly not the type who could have accepted someone on the basis of mere hope or mere hearsay. Before meeting Nityananda I had read all the major scriptures. I could not accept anything without inquiry. There are certain saints who are born perfect, and in whom divine power makes its appearance right at their birth.

Mahadev: *If God has given us an ego and emotions such as hatred, anger, and fear, then why is it necessary to transcend these in order to reach God?*
Baba: Even if God has created the ego and various emotions, you can't have a vision of Him without transcending these. It is necessary to transcend them. God might have created all these things, but has He given you any letter of

authority to make use of them? But I can certainly show you the letter which authorises me not to go near greed, anger, envy, or hate because all of these are impure passions, and that letter is in the form of the *Gita*, the *Upanishads*, and the *Bible*. God has also made poison, but how much poison have you taken?

Shaun: *During most of the day I experience Shakti in the form of kumbhak. The breath is drawn in and held in various parts of the body. Sometimes my whole body shakes. Other times great pressure builds up in the head and throat areas, and other times my abdomen and chest are drawn up. One finishes and the next one starts without an exhalation. It seems as if it could go on forever in the same breath, but unfortunately I haven't been able to last as long. Am I letting down through my own fears, or should I just take this a bit at a time? Also, my hunger has dropped off, and the least amount of food seems to fill me up. Is this natural?*
Baba: The kumbhak which you are experiencing now will increase your appetite later. That is what the main effect of kumbhak is. It increases the appetite. All that is happening to you is a sign of intense Shaktipat. You have difficulty because you don't have a correct understanding of what is happening to you. If you were to understand it correctly, all these kriyas would fill you with exaltation, and would give you more strength and power; they would not make you feel weak. After all, the Shakti is not under your control, that you can have it bit by bit. If you had gone to a shop in the market to buy something, you could have decided how much to buy. But that isn't so in the case of the Shakti. All these kriyas are taking place as a result of inner divine inspiration. You can't possibly have any control over them. Whatever is happening, let it happen. God will take care of you, and in course of time it will all settle down. Keep on praying to Gurudev that the intensity of the Shakti be somewhat reduced. But the kriyas which you have described here have great value, and these are not the sort of things which you could afford to reject; they are not so worthless.

Shyama: *All the Gopis loved the Lord selflessly, and their* *love for Him was the highest kind. Yet what was so unique about Radha that her name was always mentioned with the name of Krishna and the poets also always link them together?*

Baba: You probably remember that this question was put the other day also, and I had dismissed it almost scornfully. Yet this question has come up again. There must be some special reason which is making the questioner put this question again. If we dismiss this question this evening, also, are you going to bring it up again? I am wondering why Shyama has put this question again. She must have some superior knowledge of this matter. She must have some special fondness for Radha.

God has equal love for all beings and the question of inequality cannot arise in the case of God. He cannot be partial to one. One cannot be a special favourite to Him, and another be less dear. This is what He says in the *Gita*, "I treat all beings alike." Whether one offers Him one rupee or a million, it is all the same to Him. All the Gopis had great devotion for the Lord, and their devotion was exalted and sublime. The different poet-saints have sung eloquently of their devotion, but their devotion was confined within the bounds of propriety and decorum. The Gopis had great love for the Lord and they had an extraordinary capacity for renunciation. Their lives were absolutely pure and they had surrendered everything to Him. All the Gopis were householders; they were housewives with families and children. They were remembering the Lord and offering their devotion to Him while performing their various household chores. The Lord, out of compassion for them came right to their homes to see them. He did not ask them to go to the forest in order to have a vision of Him. The Gopis attained God-realisation through their intense devotion to the Lord.

Radha, too, was a housewife, and she, too, had children. She had a husband and a family, but she threw all social conventions to the wind, she did not care what people would say about her. She gave up her family, she gave up her home, and she set out in search of the Lord. She refused to be bound by the restrictions imposed on an individual, either by society or by religious scriptures or by other things. Though the Lord says in one place in the *Gita*, "Oh

Arjuna, all the creatures are equally dear to Me, there is none more dear than another," yet in another place He says, "I approach a devotee in the same way that he approaches Me, I answer the devotion of a particular bhakta in the same way that it is offered to Me."

Mira, too, was like Radha. Mira and Radha are amongst those bhaktas who did not at all care about public opinion, who did not bother to think how others would comment on their actions, and they did not listen to what their families said about them, and they left their homes to find the Lord. Though the ultimate state, the ultimate realisation which came to the Gopis and Radha was the same, outwardly they were different. The Gopis worshipped the Lord while conforming to social norms, while Radha and Mira worshipped the Lord by throwing up all sense of convention, all sense of propriety or decorum.

Two years ago, a certain person who held a very high position in the Congress Party came to receive initiation from me while I was in Delhi. He was asked to go and sit in the meditation room, and there he found different meditators doing different kriyas. Some were crying, some were leaping around, some were dancing. That man came out and said, "Swamiji, this isn't exactly what I came for, I do not want this kind of initiation, because I have to go and attend the Parliament meetings. If such kriyas would happen then, it would embarrass me very much."

There are two kinds of devotion: one in which the devotee conforms to social norms, and another in which the devotee does not care two hoots about public opinion, or about the propriety of his actions.

March 6, 1972

Purnama: *How many times a day should a Siddha student take a bath?*

Baba: A Siddha student should take a bath only once a day. A seeker should realise that his body and clothes become covered with particles of Shakti, and he should not wash them away by frequent baths. A Siddha student does not have to work in a factory, or say, in a field where his body would get very dirty, or covered with grime; he is given a very light job here, so he doesn't have to wash himself again and again. And the set of clothes reserved for meditation are not washed even for six months, and they are used only for meditation. My former meditation room is now kept generally locked, but sometimes I send somebody to meditate there, and whoever goes to meditate in that room is bound to have very significant experiences. Such is the effect of the divine rays of Shakti which are still present there.

I keep a separate set of clothes for meditation, and that is what I recommend for every Siddha student also, and even if you can't reserve a separate set of clothes for meditation, then you should take care that the particles of Shakti covering your body are not washed away by frequent baths. Every person carries his aura around him, and the rays of the inner Shakti are surrounding a Siddha student all the time. What, after all, makes you so dirty that you feel compelled to bathe as many as three or four or five times a day? What exactly are you doing which makes the body filthy? You are living here in a very pure atmosphere, eating very pure food, and right from morning till evening, the actions that you are engaged in are also very pure; what could make your body impure or unclean or dirty, and what is the compulsion to wash it again and again? I can understand frequent baths in the case of a person who is practising the yoga of the nightclub, and who is taking impure foods, whose actions are impure, whose thoughts are impure, and who doesn't follow any discipline in his life, who gets up any time he feels like, who would lie around anywhere, and whose body is all the time emitting a foul stink. If he washes himself again and again I would have no objection. But why should you wash yourself again and again? Your bodies are pure, the food that you are taking is pure, and in fact all of you look washed all the time whether you have washed yourself or not. And which water could ever purify the inner Shakti? It is, in fact, the inner Shakti which purifies everything it touches.

Durga: *Is there an ideal personality type for sadhana? Is it more beneficial to have an outgoing personality than an ingoing personality? Is it necessary to always maintain a smiling visage?*
Baba: It is a sign of a very advanced sadhaka. A continually smiling visage is a sign of a very advanced sadhaka. He who keeps crying all the time is a very poor sadhaka. Why should one be crying all the time? For what? If you were to look at it from the point of truth, you will find that a sadhak is even better placed than God Himself. There is nobody to look after God. The poor fellow, being perfect in Himself, has to take care of Himself, and it is He Himself who is completely responsible for Himself. While it is not so in the case with a sadhak. God is there to take care of him, so why should a sadhak worry, why should he be crying, why should he be weeping or complaining? It doesn't make any sense. On the contrary, a sadhu should be pursuing his sadhana with great love, with great enthusiasm; he should be bright and cheerful and smiling all the time.

There are ideal qualities which a sadhak should possess, the first is renunciation. That is, even when you are staying in such a prosperous Ashram, you should not be making any demands, or wanting anything, or be in need of anything. A seeker, after having performed the work which is assigned to him, should remain absorbed in contemplation of God and even when he is living in the midst of other people, he should carry himself as though he were entirely alone. He should not be addicted to small talk. A sadhak should not all the time be looking for somebody or should not feel compelled to look for somebody to have a chat with. There are some specimens who, if they cannot find anybody to talk to in the Ashram, would stand on the roadside in the hope of being able to gossip with a passerby. And if that is not possible then they like to go to Ganeshpuri to pick up an interesting conversation with somebody there. And if even that is not feasible, they go to Bombay to some restaurant and there they have conversation to their hearts' content. A seeker should have only as much contact with others as is absolutely necessary. In fact, a seeker, even while living with other people, should feel that he is in complete solitude. And this is what the Lord says in the 13th chapter of the *Gita*, "A seeker has distaste for crowds." That is, distaste for socializing. This is what the attitude of a seeker should be. Jnaneshwar Maharaj, while commenting on it says that a saint, even though living with other people, is always alone inwardly; inwardly he is always alone; he is not meeting anyone. It is always better for a seeker to remain absorbed in his inner being. Jnaneshwar Maharaj says while describing an ideal seeker, "Even while living with other people, he does not live with anyone, he is always living with himself, his own company is the best company for him, and he doesn't pick quarrels with others, he doesn't fight with others and at the same time, he doesn't try to make unnecessary contact with people. He is absorbed in himself all the time."

The mind, you know from your own experience, will begin to wander even on the slightest pretext. If you leave it free for even a moment, it will begin to perform its antics. So it is necessary for you to keep your mind engaged all the time on inward contemplation. The greatest quality of a seeker is that he has intense attachment to the Lord, he gets completely detached from the world, indifferent to the world; that is his highest quality. He is absorbed in remembering Him, contemplating Him all the time.

Barry: *Since hunger and constipation are no longer accurate guides, what body function should I use to judge the food quantities, so as not to interfere with the yogic processes when I experience uddiyana bandha and yogic heat? I had digestive ailments for so long, that I am not sure what a normal amount of food is for me. Does the fact that I have been emaciated for so long indicate an incorrect practice of sadhana?*
Baba: The uddiyana bandha that you are experiencing indicates that your sadhana is going the right way, and when this takes place, the appetite will increase itself. Take only as much food as your stomach demands. If it is somewhat less, then that would be the best. A seeker should not eat more than three-quarters of the quantity that the stomach

can hold. If you happen to eat slightly less at one meal, that should not cause any worry, because at the next meal you can eat a little more. At the same time, if you happen to eat a little too much at one meal, that too, should not cause worry, because at the next meal you can eat less. No one should think that by eating too much he can improve his health, or that he can gain weight or strength. It is only by eating in a controlled and disciplined manner that a seeker can maintain good health. It is only regular habits in regard to food that will ensure that your body has enough energy. Discipline is necessary even in ordinary life, but for a yogi, it is a must. One poet-saint says that if one wishes to become a yogi, if one wishes to enjoy inner peace, to enjoy cheerfulness right to the last moment of his life, he should follow discipline, his life should be regulated. He who becomes a slave to the senses will be overcome by stupour and sleep; and anybody who is overcome by sleep, that is an indication that he is transferring himself from the boat of yoga to a different boat, which is bound to sink in the ocean. He who sleeps regularly at night, and eats frugally during the day, is a right kind of seeker, and he will live, and his boat will carry him across the ocean. But he who does not follow such discipline is bound to sink.

Olivier: *In the morning at 4:00 it is hard for me to stand up; it is like a struggle. After, I should like to be alone without any noise, because I feel myself like a baby and I want to protect me. The more I go with the sun, the more it is good, and Guru Gita is a gift. But I am sociable around 4 p.m. in the afternoon, it is a good moment for me, good and fine harmony sometimes. Evening is good also. Why this difficulty in the morning?*
Baba: When will the baby grow up? If you do not get up at 4 every day, then the baby will not grow up, even if a thousand years were to pass. As long as you are a baby you will have to depend on others even for the ordinary needs of your daily life. Some other person will have to make sure that you are eating food, that you are taking a bath, and going around in the right manner. Therefore, this baby should learn to stand on its own feet, and it should grow up into an independent young man. If you force this baby to get

up at 4 every morning, I can assure you that it will grow up into a young man, it will grow up into a fine adult who is self-reliant and confident, and who takes good care of himself; not a miserable pathetic specimen depending on others all the time. Moreover, it is the early morning time which is most excellently suited to meditation. The brahmamahurta, the early morning time, the period from 3 to 6 is the best part of the day, and if you are awake during that part, that would promote not only your health, but your longevity, and it will make your mind still and steady and stable and will also help to purify it. Even if you do not feel like getting up early and you want to get up late, and you may feel better when you get up late, that would only make you weak and will not help you to become more steady. There are people who develop the habit of getting up late, particularly people from foreign countries, and they find if difficult to get up early, and there is no dirth of such people in India either.

If you have developed the habit of getting up late, then you can develop the habit of getting up early too. If you find it impossible to get up, or if you feel utterly miserable getting up early in the morning, well then follow your own inclination. Get up at 4, wash your legs from the knees downwards, wash your face and your lower arms, and have a stroll and see how you feel. If I wish to know a particular secret, well then that is the time which is best suited. Say, if Desai comes and reports to me that a theft has taken place, then I tell him that I will talk about it the next day, and when I get up early, the next day, I can find out during meditation who the thief is. But I can't find that out during the daytime. Such is the importance of getting up early in the morning. For some time there is no doubt that you will certainly find it difficult. When I went to America, I too, found it difficult, because what was day here was night there, and so for the first ten or fifteen days I did not feel so fresh and so vibrant; but later, it was all right, I got adjusted. When we have day here, it's night there and when it's night here it's day there, and so the body takes time to adjust itself to the new environment. There are many people coming here from Bombay and they prefer to come here in the morning, not in the evening, because they do not want to get up early the next morning.

Kedarnath: *It is said in the Siddha Gita that the mind is unreal, merely imaginary, but in our actual experience we find that the mind sits on our back like a tyrant driving us here and there, without respite, it brings all our efforts to control it to naught. In what sense then, can the mind be considered to be unreal?*

Baba: The mind is so tyrannical that it has not spared even its creator, so what respect could it have for a mere professor? The mind is realised to be unreal only after one has had the final realisation. If the *Siddha Gita* says that the mind is unreal, or imaginary, it doesn't mean that the mind is a mere illusion, like a mirage, or that it doesn't exist. The mind is nothing but consciousness, and to look upon the mind as an entity which is different from consciousness is false understanding. Who could ever describe the primal thought arising in the mind of the Lord, the thought, "I am one, let Me become many," as unreal or imaginary? To consider it imaginary shows a very inadequate understanding.

It is the mind which comes first, and then the body. It is only the mind which gives reality to Ram or to Krishna or to concepts of good and evil, or to the outer world. If the mind were to cease to exist, then everything else would become meaningless. If one were to try to dominate the mind, one would never succeed, because the mind has been dominating you right from time immemorial; you can never succeed in dominating it; that is a wild goose chase. It is never possible to dominate the mind. The scriptural texts should not be interpreted literally. If you were to look at the mind from the standpoint of truth you would find that the mind is nothing but pure consciousness. God has created this vast universe with the mind. There is a work called *Yoga Vasishtha*, which deserves the highest reverence, and should be read again and again, and the word 'lila' occurs in that work. And the sage Vasishtha says to Ram, "The world is a creation of the mind; what we call the world is a creation of the mind. When the mind transcends its own nature, then the world is no longer a world, it becomes transformed into Ram or into God."

There is no point in striving to suppress the mind or domineer it, because that effort would not succeed. Instead of that one should keep praying to the Lord; you should respect its might, and then the mind would perhaps start listening. According to the author of *Pratyabhijna-hridayam*, the mind is not a separate entity. It is not something which is made of matter or some other principles. The mind is in fact pure consciousness; the mind is Goddess Chiti Herself. When my mind begins to wander slightly then I begin to remember, or I begin to invoke Chiti, and I begin to consider my own mind to be the Mother Herself. Then the mind becomes still once again. It's because he has been trying to hold the mind firmly that he is not succeeding. If the *Siddha Gita* says that the mind is unreal, it doesn't mean that the mind does not exist. It only means that to consider the mind a separate entity is wrong. The mind is pure consciousness and the mind should be tackled through prayer, through love, and it should be filled with love and directed towards the inner Self. It is the grace of the mind which is far more important than the grace of anybody else. You may enjoy the grace of all other people, but if you do not enjoy the grace of the mind, the grace of other people would not help you at all. You have to win the grace of your own mind. By winning the grace of one's mind, I mean the state in which the mind becomes favourable, in which the mind sheds its hostility, its self-defeating tendencies, and becomes absorbed in God, being filled with love and joy from time to time. There are many seekers who have to suffer very much because they try to suppress the mind, because they try to establish their authority over it. They try to bring it firmly under their power. The best thing would be to keep on praying to the mind, then the mind will become absorbed in the inner Self.

Mira: *On several occasions some people have suffered various muscle pains, and they have requested me to massage those areas. After doing this I noticed that I now suffer from the same pain. How has this happened and what should I do or not do?*
Baba: This is what happens in the case of one whose inner Shakti has been awakened. The inner Shakti draws the pain

of the ailing person to itself, in the case of such a seeker. But then it would not afflict you for long; it would leave you after a short while. When you begin to feel such pain you should begin to meditate, and the pain will vanish. If while massaging a particular person you were in a meditative state, then the pain would not get transferred to you.

Shankar: *When I am tired my mind is very quiet, like a meditative state. The difference seems to be that when I am tired I have very little control. Could you explain the condition of a tired mind, as compared to the meditative mind? Does the mind get tired, or does something else get tired? Are there fewer thoughts when tired, and is this why sleep comes in meditation?*
Baba: When you get tired the mind gets a little beyond the reach of the body, and that is why you feel quiet. Just as during sleep the mind goes to a different centre, similarly, when you get tired the mind shifts to a different centre. It is not really the mind which gets tired; it is the inner organs, the inner subtle organs through which the mind works which get tired. But the quietude of silence which you enjoy during a meditative state while you are completely awake is a very favourable experience. In that state you travel beyond the waking state. Whether you're tired or not depends on what state you are in. It has nothing to do with the mind. In the waking state we become occupied with activities such as walking, eating, sitting, standing, etc. and in the sleep state we become completely inactive. We neither see nor hear nor sit nor walk not stand. So, when the body gets tired, the mind shifts its centre from the waking state to a different state, and it is for this reason that you feel or experience quietude. That, too, is very good, it is the samadhi of fatigue.

I have a tremendous experience of this kind of samadhi. I like to have long walks and when I get tired I come back and lie down, and I enjoy that state very much. I get up at 3 and like to go around for my inspection visit, to see different corners of the Ashram; then I come back and sit calmly. After getting up I like to visit the hall, particularly during the time of arati to see how many people are present there, and I like to visit the bathrooms to see whether the ladies are chatting, or what exactly is holding the attention of the boys in the bathroom, and I like to visit the kitchen to see what the cooks are doing there. It takes me about one hour to complete this visit. I go up through this flight of stairs and come down through the other flight, and this morning I found Davina practising asanas.

The sleep that you get during meditation is not caused by fatigue or tiredness. That shows that you are entering into a different state. The mind stays awake as long as it has something outside to hold its attention, and when in meditation the mind becomes free from all outer concerns, it retires into the sleep state. To go into sleep while sitting in a meditative posture is a very good state to get into because that indicates that the mind has become completely free from all outer concerns, and has become completely quiet. The mind stays alert and awake only as long as it has an object to occupy its attention, but the moment the mind is withdrawn from all objects, it either goes into sleep or into the state of samadhi; the mind cannot stay in a state of vacuum. What is important is that the mind should be freed again and again from all objects. It should be emptied completely. Sometimes I find Janaki sitting with her mouth wide open in meditation, and I don't know whether she is going into a very high state of meditation, or whether she is going into sleep; and if I were to put something into her mouth I wonder if she would notice. To keep awake the mind needs some object, and if no object is provided to the mind to keep it awake, it would either go into the state of sleep or into the state of samadhi. After all, what is the purpose of maintaining silence, or all these devotional practices such as chanting or recitation? They are all aimed at stilling the mind and making it silent.

March 8, 1972

Draupadi: *If a sadhak is asked by the Guru to have aham brahmasmi bhav, and is also told that total surrender to the*

Guru is the best thing to do in sadhana, can he combine the two and practise them together harmoniously, and if so, how?

Baba: In fact, the awareness that "I am Brahman" is the highest form of surrender. Very few can comprehend the mystery of this awareness, though it is of the utmost importance for everyone to understand it. There are only two divisions or categories in the world, not three: Brahman and jiva. In every field you find this two-fold division, Guru-disciple, husband-wife, heaven-hell, and so on. When one gets beyond duality one gets into the highest state, the state of supreme surrender, when the consciousness of "I am jiva," an embodied, limited soul merges in the consciousness "I am Brahman." Then supreme surrender is achieved.

In meditation the highest mantra is *Guru Om*, or *So-'ham*, and the most significant Vedantic statement is *aham brahmasmi*. Vedanta seeks to unite Brahman and jiva into a unity. That involves the surrender of the jiva to Brahman. Just as the offering in a sacrifice becomes one with the fire on coming into contact with the fire, in the same way a jiva, while merging into Brahman becomes one with Brahman; jivahood is consumed in the fire of knowledge.

This is exactly what should govern the relationship between the devotee and the Lord. As long as the devotee feels separate from the Lord or feels that he is different from the Lord, he is not a devotee. The highest form of devotion is total absorption in the Lord. If there is even the slightest self-consciousness, the slightest awareness of a separate existence, then it indicates that one is not a true devotee. Similarly, if a disciple feels that he is at a great distance from the Guru, that he is very different from the Guru, then he is not worthy of being a disciple. Through the knowledge received from him a true disciple feels complete oneness with the Guru. He identifies himself completely with him.

The attitude of surrender to the Guru, and the attitude, "I am Brahman," though apparently different, are in reality one. There is no question of combining the two because they are not really two; they are already one. There is no difference between surrender and "I am Brahman" awareness. There is a very interesting story in the *Bhagavat* and it occurs in a dialogue between the Lord and some devotees.

The Gopis and Gopas were having a discussion with the Lord, and in the middle He had to go away to attend to some urgent work. The devotees implored Him humbly not to go, but He said He had to. Then they said, "Well, if You are that keen on going, do go, but we would like to see how You can depart from our hearts." Therefore, the devotee and the Lord are always one, because the devotee is always completely absorbed in the Lord. This is also true of the Guru-disciple relationship.

Larry: *At the point when the mind becomes empty and goes into either the sleep state or samadhi, what can be done to make it go into samadhi rather than sleep?*
Baba: You have to shake the mind from sleep. If the mind retains awareness in that state, then the same state becomes samadhi. Even if you are going into the state of sleep, if you could stay a conscious witness to sleep, that too would be a state of high awareness. Sometimes while sitting in a relaxed position in my chair I go into the state of sleep, but I remain a witness to whatever happens, or does not happen, during sleep. That is a unique state because that is the state of meditation as well as sleep, the state in which I retain the witness-consciousness. It is a state of great bliss, a state of tremendous inner comfort. When it is time for me to go out, I get up from this very state and go out.

Every day I see that Janaki and Gauri fall asleep, but they sleep in the sitting position. If they are in the lying position I shake them out of it, but if they are sleeping in the sitting position, that is an indication that they are meditating. Sleep in the sitting position is highly comforting to the mind, highly soothing also. And this sleep is different from ordinary sleep; it is closer to the state of samadhi. Because after you get up from that meditative sleep you feel so fresh and energised you feel a new gladness in the brain. All the brain cells seem to be tingling with a new joy, a new vigour.

To go into the samadhi state it is necessary that one remain intensely alert and wakeful. As the mind begins to slip into the sleep state, one should be watching very alertly to see what is happening to the mind. Then one would glide into the samadhi state.

Davina Saraswati: *What daily program do you recommend if one has to be away from the Ashram for a time attending to worldly commitments?*
Baba: If it is convenient then the seeker should get up as early as he gets up here, around 5, wash hands and feet and sit for meditation. If you can't practise swadhyaya or if you have no time to sing arati, it doesn't matter, because these features belong more to Ashram life. But you must not miss meditation, because meditation concerns your own innermost being. Try to find some time in the evening also for meditation, and practise some chanting or japa.

Wherever you may go, you do not neglect the different activities of your everyday life, such as bathing, evacuating, sleeping and eating. In the same manner, you should not neglect meditation. When a seeker goes away from the Ashram, he finds time for a bath, for sleep and changing his clothes, and for various other things. So why shouldn't he find time for meditation also? Why should meditation be the only thing that is neglected? If one meditates regularly, one can feel certain that one is carrying the Ashram with him.

Malti: *What are the qualities which make a Guru truly worthy of our reverence, and what is the right attitude to have towards the Guru?*
Baba: One should not underrate the Guru. No one should think that the divine Shakti would dwell in a frivolous, unworthy fellow. One achieves Guruhood only as a result of enormous merit accumulated through countless past births.

Only people lacking in intelligence, who are themselves utterly stupid, accept unintelligent, stupid, unworthy fellows as their gurus. Are we so stupid that we should begin to worship someone even if he is worse than us? A Guru should have all the ideal qualities. Whenever they have to decide who is going to acceed to the throne of Shankaracharya, they have all this in mind. There was once a guru in Gujarat who had all the qualities, but he was addicted to playing cards. I told him bluntly that he was not worthy of being a Guru; at best he could call himself a seeker. A Guru would not be a victim of any addiction. What makes one think that a Guru who is delighting in Brahman, whose sole joy is Brahman, would come down to take delight in cards?

What could possibly make a Guru interested in all those kings and queens and 5's and 7's?

A Guru, to be truly worthy of our reverence, should be totally free from any blemish. He should be completely pure and innocent. A Guru can live the life of a householder. In ancient India there were many Gurus who were married, such as Vasishtha, Vyasa and Patanjali. But a true Guru follows the scriptural injunctions in this regard and would not do anything improper, no matter what type of life he were leading. A Guru would never be flirting with mistresses or hobnobbing with homosexuals. In our country a homosexual would never be regarded as a Guru. Homosexuals are considered to be eunuchs—disgusting, impure and inauspicious.

Celibacy is essential for one who claims to be a Guru. Shakti can be transmitted only by a celibate. One who is wasting his semen cannot transmit Shakti. In order to test the purity of the sage Shuka, King Janaka sent many beautiful, naked young maidens to him. But he remained unaffected. It is for this reason that his celibacy has become proverbial—we say, "as chaste as Shuka."

A Guru is urdhvareta. The flow of his semen is directed upwards. Even when he is in the midst of young beautiful girls his semen does not start flowing downwards. If there is a so-called Guru whose semen starts flowing downwards through homosexual or even heterosexual practices, can he be considered a Guru? There is a very significant discussion relating to this in Eknath Maharaj's commentary on the *Shrimad Bhagavat*. In the dialogue between Lord Krishna and Uddhava, it says, "A butterfly or a bee sucks the juice of a flower and finds nothing else so tasty." In the same manner, a yogi is always drinking the immortal juice which flows from his sahasrar. So how could such a yogi find any delight in the anus?

What is it that gives such a high place to the Guru? It surely could not be a glib tongue; it could not be the capacity to talk cleverly and throw dust in people's eyes. A mere wagging tongue would not qualify one to be a Guru. A Guru should be absolutely pure and fully worthy of Guruhood. All his dealings should be honest and noble. His character and conduct should be absolutely ideal. He should not deviate even in the least from the highest standards. A fellow who is charging interest on loans given even to friends, who tries to foist counterfeit goods on somebody else, who overcharges, who is cunning, does not deserve to be called a Guru.

A true Guru is perfect in knowledge, perfect in renunciation and yoga. He himself practises the discipline he sets for his disciples. His own example is the greatest example for his disciples to follow. If we are willing to settle for less, why then shouldn't we worship ourselves? To consider the Guru to be the most adorable being is the best attitude to have towards him, the highest and noblest feeling that one could have.

March 10, 1972

Malti Shoff: *We read in Guru Gita and Arati texts, "Thou art our Father, Thou art our Mother" and so on. What is the relation of personal feelings of love for the mother and father, the brother and friend with Gurubhava or devotion to the Guru?*

Baba: These personal feelings of love for the mother, father and so on have great importance; they are genuine feelings and have great relevance to the disciple's devotion to the Guru. The father and mother are worthy of ideal reverence. Take the case of the father: the father parts with a part of his vital fluid so that his child may come into existence, and after the child has been born, the father takes care of him until he grows up sufficiently to be able to take care of himself. Then the mother: the mother holds the vital fluid of the father inside her so that the child can be born. After the child has come into the world, she looks after him with tenderest care. And she goes on looking after him until he grows up sufficiently to be able to look after himself. That is why our scriptures honour the father and mother so much, and go to the extent of proclaiming: worship your father and mother as deities. If you worship your father and mother as divine beings then your children will worship you as a divine being, and this way this tradition, which ensures happiness, which ensures joy, will be continued.

The Sadguru is the supreme father, the highest father. The ordinary father gives his vital fluid to produce the body of a child, while the Sadguru brings into existence the spiritual body of a seeker. As a seeker continues with his sadhana for a prolonged period, he gets to the stage where his seminal fluid begins to flow upwards. It is only when a seeker has become urdhvareta that he becomes worthy of being treated as a Guru, or even being called a Guru. At that stage prana and vital fluid become one. In the spiritual realm no importance is attached to the downward flow of semen because that is nothing rare; that is the natural direction for the flow of everyone's fluid. If a person with a downward flow of semen could be a Guru, then you would have billions and billions of Gurus in this world. It is only after the Guru has become urdhvareta, only after his seminal fluid begins to flow upwards, that he is able to pass Shakti into a disciple. And when the Shakti is passed, what happens is that the Guru injects his own prana permeated with Shakti into the disciple. That is why a disciple is known as one who is born of mantra. The Guru is known as one who produces by means of mantra. As the Guru transmits the mantra into us, he becomes our supreme father.

Then the Guru extends protection to his disciple, and he takes care of him. He guides him in different ways, and teaches him to be disciplined and restrained both through punishment and through love. It is also in this sense that he is the supreme father.

The Guru is the mother because he takes most tender care of his disciple. He watches how his little child is growing every day and what exactly he needs and he fulfils all the needs of this tiny growing child. He makes sure that his new born baby practises the mantra and the sadhana which he has given him, regularly and in the most disciplined manner. In our worldly life we depend on other relations for our various needs, on our brothers, sisters, friends, uncles, aunts, and so on. The Guru also fulfils all the various needs by playing the role that these other characters play in our life. So when the Guru is called the supreme mother, the supreme father, the brother, friend in the scriptures, it is a true description of his complex, all-inclusive role. It is not exaggeration; it is not just empty praise bestowed upon him. The Guru fulfils all the different needs of his disciple in different ways, and he plays all these different roles. Sometimes he is the father, sometimes the mother, sometimes the brother, and sometimes the friend.

Mark: *What causes illness? What is the relationship of illness to the mind, to sadhana, to Shakti? What is the correct attitude to have towards it?*
Baba: Charak was the greatest physician of India. According to him there are three factors which cause illness: first, the atmosphere or environmental influence, second, the wrong kind of food, and third, undesirable thoughts. Mainly, it is when the regularity of one's life is disturbed and when one eats indiscriminately that an illness is caused. Unfortunately most people do not know how to eat food properly. My idea of the proper manner of eating food is not to spice it more and more strongly and to dump as much of it as you can into your stomach. It has been said in the scriptures that food should be treated like medicine, and it should be eaten in a strictly measured quantity. We do not take a medicine in any quantity that we feel like, we take it in a measured dose. There is no reason why we shouldn't take food also in a strictly measured quantity. Our food should be plain and simple. It should be pure and such as will promote longevity as well as health, and fortify our power of resistance against illness, as well as fight against illnesses which are already there. The mind keeps moving throughout the entire body, so it is greatly affected by the processes taking place inside the body. Whatever is taken into the body is bound to affect the mind. If you are not in good health, how much yoga can you practise, how much meditation? How can you do your duty? You can't even enjoy normal happiness.

Food should not be treated lightly or frivolously. We should not eat only because it gives us pleasure. Food has been considered to be very important in our scriptures, and it has been given a very high place. The Self is situated within every heart, and it is the Self who is the enjoyer. So while eating one should be aware of what the inner Self needs, and should only eat that which would be agreeable to the inner Self, which would delight it, which would fulfil its needs. If the body is sick, what kind of sadhana can such a body do? Food should be eaten discriminately, thoughtfully. It should be considered to be something which will give satisfaction to the inner Self. Then it will be quite congenial to one's sadhana.

Kalyani: *Would you please explain how the functions of the ida and pingala nadis and changes in heat and cold affect one's sadhana? Also why is it that the sushumna is most active at times of sunrise and sunset?*
Baba: The time of sunrise and sunset is the junction, the meeting point, the moment of meeting of light and darkness, which is most favourable for the sushumna to become fully active. For this reason Indian culture has prescribed prayer at the time of sunrise and at the time of sunset, and this prayer is called sandhya. The morning and evening arati that we hold here is in keeping with scriptural injunctions. Since the body is a microcosm which is fully representative of the macrocosm, whatever happens in the larger universe also happens in the body; so the same applies to the ida and pingala. The human body is not independent of the universe it lives in; in fact, the two work together. This truth is realised only in the moment of the final vision. And when the body is affected by heat and cold, the ida and pingala also get affected.

Malti Shoff: *We have so many different photographs of you, but not in a single picture do we see you in the nude. What is the reason?*
Baba: Man is considered to be superior to all other animals. But the question arises, in what respect is man superior? Man is superior because man has a sense of modesty, because man has a sense of discipline. Otherwise, man would just be an older brother to all other animals and beasts. If one has a sense of modesty, even fire would not be able to affect him, even God's wrath would be ineffective against him. I would never consider a naked sadhu to be an intelli-

gent sadhu, or to be an honourable or worthy sadhu. To me, a naked sadhu is a despicable specimen. God has bestowed us with such a beautiful body, and if one does not have the decency to cover it even with a loincloth, then one is no better than an elephant. Why shouldn't one have been born an elephant?

I'll narrate to you a story of a true event that occurred about forty or fifty years ago in Rajasthan, and I visited the spot where that event occurred. The veracity of this event has been borne out by the local magistrate, and he has vouched for the veracity of this in a monthly published by the Gorakhpur press. There was a certain king who was the head of a small state, and he had a large family and there was a couple in that family—the prince and his wife—that was not getting along well with the king; and the king, too, kept them at arm's length. The wife and the husband had great love for each other, and the wife in particular was absolutely faithful to her husband, and even though they did not enjoy the favour of the king, they were spending their days happily. It so happened that the prince developed tuberculosis, and his condition went from bad to worse so much so that he was on his death bed. And finally the doctors declared that they were helpless, that they couldn't do anything for the prince, and the prince would die shortly. The wife of the prince, even during such a crisis, was absolutely loyal to her husband, and she would serve him in a most dedicated manner; she would only partake of that food which was left over by him, and she looked after him as much as she could. One morning the husband's prana left his body and he died. And the wife at that time had gone out after having given her husband a drink of water, and she actually saw the prana passing out of her husband's body from a distance, and she immediately rushed back home. She adorned herself with her marital dress. She also wore all the ornaments that had been presented to her by her husband, and after adorning herself in this manner, she sat down. She then wanted to prepare a certain fluid which is a mixture of five different ingredients, such as cow's milk, cow's urine, and the like, so she asked five different people to go and fetch these five ingredients telling them that there was a black cow standing outside the gate. The people went to the black cow, and the cow yielded the milk and urine without the least resistance, and the people came back with those ingredients, and the woman mixed them and sprinkled them over her body, and she decided to commit sati with her husband. People tried to dissuade her, but she did not listen to anyone. And nobody had the courage to plead with her any further because her form at that time had become terrible, and she was bent on committing sati. A funeral pyre was laid to burn her husband's body, the dead body was laid on it, and this woman also got on the funeral pyre; and she laid the head of the corpse on her lap and sat there. A large number of people had gathered there to witness this most extraordinary incident, and the local officials were present there, and they passed an order saying that the pyre must not be set fire, because they would like to see how the woman could commit the sati. No one set fire to the pyre, but this woman started praying intensely to the Lord, and in a short while the miracle took place and the pyre was set aflame on all sides. The local magistrate writes that the pyre began to burn, and all the parts of the woman's body were consumed. It was only her sari which was not at all touched by the fire.

Such is the value of modesty. And one who values modesty is valuing something which is the highest in the world; one who has no use for modesty is an utter shameless fellow, and he does not deserve any respect or honour. That is why human civilisation has emphasised dress and ornaments so much—not for adornment of the body, but for the protection of modesty. Even fire cannot touch a modest person. That report says that the sari of that woman began to burn only after her body had been reduced to ashes. There is a copy available in the library concerning this account. Therefore, as far as possible, one should respect modesty.

Kedarnath: *There are some seekers who get repelled by the fierceness of Shiva or a Shiva-like Guru and take refuge in the gentleness of Rama or a Ram-like Guru. Isn't fierceness as much a part of the Guru's love and compassion as gentleness? Isn't the Guru also Rudra as well as Brahma and Vishnu?*
Baba: One who gets scared by the fierceness of the Guru is

not a true disciple. He is not even a true seeker. He is a spineless fellow looking for a spineless Guru who keeps on soothing his ego by soft words and soft teachings all the time, and that is all he is interested in. A true disciple would not be scared even of Yama or death. Take the case of Nachiketa. He followed the God of death right into his abode.

The question arises: what should the Guru take pity on? What should the Guru forgive or be gentle with? A disciple's laziness? A disciple's weakness? His addictions to drugs or alcohol? Should a Guru embrace a disciple who comes drunk and tell him, "If you have taken one bottle today, take two tomorrow?"

One who is always gentle with his disciples does not deserve to be a Guru. In fact, he shows that he is only after having more and more disciples and he is making a compromise with the dignity, with the sublime tradition of Guruhood just to attract more spineless fellows towards his spineless majesty. Only those so-called seekers who are fond of license, of having their own way, would want the Guru to be gentle all the time. Only a spineless Guru would not mind his disciples' moving around with harlots or mistresses in his presence; he would not mind their taking drugs; he would not mind their using alcohol, because he needs more and more disciples. But a true Guru does not need more and more disciples.

A disciple who is already disciplined would not merit fierceness from the Guru, and in his case the question of fierceness or gentleness would not arise. After all, a Guru is not a stupid fellow who would be addicted to fierceness or harshness. Take the case of one particular incarnation of the Lord called Narasimha, who was half lion and half man. When the Lord appeared in that form everyone got frightened except Prahlada who was completely innocent. Even in that terrible form the Lord spoke in the sweetest most soothing tone to Prahlada.

What causes destruction or purification? Can you bring about destruction with a garland of flowers or do you need a sword for that? What makes you think that the weaknesses, the defects, the bad habits of a disciple would go if the Guru were to be gentle and soothing with him all the time? No true Guru would appear in the Rudra or terrible form all the time. He would assume that form only when necessary. A true Guru would appear and behave only as a Guru, nothing else.

The Guru makes use of all four methods for correcting his disciple, namely gentleness, punishment, reward and tact. That is why the Guru is regarded as the trinity of Brahma, Vishnu and Rudra. The Guru as Rudra destroys all the defects and weaknesses of his disciple and purifies him completely; he makes him a new being, makes him a being who is pure and disciplined.

Raul: *If one has a paid job and property to manage, how can such activities be turned into a spiritual endeavour?*
Baba: If you are doing your job honestly, then you are being righteous, you are being spiritual. What makes you think that property is not divine, that property is not an image of the Lord, that property is not something to be protected and taken care of? You see how big this Ashram is and how beautiful this Ashram is, and how much care I take of the buildings and property here? I am thinking of expanding it even further. What makes you think that I am unspiritual or stupid or greedy? I am aware that all this wealth comes from the Lord; it belongs to Him, and it is here to glorify Him. That is why I am very particular that not a single penny is wasted. It is for this reason that I take the utmost care of everything here.

You should do your job with a sense of honour, and you should try to please God through it. You should not try to please the millionaire who is your earthly master. You should not consider yourself to be a servant to your boss. You should consider yourself to be a servant to the Lord. One who pursues his job with a sense of honour pleases the Lord very quickly. Do not consider your property to be different from divine abundance. It is the same Lord manifesting Himself as property whom you are trying to realise through meditation with closed eyes. There are different kinds of action. There are the sort of actions which are outgoing, which help your mind to go out, and then there are actions or activities which direct the attention of the mind inwards, activities such as meditation and chanting, and other devotional practices. Property or wealth is just an outward expression of the Lord, and you should not have contempt for it.

Carol: *Recently I have felt a violent welling up of the Shakti in the area of my solar plexus and abdomen. I used to label this hunger and eat, or anger and look for a reason for it. When I am able to see these sensations as movements of the divine Shakti, and I begin to meditate, intense feelings of anger, frustration or restlessness come up. How do I deal with these?*

Baba: You should not do anything to overcome feelings of frustration or anger or restlessness that come up during meditation. Just remain as a witness to them and they will subside in course of time. The sensation which you feel in the navel region cannot arise from hunger or anger. This is the working of divine Shakti. Your understanding of this is correct.

While asking a question you should phrase it very briefly. On the pretext of asking a question you should not write a lecture. While asking a question you do not have to state what you feel about your problem. You should only ask me what I feel about it. A question should be stated very briefly, otherwise the translator has to use too many words, and I too have to use a lot of patience; and you know I do not have too much patience with unnecessary words. Now I will ask your question: Sometimes during meditation I experience strange sensations in the navel region. What do you attribute them to? Then your second question—During meditation all sorts of feelings such as anger and restlessness arise in me, and how should I tackle them?

March 13, 1972

Cliff: *Is one-pointedness on God the same as surrendering to the Guru?*

Baba: Yes. Yes. God, soul and the Guru are not three. As long as you look upon them as being separate entities, different from one another, it shows that you haven't really attained anything, regardless of what you might be doing. It shows that you are still in a state of ignorance, and that ignorance is very much like the ignorance of a person who wanders from one sacred centre to another, from one mantra to another, without really understanding the nature of what matters. The scriptures say that that which is the Guru is Shiva, and that which is Shiva is the Guru, and there is not the least difference between the two. The difference is only in the sound of the words; the meaning is the same. Therefore, he alone who has realised that God, the Guru and the inner Spirit are one and the same, would be able to make some real progress in meditation. As long as these three are seen as different from each other, even if God is standing right before you, you would not be able to attain very much from Him.

I will narrate a story to illustrate how important correct understanding is. Once a large number of sages and seers congregated to discuss an important question. It wasn't an assembly of ordinary politicians, it was a congregation of all the greatest seers. And the question that was brought up for the assembly to decide was: Who is superior, one who engages in various austerities, such as fasting, pilgrimages, giving charity liberally, pranayama, japa, bathing three to five times every day—and there are some who go to the extent of even living in boats in water all the time, thinking that that is the best way to keep pure—or one who has correct understanding of the nature of the Lord?

Vishvamitra, the great ascetic rose up and said, "Look, it is austerities which are the most fruitful, and which impart the most power to an ascetic. An ascetic, by the force of his tapasya, can achieve the impossible. He can create a new world, he can do whatever he feels like."

Then Vasishtha said, "I don't agree with Vishvamitra. It is knowledge which is superior to tapasya. As far as tapasya is concerned, different beings and even inanimate things are performing tapasya. Look at a tree, it is standing all the time; look at the water, it is flowing all the time; look at wind, it is blowing all the time; look at a mountain, it is standing absolutely still, it has been standing in that position for centuries, for ages, in fact—and if a human being were also to practise asceticism there would be nothing special about him. What really matters is knowledge or understanding."

Vishvamitra protested and said, "No, what Vasishtha is saying is absolutely absurd, it is utter nonsense. Tapasya is superior."

Thus the two great sages began to fight with each other on this point. When the sages who had collected there saw that the dispute was getting hotter, they got apprehensive and began to wonder how the dispute would be resolved. Narada was also on the scene, and no one could beat Narada as far as coming up with the most appropriate solution to a problem. Narada came up with a very clever proposal. He said, addressing the two saints, "Look, you shouldn't fight with each other. The best thing to do under the circumstances would be to go to the nether world and see Sheshnag, the serpent who is holding the entire world on his hood. Sheshnag knows everything—all the creatures, all the mysteries of the world, great and small. Let us go and ask him which is better, asceticism or knowledge."

The disputants agreed to the suggestion and they went to see Sheshnag. When they got there Sheshnag was holding the burden of the entire earth most comfortably; it was nothing unusual for him, just as it is nothing unusual for a person to be able to bear the burden of his hair, whether it is thick, in the form of matted locks, or very thin. When Sheshnag saw the two sages coming from a distance, he got ready to receive them. He asked them how they were, and what had brought them there. So they told him what had happened—that a large number of saints had congregated to decide the question of which was the most important, knowledge or asceticism. They told him that Vasishtha took the side of knowledge and Vishvamitra took the side of asceticism, and they had begun to debate the question hotly, and when it was realised that there was no possibility of the argument coming to a happy resolution, it was suggested that they should go and visit Sheshnag and have the question settled by him. "So please let us know what is superior, knowledge or asceticism. What has more power?"

Sheshnag was extremely wise. He knew the answer to the question and he also knew his two guests through and through. He knew that the one advocating knowledge was an intelligent person and was quite dependable, but the other one, on the side of tapasya was not quite dependable— he had to be tackled with great tact, because otherwise you could never tell when he might flare up and fly at your throat. Sheshnag did not want to take any risk, because when you are confronted with a fool, he does not listen to anything that you say, however intelligent it may be. So when dealing with a fool, you have to be very tactful. Then Sheshnag said, "Look, you must realise that I am carrying such a big burden on my head—the whole earth—so how do you expect me to give you an answer when I am bending down with this burden? First, you must relieve me of this burden for a while. One of you two should hold the earth for a short while so that I may be able to answer your question, and then it will also be seen who has greater power."

Vishvamitra immediately jumped on the suggestion. He took out his yogadanda, the t-shaped stick which yogis carry, and began to brag, "I stood still for 1,000 years, and I have even chewed little iron balls. I am considered to be the greatest ascetic in the world, and now I am going to show you how much power asceticism has. My yogadanda, my stick, will hold the weight of the world. I am going to perform that miracle."

The moment the earth was placed on the top of the stick, the earth began to shake. Vishvamitra was shocked. He had not expected that the earth would not stay on the top of his stick. Sheshnag said, "Look, the earth will fall any moment." "Yes," Vishvamitra admitted in dismay, "My stick cannot hold the weight of the earth."

Then Vasishtha was called. Sheshnag took the earth back from Vishvamitra and said to Vasishtha, "What do you have to say?" Vasishtha said, "Look, here is my water bowl. If I have meditated for a brief moment with the awareness that all there is is Brahman, the Absolute, then my water bowl should be able to hold the weight of the entire world, because meditation with that understanding has limitless power."

And the earth was placed on the water bowl, and it stood

comfortably on it. Then Vasishtha and Sheshnag began to have a friendly chat with each other, "How are you, how are things in your part of the world?" and so on.

One who doesn't have correct understanding, who hasn't attained true knowledge, and who is thinking in terms of differences and distinctions all the time will always feel nervous and insecure, because he is imperfect, and an imperfect person can never stay still or steady for a long time. So Vishvamitra was feeling very restless, and he could not bear that when such an important issue was at stake, Vasishtha and Sheshnag should indulge in frivolous conversation.

Vishvamitra demanded in an angry tone, "Look, let me know what is superior, knowledge or tapasya."

Sheshnag said, "What shall I say? Isn't it fairly obvious which is superior? When the earth was placed on your yoga stick, it tilted and was going to fall any moment, but when it was placed on Vasishtha's water bowl, it sat comfortably. You can decide yourself, without my making any pronouncements in the matter, which is superior, knowledge or asceticism."

There are seekers who seem to think that if they could have a vision of Jesus, even for a brief moment, then they would be blessed, the purpose of their existence on earth would be fulfilled. But that is wrong understanding because there were so many during Jesus's time who saw him from day to day and yet nothing happened to them. There are people who entertain the fond hope that if they could have a vision of Lord Krishna, they would attain whatever there is to attain. But they forget that Krishna was present on the battlefield of Kurukshetra for eighteen days and thousands and millions looked at Him all the time. But how many of them attained liberation? If a mere look at a great saint could take you across the ocean of samsara, then thousands and thousands who came and had darshan of Bhagawan Nityananda, people in the neighbourhood who used to meet him quite frequently and even eat from his hands, would have attained liberation.

What really matters is whether your understanding is correct or not. Therefore, before starting meditation, you should first understand the true nature of your own Self, the

Guru and God. If you could just arrive at the understanding that the Guru, God and Self are one and the same, then you would be in a very high state of meditation regardless of whether your eyes were open or closed, whether you were sitting in a meditative posture or moving around attending to different activities. One-pointedness on God is the same as what is called surrender to the Guru and is the same as what is called meditation on the inner Self.

It is essential for a meditator not only to meditate, not only to try to go deeper through meditation, but also to have the knowledge, the awareness that God, the Guru and his own Self are absolutely one. Sundar, the great poet-saint, says, "Ignorance runs away from a person who meditates with the awareness that God, Guru and his own Self are not different from one another, that they are one and the same." Therefore you should continue to meditate joyfully, but never, even for a moment, consider God to be apart from you. Love the Guru with all the intensity you are capable of, but do not consider him to be different from you. Do not consider him to be a distinct or remote being. Serve the Guru, do your Ashram work with utmost enthusiasm, with all the zest you can command, but do not consider that you are inferior to God, that while God is the perfect Being you are miserable, petty, trivial, insignificant, or insecure. It is only then that the service which you render will bear the highest fruit. You may be serving the Guru and working very hard but that would not matter very much unless you are aware that God, Guru and your own inner Self are one and the same.

Ian: *Is it a good idea to visualise the letters of one's mantra during meditation, and what part can visualisation play during meditation?*
Baba: The visualisation of the letters of one's mantra in meditation has as much importance and significance as anything could have. The mantra scriptures declare that God originally manifested Himself as sound or letters. God manifests Himself as the mantra and the mantra is nothing but the Supreme Being Himself. So, if you are able, with a one-pointed mind, to clearly see the letters of the mantra with your inner eye, then you are looking at God Himself.

Correct understanding is most important. One seer says, "Goddess Chiti permeates all three worlds. She manifests Herself as the different letters of the Sanskrit alphabet from the first *a* to the last *ksha*.

You should meditate with complete absorption, and if there is still a bit of your mind wandering then you should focus on the letters of the mantra you are practising. The nectar which begins to bubble up within during meditation with a one-pointed mind as a result of intense repetition of your mantra, is the greatest nectar, that is the divine nectar itself.

Ronnie: *Is it best to combine the thumb and index finger during meditation and darshan? Is it best to hold them together in any set way?*
Baba: The position in which the thumb and first finger are held together is known as chinmudra, or the conscious mudra, and it is a sublime gesture. The inner Shakti, the inner energy, continues to flow outward through the fingers all the time. Mesmer, the man who discovered mesmerism was the first to have perceived the currents of this outgoing power. If this inner energy is allowed to flow outward, you become poorer in a corresponding measure. The secret of this mudra, the importance of this mudra, is that it stops the outward flow of the inner energy and the energy is conserved inside.

There is a great meaning behind our custom of touching the feet of a holy man, or Guru, or bowing down at his feet. It is not mere sectarian ritual, and there is nothing especially Hindu about it. The Guru's feet are touched because energy is flowing out from his toes. It is for this reason that wooden sandals with studs are worn. There are people who regard wooden sandals as a mark of untouchability, which is entirely wrong. The secret behind this practice is that if you wear wooden sandals for a long time, then the stud which you have to hold between the first two toes forces them to remain in a particular position, and in that position the outward flow of Shakti is stopped. I wore wooden sandals for a long time, as a result of which my first two toes got set in a certain position, so the outward flow of energy has been checked. It is again for this reason that great saints, such as Bhagawan Nityananda would not allow devotees to wash their feet, because if their feet are washed the energy particles are washed away. This mudra in which the thumb and first finger are held together also helps you to achieve one-pointedness of mind in meditation.

Janaki: *What should one do in the hot season to avoid becoming overwhelmed by tamas, particularly after lunch? How can we maintain our mental and physical energy during this season? How should we regulate our food and rest so that we can function in the best possible way at this time?*
Baba: The summer season will not last forever, and while it is hot you can rest for a short while, say for fifteen minutes after lunch, and that should refresh you. Once you become accustomed to the heat, you will not feel its effect any longer. One should try to eat only two or three times, and overcome the habit of eating too frequently. If you need some rest, then after lunch you can either sit or lie calmly anywhere for a short while. It is only during the period of transition from winter to summer that one begins to feel low. After the period of transition, everything will be all right again. It doesn't mean that you are getting overcome by tamas. It only means that the heat of the season is proving a little too much. For the first week you may feel a little uncomfortable, but later you will get accustomed to it.

I used to get pain in my knees, and this time I decided not to use my air conditioner. I haven't used it for a long time, and that has helped me to get rid of the pain.

So, it is always good to accustom your body to the rigours of the season. The Matru Mandir is a quiet and cool place, and you can go there and sit or lie calmly. At present we are passing through the period of transition, so I am not surprised that you are feeling uncomfortable, but it will soon pass.

Continue to eat regularly as before. Whenever there is a change of climate or food, everyone has to bear with a certain amount of distress or discomfort, but after you have been exposed to a different climate or food for a time, you become habituated to it.

Kedarnath: *What should a seeker do if in spite of his pro-*

longed efforts and repeated prayers he has not been able to overcome a certain strong inner craving?
Baba: This was exactly the kind of question that was posed by Arjuna to the Lord, and the Lord's answer was, "You should cut your cravings with the sword of perfect dispassion, varaigya." Cravings can be given up only through firm varaigya, unflinching varaigya. It is only these small cravings which pester a person so much. It happens quite often that you are able to overcome formidable enemies but submit in the most miserable manner to petty insignificant ones. It is a strange irony that one should be able to renounce most precious things, yet should feel so helpless in the grip of a certain craving that one is forced to keep two pieces of chocolate under his pillow during the night. It is just like defeating an elephant, but being defeated by an ant.

Nathalie: *What should I do when I feel nervous, aggressive or angry against people or against material objects?*
Baba: Such feelings, emotions and passions keep arising from inside all the time, but the saving grace is that all of them are ephemeral, fleeting. You should not attach too much importance to any of them. At that time become completely silent and still. Everyone experiences these emotions and passions from time to time, and if you could develop the power of substituting that emotion or passion with something else, that, of course, would be the best.

Pratibha: *If there is a seeker in whose case such mantras as So'ham, Shivo'ham and aham brahmasmi begin to arise spontaneously within, what does that indicate? Does it mean that the seeker has understood their meaning perfectly, and it is because of that that these mantras are arising? Or does it mean that the time has now come when the seeker would be able to understand their meaning thoroughly?*
Baba: The fact that this question has come up shows that the meditator has not been able to understand the meaning of these mantras. If you had understood the meaning of these mantras, then you would not have put this question. It is quite obvious that you haven't understood the mantras,

otherwise you would not have put this question. You should take it that after these mantras have begun to arise spontaneously from within, the time has come for you to understand their significance fully. And even if the time hasn't come as yet, it will come in the future. Various thoughts keep arising in the human mind. Nathalie just complained about thoughts of anger. Similarly the thought that "I am Brahman," the Absolute, also arises spontaneously like a thought of anger, because this thought too has been embedded deep in the human psyche through the spontaneous repetition of this mantra going on inside through countless births. Whether you are Hindu or Muslim or Christian, whether you belong to India or some other country, this mantra of *So'ham* is going on in you all the time. In your present birth you may be Hindu, Muslim or Christian, but who knows what you were in your last birth? Just as old impressions throw up thoughts of anger, similarly, they also throw up these sublime thoughts of identity with the Absolute, and that is the correct understanding of this matter. But there is no doubt that a seeker would be able to understand their meaning fully in course of time; if not today, then tomorrow. Just as you come to know anger from within when anger arises, just as you get to know greed directly when the passion of greed arises inside, similarly, you will realise the inner meaning of a mantra when it begins to throb inside spontaneously, provided that that throbbing is quite genuine.

March 15, 1972

Ronnie: *I often chant Guru Om and sometimes your name. Is it better to concentrate on Om namah Shivaya; or are these three mantras equally good? If it feels best, can I mainly chant Guru Om?*
Baba: Once you have begun to chant *Guru Om*, and once

Guru Om has penetrated your heart, what's the point of starting chanting *Nityananda* or *Muktananda Om*? And what makes you think that *Muktananda Om* is different from *Guru Om*? Therefore, it would be best for you to continue with your japa of *Guru Om*. *Guru Om* is the same as *Om namah Shivaya,* and it would be good if you were to chant *Om namah Shivaya* also, for a while. But if you don't like to, it doesn't matter, it's not compulsory. The difference between Guru and Shiva is the difference between *pani* and water. Which do you prefer, water or *pani*? These mantras are different from each other only in their sound; their inner meaning is the same. There is a great saint who says in his poetry, and what he says is absolutely true, "No matter how much you practise austerities, japa or worship, or how many scriptures you read, until true knowledge arises from within all these practices have no use."

For liberation, knowledge is indispensible. If liberation could be attained without knowledge, there would have been no need for Krishna to impart knowledge to Arjuna. In the *Gita,* also, knowledge is given a place of honour and the Lord says, "There is nothing so purifying as knowledge." So knowledge has the highest significance. The other day, also, we compared knowledge and austerities and found that knowledge has much greater power. Knowledge has the divine power of consuming all one's impurities and taints in a moment.

It would be very good for you to continue to chant *Guru Om*. However, *Guru Om* and *Om namah Shivaya* have the same meaning. You should carry on your japa with utmost intensity. In fact you should merge yourself so completely in this practice that your condition should become like that of two friends who meet each other after a long time on a railway platform and become so absorbed in each other that they don't even notice the train that comes and leaves. That is how you should merge yourself in the japa. One who practises a mantra calmly without letting any doubt arise in his heart, with single-pointed devotion and utmost fidelity, is like one who has taken to a route with utmost determination and who keeps on pushing ahead with steadfastness, and who is bound to reach his destination after covering the different stages on the way. So once you have received the mantra from the Guru, it becomes absolutely unnecessary for you to look here or there, or to read too much, or to seek some other method of liberation. It would be enough for you to stick to the mantra with full faith, with full fidelity. And nothing else should matter to you.

Carol: *I have been drinking four or more cups of water a day since the weather became hot. Is this too much?*
Baba: This is the period of transition from cold weather to hot weather, and one has to be very careful. One shouldn't drink too much water, because water cools the gastric fire, and it may also cause dysentery. Once you submit to this need for more and more water, there is no end to it; you keep on drinking water throughout the day. However, one does need a little more water in hot weather than in cool weather. Therefore, exercise self-restraint, and the thirst arising from within will subside itself. Quite often you will be served a piece of onion at mealtimes, particularly in the evening, and whenever you get a piece of onion you should chew it thoroughly because that is the best, the most effective antidote to heat.

Pratibha: *Is there any difference between the Shaktipat received from you and the Shaktipat received from a disciple of yours who is not perfect like you? Do the disciple's imperfections affect the progress of the seeker who receives Shakti from him?*
Baba: Shakti is always perfect. However, one who is performing Shaktipat may be imperfect. Even when Shakti is transmitted through a medium, one should not think that the Shakti is coming from an imperfect person; one should believe that Shakti is coming from the perfect Being. The Shakti which has been working comes through the line of descendants. And our attention should be riveted all the time on the very source of Shakti. Even when it seems that a particular disciple is performing Shaktipat, that is not so. It is not the disciple who is performing Shaktipat; it is the Shakti who out of Her own pleasure is transmitting Herself into a seeker; because the disciple does not know anything about Shaktipat and the disciple has not been taught how to transmit Shakti. Until the time when the Guru himself

tells his disciple that he has achieved perfection and he is now worthy of carrying on the tradition on his own strength, and he gives him the command to go and perform Shaktipat, assuring him that the Shakti will pass from him into others in full measure, one should not think that the Shakti is flowing from the disciple. One should think that the Shakti is coming from the original source. After a disciple has been thoroughly authorised by the Guru, then you can take it that the Shakti is now coming from the disciple. The disciple is only a pretext, he is just a medium, just an instrument. The disciple's imperfections would have no effect, because behind the disciple's imperfections, the perfect Being is present.

In any case, a disciple from whom Shakti is coming into you will always remind you of the Guru who is the original source, and he will never try to stand between you and the Guru, regardless of the state that he might have attained. This very morning while writing a commentary on one of the verses of the *Guru Gita*, I described the state called swatantra. Swatantra means the state of freedom, and the state of freedom is not the same as the state of license, or self-will, or the state in which one would do whatever he feels like. It is, on the contrary, the state of supreme freedom which the greatest saints attain after passing through a period of intense discipline, and this was the state that Bhagawan Nityananda was in, this was the state that Zipruanna was in.

A saint who is established in this state is no longer amenable to our ordinary moral criteria of judgment. Take the case of Kabir, or Goraknath, or Jnaneshwar. They had highest talents and they were most powerful beings, particularly Jnaneshwar. Jnaneshwar had so much power that he could even command an inanimate wall to move. He was a perfect yogi. All of them had achieved the state of supreme freedom, and yet whenever Jnaneshwar writes, he makes it quite clear, he does not serve as a screen to the glory of his Guru, on the contrary, he brings it out more fully. Everywhere he says, "It was by the grace of Nivrittinath (who was his Guru) that I am writing this. It is by his gracious favour that I am able to compose this verse." That is what he keeps repeating again and again.

If the disciple is imperfect, but behind him stands a perfect Guru like a solid primeval rock, the disciple shouldn't worry. A disciple, by merging his separate individuality in the Guru, becomes the Guru himself. He worships the Guru by becoming one with him.

Bill: *How may I come to fully know that the Guru's feet are the root of worship, how to fully know what the water or the dust of the lotus feet is, and how fully to drink that water, or kiss that dust?*
Baba: It is a great mystery which can be revealed only when you rise to a certain state. This is not a question that can be answered in a session of this sort. Let's see what the Guru's feet mean. The Guru's feet refer to the Being in whom the Guru stands rooted, and that Being is the Supreme Being, that Being is the highest truth. The root of worship is the state of the inner centre in which the mind completely merges itself in the course of meditation. The water of the Guru's feet is in fact the nectar which begins to flow from that root-source when one has achieved perfection through meditation. It is only when through meditation one gets into the state which is beyond the distinction of you and me, which is beyond the distinction of mine and thine, outer and inner, Guru and disciple, that one begins to drink this nectar, the water of Guru's feet. Do you find it much too subtle, or are you able to grasp it? The source of peace, the source of stability which the Guru has become one with, is the root of worship and when the Guru becomes centred in that source, the vibrations arising from there constitute the dust of the Guru's feet and drinking the water. After all, spiritual knowledge isn't that easy to grasp. It's not enough to write one or two books and begin to feel that one has come to know everything that one needs to know, because spiritual knowledge deals with the subtlest mysteries, and it is only after your heart actually opens more and more that you are able to understand those mysteries.

Purnama: *Could Baba explain the role of work for the Ashram in the relationship between Guru and the Siddha student/disciple?*

Baba: As long as the Guru and disciple, the father and son, remain different from each other, each of them feeling that he is separate, the relationship between the two will not have any validity, and it will not last because it will be without any true firm basis, it will be a bogus relationship. A son is the father himself in a different form, in every sense of the word, and he is heir to all that the father has. Likewise, a Siddha student is the Guru himself and is heir to all that the Guru has. One does not become aware of the full glory of the Guru because one has not yet become a perfect disciple. Once Hanuman was massaging the feet of Lord Rama and suddenly Ram asked Hanuman, "Can you say something about our relationship? What would you say if I were to ask you, who are you?" Hanuman answered and his answer is most significant. He said, "Now I am serving you so at this moment I am your servant. When I worship and adore you as the supreme Lord then I am your devotee. And when I become fully aware of the highest truth then I know that there is not the least difference between You and me. Ram is Hanuman and Hanuman is Ram."

And this is an authentic state. If a disciple were a true disciple, he too would be in the same state that Hanuman was in. And when a Siddha student is engaged in Ashram work, if he happens to be a true Siddha student, it's not a tree that he is watering, it's not a bathroom that he is cleaning, it's not a floor that he is sweeping, but he is rendering direct service to the Guru's body. If you can't look beyond a particular job, if you cannot see beyond what lies right before you, then you would not gain much. Say, for instance, if you are picking up leaves, if you think that you are only picking up leaves, then you cannot gain much through that service. Correct understanding would be that the Guru is the Siddha student, is the Ashram. The Guru, the student and the Ashram are one and the same.

Uma: *Exactly what type of self-effort should a sadhak living in the Ashram make?*
Baba: The highest object of self-effort of a seeker living in the Ashram would be to keep the mind, which is wandering all the time, firmly riveted on the mantra *Guru Om*—not to let it move, like the head of a person in the hang-man's

noose. Then a student should realise that the Ashram is nothing but an extension of the Guru's body or the Guru's form, so whatever belongs to the Ashram, all the Ashram property, all the Ashram things should be taken very good care of. An ideal student would make sure that all the things in the Ashram are kept neat and clean and they are handled carefully, and they are properly organised. The first, most important thing for a seeker is to achieve fullest concentration of mind, to make the mind completely one-pointed, to absorb it fully in meditation. And next comes the Ashram. A sadhak should consider the Ashram to be the most sacred place that he could live in, and surrendering himself fully to the Ashram, he should start working to ensure and maintain the purity and neatness of the Ashram.

Durga: *If one should have the attitude "I am God," rather than "I am a sinner," how is one prevented from performing bad actions and feeling justified through this attitude?*
Baba: How would such a person feel if somebody were to whip him half a dozen times? Because it is God Himself who is whipping him. The scriptures which tell you that everything is Brahman also enjoin upon you to keep away from sins, and you should not forget the latter part. Shall I narrate a story in this context? Shivaji was a king of Maharashtra, and he had an elephant. You know elephants are full of great love, but sometimes they run amuk, and that is what used to happen in the case of Shivaji's elephant, too. One day it so happened that the elephant flared up and became violent and destructive and began to uproot trees and plants and to dash people against rocks. That same day Ramdas was holding a big congregation, and all his followers had come to attend that meeting, including his chief disciple, Kalyan. The subject of the discourse was the all-pervasiveness of Ram. Ramdas began to deliver the discourse and he said, "By the grace of the Guru a seeker begins to realise that everything is permeated by Ram, there is nothing but Ram. Whatever is, is Ram, and whatever is not is also Ram." And Ramdas said in the end, "I proclaim in the name of God, that Ram and Ram alone exists."

This delighted all the listeners, most particularly Kalyan, the chief disciple, so much so that he became intoxicated like the elephant. After the congregation was over, Kalyan rose up and began to exclaim, "Ram is present on the right, Ram is present on the left, and Ram is everywhere," and he began to run in the direction that the elephant was coming from. In the meantime, four or five devotees rushed and seized Kalyan telling him, "Swamiji, it is true that everything is Ram, but that elephant has run amuk, and you should not run towards him."

But Kalyan did not listen to anyone. He rushed headlong, and the elephant got hold of him with his tusks and threw him a great distance. Then the elephant was brought under control and Kalyan was given some first aid, put on a stretcher, wounds bandaged, and he was taken to the Guru. When he came to, he said to the Guru, "You are a liar. You told me that everything was Ram, and I rushed towards the elephant taking him to be Ram, and this is how I have been treated by the elephant."

The Guru said, "Look, people warned you against rushing toward the elephant. Why couldn't you see Ram in that warning? Because you didn't see Ram in that warning, you had to suffer."

So suffering is the consequence of sin, and one should be able to see God in suffering also. The important question is, who is reaping the consequences? Ram will never resort to sinful actions, and Krishna never will. Therefore if you resort to sinful actions thinking that you are God, then you will suffer as God. This truth proclaimed by the *Vedas* that everything is Brahman should not be misconstrued to justify license and corruption and immoral conduct. This truth has been proclaimed in order to cultivate the vision of equality, equal love for all beings. And the knowledge that everything is Ram, that everything is Brahman, is not meant to get into the samadhi of conflict or strife. It is meant to get into the samadhi of equality-consciousness.

* * *

Now that summer is approaching, you have to be much more careful. Don't drink too much water. Exercise self-restraint and discipline. I am happy that all of you are working punctually and all of you are living here in a very nice manner, yet I would like to emphasise that everyone living in the Ashram should follow the Ashram discipline with complete fidelity: everyone should get up at the right time, go to bed at the right time, exercise restraint while talking to each other, and should carry on the Ashram work in a regular, disciplined manner. Whatever you do should have some order to it. Now that you get more free time in the afternoon you should read a little and you should also meditate a little. If you do not live a life of discipline and regularity, it means that you are not aware of your human dignity; you are reducing yourself to the level of germs and insects, beasts and animals.

Therefore keep on honouring your own Self; do not look down upon yourself. Nobody has attained anything without sadhana. If there is no kitchen, then no food can be cooked. So all this talk about instantaneous bliss, instantaneous realisation is bunk. You should realise that it is all ephemeral—this instantaneous bliss vanishes instantaneously. Therefore do not feel shy of sadhana, prolonged hard work. It is only then that you will be able to attain lasting bliss. There may be people uttering eloquent harangues, holding out all kinds of things, dealing out illusions most liberally—I can also write a book tomorrow saying that I could make you realise God by evening if you came to me in the morning, but that would be a lie. You should all be ready for a life of sadhana and work. You should all love discipline and regularity and you should not bother about what others are saying or doing. Remain concerned with your own Self, and live joyfully in the Ashram. If you were to study the life and character of the saints who achieved the highest realisation, you would realise that the highest realisation did not come to them in an instant. They had to work very hard for it, and they had to pass through a prolonged phase of intense tapasya and discipline. You must never forget that.

March 17, 1972

Penny: *Please explain the significance of animals and in-*

sects and how they should be treated.
Baba: Animals and insects do not have much intelligence, and they do not understand their situation, while we have been endowed with understanding and knowledge by the Lord, and we should treat them with an awareness of this difference. This is as far as the ordinary treatment of them is concerned. The spiritual viewpoint is entirely different from the worldly viewpoint, and the spiritual viewpoint does not take cognizance of outer form. To a spiritual person an animal is not an animal, an insect is not an insect, but his attention is focused on the inner essence of all life. Take, for instance, two persons who are looking at a gold ornament. One considers the ornament as an ornament and values it as such, while to the other the ornament is nothing but a piece of gold. Ordinarily our attention is attracted by the outer form, face and shape of the ornament, while the goldsmith is only concerned with the amount of gold in that ornament. From the worldly viewpoint, an animal should be considered as a creature who is without knowledge and understanding, while we have been endowed with knowledge and understanding. But from a spiritual point of view, an animal is a manifestation of the same Being that we are a manifestation of.

Noni: *During sleep and meditation I get a lot of dreams. Is there any way to induce or control it and convert it to deep sleep?*
Baba: How do you get dreams during meditation? Do you fall asleep? Then you should phrase your question differently and say, "During meditation I fall asleep and during sleep I have dreams." It is quite natural to have dreams and in any case dreams do not harm you in any way. For enjoying deep, dreamless sleep you should immerse the mind completely, at least for a while, in inward contemplation of God. Deep sleep is enjoyed by one who does not allow his mind to think too much and keeps it silent and still all the time. If there is anything for man to learn, it is to keep the mind silent, to keep the mind free from thoughts. The longer you can stay in this state of silence, the deeper your sleep will be.

You will not get dreams during meditation; you may get

thoughts. No harm is done if thoughts come into the mind. All that you need to do is to stay a witness to them. A wise person, a person with a true subtle understanding of things, would be concerned more about witness-consciousness during meditation, and he would not be bothered about how a particular thought arises, why it arises, why it is coming into the mind, and so on. You cannot change the nature of anything. For instance, the winter has passed and summer is approaching. And if winter has gone, then the cold is also gone. You cannot stop the cold from going, and you cannot stop the heat from coming, and if you were to make an effort that would be useless. You may be able to retain the cold or to stop the heat for a while, but you wouldn't be successful if you were to try to do it permanently. If it gets very hot one turns on an air conditioner, and if it gets very cold one turns on a heater. But a heater and an air conditioner are artificial gadgets, and you cannot change the course of nature by means of them. You may be able to save yourself temporarily from heat or cold, but you cannot eliminate them from the scheme of things. Similarly, it is the nature of the mind to keep on thinking one thing or another all the time. And the nature of the Self is to remain an impartial witness. Only when you become involved with the nature of the mind and you begin to disregard your own true nature are you in trouble. You should not be too concerned with the thoughts that come into the mind; keep on witnessing them as if from a distance.

Kedarnath: *It is sometimes seen that in spite of an earnest practice of the divine Name lasting for years, tendencies such as jealousy, egoism, pettiness of heart and narrowness of mind continue with unabated fury. What is the reason?*
Baba: The reason why these evil tendencies continue is that the devotion of a seeker is not aimed at self-transformation or self-purification or the experience of the inner Self or the Lord. It is flowing from some other motive. These tendencies do not abate because he does not make an effort to overcome these bad tendencies and inculcate good qualities. Passions such as lust, greed, jealousy and conceit have a strong effect on the mind. But there is no reason why the Name of God should not have an equally strong effect. The

reason why these tendencies persist is that the seeker does not perform sankirtan with the firm resolve that he shall overcome these bad qualities and defects.

It is very difficult to change one's character. It takes a very long time. Otherwise, an inner change must follow the practice of the divine Name. Tukaram said that as his love for the divine Name increased, his experience of bliss through the divine Name also became stronger. As more bliss floods the soul it is natural for misery and sorrow to vanish because the two cannot stay together in the same place.

Some seekers are only concerned with making a show of enjoying it excessively. But devotion bears full fruit only when one becomes completely free from slavery to public opinion. If a seeker is concerned all the time with what people are saying about him, whether they are speaking ill of him or praising him, if he is practising devotion only to win public approval, this is not true devotion. He is devoted only to public opinion, not to God, not to the inner Self. There is a very interesting conversation between Radha and her companion. Her friends tell her, "People are saying all sorts of things about you because you are neglecting your family and your husband and running after Krishna."

Radha replies, "Would you like to know what Radha says? I am so deeply engrossed in my love for Krishna that I have absolutely no time to listen to what people say about me."

This is the secret of devotion. It is only when a seeker turns to devotion with an ulterior motive such as trying to win praise from others, trying to show off, or trying to overcome the effects of a calamity, that he doesn't experience the depths of true devotion and consequently his character does not change, he does not become pure. The joy of true devotion is absolutely unique and whatever is not true devotion is a mere mockery.

Kabir talks about the character of such fake devotees in one of his songs. He says that such a one visits sacred centres, goes from place to place and conducts chants and devotional songs with such skill that his audience gets completely absorbed in the chant. But he himself is not aware of his true inner Self. He does not understand where he is, how much he has purified himself and how much of the distance he has traversed. One must find out why one has been born in this world, where one has come from and what the destination is. Kabir gives the example of a heron. He says a heron simulates meditation in a perfect manner. When he stands rapt in a meditative state it would be impossible for anyone to find out that he is only pretending. From the outside he looks like a perfect meditator, but his mind is completely impure, even despicable, because his motive is not to find God, not to achieve Self-realisation, his motive is to catch fish. By fish is meant the craving for honour, status and so on. Kabir says that a fake devotee never finds out about the inner Self; he is always entangled in outer worldly things. Therefore you must keep away from pretense, from mere show. If you were to take a true interest in sankirtan, in chanting the divine Name, it would not take you long to be transformed.

Barry: *What is the inner difference between mala japa, ajapa japa and meditation? Is there any daily limit to mala japa? Is writing a mantra of any value?*
Baba: Japa is a means to make the mind one-pointed. It is much better to do japa on a mala than to write a mantra. For meditation you do not need the mala so much; you may need it in the initial stage, and you may use it then, because in mantra repetition, it is not the outer beads which you keep turning, it is the inner beads. You should combine your mantra with your breath, repeat it once while inhaling and once while exhaling. Sit quietly in a corner and practise this method and then it will feel quite natural.

In my case the mantra japa goes on with breathing even during sleep. If you were to practise your mantra with deep faith and devotion, with genuine interest and great, intense love, you would find the mantra chasing you all the time. Now it is the other things which you take interest in which keep overpowering you; but after you have practised the mantra for some time with earnest devotion, then the mantra will overpower you. You should have intense craving for japa and do it with enjoyment, with profound inner taste all the time. If you were to practise it in that manner, you would find that japa would go on automatically in you even if you were unaware of it. What is of importance here is the intensity of one's interest in japa.

Unfortunately we do not know how to become fully aware of the meaning of the mantra that we are practising, like we become fully aware of the meaning of ordinary words in our daily life. It is of utmost importance for one to understand the full significance of the divine Name, to be fully aware of its meaning and importance. Read the writings of the great saints on the theme of the divine Name. See with what intensity they practised it and what they gained as a result. In Maharashtra there have been so many great saints who have practised japa and written extremely good books on the subject. I used to study them with great care.

In our everyday life we find that words have a strong effect on us. Even while we are reading our mind gets affected. Sometimes you happen to read an article in the newspaper with which you are not at all concerned, and which is not at all concerned with you, and yet you begin to feel that article is aimed against you and you begin to boil inside. In our daily life we can see what power sound, word, or language wields. Now I am speaking, and what I am saying is being recorded on tape with utmost fidelity. Similarly, the japa, the mantra that we do should become imprinted on our inner heart. What is recorded on tape will have great power, as much power as words coming from my mouth, and the same is true of japa.

We should track the course of a particular mantra right to its source—say a mantra such as *Guru Om* or *So'ham* or *Om namah Shivaya*—resting in that state of stillness from where the mantric sound emanates. To dive deep into one's inner Self along the ladder of the mantra is an activity which is full of great joy, great bliss. It releases tremendous love inside, and it floods the being with great sweetness. If one doesn't experience this inner sweetness, this inner joy, this inner bliss, which attends mantra repetition, it is only then that one begins to doubt the efficacy of japa, or he begins to blame other people.

Girija: *When I feel devotional it seems that in addition to feelings of joy, there is also a deep yearning for even closer*

contact with the Divine which is painful and frustrating. It is as though there is no way to get close enough. Did the great bhaktas such as Tulsidas and Sri Ramakrishna experience this, or did they enjoy devotion without pain?
Baba: You have completed one year of your stay in the Ashram today, and I am very glad to know that. You have served the Ashram in a most beautiful manner, and we haven't had any complaint against either of you, and thank you very much for that.

I am quite aware of the yearning and its pain. The sport of the Lord consists in this experience of bliss followed by separation. The state of viraha, or separation, is a very high state of sadhana. If one were to become proud whenever bliss begins to flow in the heart, then that bliss vanishes. This state of separation in which one feels acute pain for the Divine is a very good state. Paradoxically enough, this pain does not indicate any lack. It is pain that springs from fullness. Every bhakta experiences pain.

Whenever the ego begins to stir inside, it is followed by separation and separation is painful. When the ego vanishes and So'ham fills the heart, then there is pure bliss. I am not referring to the petty ego of worldly life, or the ego which craves honour and status and position. There is also a kind of ego which is associated with love, which begins to take pride in the intensity of its love. In the *Shrimad Bhagavat Purana* there is a portion called the Raslila which deals with a profound mystery. Different commentators have commented on it in different ways, and it is a theme of utmost importance. It is difficult for the intellect to fathom its mysteries. All the devotees were constantly praying to the Lord, "Lord, please show us Your true nature one day, the nature which the *Vedas* are unable to describe except by saying 'Not this, not this', the true nature which is beyond the perception of even yogis. We would like to see You as You are in Your innermost nature." This is also called mahabhav, the supreme state, the state of the Lord as He is.

To reveal one's own true nature is not an easy task; it is not like cooking puris or malpura. Somebody asks you to cook them and you cook them and that is the end of it. It was difficult for even Krishna to reveal His true nature.

229

Even though the Gopis had been with Krishna for a long time, they were not aware of His true nature. The Lord fixed a certain day to reveal His true state. The time of full moonlight was fixed for that purpose and the Lord instructed the Gopis saying, "Look, the moment I begin to play My flute, come running. I am not going to hear the plea that you could not respond to My call immediately because you had to take care of your husband or because you were held up by a baby who was crying, or you were busy cooking and you did not want the food to get burnt. Come the moment you hear the sound of the flute. Do not say that you could not come because you were busy putting on make-up, or you were out shopping and you did not hear the call." (Krishna was also aware of the fact that women have a weakness for shopping and once they go on a shopping spree, it is difficult to bring them back.) Now the appointed full moon night came, and the sun went down in the west, and the moon came up and all Nature was aware of the unique significance of that night because it was on that night that the Lord was going to reveal His true state. So the moon began to shine even more brilliantly, the Jamuna began to flow with much greater delight, the breeze began to blow with far more joy. A certain spot on the bank of the Jamuna had been fixed for this purpose, and the Lord had instructed that He would play His flute twice. The first time would be a warning, and when He began to play his flute for the second time, all the Gopis should be there. He would not tolerate any latecomer.

The sun had gone down, the moon had come up and the Gopis were getting ready for the great experience. One had loosened her tresses and was tying them up in front of a mirror. Another was giving suck to her baby. A third was giving food to her husband, and a fourth was playing with her children. Thus, each was busy with some chore or another. In the meantime the first sound of the flute floated in their direction. The minute the Gopis heard the first sound they forgot themselves completely and rushed towards the spot fixed for the great revelation. They forgot themselves to such an extent, that some of them were without upper garments, others were without lower garments, and there were yet others who were completely naked. There were some whose tresses were flying, but the only thing that they were concerned with at that time was the experience of the divine nature of the Lord, and no worldly consideration could hold them back.

Then each of these Gopis had a unique experience. As she was running towards the destination, she saw Krishna running towards her. None of the Gopis was looking respectable, because none of them had time to dress properly and yet each Gopi saw Krishna rushing towards her. She clasped Him with great love, forgetting everything else in the world. Each Gopi in this experience thought that she was the only one present with Krishna, there was nobody else around, and so she clasped Krishna with all her might and became completely immersed in that divine feeling.

When you are experiencing great bliss, that should make you completely silent. But what went wrong with the Gopis was that they became conscious of the fact that they were supremely fortunate, they were possessing the Lord in their very arms, so they began to emit grunts of great inner satisfaction. The moment a grunt came out of their mouth Krishna vanished from their arms, and each Gopi found herself grasping her own bosom. They glanced up and found Krishna sporting with Radha. As Radha looked towards the Gopis she felt a little contempt for them; she felt proud that she was the only one with the Lord in her full possession. Krishna vanished even from Radha's grasp, and Radha discovered to her dismay that she was only holding a tree in her arms.

As Krishna vanished the Gopis were plunged into acute inner agony. They began to cry and groan and weep and complain very bitterly, but to no avail. They had to return home in that state of great distress and pain.

The seer Shuka, while commenting on this experience, writes that the experience of love is so subtle, so profound, that even the consciousness, "I am enjoying the Lord," goes against it. That is what makes the experience of divine love so unique. When a seeker merges himself completely in the love which bubbles up within, great bliss is experienced. But the moment the seeker becomes aware, "I am experiencing such great love, how fortunate I am," then love vanishes, and it is only the ego which remains. And that is the pain. Ruskhan says in a song of his that whenever he achieved self-oblivion he found the Lord; but the moment that he became conscious of his separate existence, he lost the Lord. This is what must be happening in your case.

* * * *

Summer is approaching and you shouldn't drink too much water. And be extremely careful about what you eat. Keep pursuing your sadhana earnestly, meditate regularly, and do everything punctually. You should not fall a victim to smugness. If you were to enjoy a couple of malpuras on a particular day, that should not make you fly into ecstasy, feeling that this is the purpose for which you are here. Continue to meditate with great love, continue to do your sadhana with great love.

March 20, 1972

Shankar: *The main trouble I have in sadhana is finding the right pressure to maintain—not too loose, not too tight. Can Baba give me advice on this? Is it ever justified to tighten up so that your joy is decreased?*
Baba: You must realise that sadhana is tapasya—it is hard work, it is not a bed of roses. To walk on the spiritual path is not like touring the country as a wealthy tourist, staying in big hotels and seeing beautiful gardens and eating rich foods. There is no such thing as tightening yourself too much. It is only those people who have not been doing any sadhana who begin to feel that they are tightening themselves too much. Take for instance a person who has never practised the lotus position. If he were to sit like that even for a few minutes, he would begin to feel the strain, while we can sit for hours without being conscious that we are sitting in a particular posture.

Discipline or self-restraint is necessary, not only for a yogi, not only for a seeker, but also for a person who is living an ordinary life in the world. Restraint must be exercised in the matter of food and sleep and so on. If in your ordinary life you do not exercise any self-restraint then you end up in a nursing home. Even in your everyday life you have to control your sleep, your food, and your recreation, and if you don't do that you won't be able to live life successfully. If you go to bed late at night you get up late in the morning, and you are not saving any time by going to bed late at night. We go to bed early at night and rise early. As far as conversation is concerned, you should talk only as much as is necessary; there is no need to talk more than that. Do you remember the story I told you the other day about Kali Yuga appearing holding his tongue? A talkative person cannot keep his mind focused on the Lord. He cannot do japa either, nor can he hold sublime thoughts in his mind, nor can he reflect on them. You should talk only as much as is necessary for your normal life. You shouldn't talk too much and you shouldn't talk too little. You don't have to become absolutely indifferent to your friends, and at the same time, you don't have to become too friendly with them. It is just like putting a limit on the amount of food that you are going to eat. Once a great professor from Iceland or Greenland came and stayed here with us for quite some time; he used to wear khadi. He would sit in my presence for a quite a few hours, at a distance, not utter a single word, and then leave. When he came the only word that he uttered was, "Good morning." At that time I was practising vigourous control in food. I was only taking coffee and dry bread. At the time some devotees brought bread for me on Saturday and I had to make it last me until the next weekend. Babu Shetty, Desai and Venkappa, when they came here, would bring some loaves of bread and that would last me until the next weekend. Usually it so happened that he came when it was time for me to take coffee. I would give him bread and a banana and coffee only on Sundays, because until Sunday whatever had been brought to me would be fresh, but on other days it would become stale, so on other days I didn't give him anything. In spite of the fact that I was a disciple of such a great Guru, I did not let anyone know what my condition was, I didn't let anyone even suspect it. For a long time that professor came every day and sat silently for hours together and then left. He followed that routine day after day, and I would keep sitting there exchanging conversation with devotees who came along, like I do now. Then after about five months there came a certain devotee who happened to know English. Now that I had found an interpreter I asked the professor from Iceland if he didn't ever feel like asking me anything.

The professor said, "I have nothing to say, because I am making an effort to get your love without exchanging any words with you."

Then I said, "Look, if we were to begin to talk to each other we would have a stronger relationship between the two of us, and we would understand each other much more and our inner link would become stronger." He was also a great poet.

He said, "That may not be the case necessarily. On the contrary what may happen is that if we begin to converse our love may begin to change."

And he narrated a story. An English girl married a Russian boy and the love between the two of them was a silent love, because they didn't know each other's language. They were communicating with each other on a subtle level, and they were living very happily. Thus a number of years passed and they had three children and yet weren't talking to each other. One day it so happened that a scholarly guest who happened to know both languages, Russian and English, landed at their place. Both of them honoured him very much, and they asked him to stay with them for some time. The husband and wife would hold conversations with him separately, and they would talk to him with great love, but he never found them talking to each other and this surprised him. One day he said to them, "Look, I have been here quite some time and I haven't heard you exchange a single word with each other. How can you possibly love each other if you are not able to speak to each other?"

They said, "For love we don't have to speak to each other, and even though we haven't exchanged a single word with each other we have had three children and we are quite happy with each other."

The professor wanted to know the reason and the husband said, "Look, I don't know English." And the wife said, "I don't know Russian."

The professor said, "Look, you shouldn't have any worry on that account, because I know both languages," and he began to teach English to the husband and Russian to the wife, and the husband and wife began to talk to each other. The guest did not stay with them forever. After some time he left. Before the scholarly guest had come they were loving each other on the basis of subtle inner understanding, but now that gave way to superficial contact through words. Now that the two could communicate with each other on the level of language, sometimes they would say things that would hurt each other, sometimes they would talk too much and sometimes they would talk less. The perfect harmony which was between them was upset and they began to have more and more quarrels. One day they had such a bitter quarrel that they decided to divorce. They then separated. They started living in different houses.

After a few days that professor appeared on the scene again. He was on his way back and he wanted to say hello to them again. He asked the neighbours where that couple was and he was told that the two had fallen out with each other, that the girl lived in that room and the boy lived in that room. So he went to meet both of them. He asked them in a tone of surprise, "Look, you loved each other so much, and you even had three children. How could this present rift come between you two?"

Both of them said to him, "Look professor, if you wish to know the truth, this is your gift to us."

It appears that the same holds true between us. We understand each other on a subtle level and that is one reason I am not learning English, because if I were to start learning English I wonder whether the same thing that happened to that couple would happen to us.

It is always better to talk less rather than more. Because if you talk less then you will be spending more time in the remembrance of the Lord.

However, you should not strain your body while practising a particular discipline. If you can sit in a meditative posture and meditate for one or one and a half hours that would be enough. Besides that you should be doing your work assignment most punctually without anyone having to check you. During the remaining period you should learn to keep your mind still, to keep it empty and you should make a vigourous effort in that direction.

To fall asleep during meditation doesn't mean that your mind is weak, it only shows that the mind has stopped thinking. Whenever the mind stops thinking it falls into sleep. It stays awake only as long as it keeps wandering among external objects. For some time you shouldn't interfere with what is happening to you. You shouldn't force yourself to stay awake in meditation. There will come a time when you will pass beyond sleep. As you go beyond this sleep you will be able to slip into higher consciousness, the state of tandra, where you will become aware of many things you cannot perceive with your gross senses. But as far as conversation is concerned, you should reduce it to the minimum. And that applies to everyone present here. I, too, do not like people who talk too much. You should talk only when it is necessary, and if it is not necessary to converse, then keep silent. Silence is the best way of honouring other people, and besides, then you will not be getting on each other's nerves. Talking too much is a disease and it doesn't show any intelligence on the part of those who indulge in conversation.

Ram: *I have been alternating between muttering my mantra and repeating it inside with my breath. I wonder whether I should continue this method of a fixed number of japa or increase it? Should I devote more time to witness-consciousness methods and object meditation and less to the regular japa meditation that I have been doing?*
Baba: Whatever limit or number of malas you have fixed for yourself, first do that. After that you should begin to use the mala of the prana or the mind, which is much superior. Repeat your mantra once while inhaling and once while exhaling. That is very fruitful. As you keep on doing your mantra with the breath, witness-consciousness will come to you naturally. There is no such thing as exclusive practice of witness-consciousness—leaving everything aside and devoting all your attention to witness-consciousness. I understand there are teachers who are holding courses in witness-consciousness and who teach people how to stay a witness. I have no objection to that. After all, it is a new age and novel techniques are in the air and there is nothing wrong

with them. But then the question arises, what exactly is the nature of witness-consciousness? I can explain it by a very simple example. Here Amma and Uma are taking notes. I don't know exactly what they are writing, I am only watching them write. And that is what witness-consciousness is. There may be another person meditating and if I am watching him from a distance I am in witness-consciousness. If a criminal dispute arises between two persons and the case comes to a court of law, then the judge while interrogating the victim would ask him, "Well, I accept the fact that you were thrashed and it is quite obvious that somebody did hit you, but I would like to know if you have a witness who would testify?"

Similarly, to keep on watching while inhaling and exhaling whether you're saying your mantra or not, that is what witness-consciousness is. The inner witness is awake all the time, and is watching whatever is happening. It is not at all difficult to watch what is happening there and you don't have to take special training for that. To keep on watching whether the mantra repetition is going on with the respiratory rhythm or not is a very simple form of witness-consciousness and you can practise it wherever you are. But the inner witness is of the highest importance, and a meditator should meditate on the inner witness. It is that inner witness which is the goal, the object of meditation. The sages say that the inner witness is without attributes; it is pure consciousness, the Lord Himself. It is the inner witness who is the Sadguru and you should always be aware of that inner witness.

Purnama: *Is the process of the ascent and transformation of the seminal fluid the same in women as in men?*
Baba: The fluids of men and women are different. In our scriptures man's fluid is called virya. There is a different word for woman's fluid and that is raja virya. But the process of the upward movement of virya or raja virya is the same in man or woman, though the fluid may be different. After your inner Shakti has been awakened your virya or raja virya will begin to ascend upward above the navel chakra. For that one should meditate more and more intensely. This process of the upward flow of the seminal fluid

is an exceedingly joyful process. This is the most significant process. The fluid begins to move upwards until it has reached the sahasrar and then it begins to flow downwards and again it moves upwards and that cycle goes on continuously. The technical term for this process is urdhvareta. When the time for this process arrives, it is preceded by the drawing upwards of all the abdominal and pelvic organs. When that begins to happen you can feel certain that now the time has come for the fluid to begin flowing upwards. When that happens all these organs, visceral and abdominal, are drawn upwards and a pit is formed. It is only after you have become established in this upward flow of the seminal fluid that you begin to enjoy true joy. The joy which you experience through the downward flow of the seminal fluid is not joy at all. True samadhi comes after that, not before.

There is absolutely no difference between men and women with respect to chakras or the nerve structure or the Kundalini Shakti. It is the same in both, identical in both.

Olivier: *Now I feel that the essential part of my body is my abdomen; it is hot, and when I walk to the garden, for instance, it is as if I carried it. During meditation all my concentration goes to my abdomen. I am very quiet, sure, solid as a statue and with my inner eye I can see my body sitting in place meditating, and often I fall asleep. What is the meaning of concentrating on the abdomen, of seeing my body in meditation and of falling asleep?*
Baba: Where exactly on the abdomen does your mind get focused? On the navel chakra or the solar plexus? Very good. In fact, there is a recognised method in which the seeker is asked to concentrate all his attention on the navel chakra and as a result of the Kundalini awakening, this method comes spontaneously to certain people. How is your appetite? (Good.) What you are saying is quite correct, because when the attention becomes focused on the navel chakra the digestive fire begins to burn more intensely and the appetite is increased. The abdomen is the breeding place of all diseases and through this concentration all illnesses will get burned.

If you are seeing your body like you see somebody else

sitting at a distance from you, that indicates a very high state; and that is the state of pratik darshan, the vision of one's own physical form. You shouldn't resist sleep during meditation because sleep indicates that the mind is getting free from anxiety and becoming one-pointed. However, you can tackle sleep on a very, very subtle level and if you could overcome it on that subtle level then you would enter into the realm of pure light. All the Hatha Yogic processes are, in fact, meant for the purification of the abdominal region. There is a poetic saying in the Marathi language and people interpret it to suit their own weaknesses and the saying goes like this—"The stomach comes first, and the Lord afterwards." Now people interpret it to mean that first you must pack your stomach with all kinds of food, then remember the Lord. But the true meaning of that saying is that first you should purify the abdominal region. The six purificatory exercises outlined in Hatha Yoga are meant for that purpose. It is a strange irony that these days one finds the tummies of Hatha yogis bulging out. What is the use of practising Hatha Yoga then? It is very essential to keep this region pure, to keep it in good shape. What is happening to you is quite valid.

Rana: *Is it not enough if I can have the darshan of my Sadguru in my daily meditation? Is it necessary to see all the various lights and so on?*
Baba: You get a vision of the Sadguru in meditation only after having crossed all the other stages, after having seen all the other lights. After you have seen the Sadguru, what's the point of minor experiences, because that is the highest experience. One poet says, "If I have had a dip in the ocean, what is the use of my having a dip in a pond or in a river?" If you are envisioning the Sadguru, what is the point of all other minor or secondary experiences?

Bill: *How may I, above all, be true to myself in act, in words, written, spoken and sung, and in feeling, desire and thought?*
Baba: What is your condition now? Are you true to yourself now or not? What exactly is the point of your question? In this connection Tukaram Maharaj says that he who is him-

self practising what he is teaching to others, so understanding the full value of what he is telling others, he is not deceiving himself. He is being true to himself. To have no faith in oneself is to deceive oneself, to be untrue to oneself. To have faith in yourself is to be true to yourself.

One form of self-deception is to appear to the outside world in a manner which is different from what you really are inside. There are many seekers, in fact, there are many of this type amongst my students, also, who keep on praising me to the skies in my presence, saying that they have gained so much from me, they have gained this experience and that experience, and what not, and I keep on listening to them silently. But it is seen that when the time of test comes, such seekers turn away without the least difficulty and this is what is meant by self-deception. One who is not pretending to be other than he is, one who is not showing off, one who is not projecting an image of himself which is quite contrary to his inner reality, is being true to himself, he is not being his own enemy.

March 22, 1972

Virendra Kumar Jain: *If a devotee has a very strong desire to drink the sacred water of the Guru's lotus feet, does the Guru fulfil his desire?*
Baba: The questioner is a poet and a poet always puts a question which puts the speaker in difficulty. Why won't the Guru fulfil it? In fact, he must. There is a certain episode in the *Ramayana* in which Kakabhushandi and Bharadwaj, the two great sages, meet each other. In the course of their discussion it is brought out that if you have a very strong desire for something, and if this desire arises from pure love, from pure devotion, it is bound to be fulfilled almost immediately.

It is true that the water of the physical feet of the Guru has some importance, but its importance is not that great.

I have seen many teachers, who after initiating their students would stick out their legs so that the student could wash them and drink the holy water. I am dead against this attitude. I don't permit people to wash my feet. I hardly even permit people to touch my feet. There is no point in assuming Guruhood or pretending Guruhood. If Guruhood descends on you, if it comes to you from the Divine, then there is some point in washing the feet and drinking that water. But to wash the feet of a pretender won't do any good. To drink that water would not benefit you, in fact it may bring you harm. From an Ayurvedic point of view, it is obnoxious. You are not drinking anything sacred, you are only drinking dirt, despicable dirt. It is not the water of the Guru's physical feet which will make you immortal, it is only the nectar flowing in the Guru's abode situated in the sahasrar which will make you immortal and that nectar can be received by the grace of the Guru.

In the course of your meditation, when the mind becomes stabilised in the sahasrar, this nectar begins to flow. Only after drinking this nectar can you be said to have drunk the water of the Guru's feet. The Guru is bound to fulfil a true desire of his devotee, but I must repeat again, that it is not the water of the Guru's physical feet which matters. The true feet of the Guru lie in the sahasrar; it is the nectar flowing from them which gives immortality. A meditator can gain access to this nectar only through meditation, only through the grace of the Guru.

Kedarnath: *You have said many times that the japa should go on in the throat region. Please tell us how we should get the japa to the throat region from the tongue and what is the difference between the two.*
Baba: You should not confuse the physical part of the tongue with the whole of it. In fact, we have not just one tongue, but four tongues, and these four tongues belong to the four bodies. The physical tongue belongs only to the physical body, and functions for the physical body. If you keep repeating the mantra with your tongue for a certain length of time, being fully aware of its inner meaning, the mantra itself will descend to your throat region. You can not make it go deeper by your own effort. Even if you tried you

would not succeed. The japa which is practised with the tongue is on the gross level of speech and no matter how long you practise it, it will not bear much fruit. The japa must pass from the gross level to the subtler levels to bring you the inner fruit. As one keeps on repeating a mantra with the tongue, with great love, in course of time the japa descends to the throat region. While seated in the throat region the individual soul passes into the world of dreams.

As its power increases, the joy increases. The bliss of japa on a subtler level is indescribable. You also begin to have visions of gods and goddesses and you begin to get into the state of tandra, the state of higher consciousness. There you perceive all sorts of things that you cannot perceive with the physical sense organs. That is the throat region.

From there the japa must descend to your heart, and the third tongue is situated in the heart. When the japa descends to the third level, the Pashyanti level, the heart, the bliss increases greatly and one becomes so overjoyed that he begins to dance. It is at this stage that one begins to experience God as sublime bliss, as supreme delight. At this level one comes to gain many other powers and advantages. The centre of knowledge becomes available. Talents of poetry, music and art and others are also realised, and one also acquires supernatural powers, not only for exhibition, but powers by means of which he can promote the good of others. Then one's word comes to have power and whatever one happens to utter is bound to bear fruit, bound to come true. But that isn't the end of the journey either. You have to go beyond the heart to the navel region. You have the fourth tongue in the navel region, the deepest level of speech. When japa goes on in the navel region you can hear it and also feel it. This is the stage in which one gets the highest vision, the final vision.

The path of Japa Yoga is a simple, straight and easy path and one can follow it without any strain, without the least difficulty. Lord Shiva tells Parvati that siddhis come through japa, and Lord Krishna also says in the *Gita* that of all sacrifices, He Himself is the sacrifice of japa.

It is of the highest importance. If you were to make a deliberate effort to get the japa from one level to another, you would not succeed. In fact there is no method by means of which you could succeed with that. The only way for a seeker is to continue to practise japa with single-minded, undivided devotion, and then the japa passes on of its own accord.

Malti: *What are the signs of a jivanmukta? How does an enlightened being conduct himself? What qualities should a Sadguru possess that would cause us to remember him every morning, and perform worship to him twice every day?*
Baba: There are two states, the state of the soul in bondage and the divine state, that is the state of freedom. And these two states correspond to two different levels of knowledge and understanding. What you think of yourself, how much awareness you have of your own worth, what the extent and depth of your knowledge is, all depend on the state which you are in. Let's take two states, waking and dream. A millionaire with a vast retinue of servants to attend him, enjoying all comforts and luxuries and power, with guards posted at the gates to his house, retires for sleep. During sleep he passes into a dream state and sees himself as a beggar who is afflicted with some ailment, and he begins to beg from people passing by. And everyone only looks at him with contempt, paying no attention to his groans and pitiful condition. In the dream state he is not at all conscious of the fact that he is not a beggar, but a millionaire, because that knowledge belongs to the waking state.

Therefore, your idea of what you are depends on what state you are in. There is yet another state which lies between these two states, the waking and dream state, and that is the state of lunacy, and in that state one is not at all conscious of one's duties or responsibilities. One no longer respects his mother as his mother, his father as his father. He would enter any house and would be thrown out forcibly without understanding what is happening to him.

There are different views of man, philosophers have stated different theories as to the nature of man, but the fact is, that man is nothing but the state that he is in at a given moment. It is a result of the state that he is in at a given moment that he experiences happiness.

In the state of bondage, the individual passes from one state to another, from the waking to the dream, from dream to deep sleep, from deep sleep back to waking and this cycle goes on endlessly, interminably. This is the ordinary state of bondage. It is in this state of bondage that the individual continues to experience pleasure and pain, and sometimes it happens that he experiences pain in the midst of pleasant circumstances and pleasure in the midst of unpleasant circumstances. As a result of the strength of the merit he has gained, he comes to meet his Guru and receives his blessing and his inner sadhana begins. As a result of that inner sadhana, which has been made possible by the Guru's grace, he advances to the state of Turya and it is in that state that he becomes liberated, that he attains divinity.

Before becoming liberated the individual is conscious of himself as a limited being, he sees himself as belonging to a certain caste, having a certain status, belonging to a certain race or country, as having a certain amount of power, a certain amount of wealth, and his vision does not go beyond these categories. He remains in the limits of these identifications. But once he is able to attain the state of Turya, through the grace of the Guru, he begins to feel, "I am Shiva, I am perfect, I have no caste, I have no country," and his consciousness of himself as being divine is as intense, as full as his consciousness of his being a particular individual was in a different state. So this is the state of liberation, and that was the state of bondage. In the state of bondage, one thinks of himself as being an individual, but in the state of liberation one looks upon himself as being divine. In the state of bondage one is aware of himself as being a body, but in the state of liberation one is aware of himself as being pure spirit, Shiva Himself. You may call it egoism if you like, but that is what it is.

In the second chapter of the *Gita* the Lord describes the various characteristics of the enlightened being or a sthita prajna. This term consists of two elements, prajna means reason or intellect, and sthita means to make it steady or stabilised. So a sthita prajna is one who by means of meditation makes his intellect steady, centres it. Such a being is never affected by the good or bad consequences of the actions which he may happen to perform in his daily life. And his reason is so firmly rooted in the Divine Being, that whatever actions he may be engaged in in his daily life, he will not be affected by them in the least. Whether his actions are brutal, cruel, or gentle, his inner state remains uncontaminated by what is happening on the surface. His intellect is so firmly established in his divine source that he will pick up weapons and go and fight a war with the same faith, with the same zest, with the same adoration with which he would worship the Lord, pray, or meditate. For him, all activities are alike.

It is only as long as our reason remains unstable that we remain victims of a discriminating mentality, or a mentality which distinguishes between high and low, ferocity and mildness, gentleness and harshness. Last year, or maybe two years ago, when I was going to the south there were a few students of mine who were in a serious accident and were placed in a hospital in Madras. When I reached Madras I was very keen on visiting them in the hospital, and I went there. There was only one thought in my mind, and that was to go visit a couple of girls. When I came into the corridor a man came up to me and asked me rudely, "Where are you going?" I said, "I am going to ask about two students of mine who are here." The man said, "You can't go in there, it is the ladies' ward." And I said to him, "Then what are you doing here?" And Colonel Rao was behind me, and he hinted to the attendant that he shouldn't get into an argument with me, and he took him aside, and I went in and saw the girls and came out. I was not at all conscious of the fact that I was in a ladies' ward where I was not supposed to be, that there were women who were half naked and others who were completely naked. I was only concerned with a couple of students of mine. I was so possessed by the thought of visiting my students that at that time I could not be made conscious of the fact that the ward that I was going into was a woman's ward and I was not supposed to go in there. So such is the power of an intellect when it becomes steady.

An enlightened being performs all actions in a state of total freedom, without being affected by the limits of social demeanour, without being aware of the purity or impurity of what he is doing. It is prajna which is the superior faculty in man, and it is this which enables one to become an orator or a good writer. Unless this faculty has begun to function one cannot do very much in life.

We recite the *Guru Gita* every morning and we also hold a group worship of the Guru thrice every day. There must be many seekers here who are worshipping the Guru more than three times. There are different kinds of teachers in this world. I met so many different kinds, but I could not worship any of them as a Sadguru. I did respect some of them and I did learn certain skills from them, I did acquire certain knowledge from them, but I could not worship any of them as a Sadguru. It is one thing to be a seeker, it is one thing to be doing sadhana while being a householder, but it is something else to be a Guru. Guruhood is the noblest institution. Even Divine Beings like Ram and Krishna worshipped the Guru, and bowed at the feet of the Guru for enlightenment and knowledge. So such is the true glory of a true Guru, and his abode. A Sadguru is a most extraordinary being. His birth is an extraordinary event, his life is full of extraordinary events, all his actions are extraordinary, and the way in which he leaves his body is also extraordinary. A Sadguru must have a pure body. He must possess knowledge in its completeness. His range of knowledge must include everything in this world, right from the *Vedas* to archery, Ayurveda and other skills to the most ordinary arts. A Sadguru by the power of his Guruhood divests even his physical body of its grossness and endows it with full consciousness. He has achieved total self-mastery. A Sadguru is in complete possession of himself. None of his sense organs can ever lead him astray because he rules over them like an unchallenged sovereign. The flow of semen of a Sadguru must be directed upwards, and in the ancient times the Gurus were tested as to whether they were urdhvareta or not. When the seer Shuka went to King Janaka, he was put to a test. Shuka, a young boy, was made to live in the palace where beautiful queens lived for many days, yet his semen never started flowing downwards. A Sadguru does not get into the state of bondage even for a moment. If he were in a state of bondage, we would not be worshipping the Sadguru, we would be worshipping bondage, and what's the point of worshipping bondage? We might as well worship ourselves in that case. We could wave lights to ourselves and stand before a mirror and perform worship, and in a mood of self-congratulation, feel elated. But a Sadguru is continually established in the sahasrar, and he does not come down from that state even for a second.

Another mark of a Sadguru is that if you live with him, in course of time you lose your bondage and you become liberated like him; you become him, in fact. You do not live with him for the sake of petty advantages, things you may receive from him. Purandardas was a great poet. He was honoured recently by the entire country and some of his poems are in the form of questions and answers. A question was put to him once, and that was, "How does one recognise a Guru? On the basis of what qualities could we say for certain that a particular teacher is a Sadguru or not?" Every year a large number of devotees used to visit him and one year one devotee put this very question to him. "How to know a Sadguru for certain?" Purandardas said, "A Sadguru is one from whom you receive initiation. Your inner sadhana starts, and in the course of fifteen months, if you are able to have an experience of the samadhi state, then you can feel certain that the teacher that you are with is a Sadguru." People used to gather there every year on a particular occasion, and the next year the same gathering was held and the same devotee appeared and the same question was put. And then Purandardas said, "A Sadguru is one by living in whose presence you will have the actual experience of samadhi at least three times." The third year the same devotee appeared and put the same question. Purandardas said, "Well, do not put this question again. The Sadguru who is worthy of our highest worship is one in whose abode the moment you enter you enter into samadhi, you become samadhi itself."

A Sadguru is one as a result of whose influence we undergo an inner transformation and in whose presence we automatically go into a state of samadhi. A true Guru is one who transmits his own divine power into his disciple and as a result of that initiation, the various yogic practices take place within the disciple, and in course of time he transmits his own state to him. A Guru is one who transmits his own inner state to his disciple, who transforms a disciple totally and makes him utterly like himself.

March 24, 1972

Jag Bhandari: *How does one dedicate all activities, both religious and secular, to the Guru?*
Baba: When a disciple becomes a true disciple of the Guru, he doesn't have to dedicate his activities—they become dedicated themselves.

Where is the person who put this question? (In Bombay.) How can he listen to the answer? Are you going to send it by post? Why are you going to all this trouble? What stops him from coming here once a week to attend a session? If I wanted to put a question to the questioner right now, how would I do it?

You don't have to dedicate your activity if you dedicate yourself. If you surrender yourself, all your activity will automatically be dedicated to the Guru. Once a devotee has become completely the Lord's, he doesn't have to make another independent effort, a separate effort to dedicate his worldly activity to the Lord. Take the case of a person who comes to the Ashram and says, "Baba, I feel that I belong to you totally." Then the next moment he were to ask me, "Baba, here is a beautiful coat that I am wearing, how shall I dedicate it to you?" How could I answer this question? All that I can say is, "Have you left your coat outside at the flower vendor's? If you have left it there, then it is all right, you can dedicate it, but if it has come with you, when you surrendered yourself, the coat has also been surrendered as part of it. If you have left it outside then probably you will have to dedicate it to me later." Therefore, when the devotee becomes the Lord's completely, whatever he has, whatever he does, is automatically dedicated to the Lord in full awareness of Him all the time.

I'm sure you remember the story of King Janaka which I narrated to you once, of how a brahmin came to his court and began to abuse him. A congregation was being held at the court of Janaka, and Yajnavalkya was present. Yajnavalkya was speaking and Janaka was listening. In the meantime, a brahmin appeared and asked Yajnavalkya to stop for a minute, and asked money from Janaka. The king kept silent, he did not give him anything, and the brahmin began to use very harsh words for the king, but the king did not react. The brahmin became so irritated that he began to abuse him. He did not stop at that. He got so angry that he lifted up his hand to hit the king, saying, "Look, you are the king of the land, the ruler, and you are supposed to be the protector of all of us, and you have so much wealth. I am in such trouble, I have to perform the sacred thread ceremony for my sons and yet you are not willing to part with a single penny. What kind of king are you, you insensitive brute." The courtiers thought the brahmin had gone out of his mind and so he was driven out. Then the courtiers asked the king, "You have so much wealth, and yet you did not give him any, in spite of his repeated entreaties. Not only that, when the brahmin abused you, you remained silent. You are supposed to be such a great hero, such a valiant warrior, what happened to your valour, what happened to your heroism when you heard all those terms of abuse?"

For three days it went on like that. Janaka had surrendered everything to his Guru, even royal authority. After three days Yajnavalkya returned everything and said, "Janaka, now rule the kingdom on my behalf." What makes you think that the Guru would not behave like Yajnavalkya? If you have surrendered everything to the Guru, won't the Guru return everything to you? What possible use could he have for the things which you possess?

Raul: *After some time in the Ashram I have come to love you and I am very grateful for the opportunity you have given me to improve myself, yet I haven't been able to feel that you are really my Guru, despite the things I have learned here. Is it that you are not to be my Guru, or is it that my ego is so impure that I am blind to the fact? Please help me clear up my mind.*
Baba: It is only when you become a disciple that I will become your Guru. If you do not become a disciple, how can I become your Guru? The question of the ego being pure or impure does not arise here. How can one become your Guru if you haven't become his disciple? Once during my school days I read a humourous story. There was a boy and a girl. They were great friends to each other, yet the girl would say

to him again and again, "It doesn't seem as though you are my husband." And the boy would say, "Look, you haven't married me, so how could I be your husband?" So how can you accept me as your Guru if you haven't become my disciple? The question of ego is entirely irrelevant here.

Carol: *For a few days my feet have been burning. A friend told me that this is sometimes a symptom of vitamin B deficiency. Is this true in my case?*
Baba: I can see that you are meditating very intensely. Whenever you sit you glide into meditation, and you are meditating as much as any seeker should. When one begins to meditate intensely, the Shakti begins to eat up some of the flesh of the feet, and it is then that you begin to get the burning sensation. But there would be no harm in your taking vitamin B, because that, too, is food. You can take one pill every day. I keep watching you: your meditations are very intense and during intense meditation it does happen sometimes that when the Shakti is eating up the flesh of a particular part, it does begin to burn.

Kedarnath: *How can a seeker save himself from all kinds of deliberations and thoughts and fancies and imaginings and passions such as greed, and desires which he had forgotten a long time ago, which become active in his mind once again?*
Baba: It may appear to you that you have forgotten certain things, but those things remain present deep down in your mind, and it is very difficult to forget them at that level. All these desires and thoughts lay embedded in the knot of the heart. The impressions of countless births remain latent in the sushumna nadi. Sometimes they rise to consciousness. However, once the Kundalini awakening has taken place and one has begun to meditate very well, then all these impressions are brought to the surface by the Shakti in easy installments and expelled from the system in course of time.

There are three kinds of seekers. The highly deserving, the moderately deserving and the very, very ordinary. As far as a very highly qualified seeker is concerned, he is not bothered by these thoughts and desires, whether they are good or bad. He knows that the food which he eats every day also produces some waste matter, and waste matter is being continually discharged through the different openings of the body—through the eyes, through the ears, through the nose, and the anus—he knows that old waste matter is being thrown away and new waste matter is being formed continuously. A highly qualified seeker knows that it is the characteristic of the mind to keep on producing all kinds of thoughts and desires, good as well as bad, from the inner void; they keep on arising all the time.

Knowing this, knowing the true nature of the mind, he does not get upset by these contents, which appear from time to time; he keeps watching them impartially like a witness and he is not bothered by their goodness or badness; he remains calm and tranquil.

Take the case of an obscene painting. There may be people who would be shocked when they looked at such a painting, but as far as the painter is concerned, to him that painting is nothing but a pattern of the colors made with the same brush with which he is painting other pictures as well. Likewise, in the mind all kinds of thoughts, passions and desires keep arising. The seeker is not concerned with them at all; he watches them from a distance. His composure is not disturbed in the least, because he knows that all kinds of things, all kinds of contents keep on coming up to the surface. And he makes no effort to drive these things out of his mind; he remains calm and tranquil all the time. As a result, his mind also becomes steady in course of time. The mind sheds its restlessness and it begins to become one-pointed also. He is also aware of the truth that all these thoughts and feelings and desires are nothing but the divine substance itself. It is the divine substance which is throbbing through all these forms, some of which appear ugly and bad to us, while others appear to be beautiful. As he understands this supreme truth, he stops fighting with the various mental contents and stops trying to get rid of them. This is the way of knowledge, this is witness-consciousness, true witness-consciousness. The other two kinds of seekers would get after their bad thoughts, fight with them, try to overcome them, try to push them out of their minds, and they would engage in constant warfare with themselves. In the course of time they may succeed in overcoming these so-called undesirable thoughts. What could Kedarnath possibly lose? Say there is a certain bad thought which has arisen in the mind. That hasn't made you smaller—the real you—and when that thought goes out of the mind again, you do not become bigger as a result of that. You remain the same. High meditation consists in watching, in the understanding that the seer is much greater than the seen, the thinker is much greater than the thought. And this understanding makes a seeker absolutely calm.

Girija: You say that there is no knowledge of the waking state while in the dream state, yet I feel that my dreams are becoming more conscious. Often I am aware that I am dreaming, and try to change a dream if I don't like it. Also, I remember that I am doing sadhana, and have to be careful of what I do. It seems like a mixture of the dream state and meditation. What is this state? Also, should we think about our dreams afterwards as you recommended with meditation?
Baba: In the dream state you are conscious of dreams, you are not conscious of the waking state. The state that you are experiencing lies at the meeting point of the dream state and the state of meditation; it is neither full meditation nor full dream state. I still say that in the dream state you are no longer conscious of the waking state. You can, however, become conscious of the dreams that you are having. Each state has four aspects. If you get fully absorbed in a state, whether meditation or dream, you would not be conscious of another state at all. When I am trying to sleep, there is a phase in which I am somewhere between sleep and waking, and in that phase, I am partly conscious of what is happening in the outside world, and partly unconscious. But that doesn't mean that I am in the sleep state and yet conscious of the outer world.

The experience that you have described shows that you are very alert. To be able to remain conscious even while dreaming shows that in meditation you are very, very alert and wakeful. You must be meditating at a very subtle level. What is happening is that while meditating you glide towards sleep, and you don't cease meditating. So as a result of that you remain conscious of your dreams. If in that state, sleep tries to overcome you, let it overcome you and see where it leads you. There is a certain state, a very high state of meditation, in which you are neither awake nor dreaming, nor asleep. People say all kinds of things. There are some people who come to me and say that they are experiencing very deep meditation, and I ask them, "What's happening?" They say that they are very conscious of what is happening to them. Some people complain that they remain conscious while they are in deep meditation, and I say, "Look, deep meditation does not mean that you become a stone. Deep meditation doesn't mean that you lose awareness. Deep meditation doesn't mean that you become divested of understanding. If you were to lose consciousness, then who would know what is happening to you during meditation, and who would experience the samadhi state?" The true state of meditation is a state of full consciousness, a state of full awareness. Yet it is a state which is neither the waking state, nor the dream state, nor the deep sleep state. It is different from all these three, and yet it is a state of full awareness. If you were to lose your awareness, then there would be no difference between you and a mass of inert matter. The fact that you are aware that you are dreaming shows that you are becoming more centred in witness-consciousness. Do you see any light, soft light in this state, light which is neither white nor black nor blue nor yellow, slightly saffron? As you go further, a soft saffron light will arise in this state and envelope you. If you were to have a vision of this light, you would sometimes be able to see the outer world in this light. In the state of meditation, one should stay fully aware, fully alert, fully vigilant. One should get away from the waking state, from the sleep state, from the dream state, and at the same time one should not get away from the meditational tandra. There is no need to understand it on the intellectual level so much. As you begin to meditate, further experiences will come to you themselves.

Larry: *Would you please speak about the practice of Gurubhava, and the secret of making it steady?*

Baba: If you let go of your consciousness as a disciple completely, then whatever remains will be the Guru-consciousness. Gurubhava is the state of pure consciousness, which is different from all thoughts, whether good or bad, all feelings, whether desirable or undesirable. Don't you sometimes have the experience of self-forgetfulness? It may be occasioned by anything. That is Gurubhava, and that is a true state. If you completely overcome your consciousness of being separate from the Guru, or being a disciple, if you eliminate all other thoughts, what remains behind is Gurubhava or Guru-consciousness. Radha was established in Krishna-consciousness. That was the reason Radha was honoured so much. The other day someone asked me why Radha was considered to be more important than the other Gopis. Radha would get so completely absorbed in Krishna-consciousness that she was no longer conscious of herself as Radha—so much so that she would even begin to ask her companions, "Where is Radha? What has happened to her, where has she vanished?" The on-lookers would look at her and wonder what had happened to her. And if there were some clever, modern types among them they would have probably caught hold of her and locked her up in a mental hospital. You should get rid of your consciousness of Larry.

Kalyani: *Would you please explain the relationship between tapasya and inner growth. Was the suffering experienced by the great bhaktas as a result of their separation from their beloved sufficient tapasya, or did they undergo other austerities?*
Baba: Inner growth comes as a result of tapasya. When your tapasya begins to bear fruit, you begin to grow inwardly. This separation from the beloved is a very effective means to union with Him. The more acute the pangs of separation are, the sooner will a devotee be united with the Lord. Poet-saints have described this state most beautifully. The condition of a devotee who is suffering from a sense of separation from the Lord is like that of a fish out of water. A devotee is troubled only because he feels separate from the Lord. Though he has already become one with the Lord, he feels separate from Him. This is not the state or condition

of one who is actually separate from the Lord and trying to become one with him.

Pratibha: *What exactly is it that moves a person established in the state of perfection to make decisions or undertake different works? Is he acting from his own independent intellect, or is the Chitshakti driving him and making him move and act, while he remains a witness?*
Baba: If there is still something left for a person to do, it means that he hasn't achieved perfection—he is still imperfect, because the state of perfection implies that he has done all that was necessary for him to do. There are many clever, educated people who used to raise this question about my Guru, Baba Nityananda. They would say, "This man has such enormous power, and yet he does nothing for the good of the world." But these people forget that as long as a saint is aware of the world as the world, he is not a saint. He becomes a saint only when the world has vanished completely. So for Nityananda, the world existed no longer. So what was he going to reform? It is only for an ordinary reformer that the world exists as a separate entity.

Once I read a poem of a saint who used to live in Poona. He was enlightened and he was a great friend to me. I was very fond of him. He says in his poem, "O reformer, your own heart is the world, so first reform it. When you yourself become reformed, or when your heart becomes reformed, then you will find the world to be in a perfect condition."

So-called social workers don't seem to be conscious of what they are doing. They build a new bridge. The old one is breaking, and the new one will also break, and they will have to build another. There will never be respite, because while they build a new dam, the one which was completed yesterday has burst.

If one has achieved perfection, it means that one has done everything that was necessary. However, there is such a thing as the invisible hand of destiny, and as a particular being has certain functions to perform in the world, destiny impels him to perform that function. You should ask this question again next time.

March 27, 1972

Draupadi: *Babaji does not approve of the actual pad-puja to the Guru. What about mental pad-puja to the Guru?*
Baba: When you are doing pad-puja, or when you are worshipping the physical feet of the Guru, it is the Guru that you are honouring. And when you are worshipping them mentally, it is your own Self that you are honouring. Manas puja, mental worship, depends entirely on the pleasure and sweet will of the worshipper. Your mode of worship depends on the sense organ or instrument which you are using for that worship. The quality of worship depends on the quality of the instrument which you are using. The Lord says, "Of all the sense organs, I am the mind." That implies that the mind is superior to all other organs. Therefore, mental worship is a million times superior to physical worship. No other worship can compare with mental worship. It is usually seen that the wise do not perform gross worship, they perform mental worship, sitting quietly some place. Likewise, they perform japa mentally, and they go on pilgrimages also mentally, not on the gross level.

In our ordinary conversation, we sometimes ask another person, "Are you speaking from your heart, or are you only pretending?" Kabir says in one of his songs, "There is a certain sacred centre which is dear to me, and I would like to know who is it who would undertake a pilgrimage to that? Who would like to worship that sacred centre?" He says, "I take a dip in the holy Ganges mentally, I also visit Kashi mentally. Who is prepared to undertake this kind of pilgrimage?" The water of the Ganges, and soap and all your cosmetics may be able to wash and adorn your physical body, but can they ever penetrate to the inner Self, or to the mind? He adds, "I sit inside the mind and I meditate inwardly and then I plunge into deep peace. So, who will undertake this kind of pilgrimage?" Kabir says, "O, you sadhus here, who has the time to wander from one place to another?"

Therefore, whatever is done with the mind comes to have a very great importance. And in another poem, Kabir says, "He who has not seen the inner Self, who hasn't purified the mind, who hasn't removed the stains from his heart, what would he gain, even if he could sit in a posture for a long time?"

Among the Pandavas, it was Bhima who was performing mental worship. All the people used to complain to the Lord about Bhima, saying that he was utterly indifferent to all spiritual practices and obligations, that he didn't bother to get up early and wash himself, he didn't bother to do japa or meditate, that he was just fooling around, or sitting like an idiot. It is like some people here complaining about some of their companions, that they don't get up early, they don't do this, they don't do that. People were complaining against Bhima constantly and one day the Lord said, "Look, mind your own business. Don't bother about Bhima. He will mind his own business."

Finally Arjuna got completely fed up and said to the Lord, "Lord, it is too much. It is far more than I can bear. Bhima eats like a pig and he either sleeps, or when he sits up he doesn't seem to do anything, he sits idly, his lips don't move in a gesture of japa, and he does not count the beads, and he doesn't show interest in any ritual. What should we do with him?"

The Lord said to Arjuna, "Look, Arjuna, you should not get upset about it, because I know Bhima through and through. Bhima is a very great aspirant, and he is performing all his spiritual practices mentally. He is offering worship mentally, meditating silently and inwardly, and you shouldn't worry about him. Bhima has enormous strength, he has got so much power that he can even raise the Lord before him. So you should not worry about him." The Lord also added, "Bhima could accomplish easily what it would require you to undertake long penance to accomplish."

But Arjuna did not feel satisfied and again complained, "Lord, Bhima is utterly idle, and he doesn't practise any of the disciplines."

Arjuna was very particular about external forms. He had learned how to perform the correct worship and so on, and he thought that anyone who did not practise these external modes was utterly lousy and an inferior creature. Then the Lord suggested, "Arjuna, sit down calmly and begin to meditate inwardly and try to find out whether

Bhima has practised tapasya or not, and how much power he has acquired."

Arjuna began to meditate and he got so absorbed that he traveled to a different loka, called Satyaloka, which is quite close to Siddhaloka. He saw that in that loka there were thousands and thousands of people carrying huge baskets of flowers and moving in a certain direction. In that vision, Arjuna asked them, "Where are you carrying all those flowers?"

They said, "To Satyaloka, because in Satyaloka flowers don't fade and we are going to preserve these flowers there for a long time, and wait for a certain mortal to arrive there from earth. The name of that mortal is Bhima. Bhima is a great aspirant, because he is worshipping the Lord mentally all the time in a proper manner, making all sixteen offerings to Him. We are waiting anxiously for him to honour Him."

This amazed Arjuna. He was so amazed that he came out of meditation and opened his eyes and saw the Lord sitting by his side. He addressed the Lord saying, "Lord, I have seen a most miraculous vision. Could You explain it?"

The Lord said, "What you have seen is true. That is what will actually happen."

Mental worship has a great importance. I worshipped the Shivalingam mentally for a long period of time. I would perform that worship in the elaborate scriptural manner and it would take me about two to two and a half hours to finish it. But this was all on the mental level. I would create all the articles for worship from imagination. As a result my mind would get completely occupied. In fact, I wanted just a part of my mind to get a little restless, so that I could create more articles for the Lord. I used to create so many different things that my mind would get completely absorbed, completely focused, and I would start wishing that it would get restless again. I would imagine that I was worshipping Shiva and after all, all that we experience is imagining, and the best thing is to get rid of one kind of imagining with another train of imaginative thought. So in my imagination I would build up a temple, and that temple was studded with the most precious gems. And in that temple I would install a Shivalingam with diamonds and I would have a gold jar with which I would pour water on the lingam. Afterwards I would get cow's milk. Then I would wash it with coconut water, then pure water. Then I would wipe it with a precious bit of cloth, and rub a piece of sandalwood and prepare paste to apply on it. And I would not let this train of thought break at any moment. Since I would not have to prepare anything on the physical level, I could afford to imagine anything. After applying the sandalpaste I would create prasad. First I would create gold vessels, gold plates and other gold utensils and I would also imagine all sorts of flowers and I would arrange them around the lingam. While arranging them I could visualise the lingam very clearly. I could even inhale the fragrance of the flowers. And I would conjure up the images of all the flowers that I knew, and then I would make offerings of rich sumptuous meals to the lingam. I would fill my different gold utensils with kheer, basundi and seera and all the other delicacies I could think of. That was the way I rendered mental worship to the Shivalingam.

In Patanjali's *Yoga Sutras* there is an aphorism which reads, "When the three become one, then you achieve what is called samyama." The three are dharana, dhyan, and samadhi. I would get completely absorbed—so absorbed that I would completely forget myself, and that was how I was practising this aphorism. There are yogis who, in order to practise the technique embodied in this aphorism, practise tratak. They try to fix their gaze on a particular spot. Many of them damage their eyes in the process, or they damage their respiratory rhythm. But I was practising samyama in the most easy and natural manner by performing mental worship. My mind would get completely focused, completely centred. All the miraculous powers come at this point. God-realisation is still far, far away. It is as a result of this mental worship or this inner concentration that a yogi comes to acquire all the miraculous powers. That wasn't the end of the mental worship, there was still another phase of it, and that was the phase of meditation. I would turn to myself and regard my body as a temple of Shiva, and my inner Self as identical with Shiva, and my intellect as Shiva's consort, Parvati, or Girija, and my sense organs as Shiva's companions and this way I would begin to meditate, identifying myself with Shiva, with the mantra *Shivo'ham*,

"I am Shiva." I would be lost, rapt in meditation for a while and this is how my mental worship ended. After some time I stopped performing mental worship to the Shivalingam and I began to render it to my Guru, Nityananda Baba. I would install him in all the different parts of my body—he is in my feet, my legs, and thighs and so on—and thus I would achieve complete identity with him, complete oneness with him. And thinking myself to be Nityananda, I would meditate.

The various miraculous powers have their origin in the mind, not in divine consciousness. The mind, which keeps wandering all the time, should be brought under full control by this method. In the beginning, a seeker may feel slightly bored. But as he persists in this mode of mental worship, after a while, he begins to enjoy it. He also begins to have most marvelous experiences. The image which is being worshipped mentally soon acquires a certain radiance, it begins to emit light, it begins to glow, and then many other experiences occur which are most amazing. We know from our own experience that when we think of a beloved friend our mind is filled with love and joy, but when we think of an enemy, our mind is filled with hostility, with anger. Therefore, anyone who hasn't been able to acquire control over his mind can acquire control by performing mental worship. Those whose minds keep wandering too much, whose minds are far too restless, could practise mental worship with tremendous gain.

Uma: *Does external behaviour eventually change internal feeling? For example, if I remain silent or pleasant to someone when inside I feel he is an incompetent fool, am I doing the right thing? Isn't it hypocritical to act one way but feel another?*
Baba: What makes you think that all the people in the world are wise or clever? Baba Nityananda was fully enlightened, but are all people fully enlightened? He knew that there were so many fools around him, and yet he would look at everyone as an embodiment of the same Lord, and he would not regard them as fools, much less call them or treat them as fools. There must be many in this assembly who must be quite foolish, even stupid, yet does that mean

that I should start treating them as fools, or I should scorn them or despise them as fools?

During the days of my wanderings, I would meet all kinds of characters, including thieves and robbers. In those days I had hardly any possessions, I used to wear just a loin cloth and have a wrap around my trunk, and there was nothing with me which could be stolen. On the contrary, if I hung out with thieves, they had to feed me. Once I ran into a character who was later on caught by the police and hanged. I asked him, "Why do you rob people?" He said, even proudly, "It's my family tradition, I come from a family of illustrious robbers." And he took great pride in his particular kind of crime.

Now from my point of view, what he was doing was utterly foolish, but from his point of view, what he was doing was a matter of pride. He was trying to live up to his family tradition. I did not want to impose my notions of wisdom or cleverness on him. I said to myself, "Look, what he is doing is his concern, not mine." I was quite happy with the meal he fed me, and left the next day.

Then there was a very great man, a most strange character living in Karnatak, named Nagalinga. He behaved in the most strange manner. During the day he would hit people with his stick mercilessly, and at night he would give the most enlightened discourses on spiritual themes.

In the Vedantic scriptures there is a mantra, the meaning of which is, "When a householder looks at an ascetic, he says to himself, 'Look at that bum. He is utterly useless. He isn't doing anything for society. He is a parasite, living off others, and he is utterly stupid'. When a sadhu looks at a householder, he says, 'Look at that wretch, that sensual slave. He hasn't realised the utter futility of pleasure, and he is still rolling in piggish mire'." The householder thinks that the sadhu is a fool, and the ascetic thinks that the householder is a fool. Who is going to decide who is actually foolish?

We should be concerned about what really is our concern. There is absolutely no need on our part to overstep the boundary of what should concern us. Just a few minutes ago, Sudhaka came up with a note containing a question, and I did not accept it. I sent him back, and I shouted at him, because it is not his job to give people's questions to us. And what was the questioner doing for the last three days? How come he thought of it at the very last moment? So right in the middle of my lecture, I began to shout at Sudhaka because he was doing something that wasn't a part of his job. One should first make oneself sure of his particular field. Therefore, one should be concerned only with one's particular department or sphere, and one should not be concerned with what is happening in a field which doesn't concern him.

During your spare time you should be absorbed in the inner Self. Also, why should you waste time and energy on trying to reform another character? In many cases you may just be spoiling yourself in an attempt to reform another person. Why should you disturb your own peace of mind? You should not butt into what you are not concerned with. It is, of course, true that one should not be arrogant, or egotistical, or conceited, but it doesn't mean that one should lose discrimination.

Now, if somebody comes to me and asks me whether there is room for him in the Ashram, I tell him to go ask Desai. Does that mean that Desai is my master? Does it indicate that I am subordinate to Desai, or that he is lord over me? Or that I can't make a decision in the matter myself? It shows that I have entrusted this job to him, and I rely on him for that job utterly. Then there are other people who come for darshan, and after taking darshan they tell me quietly that they want to see the gardens. But I tell them, "Look, I am only authorised to bless you. If you want to see the gardens, you should go and talk to Shankar about it." But does that mean that I am scared of Shankar, that I myself can't ask somebody to go with that person and show them around? If I have given orders that the office must be closed at a certain hour, then it must be closed at that hour, regardless of who is sitting inside; even if Secretary Desai is sitting inside, he should be thrown out and this is what I told Sharda Amma very clearly. If there is anybody who wants certain things from the store, then I ask him to go approach Durga because that is her job. Some of the local boys who are employed here come to me sometimes sneakily and ask me permission to go on leave for a day or two. I ask them, "Did you ask Venkappa? It's not within my power to grant you leave." This is what organisation means, this is what discipline means. No matter who a person may be, whether a trustee or somebody else, I would not tolerate any interference from him as far as the organisation, the administration of the Ashram is concerned. It is, of course, true that there are men and men, and there are people who need to be reformed.

Therefore, one should exercise restraint. If there are feelings which have become strongly entrenched in you, they will not be changed by external behaviour. There was a great Vaishnava who was a butcher, and though he was slaughtering animals, inwardly he was a great devotee of the Lord, and his external behaviour did not affect his inner devotion. Take the case of Kanupatra who was a dancing girl. If there is an attitude which becomes firmly established, it doesn't change, whatever your external behaviour may be. Take the case of Sergeant Kumar who was here a few days ago. He is a naval officer, and he fought very bravely in the recent war, and he is a very good meditator. Though he fought bravely, that war did not affect his inner heart or mind.

Try to stay composed as much as you can and look upon all equally.

I could speak for at least two hours on mental worship, because that is a subject that is very dear to my heart. I spoke very briefly, yet the time is up.

March 29, 1972

Visitor: *What is the cause of diseases such as diabetes, epilepsy and cancer spreading so much these days? Do they result from the bad karma of the past life or the present life? Is it possible to conquer these diseases through the repetition of the divine Name, through mantra japa? Can one acquire the fortitude to bear with them?*

Baba: These diseases can be completely conquered through repetition of the divine Name. Tukaram Maharaj in one of his verses asks, "What is it that cannot be accomplished through the repetition of the divine Name, can you tell me?" Generally speaking, it is true that the roots of such diseases are in a past life, but they arise in the present life. It takes, for instance, a long time for epilepsy to develop, and if there is a child who is suffering from epilepsy it would be difficult to understand how he could have got it, if you reject the theory of past karma. Through repetition of the divine Name, self-control and regularity in daily life, one can attain not only supreme peace, but one can also conquer all these diseases.

Whatever happens in this life has its roots in past lives. Our present body owes its existence to the contact of the bodies of our parents, which occurred before this body. Therefore, one should think good thoughts again and again, and one should try to understand the truth with subtle penetration. One should not be after purely fleeting advantages. One should be far-sighted and try to achieve a state which will last, which will endure and for that it is necessary to practise tapasya or self-control for a long period of time. Japa, or repetition of the divine Name is a very great method.

Visitor: *The body is inert, without consciousness, so it cannot experience pleasure or pain and the soul is completely detached, it has nothing to do with the body, so what is it that experiences pleasure or pain?*
Baba: It's a very strange question. You are experiencing pleasure and pain every day in your life, and you want me to answer your question. This reminds me of a story relating to Ram Tirth. He was going abroad in a ship, enjoying looking at the sky and the blue ocean very much. Poets and saints enjoy the sight of the sea and the sky very much, because the sea and the sky are like the Self which is always detached. There was a passenger who was lying by his side, who had fallen asleep. That fellow began to have a dream and in that dream he saw a tiger with three horns rise from the sea. The tiger came into the ship and hit him in the ribs, as a result of which he began to suffer from acute pain, and

he began to scream and this woke him up. He was greatly frightened, and in that state he said to Ram Tirth, "Swamiji, where is the tiger?"

Ram Tirth asked, "Which tiger?"

"Didn't you see him? The three horned tiger who hit me just a few minutes ago."

"Our ship is moving in the sea, so how can a tiger come here?"

"I saw him myself in a dream."

"When you saw him you were dreaming, but I am in the waking state, so how can I see what you saw in your dream?"

This question is just like the question of the man who was hit by the tiger. It is he who experiences pleasure and pain and he wants me to tell him who experiences pleasure and pain. Nonetheless, it's a very good question, a question of a high order, and one which we should think very deeply about. First we have to find out whether we are experiencing pleasure and pain all the time or only in certain moments. The experience of pleasure or pain is not a fixed experience. Quite often it happens that we are experiencing pain in the midst of happy circumstances and pleasure in the midst of very bad circumstances. So the experience of pleasure or pain depends on time and place and our condition or state. Here we are feeling the heat so much, but if this very heat could be transported to Srinagar, the people there would be very happy, because they are freezing at this time. The people in Kashmir are suffering very greatly from the cold, and if that cold could be brought here, we would be happy about it. What is giving them pain would give us pleasure, and what is giving us pain would give them pleasure.

The Lord explains it beautifully in the second chapter of the *Gita*. He says that pleasure and pain belong only to the antahkarana, the inner mind, and they are felt when the mind comes into contact with the outer objects through the sense organs. Experiences of cold or heat, or pleasure or pain are momentary. They arise and subside, and the best thing for a wise man to do is bear them with fortitude. Take the case of a man who is suffering from acute pain in his lower arm, and the pain is so acute that he is screaming and waiting for sleep to be able to forget this pain for a while. He happens to glide into sleep and even though the pain is present, he doesn't feel it. After he wakes up he begins to groan again, because the memory of pain returns and you find him saying, "I slept peacefully for two hours and during sleep I wasn't at all conscious of the pain. It is only after waking up that the pain has started harrassing me again."

Take the case of another man who is mentally disturbed and who has most frightful dreams, so he is scared of falling asleep. He takes every possible measure to prevent himself from falling asleep. On the one hand you have a man who wants to fall asleep to overcome his pain, and on the other hand you have a man who doesn't want to fall asleep because he is afraid of the pain that he may experience during sleep. It would be difficult to say which state the experience of pain belongs to—the waking state, or the state of sleep.

It is a very important question, to decide who experiences pain and pleasure—the body is without consciousness, so it cannot feel pain or pleasure. And if it could feel pain or pleasure, then this chair would also experience pain or pleasure. The soul does not experience pain or pleasure and the soul lies much beyond the state of sleep. Sunderdas, the great poet-saint says in one of his verses, "The body or the five sense organs, the five organs of knowledge and perception, and the five organs of action, and the four-fold inner antahkarana cannot experience pleasure or pain because they are without consciousness, and the soul too, will never experience pleasure or pain because the soul is pure consciousness, the soul is always beyond the reach of such experiences. It is only as a result of the union of the soul and the body that the experience of pain or pleasure is had."

It is during the present state that the soul seems to be one with the body. This is the state of ignorance, or the state of delusion. One can see this state clearly only in the highest state of liberation. So, it is only when we are identified with the body, when we consider the body and soul to be one that we experience pleasure or pain. It is only in the state of identification with the body and the mind, the state in which we consider the eyes to be 'my eyes', the ears to be 'my ears', the mind to be 'my mind', that we experience pleasure or pain. To understand the immense power of delusion, the immense power of this false identification, we can take an example from our ordinary life. Take the case of a village where two families are living in two opposite houses. There is a street between the two houses and there is a girl in one family and a boy in the other family. Now the girl and the boy have had nothing to do with each other for years and years, they don't even know each other, and one day it is decided all of a sudden that they are going to be married and they get engaged. Now each begins to identify with the other, each becomes attached to the other. In course of time, the attachment between the two becomes so strong that each begins to feel happy in the happiness of the other, and unhappy in the unhappiness of the other. If one begins to suffer from the least pain, then the other one goes into agony—so much so that if one happens to run a slight temperature, the other almost loses his mind and in sheer agony may fall unconscious and the doctor may have to come to give him an injection to bring him back to normal consciousness. This is the result of identification of two people with each other, two persons who never knew each other before.

Nothing on the surface of this earth lasts. All relationships seem to be transitory. After some time it so happens that the boy and girl fall out with each other and they decide to break up their relationship and after the relationship is broken, again they become indifferent to each other. One's pain or pleasure does not affect the other at all. Now though the two still exist, one is not affected at all by the other. And what has happened? Who was experiencing all that pleasure and pain when they were attached? And who is it that has stopped experiencing the pleasure and pain when that relationship came to an end? It was obviously false identification, wrong understanding which caused all this pleasure and pain—avidya, or ignorance, which is not a separate entity, which is only a name of lack of right knowledge or lack of right understanding. It is this which produces false identification of the Self with the body, and it is on account of this that the experience of pleasure or pain is had. The experience of pleasure or pain belongs neither to the body nor to the Self. Both are free from it. The spirit is without any stain, and so is the body. It is only the intermediary who joins the two in a wrong connection who experiences pleasure or pain. But to see clearly, to perceive it directly, one has to meditate very deeply and get into the state of Turya. If a person is even slightly intelligent, he would be able to understand it by taking the example of a person who is under anesthetic during an operation. Even when he is being cut by a knife he doesn't experience any pain. And this is due to the fact that the connection between the inner centre of feeling and the seat of pain has been broken. It is the antahkarana, the four-fold inner instrument, which makes it possible for us to have the experience of pleasure and pain. It is, in fact, the antahkarana itself which experiences pleasure and pain. The soul is supremely pure, it is without the slightest stain, it is the Supreme Being itself, so it is beyond the experience of pleasure and pain.

Miss Borse: *Christians criticise the Hindu religion on the grounds that it preaches individual salvation with no concern for one's fellow beings and their happiness. This is why, they say, India is in a state of mass degradation. Do you agree that the Hindu religion is individually oriented and that it lacks in social conscience?*
Baba: Can you have society without individuals? It is individuals who compose the society. It is only when a certain number of individuals come together that a society comes into existence. If an individual were to aspire for liberation would he be doing sadhana for himself, or would he be able to save all the others belonging to that particular society? Which religion is it that can distribute salvation to all the members of a society like you distribute cloth to the poor, or sweets or something else? If there is poverty in India, it is not because individuals in this country have been seeking liberation, it is because of dirty politics prevailing in foreign countries. It was foreign nations that sucked the blood of India; and since we attained independence, poverty has been overcome to a great extent. When you come to India again you will find it even in a much lesser degree.

I have been abroad and I can say that you don't find so much degradation in India as you find in other countries. If you go to other countries you find that people are swallowing more and more medicine and pills and more and more hospitals are being opened up, and more and more doctors are being needed and the surgical science is making rapid advances. What does that indicate? Does that indicate progress or degradation? It only depends from what standpoint you look at a particular country. From a certain standpoint I could find the same degradation prevalent everywhere. It all depends on your approach to a particular country, and if your approach is defective you will find that country extremely degraded.

When I was in Oakland a boy asked me, "Is it true that there are many beggars in India?"

Then I asked him, "Do you have any beggars from India in your country?"

He said, "No, we don't have them here, they don't leave their country."

Then I said, "Look, India has large numbers of beggars from your country." (That boy's friends were very angry with the boy for having put that question.) If India is poor, it is because of the bad policy of other countries. But now, of course, we are no longer victims of foreign countries and we will overcome poverty and enter into a new era of prosperity.

If there is anyone who criticises another religion, whether he is a Hindu or Christian or Muslim, he is absolutely stupid and this I can declare without the least fear, and I will declare it anywhere. What do they know about Hinduism? This kind of criticism springs only from illusory understanding, and in fact, it is gross selfishness, it is partisanship which is behind it. Inner peace is not the exclusive property of any particular religion, whether Hindu or Christian or Muslim. God has not appointed an exclusive middleman. He never authorised anybody to go and tell others that if they were to approach God through him alone they would achieve salvation. I am against any narrow, fanatical concept of religion or any narrow mentality, and I am also against 'isms', though I am a great worshipper of God; because God is beyond all this religious strife or these religious differences. Those who turn their ideas away from the path of truth and begin to criticise another religion are only behaving like petty traders who would advertise their goods, saying that our goods are far superior to the goods produced by another factory. Criticism of one religion by another would only produce differences. If there is somebody who is criticising another religion, then the followers of his religion will begin to doubt the validity of the religion which he is defending.

You cannot attain liberation by building beautiful highways, or by building high dams or very big factories. You can find liberation only by turning your attention within. There is no such thing as communal salvation, because liberation, strictly speaking, is the inner state of a particular individual who has striven towards it. Whatever religion it may be, it cannot grant salvation to entire mankind, or to a whole society.

David: *Because all Gurus are the same, divine, does it follow that the disciple does well if he leaves the one meant for him to follow another?*
Baba: Take the case of a person who claims that you can get complete satisfaction regardless of which hotel you are staying in, yet he changes his hotel. What does that indicate? If he is feeling fully satisfied with the hotel that he is staying in, is he leaving that because he is fully satisfied with staying there, or is he leaving that because he is dissatisfied there? Then the question arises of a particular seeker who has been initiated and set on the path of sadhana by a certain Guru, and who has been practising his sadhana for a length of time—whether he is leaving him after he has completed his sadhana, or in the middle of it. If he has already achieved perfection, what need is there for him to go to another Guru? And if he hasn't achieved perfection, if he is still struggling, is he going to another Guru so that he may be able to advance from the point that he has reached under the guidance of his present Guru, or is he going to a different Guru to start from scratch? Take the case of a student who has been studying at a certain college, a college which is properly organised and has a certain discipline and which follows a certain system. He has taken up a certain course of study there. Would you regard him wise if he were to leave it half way and seek admission to another college? Because there he would have to start from scratch.

I can assure you that whatever Guru you go to, there is

no escape from sadhana, there is no escape from discipline. If salvation could be granted just by a wave of the Guru's hand, then it would be granted to everyone in the world. And it would be better in that case for such a glorious Guru to get on the top of a mountain—on the top of Mount Everest—and wave his hand from east to west, north to south and grant liberation to entire mankind. Those people who think that you get liberation without sadhana, with just a miraculous wave of the Guru's hand, are labouring under an illusion.

It is, of course, true that all the Gurus are the same. Let's say, the Gurus who belong to the Vedantic path would say the same thing more or less. The Gurus belonging to the devotional schools would have obvious similarities. The Gurus belonging to the systems of yoga would be very much like each other. But what need is there for a particular seeker to keep on wandering from one Guru to another? I am not against changing one's Guru if one doesn't find the present Guru answering his particular needs or corresponding to his particular temperament or condition.

Girija: Because of unfamiliarity with traditional Indian puja, I have done my own version of manas puja, which involves entertaining Baba in America. There is a lot of shopping because I must design a house with Baba's quarters, etc. Since there is no prescribed ritual to follow, I can follow my mind wherever it leads. Is this manas puja, or mere fantasy?
Baba: It is the sincerity of one's feeling which has the highest place in manas puja; in any mode of worship it is the feeling that is far more important than the ritual. There is, however, nothing like feelings coming together with ritual. There was a great woman saint in Maharashtra who was called Bahinabai, and it was said that she had seen the Lord in a vision. In a song of hers she celebrates the glory of feeling. She says that by means of intense feeling one can achieve liberation without any difficulty. So it is the purity of feelings which is of the utmost importance in mental worship. The inner Self has infinite power and through entertaining a strong thought, one would be able to accomplish what one has in mind. I am quite conscious of what you

are up to, and you will succeed. But you won't be put to too much trouble if I come to America. My food is very simple. I just take rice and one vegetable, so you won't have to labour very hard. While I am in India, I take spiced foods, but when I went abroad I took only boiled food, so it would be less trouble for you. While I was in America I was eating boiled vegetables and rice. I am fond of strawberry yogurt which you can buy in any store. When I was in Utah staying with Prof. Salunkhe, one of the local papers mentioned on its front page that I was fond of strawberry yogurt.

God is the religion which transcends all religions. God is the kind of businessman whose goods you can buy without any middle man. You should try to gain direct access to Him.

March 31, 1972

Chandra: *For the last four months my relationship to you seems to have changed. Whether I stand near you or not seems to make no difference to me. At the same time my love for you has not lessened, but the quality seems to have changed. I seem to experience you more inside than outside. Is this feeling real, or am I just deluding myself?*
Baba: The fruit of worship is that one begins to experience the deity within rather than without. The worship of the Guru is not like the worship of a deity where the worshipper looks upon oneself as being different from the deity. In our life in the world also we find that we may honour or love or respect a person very much, yet we consider him to be different from us, and we never achieve oneness with him. It is very different in the case of the relationship with the Guru. The Guru has to be realised within. It is not just enough to stand for a while in his presence, or to extend reverence to his physical form. After all, how long can you do that? The reward of true worship is to feel close to the

Guru from within, to realise the Guru within one's own heart, and to begin to rely on the inner Guru more and more. As far as the outer Guru is concerned, it is quite possible that sometimes you may feel offended with him, and at other times you may feel great love for him, and in a moment of anger with him you may feel that you want absolutely nothing to do with him.

When I arrived in Melbourne, a certain person who when he was here claimed to be a student of mine, did not come to meet me. It was only after a few days that he came to meet me. I asked him why he had not come on the first day and he said, "Well, I didn't come because I was angry with you."

I said, "Why were you angry with me?"

"Because I haven't been blessed with a child so far."

I said, "It's strange that you should accept me as your Guru just to be blessed with a child. As far as I am concerned, I have nothing to do with the child, nor am I very much aware of how a child is born." Then I said, "All right, you haven't got a child yet, but how are you?"

"Now I have adopted somebody else's child and we are feeling much better."

Then I said, "Look, if a yogi were a beggar like you, then how would people ever believe that a yogi is an ideal being?"

Therefore, when you begin to worship the Guru, you should not worship him with some ulterior motive. You should not worship him to have some material gain from him. You should worship him from within. You should worship him for inner transformation. The institution of the Guru would have absolutely no meaning if people thought that a Guru was meant only to perform petty miracles. One should be able to realise the Guru within one's own Self. The worship which one renders with true feeling has great power, and so one should adore the Guru with true devotion, with intense feeling. As one continues to adore one's Guru, in course of time, what happens is that a new being seems to arise within oneself. And that is the Guru. That shows that the Guru is feeling very pleased with your worship. As a result of your worship of the Guru, you should be able to overcome your consciousness of being a disciple, and completely merge your separate identity in the Guru and become one with him.

This is exactly how the Gopis used to adore the Lord as their Guru. Shall I tell you a story? It's a humorous story, but if you were to turn this story against me, then I would be in a very embarrassing position. One day all the Gopis got together and entreated the Lord again and again, "Lord, please stay with us for the whole day, at least today, so that we may worship You to our heart's content." There is an aspect of love which is very vital, and that is separation. Love seems to flourish on separation. And the Lord, in order to give the Gopis an intense feeling of separation, began to make pretexts. "Look, I am not free. I have to go here, I have to go there, and I have to meet people there."

Then the Gopis said, "Look, Lord, we request You again to be with us at least for a few hours so that we may get an opportunity to worship You at least for that short period without any interruption. If You are so particular about going away from here, then we won't stop You. But we would like to see how You can depart from our hearts. Because within us You have taken a new form, and it is that form which we are worshipping and feeding and loving every day. The form which has been born within us, which has emerged within us can never leave us, though You may leave us."

As the Lord heard the words of the Gopis He felt very happy, and He said, "Very good. That shows that you have really attained something."

A true Guru on the path of the Siddhas does not feed you with mere hope. He doesn't hold out the hope that if you continue to practise or pursue your spiritual discipline in this birth you will get the reward of it in the next birth. On the contrary, this path insists that you should be able to see the Lord within you with these very eyes, that you should be able to experience immortal inner bliss in this very body. Being with the Guru is not like being a beggar who receives a few pennies today and hides them away to serve him in good stead the day after. The Guru is not a miser. The Guru gives liberally. In fact, the Guru gives fully of himself, and the Guru makes the disciple like him. Eknath Maharaj says paradoxically, "Lord, I have pierced the sense of difference between us which was afflicting me, and I thus achieved oneness with You. But after achieving oneness with You, for the purpose of worship, I again started feeling that we are not one, we are two."

Pratibha: *Whatever yogic kriyas occur to a seeker during the initial stage of sadhana are not manipulated by him, but are the spontaneous works of Chiti Herself. Once when I was in the state of tandra for two or three days together, I experienced that my ego had become completely quiet and silent and that the words that were coming from my lips were not coming from me, but it appeared as though they were coming from somebody else. What exactly happens after the attainment of perfection? Does a perfect being act and make decisions by relying on his own intellect, or is it the Chitishakti which animates, which acts for him, and which makes decisions through him, while he remains only as a witness?*

Baba: To achieve perfection and to retain individuality are two things which are absolutely contradictory. It is only when one's individuality merges in universality that one is said to have attained perfection. As long as ego is present, as long as one feels that one has a distinct separate identity, one has not yet attained perfection. It is, of course, true that many different kriyas occur during the course of sadhana, and all these kriyas are the work of Chitishakti. Yet that doesn't mean that ego leaves a particular seeker. A seeker still remains in the state of bondage and keeps on experiencing the ego quite strongly. After one has achieved perfection as a result of sadhana, he ceases to exist as a separate individual, as a distinct entity. Nothing remains for him to do. If something to do still remains, it means that he hasn't achieved perfection, that he is still in the state of sadhana. Such a seeker would be like a student who takes up a course for the B.A. and leaves it in the first year. People start calling him a graduate in spite of the fact that he hasn't yet completed his studies. It happens in many cases that seekers begin to have experiences of the Lord from time to time. Yet they do not get established in the state of perfection and they happen to give up sadhana before achieving perfection. Then they begin to feel that there is a lot of important significant work for them to do, that they have to save mankind and help the world, or that they have to reform mankind. This is the most powerful illusion which strikes not only ordinary people, but also highly educated people. It seizes great leaders, ministers, intellectuals and even writers. The idea that one is going to work for the welfare of the world is the most potent illusion. However great one may be, it is difficult to overcome this illusion, because this illusion is always more powerful than the power of self-control that you may have at a certain stage. The world has existed since time unknown, and it will continue to exist, and yet you find a person, when he becomes old, worrying about his children, worrying about his family. You find him saying to himself, "Now that my death is so near, who will take care of my children? Who will take care of my family?" He seems to be oblivious to the fact that his family will continue to prosper in spite of him. He keeps on worrying about them, and he doesn't bother to worry about his own salvation. This is exactly what is happening with most leaders, and most institutions. They worry about the world, they try to save others all the time. I am not suggesting that one should be indifferent to the lot of others, or that one should turn against them. But what is usually seen is that under the cover of working for others most people are only seeking to serve their own secret, personal, selfish ends.

So, therefore, there is absolutely nothing left to do for one who has achieved perfection. There were many people who used to raise this question about my Guru. They would say that he is such a great saint, he is established in such a high state, and yet he isn't doing anything for the world. But then, it is only he who is conscious of the world who will be able to do something for the world. He who isn't at all conscious of the world, who has risen completely above the world, what shall he do for the world? It was only the other day that somebody suggested, "Swamiji, it would be very good if you would undertake some welfare project outside of the Ashram. You are quite intelligent and you would be able to do a lot of work."

I said, "Look, the country is already too full of reformers, and there is no room even for you, so why are you dragging me into that field?"

Once a seeker achieves perfection, the world ceases to exist as the world for him. The world no longer appears to be real, nor does he feel any strong attachment to it. He is no longer like a reformer to whom the world is very much there, and who is helplessly attached to it.

There are some very high saints who work for the welfare of mankind, and there are others who don't, and how do you explain this apparent disparity? Man is governed by his destiny and in Vedantic philosophy, the role of destiny is emphasised very much. It is destiny which makes some people act and live in the outer world, and again it is destiny which turns the attention of other people towards the inner Self. It is only as long as a saint has not achieved the highest state, the state of perfect equality or perfect equanimity, that he obeys outer rules. But once he has achieved that state, he goes beyond all rules and conventions. After having realised the highest truth, a saint becomes established in that and this absorption in the highest state may take many forms—there is no one standard form for it. After attainment of perfection, some saints live like idiots, like characters who cannot take care of themselves and who have to be looked after by others. There are others who live like madmen and yet there are others who move like unclean spirits. And there are others who move in the outer world very intelligently, who go about giving very meaningful discourses, and who do a lot of work, who write a lot, and compose poetry and scriptures.

Bhartruhari describes the state of a fully realised saint, a saint who has become absorbed in Brahman in a most beautiful manner in his poetry. You can read it if you are interested. He says, "There are certain saints who after having become absorbed in the Highest Being keep lying naked on the bare earth like pythons, completely unaware of what is happening around them. There are others who live with the splendour of a king—in fact, even the splendour of a king would pale before their splendour."

If there is a saint of this quality who turns himself to work for the world, he does so only on receiving inspiration, either from the Lord or from his Guru. It's his prarabdha, his karma, his destiny, which directs him, as he does not work in order to accomplish a certain objective or purpose.

He works because he is being driven by divine inspiration. As far as he is concerned, the world doesn't exist. A fully realised saint, while dwelling in the body, remains different from it, watching it like a witness all the time. He is not affected by its joy or sorrow. Similarly, when he is participating in social actions, he remains detached all the time, observing all the while like a witness. Whether his work results in success or failure does not affect him at all, because he does not identify himself with the work he is doing. Most people's problem is that they become identified with what they are doing, and hence they begin to experience pleasure and pain or joy and sorrow.

The Vedantic philosophy is divided into four parts, and it is the fourth, the vital part, where the condition or the state of the fully-realised saint is described. A fully-enlightened saint has a vast store of merit which has come to him as a result of his noble deeds through countless births. He has performed tapasya through countless births, so he has to exhaust this merit. Even if he doesn't exhaust it in his own person, after he has given up his physical form, the place where his body lies, his samadhi shrine, gets all the rewards, all the fruit of the merit which he has earned. Though such a one lives in the body, he is not affected by what happens to the body, whether good or bad. Even when he participates in outer life, he is not at all affected by its joys and sorrows. A witness will always be a witness regardless of what he is observing, whether sinful deeds or virtuous deeds. A fully-realised saint does not make decisions, and if there is anybody who thinks that he makes decisions, he is entirely mistaken. It is his destiny which is making him work by acting within him as inner inspiration. It is only because of this that his work, even though it appears to be so very difficult, even though it appears to be so stupendous to others, is accomplished with the utmost ease—because his destiny is with him, because the divine source is behind him.

I never wanted to write *Chitshakti Vilas*, nor did I go to Mahabaleshwar with the purpose of composing that work. It was only after reaching there that one night I was seized by inner inspiration and I began to write. I finished only after the work was completed. During that period of composition, I did not consult any other book, any other source, nor did I discuss the matter with somebody else. Whatever flowed from my pen flowed spontaneously, as a result of inner inspiration. Take the case of this Ashram, which has grown in a most astonishing manner in such a short period. I am sometimes amazed when I think about at what a fantastic speed this Ashram has grown.

Therefore, such a saint or perfected being does not act from his own will, or from his own mind. It is destiny which works through him, and that is why whatever he does is accomplished with such ease. Once one has perfected one's sadhana and becomes established in the state in which one sees the Lord in everyone, what remains for him to see or experience? But there are some of these saints who seem to be compelled by the Lord to go out and work in the world and their destiny cooperates with them fully.

Kalyani: *It is often seen that seekers become self-righteous and fanatical about their spiritual progress. How can this be avoided?*
Baba: It is only when in the course of sadhana a seeker loses the qualities which make him a seeker that he becomes self-righteous and no longer remains a seeker. Generally speaking, it is true that one is always looking upon another person as a rival and comparing himself with him, and to his disadvantage. Even though you may be inferior to the other person, you feel that you are superior. A seeker becomes self-righteous because he himself is deficient in some way. If he had really achieved greatness, then he would not become self-righteous, and he would also look upon others as being great. Whenever one finds fault with others, it shows that he himself is suffering from the same faults. You find that a pure, stainless being will not look for defects in others. Take, for example, the case of a person who has achieved selflessness. Would there be any room in his heart for selfish desires? If such a person sees selfishness in others, it shows that he, himself is selfish, because if he had really become selfless, then he would not be able to see others as selfish.

If you have really achieved equality, then the question of your seeing inequality in others would not arise. When a seeker begins to feel self-righteous again and again, he can be certain that a great obstacle is obstructing his path. It is because of his own pettiness that he begins to regard others as petty, though they may be much greater than he. A conceited person suffers a lot. It is only ego which brings you to birth in this world, nourishes your chains and bondage, and makes you suffer. If you are able to overcome ego, then you are no longer in bondage; you become one with the Supreme Being. It happens quite often that a seeker falls a victim to a certain weakness, and these weaknesses grow so powerful that it becomes impossible for him to become free from them. One should only be concerned about his own progress, and he shouldn't worry about what is happening with others. Because in any case it would be very difficult for you to know what exactly is the state of another seeker. You should conduct yourself in such a manner that the inner Shakti will always be pleased with you. If you were to fall a victim to pride, even for a short while, then for the next few days your sadhana would be impeded. Passions such as greed, lust and anger are as intoxicating as drugs which hippies are so fond of. And one who is under the sway of these lusts is also a sort of hippie. It is only when he becomes happy instead of hippie, when he becomes free of these lusts, that one should congratulate oneself. As long as one is addicted to these inner passions, one would never be able to achieve happiness. If one is seeing defects in another, again and again, if one is getting irritated again and again, one can feel certain that that is an indication that one is going to suffer very much, or one is going to fall very soon in the future. Therefore, one who is seeing faults in others all the time, who flies into anger all the time is inviting trouble for himself.

Jon: *Are the directives from the Guru based on omniscience rather than on the information provided him, and is that why he should never be questioned?*
Baba: It does not matter. Even if the Guru were not omniscient, even if his knowledge were limited, as long as he is giving you sane advice, you should follow it. For instance, if he tells you to avoid a certain path that is full of thorns, you should avoid it. And if he tells you it is not good to

expose yourself to the sun, well don't expose yourself to the sun. You don't have to start wondering whether that directive is coming from his omniscience or not. To be able to live one's daily life effectively, one does not need omniscience. What one needs is intelligence, good principles, not omniscience. In fact, omniscience is a relative concept. Omniscience is relative to limited knowledge, and the Guru is beyond both. Let's say there is a person who does not understand anything in daily life, and we call him stupid, and there is another who understands it intelligently, that does not necessarily mean that he is omniscient, or that he is a Guru. Take for instance, the case of a radar installed in Bombay which will be able to tell you exactly what minute a certain plane left a certain station in Pakistan: would you call that radar a Guru?

The Guru is established beyond knowledge. Full knowledge and limited knowledge are only relative concepts and the Guru transcends them both. A so-called omniscient person can be as stupid as a person who is said to be limited in knowledge. The Guru is absolutely beyond the reach of knowledge, whether it is full knowledge or limited knowledge. As far as knowledge of every day affairs is concerned, whether it is full, or limited, still keeps one in the realm of ignorance, in the realm of avidya. How can you compare the Guru to a very sensitive radar?

April 4, 1972

Jon: Chiti is in all and all is Chiti. How should I look upon illness—as a manifestation of Chiti, or the divine will in me, or as imperfection of the body which I have not purified? Chiti, or the Guru, pervades all cells in the body, and you said faith has enormous power. Can I cure an illness by faith in the Guru alone, who has all power, or should I see

the Guru in Chiti through discrimination which makes me select the means of curing the illness, through medicine, control of food or fasting?
Baba: Food is health, and food is disease. If you take food regularly, then it is pure nectar, but if you take the same food irregularly, it turns into poison. If one cannot resist the tendency to overeat because of one's sheer greed for food, and if an illness comes as a result of overeating, how can you attribute it to the will of God? What makes you think that God feels happy if more and more people are sick or if more and more people are suffering from more and more impurities? If God were taking pleasure in creating more and more of these petty problems for people, then God would be less intelligent than an ordinary person. The Lord says, "All beings are equal to Me. None is especially dear, none is especially hateful."

In the dining hall, the servers come around with food to serve to you, and they give you as much as you ask for, and if you happen to overeat, or if you eat more than you can digest, you can certainly not lay the blame on the servers. The servers have nothing to do with it. Just as sorrow or happiness arise from Chiti, in the same way, discrimination or knowledge also arise from Chiti. Discrimination should be applied to deciding that one is not going to eat more than a certain amount.

Once I flew to Hyderabad and in the plane the air hostesses wanted me to have something to eat. They kept coming to me again and again with something or other to eat and I told them, "Look, this is not the proper time for me to eat, and if you are so particular for me to eat something, you can bring whatever you want me to eat to the Ashram."

I do not treat my stomach as a freight train which can be packed with all sorts of foodstuffs without discrimination.

Disease results from a number of factors coming together—irregularity on our part, changes of weather. And one should not bring the will of God into the picture. There is nothing like your overcoming a certain illness, particularly ordinary illnesses, through the exercise of discrimination, through control of food. Just as an illness comes through irregularity on your part, similarly, it can be eliminated if you become regular. If you happen to overeat and if that causes dysentery, then you must immediately exercise self-control. There is no harm in partially starving yourself, but overeating is positively harmful.

Whatever one may say in this matter, there are people who would like to approach the Guru for the cure of even their ordinary ailments, and they would like him to use his Shakti for that. People go to Gurus so that they may manifest sacred ash or perform some other miracle to rid them of an ailment that they have contracted. But I feel that this is not at all reasonable. It doesn't make any sense to me to consume the supremely blissful divine Shakti to overcome an ordinary ailment like dysentery which can be cured by a pill of Enterovioform. Why should one equate the divine Shakti with Enterovioform? If one's faith in God were to be used only for curing dysentery, then God would no longer be Maheshwara or Mahadev, God would be "Enteroviofor-meshwara."

I'll narrate a true incident. It happened during the time of Tukaram. Tukaram Maharaj had taken a pledge that on every Ekadasi day he would go to Pandharpur and have darshan of the Lord, because he was a firm worshipper of the saguna. If somebody were to raise the question, "Why should such a great saint like Tukaram take such a pledge?" all that I would say is, "It all depends on what one gets addicted to." For instance, I am addicted to getting up at 3 a.m. and going to the hall and looking at Baba through the hole in the wall. And if someone were to ask me about it, all that I would say is, "I am addicted to it, and that is all there is to it." It is of course a noble addiction. While Tukaram was about to leave, a great yogi happened to come to his place. This yogi had practised some of the advanced techniques of yoga and was reputed to have attained certain powers through them. When he looked at Tukaram and all that Tukaram kept himself busy with, he began to despise him because he did not find Tukaram practising any of the yogic techniques. Tukaram appeared to him to be much too simple. Here was a fellow who while sweeping would be chanting *Jai Jai Ram Krishna Hari*, or who would dance like a lunatic while chanting the divine Name. Tukaram did not practise any postures or pranayama, did not know how to direct his prana upwards or downwards. While the yogi was busy making his estimate of Tukaram, Tukaram happened to say to him, "Yogiraj, I have to go to Pandharpur. What are you going to do with yourself?"

"I, too, will come."

"Very good."

So both of them set out for Pandharpur. They had to cross a big river on the way by taking a ferry. As soon as the ferryman saw Tukaram, he welcomed him and said, "Maharaj, come and sit in my ferry."

And Tukaram went there immediately. In those days we had old coins, paise coins, and Tukaram gave two to him. Then he invited the yogi to come and sit with him in the ferry. The yogi said in a tone of scorn, "Tukaram, I thought that you had some intelligence, some realisation, to your credit, but I see that you are utterly blank and ignorant and mediocre. Should a yogi like you sit in a ferry to cross the river?"

Tukaram replied, "I only know the Lord Pandurang, and how to chant His divine Name in ecstasy—so much so that I begin to dance while chanting His name, and that is all that I know and all that I need to know."

The yogi said, "If you are interested in crossing the river in an ordinary way, go ahead, and I will show you how I cross the river."

Tukaram went across in the ferry, and went to the temple, had darshan of the Lord and began to return. The yogi sat on the bank of the river and started performing certain yogic exercises. First he flushed his stomach and intestines, then he sat in the lotus posture, he held his breath and applied the three bandhas and he slowly descended into the water and it took him five or six hours to cross the river in his yogic fashion. The moment the yogi reached the other side of the river, Tukaram also reached there, and Tukaram again got in the ferry. The yogi shouted, asking him, "Have you already returned?"

Tukaram said, "Yes Yogiraj, I had a most wonderful darshan of the Lord."

Then he said, "Are you aware of how I crossed the river? I crossed the river by means of my yogic powers."

Tukaram said, "Look, what you have earned through yoga only costs two paise. What you could achieve through yoga I could obtain by paying two paise to the ferry man. That's all that you have gained through yoga."

Similarly, you don't have to spend the divine power, the divine Shakti, to cure an illness which can be cured by buying a pill from the market which would not cost you more than two or three paise. In fact, one who really understands God, who really loves God, would never stoop to the level of indulging in cheap displays or using divine powers for these petty ends. Only atheists would indulge in such miracles. The divine Shakti is not meant to be consumed in miracles. Say you have a cold today, and you have cured it by consuming some of the divine Shakti. The cold may return after four days—are you going to use the power gathered through your chanting *Hari Ram* just to cure the cold again and again? That yogi could have crossed the river by paying the ferry man two paise, but to cross the river the yogic way took about five hours.

The best course for a wise man is to overcome illness through self-restraint and discrimination. The body will always be down with some ailment or another, because that is its very nature. And if you have been able to cure one, another will come. You may travel throughout the entire world and you won't find anyone whose body is completely healthy or completely happy. There was a great Guru called Samartha Ramdas Swami and he had great divine power. He would always ask this question: "Is anyone on the surface of the earth happy?" Exactly when does one feel happy in worldly life? Eating or digesting what has been eaten, or excreting the waste products, or sleeping, or waking up from sleep? Therefore one should not use the power gained through spiritual practices for these petty ends. Save that and exercise discrimination and self-control. If you love God, if you are constantly praying to Him, all that is evil will itself drop off, and you won't have to make a special prayer to the Lord to free you from disease or from other evil things. There is no doubt that faith has enormous power and illness can certainly be cured through faith. Incurable diseases could be cured by faith. You will meet a certain devotee who is at present in England, but who will return very soon. He is one of our most distinguished mountaineers. He recently conquered Trishula, and while returning he got frostbitten. The doctors in Delhi told him that his toes would have to be amputated but he said that he would first talk to me and then decide about it. He came here to see me on his way to England, and I said, "There is no doubt that God has limitless powers, and if you have faith in Him, if you pray to Him, your illness will be cured. Keep praying to Him, and don't have your toes cut off, and see what happens. Tell the doctors to treat your toes only from the outside. But you should give them inner treatment through japa, through concentration on the frostbitten toes and combining japa with that."

Now he has completely recovered and even the doctors in England are amazed at his recovery. He has written that he will come first to the Ashram and then go home, so you all will meet him. The mantra has enormous power.

Amrita: *Why do we hold swadhyaya many times a day? And is it necessary to read from the book even if you know a certain chant by heart? What is the importance of reading from the book?*
Baba: Swadhyaya is a most exalted bath, a most exalted nourishment for the inner Self, the inner organs and the inner mind. However beautiful a person may be, and he may be wearing the most expensive clothes, clothes that have been very well ironed, but if he hasn't had a bath, his body will give out a terrible odor. The body may be very well formed, it may be quite shapely and symmetrical and the complexion may also be very attractive, and the features of the face may be quite fascinating, and the person may be using the most expensive cosmetics in the world. But if she doesn't take a bath for a few days, though she may look attractive from a distance, her body will give out a foul odor. Likewise, no matter how much one may eat, how much one may drink, what one may wear, and in what style one may live, if one's mind is not pure, what peace or happiness can he enjoy in life? What possible radiance could his heart have? If your mind is impure, if your mind stinks, if your mind is filthy, then you may use the most delicate perfumes on the outer body, but they will not be able to purify the

mind. Only other people would get the fragrance of the perfumes, not you. You would only inhale the foul stink of your mind.

Swadhyaya is a regular bath and regular food for the inner Self. It is the best nourishment for the spirit. Through swadhyaya the mind is washed every day, and new impressions are also formed in the mind. The scriptures talk about shravan samadhi, samadhi attained through sound, through hearing. There is a portion of the *Vedas* which is didactic, where the Guru gives instruction to the disciple. In this section, there is a most significant verse which says, "You must never neglect swadhyaya, you must practise it with absolute regularity."

One session lasts for about an hour or an hour and a quarter. During that period one gets the opportunity to master at least one sitting posture and to achieve concentration. Then there is a technique called tratak—gazing fixedly at an object—which is used to still the thought waves arising in the mind, like holding your book at a certain distance, in a certain position. I ask people again and again not to be lax in the matter of holding their books. They must be held up straight before the eyes. When you are holding your book in that manner, you are practising tratak in the most natural manner, because your eyes are fixed on the words of the text all the time. Thus while practising swadhyaya you are practising tratak. You are also perfecting a sitting posture, and pranayama also comes in a most natural fashion. Your inner spirit is getting all the nourishment it needs, and the mind is also becoming more and more focused. So swadhyaya has all these advantages. In fact it is even more advantageous than meditation. There is a certain mudra in yoga by means of which all the openings in the face are closed, the ears are closed by putting fingers in them; the eyes are shut placing fingers above them, the nostrils are also closed; the mouth is also closed and this mudra is called shanmukhi mudra, a mudra which has six aspects. But through swadhyaya you are practising a mudra which is even more effective than the shanmukhi, and which is even more purifying. When you are holding the book firmly, your hands are engaged. With your eyes you are reading the words of the text. With your ears you are hearing the sound of the text, and with your lips you are chanting the text. Thus the mind becomes focused very easily. That is why I insist that you read from the book. Your eyes should be focused on the text and you should be going from one word to another mentally. You should constantly listen to the sound of the chanting, because this is a most mysterious yoga. Swadhyaya sessions are quite expensive from a strictly monetary point of view. We consume electricity, and electricity is not cheap in this country. And the musical instruments that are used for accompaniment are quite expensive. The harmonium cost more than Rs. 1000/-. The tambouras do not cost less than Rs. 500/- each, and more over, some of my most trusted workers are held up by swadhyaya. If swadhyaya sessions did not have any utility, I would not waste all these valuable resourses on them. Probably many of you are not aware of this aspect of it: how much it costs, and how much our different things get worn out through being used so much.

Shyama: *There is a certain temple in Poona where boys below 14-16 years old are not permitted inside. Does it mean that boys of that age do not need God?*
Baba: What is the point of admitting young children into a temple, children who only disturb others' concentration? Why does a meditator from Bombay, after all, like to go to a certain temple in Poona, or like to come here? He obviously is spending Rs. 10/-, 20/- or 30/- on the fare, and much time in the journey. There must be a reason. The obvious reason is that he comes out of Bombay to these places in the hope that he will be able to meditate in a pure atmosphere, that he will be able to get away from the noises of city life. If after coming to an ashram, you find children crying around you all the time, and mothers who do not know how to look after their children inspite of the fact that they have given birth to them, what's the point of coming to an ashram? Quite often I find that quite a few women come with their children and during swadhyaya, they give the swadhyaya books to them and the children begin to tear them merrily. And I begin to wonder whether these women have come to earn a little merit, or to lose the little they may have earned before. If the children are not causing havoc

with the swadhyaya books, they will be causing havoc in the gardens, running around and disturbing everybody. It is for this reason that children below fourteen are not permitted in that temple in Poona. I myself have read it and I don't find anything wrong with it. If I am present during a swadhyaya session and if there is any child who begins to cry, I ask the mother to take the child out, because the swadhyaya time is not the time to indulge a child. It is the time for swadhyaya, and if a child cannot be kept silent or under control, he has no business to be there in the swadhyaya sessions. Parents, before bringing little children to the Ashram, should first make sure what exactly the nature of the place is. The meditation room is, after all, not like the Chowpatty Beach, or the Hanging Gardens or a railway platform. It is not a public garden. Therefore, the notice which has been put up in that temple is absolutely justified, and in fact, I, too, am going to put up such a notice here.

Barry: *Often when I sit for meditation I have to exert great force to merge and remain merged with the mantra. The greater the effort, the more violent the kriyas which pull attention from the mantra. There also is an energy drain, and I go from periods of awareness to semi-unconscious states. This also occurs during the day when trying to witness my various methods. Are my efforts being misdirected? Is the energy drain real, or due to attitude?*
Baba: You are making the right sort of effort. During kriyas, if the mind moves away from the mantra, it doesn't matter. When kriyas are taking place, you should not worry about the mantra. You should only try to stay as a witness to the kriyas. However, it is the mantra which is the very life of the kriyas, which has caused those kriyas. A phase of violent kriyas will always be followed by a phase of complete stillness of the mind, or the sense of a feeling of detachment. During that phase it may appear that your energy has been drained, or that you are falling into semiconsciousness, or unconsciousness, but that feeling arises from wrong understanding. This is the natural result of kriyas, and there is in reality no energy drain. Keep practising your mantra and hear the mantra when you repeat it. Also watch whether you are repeating the mantra and hearing it or not.

This way you are practising witness-consciousness along with mantra repetition, and this is a most joyful state, a state which will enable you to experience inner ecstasy. There is no loss of energy. What happens is that one becomes perfectly still. After that phase is over, all the energy that appeared to have been lost comes back. How do you feel when you wake up from deep sleep? What happens is that during sleep your mind is pulled inwards, and during the waking state your mind is drawn outwards. Similarly, during meditation, during kriyas, your mind is pulled inwards while in your ordinary state the mind is drawn outwards. And when you pass from kriyas to your ordinary state, it may appear for a moment that you have lost some energy, but in reality there is no loss.

Right understanding is of the utmost importance. Take another case. You have had a very good delicious meal, and you have eaten to your heart's content. For a while you feel absolutely satisfied. But what happens is that your body becomes heavy or dull. This is not because you have lost energy, or because of the good food. What happens is that in that state of contentment your mind is drawn inwards, and when the mind is drawn inwards, your body is left as a corpse. So you should understand what is happening to you. Whatever is happening to you is quite right. However, during meditation you should constantly try to remember the Lord, to remember the inner Self, because it is this remembrance that will release more and more bliss inside.

I find many ritualists performing elaborate rituals, but since they do not have any faith in the Name of the Lord, they do not use it at the time of the ritual, and those rituals remain dry and joyless. Then there are others who practise all kinds of yoga, all the advanced techniques of Hatha Yoga, or Raja Yoga and all other yogas, and yet when you look at them you feel so sad, because their faces are without any light, without any life; and it is because they have no faith in the Name of the Lord. Take the case of an intellectual who is fully conversant in all the schools of philosophy, who reads and talks very brilliantly. He too remains dry and joyless because he has no faith in the Name of the Lord. The Name of the Lord is pure nectar, but unfortunately people leave nectar aside and turn to what has no savour or joy, no nectar. Therefore, be constantly conscious of the Lord, because it is there that bliss lies.

April 5, 1972

Larry A.: *Sometimes I experience mental blankness, such as being unable to do the simple addition of a column of figures. Could this be a temporary result of meditation, or does it indicate that something is wrong?*
Baba: There are different states of the mind, and the state of blankness is just one of them. And it is a passing phase only. This condition, too, is quite good. Since you do not understand its value, you get upset about it. Otherwise, that state is the state in which you are neither conscious of pain nor pleasure, joy nor sorrow, outside nor inside. If you could stay in this state for a long time, it would be very good, it would give me great pleasure, and I would feel that your stay in the Gavdevi Ashram had been fulfilled. It is for achieving this state that we practise different kinds of yoga, that we offer different forms of worship, and perform different religious rituals and engage in other spiritual practices.

Ramesh: *Is it good for a seeker to sleep during the day or not?*
Baba: To sleep during the day and keep awake at night is not good, not only for a seeker, but even for a person who is immersed in worldliness. You can find out from your own experience. If you sleep during the day, day after day, your mind becomes dull, your body also loses its agility and some of its vigour, and in course of time you become quite feeble. According to one of the important Ayurvedic treatises, written by Charak, to keep awake during the night but to sleep during the day is to welcome all kinds of diseases and ailments. The sun and health are closely related, and so are the sun and the sexual fluid. One who sleeps during the day can

never have as strong and pure sexual fluid as he should have. However, those who have no choice, those who have to be on duty at night, or who have to attend to work at night, may sleep during the day, because they have no choice. But those who do not have to work at night, who have the entire night at their disposal, should sleep at night, and not sleep at all during the day. If you feel extremely tired, if you have laboured very hard, or if something else has gone wrong, then you could have a short nap for about fifteen minutes, lying on the left side. That is permitted. But to sleep for two or three hours in the afternoon or to fall asleep at noon and wake up in the evening, and keep awake during the whole night is certainly not the yogic way of life. You can verify it by your own experience. Do not sleep during the day for a few days, and see how easily the food you eat gets digested, and how active you feel. But if you sleep after a meal, the digestive fire becomes dull, and the body feels like dead weight. If you were asked to eat after having a full meal, however delicious the food might be, you would not enjoy it. You would not be able to relish whatever juices it may contain. So if you are sleeping during the day, how could you have deep peaceful sleep during the night?

Amrita: *I am, of course, working, but I feel that I put in very little. I have the capacity to do much more, but my problem is that I am not able to organise my time, and my Shakti, in spite of my best efforts. I spend most of my time drinking, eating and sleeping. How may I organise my time and my Shakti so that I can do the maximum amount of work?*
Baba: How can you spend most of your time eating and drinking? Somebody else is cooking your food, you finish your meal in about five minutes. And how much water could you be drinking? You surely couldn't be gulping down gallons and gallons. You don't have to cook, we have a regular cook in the kitchen who does the work for you. You only have to eat, and that doesn't take much time. However, if after finishing your meal you spend time on gossip, that isn't good. If you have put in writing work for about four or five hours, that is enough. If you can put in intellectual work of four or five hours, regularly, that would be more than enough for our purposes. I am sure most of your time must

be spent on adorning all the different deities you have in the Ashram; you must have at least fifteen or twenty. It would be much better for you to have just one and take full care of Him. When I come up, I see that you have one deity in each corner, and you have one by the side of your bed also. It must take you at least half an hour to adorn one, so if there are ten gods that you have to take care of, five hours are gone. And as far as the day is concerned, it cannot be made longer for your sake. You can save a lot of time by offering worship to all the deities collectively in one place, and calling upon all of them to partake of it right there, without your having to worship different deities separately. Then you are putting a turban on one deity, and beads on another, and adorning the third in still a different manner. This afternoon I went up on inspection and it took even me a half hour to have a good look at all the different gods that were present in that section.

You are putting in enough work, and what you are doing is enough for a renunciate. If you are working for five or six hours, that is enough. You must not reduce your sleep, because if you cut down on sleep for four days, you may fall ill on the fifth, and the next week will be wasted on your recovering from the illness. So how much time will be gained that way? If you choose one field and concentrate all your attention then you can do a lot of work in that field. In any case, no one can keep on working endlessly day after day. A person who travels twelve miles today will not be able to walk the same distance every day. You should sleep when it is time to sleep and eat when it is time to eat, and work when it is time to work. And if you make the fullest use of the work time, that should be enough for the Ashram. However, in time of emergency, you may have to work during the night also, you may not get any sleep. But that doesn't happen every day.

Judith: *I cannot say that I believe in God. I cannot say that I have faith in the name of the Lord. But I do have a longing for that belief. Can one acquire a conscious faith in the Name of the Lord by living here, coming to love the Guru and chanting, meditating and working to the best of one's ability? Or should one have this conscious faith beforehand?*

Baba: There is nothing like coming here with faith. However, if you don't come here with faith, and if you develop it during the course of your stay here, that too is equally good. Your question shows that you already have faith. It is just like saying that even though I am talking to you, I am asleep. There is no difference between longing for belief and belief. You will certainly acquire a very strong faith by living here, loving your Guru, and doing the Ashram work conscientiously. If you do the Ashram work without any selfish motive, then you will gather enormous Shakti within you, regardless of the nature of the work that you are doing. It is only an unintelligent person who would distinguish between different kinds of Ashram work. To an intelligent person who has the right sort of understanding, all forms of work are equally as valuable, because they are all service to the Guru. One who performs worship inside the temple is doing Ashram seva. One who keeps watch at the gate is doing Ashram seva and one who sweeps the floors is doing Ashram seva. It is only unintelligent people who think in terms of superior and inferior kinds of work. To a true bhakta, to a true lover of the Guru, it is all Guru seva, whether he's keeping watch or performing worship, or writing or sweeping.

First you should begin to love your own Self. If you are able to love yourself, you will be able to love everybody else. A man should never fall into dejection and despair by constantly harbouring thoughts of inferiority, self-pity, or self-abnegation. You should always remember your own inner Self with great love. You should always think of the dazzling flame of love which is present inside. That will fill you with great delight, great happiness, great zest. If you begin to take care of your body, remaining aware that your heart is the seat of the effulgent Lord, and if you wash and clothe the body with great love, if you feed it at the right time, and with an adequate amount of food, if you do not neglect it, then you will find great love welling up inside you. And that love will also keep you buoyant and zestful all the time. In fact the work that you engage in during your stay here will do that also.

First you should learn to remain content. You should keep trying to feel more and more contented by going deeper into your own Self. Faith will certainly come to you by living here. You will acquire most sublime faith if you continue to live here and participate in the Ashram routine and do the Ashram work with love and devotion.

Uma: *What is the significance and the purpose of a yajna such as was held here last year and will be held this year on your birthday? What offerings are made, to whom, and what do they signify?*
Baba: The science of yajna is very vast; it is as vast as the earth. While describing the nature of the yajna, the seers say that yajna is Vishnu Himself, yajna is Shiva, and yajna is you, your own inner Self. To understand the importance of a yajna, we should go back to the ancient times when at the end of a yajna the deity who was invoked and worshipped during the yajna would reveal himself, and the sacrificers who were performing the ceremony would obtain the full fruit of the sacrifice they performed. Even today, modern science bears witness to the validity of the yajna. When a small atomic bomb is exploded, even for test purposes, it creates an enormous disturbance in the atmosphere. It affects the atmosphere for thousands of miles and upsets the sequence of seasons. It may cause a rain storm in one place and some other disturbance in some other place. It upsets the balance of the five elements. Once a scientist was explaining what exactly happens when an atom bomb explodes. How is it that such a small bomb can cause such enormous havoc? What happens when this tiny bomb explodes is that a bomb of air gets formed, as it were, and that explodes, and after that explodes, another bomb is formed, and that explodes, and this series of explosions goes on and this is how a vast area is affected. Yajna is like an atom bomb. It has the same power, but its power is not destructive. A yajna is not held to destroy a country, or destroy a city, or to kill large numbers of people, or to cause devastation, or destroy crops and other things. A yajna is held to destroy only impurities, to purge the atmosphere of all the impurities, of all the unhealthy germs which may be present. A yajna brings happiness to all concerned. During a yajna, herbs of the finest kind—almost divine herbs—are collected, and pure ghee is used, and these herbs along with

the ghee are offered to the fire. The smoke of the yajna spreads through the entire atmosphere and purges it of all the impurities that may be contained and thus it ensures good health, happiness and purity for all the people. It also results in timely rains. Such is the importance of a yajna.

When you worship a deity, you get the satisfaction yourself, because as far as the deity is concerned, he is ever content and he doesn't need anything from you. So the fruit of worship is earned by your own Self. But that fruit remains confined to you or to a certain number of people who are present, and may also partake of it. But this is not the case of a yajna. The effect of a yajna is much greater. It is much more pervasive, because when a yajna is held, not only the people who are performing it, not only those who are actually present at the ceremony, but also the people who live in the surrounding areas and also the people who inhale the air which is laden with the pure perfume of the yajna offerings, are purified, and they get all its benefits. All four *Vedas* celebrate the glory of yajnas in the most lyrical terms, and the *Gita* also speaks of the great importance of yajnas. The Lord says that when a yajna is performed, the atmosphere is purified and rain-bearing clouds are produced. And timely rains are caused, as a result of which food grows properly and abundantly on the earth. And food promotes life, ensures the continuity of human life, and as its continuity is ensured, then peace and joy follow. I can say that a yajna is a great friend to man. A yajna increases inner sattvic radiance. I would go to the extent of saying that a yajna is God Himself in a manifest form.

Kedarnath: *Last time you spoke about mental worship. Please tell us how long this worship should be carried on and does it continue for the whole time, or does it come to a stop automatically during the course of meditation? And what is the relationship between such worship and the mantra?*
Raul: *Your description of manas puja last time was most interesting. Could you please expand on this topic?*
Baba: A question should be very carefully phrased and it should be brief. It should also be written in a neat legible

hand, and not in a manner that corresponds to the irregularity of your everyday life. If somebody were to give me a question or a piece of writing which is not properly written, I would throw it away. One shouldn't write a question as carelessly as one would put on a cap or one would sit, or put on a scarf. One should write a question very neatly. If the questions are not neatly written they will not be accepted, they will be thrown away. You have all the time in the world to write your questions carefully.

You should find out from your own experience whether it continues, or whether mental worship comes to an automatic stop. Find out from your own experience how long it continues and exactly what form it takes. The question of performing such worship for a certain length of time does not arise. As long as your mind is active, the worship will continue. Find out from your own actual experience what really happens. You cannot fix any time, say three minutes of five minutes or ten minutes in such worship. It all depends on how elaborately you perform it.

You should continue to perform mental worship regularly. The mantra is the very root of mental worship. Mantra is absolutely necessary for such worship. If such worship comes to an end, and there is still some time left, that time should be spent on japa. Mental worship doesn't really end. What really happens is that your mind wanders to something else, so the worship gets interrupted. However, after this worship is consummated, great peace and calm fill the mind. Mental worship and the mantra are very closely related to each other. The mantra is nothing but a way of remembering the Lord. Mental worship promotes meditation. Those whose minds are very restless, whose minds are overactive, should engage their minds in very elaborate mental worship so that there is enough work for the mind to do. Even though in the beginning you may perform it only with your mind, later on it begins to emerge from deeper levels and you achieve something very valuable. If while performing mental worship, say you are offering flowers to a deity, which may be a Shivalingam or some other form, you offer those flowers with full attention, you will be able to inhale the perfume, and when you are able to inhale the perfume of the flowers that you are offering mentally to the deity, you can think that your worship has been consummated.

Mental worship could also be very useful for psychologists. If those who have dull minds could be made to perform mental worship, their minds would become very agile, very sharp and very strong. While performing mental worship one should not bother about the controversy between form or formless. One's only concern should be how to tackle the mind, which is so restless or overactive. Mental worship is a very easy and simple way to gather all the mental energies and focus them on one point, and thus strengthen the mind. When the mind becomes completely focused during mental worship, the things which you are offering will be clearly visible to you—so much so that you could even touch them.

Pratibha: *New visitors to the Ashram are not able to eat all the food which is served to them, so a part of it is wasted. Can we stop this waste? My mind is filled with disgust when I see so much food wasted.*
Baba: It should be explained to new visitors that they should not waste food. Visitors should exercise discrimination, and have the good sense to realise that it is not good to waste Ashram food. The servers, too, should be careful. There are quite a few guests who show up about the time of the forenoon arati and then they barge into the kitchen and they eat the food which is served and most irreverently waste a considerable portion. I feel that by coming to the Ashram they are not earning any merit. Just as they are only committing various sins while living in Bombay, by coming to the Ashram they are only adding to their store of sins. If you were to buy your food at a restuarant, you would not waste it, because you have to pay for every little thing you get there. It is only when food is served free of charge to you, when it is served with love, that you begin to waste it. And it is a matter of great shame, and great regret and sorrow at the same time. There are some visitors who go to the extent of even throwing away the bowls along with the leaves, and I begin to wonder whether these specimens are coming straight from a mental hospital or a lunatic asylum, or whether they have any common sense at all, and what

exactly is bringing them here. If a person had even the least intelligence, he would think ten times before doing such an act. It is only because the food is served here freely and with great love that people tend to waste it, and I wonder what these people would say to the Lord if He were to question them about what they did when they came here. If there is a person who doesn't know the capacity of his own stomach, who doesn't know exactly how much his stomach needs, what can you expect of him? What can he do in life? Isn't he a mere burden on the earth? You can ask the people who attend me and cook for me, how much food is left after I have finished eating. They don't find even a grain on my plate; they have to wash the plate in order to get some prasad. It is because I have honoured food that I am being honoured by food now. Those who disregard food, who dishonour food, will always be starving, they will never be honoured by food, and they will always be begging for food. This is highly improper and we should regard food with great reverence, whether we are here or elsewhere.

April 7, 1972

***Raul:** In the last few weeks I have been doing asanas and calesthenics, then taking a bath before sitting for meditation. The body feels awake and stable, thus permitting faster concentration. Do you approve of this practice?*
Baba: It's all right to practise asanas before meditation, but you shouldn't do calesthenics after asanas. The asanas may appear to be very easy, very effortless to an onlooker, but the fact is that the exercise that you get from the asanas is at least fifty times what you may get from calesthenics. Asanas give you all the exercise that you need; there is no need to exercise through calesthenics. If you are performing calesthenics after asanas, it would be just like having a full satisfying meal at one restaurant and then going to another

restaurant to eat more. If you have already had a full meal, what is the need of eating more? If you want, you can practise five or ten asanas more. But do not practise calesthenics after asanas; you can practise the corpse pose after asanas. Even if you are doing calesthenics before asanas, it is not necessary at all. You can increase the number of asanas. The rest is quite all right. Asanas help meditation very much. Through asanas, the prana, the mind and the heart get purified. As a result of this purification, meditation comes much sooner.

Kalyani: *Is there any value in keeping a spiritual diary? If so, what should be recorded?*
Baba: A spiritual diary has enormous value. *Chitshakti Vilas, (Guru or Play of Consciousness)* is nothing but my spiritual diary. You should not consider it to be like other books. Though it contains philosophy, it is not a philosophical treatise; it is my spiritual diary. It is not possible for every seeker to remember the details of all the experiences that come to him, and even I have not been able to give all the details of all the experiences that I had. In fact, what has been left out could fill another two volumes, and I am thinking of writing more on the subject.

Maintain a regular diary, and record the experiences that come to you during meditation. This will be good not only for you, but also for others, and you will realise its value in the future. It was only this afternoon that we received a letter from California which said that more and more people are getting interested in the answers to the questions put here, and more and more people are buying the *Newsletter*. What is the *Newsletter*, after all? It is just a diary which records what is happening here. The inner miracles which occur during meditation are far more valuable than all the external miracles of the world. It is very advisable to record these experiences in a diary, and the writer also should keep reading the diary from time to time. If you read a record of a certain past experience, that will give added delight to your heart; you will become aware of what happened to you on a certain day.

There is so much more left to be recorded from my spiritual diary. It could fill another two volumes. I am going to write more, but I will begin to write only when I receive the command from within.

Durgadas: *Many seekers get very good meditation, and they also get good spiritual experiences and visions. Yet, they are tormented by sexual appetite. In spite of their best efforts, it doesn't leave them. How do you explain this?*

Baba: The torment from the sexual appetite that you experience during meditation is very different from the ordinary sexual appetite because during meditation it arises in order to be expelled from the system. The reason is that all the cravings and appetites are lying stored up in man through countless births. Just because you get good meditation, and have meditated for a while, it doesn't mean that you have become completely pure. In the human body, there is a nerve, the central nerve, called the sushumna, which serves as the support for all the nerves throughout the body. It is this central nerve which is the abode of the Kundalini. It is in this central nerve, the sushumna, that the impressions of all the actions we might have performed during all our previous births are embedded. These impressions are just like the voice that gets recorded on tape. From time to time, an impression arises from the sushumna during meditation. It may be anger, greed, sexual desire, or something else, and it begins to torment the seeker. In spite of the temporary emergence of one of these passions in the mind during meditation, if the seeker has devotion for the Guru, he will soon find that such passions give way to a very high and sublime feeling, so much so that the seeker will feel amazed how it is that after the attack of such an impure passion, he could soar so high.

However, one who understands the purpose of the Ashram, who understands its significance and values and who is abiding by the discipline of the Ashram, will not be so tormented by such passions. Even if one of these passions should arise, it would subside very soon.

Once I read the life story of a very great saint, one of the greatest saints of the world—so great that it's difficult to describe his greatness; even he, during meditation would be attacked by foul, lustful thoughts and he would not even be able to express them. He would feel so ashamed of them.

The only way out is total devotion for the Guru, and discipline.

Shall I narrate a story? There was a king who used to love his Guru very much. He loved him with mind, speech and thought. Whatever new gifts were offered to him, he would first offer them to his Guru. There were certain physicians who were interested in gaining the favour of the king by hook or by crook. The trouble with most such people is that they are only interested in gaining certain very special rewards, without bothering about the means employed. So these physicians suggested to the king that they would prepare a certain medicine for him, by taking which he would be able to satisfy a number of women—so he could marry a few more. The pill was prepared and put in a box and the box was offered to the king. The king, as was his custom, offered the box to the Guru, and the Guru took out two pills and put them in his mouth and had a drink of water right in the presence of the king.

The king, on returning home, took one pill, just to test its efficacy, and it excited him so much that he was tormented by lust throughout the night, and he was not satisfied even after having mated with all his queens.

The king got up in the morning, had a bath, sat for meditation and started performing worship to his Guru. Immediately he remembered that he had given two pills to his Guru, and that worried him very much. He said to himself, "Look, I took only one pill and this is what happened to me. All the queens in the house could not satisfy me. What must have happened to my Guru, who took not one, but two?"

He immediately got in his car and rushed to his Guru. When he reached the Guru's abode, he found the Guru sitting there as usual; he was as calm as before. The Guru called him and said, "Your Majesty, what brings you here in the morning? You usually come in the evening."

The king said, "Sir, how are you? As a result of taking just one pill I got into a very bad plight, and I feel so ashamed that I offered those pills to you, but I couldn't help it because it has been my custom to offer you whatever has been offered to me. How are you? I am really sorry that I gave those pills to you."

The Guru said, "Well, I have absolutely no idea what those pills are meant for, and what their effects are. Those pills have had absolutely no effect on me, because I am feeling absolutely the same as I feel every day."

The king said, "I took just one and you took two." And he began to wonder just exactly what the matter was, and his mind was filled with doubt and he sat down and began to think about it.

The Guru said, "Your Majesty, you shouldn't think too much about it. I will explain it to you tomorrow. Come tomorrow and bring that famous wrestler with you."

The wrestler was brought, and the Guru asked the king to give two pills to the wrestler. The Guru said, "These pills arouse a very strong sexual desire. After taking these pills, if you feel like it, you can visit a certain nightclub." (There are nightclubs in all countries.) "Do not go there before seven in the evening and stay there for the whole night."

The wrestler began to wait anxiously for the auspicious hour. He already had so much physical vigour, he had had two very efficacious pills, and above all he had been blessed by the king of the realm and also by the Guru. So no wonder he was waiting so eagerly for the evening. As soon as the wrestler got into the nightclub and sat down there, a drum was beaten and a crier began to make an announcement. The public crier announced: Tomorrow at 7 a.m., so-and-so wrestler will be hanged at such-and-such place.

As soon as the wrestler heard that he was going to be hanged the next morning, he was shocked out of his wits, and he began to call upon the Lord to save him, and he forgot completely about those pills. The effect seemed to have melted away because he was now worried about his life.

Half an hour before the hanging, the wrestler was called to the Guru's Ashram. The king was also there. The Guru said to the wrestler, "Look, you took two pills yesterday and you went to the nightclub. What exploits did you perform there?"

The wrestler said, "Guru Maharaj, the pill which I received through the ear was far more efficacious than the pills I received through the mouth. In fact the pill I received through the ear was so efficacious that it completely nullified the effect of the pills received through the mouth. The moment I became aware that I was going to be hanged in the morning, the thoughts of lust left me completely. Now there is only half an hour left before I will be hanged, and Sir, you were so kind to give me two pills yesterday, now be so kind as to save me from the noose."

Then the Guru said, "Oh king, only that person who wishes to have sensual gratification would be affected by such pills. But one whose thoughts are completely turned away from sensual gratification would not be at all affected by such pills."

Therefore, if meditators regarded sexual thoughts as death itself, then they would not bother them so much. It is only when they begin to consider those thoughts valid, or begin to feel happy about them that they will torment them more and more.

I heard this story thirty-five years ago, and I remembered it all of a sudden this evening. Such things do happen during meditation, but if you have sufficient devotion to the Guru, those thoughts also melt away very soon.

Malti: *It is said that when the Guru feels pleased one receives all powers, all knowledge. But the Guru is sublime bliss iteself. How do you explain the contradiction?*
Baba: It is true that the Guru is full of bliss all the time and is fully contented within himself. His inner contentment has nothing to do with any outer factor. It is his very nature to remain fully contented. But that doesn't mean that the Guru is satisfied with the progress of the disciple. The Guru is satisfied with himself, he is pleased with himself; he is enjoying absolute inner contentment, which has no relation to any outer factor.

A very important question is raised in Vedantic philosophy: "Are you going to attain what you haven't attained, or are you going to attain what you already have?" If you say that you are going to attain what you do not have now, it does not make much sense because, if you don't have it now, it's quite possible that you will lose it some time after attaining it. Then the sages add that you attain what you already have, not what you do not have. He is already there. The

Lord has been here all the time, and it is only on account of wrong understanding that you feel that He is not present within you. And when that wrong understanding goes, you realise His presence within you. So it means that you are attaining what you already possess, what you already have.

The Guru is completely content within himself, and this contentment arises from within him. He is not contented because his disciples are serving him well, or because his disciples are performing tapasya. He is contented in spite of what his disciples are doing. When the Guru, who is always self-contented, becomes pleased with the disciple, then the disciple by his grace receives all powers and all knowledge. But the Guru's own contentment has nothing to do with what a disciple does or does not do. The Lord says in the *Gita*, "All beings are equal to Me. To Me a great saint has as much value as a tiny ant, or a small bird, or some other creature. Though I have killed so many, I have absolutely no malice for anyone, and though it looks like I love so many, I love thousands and have bestowed so many gifts on them, the fact is that I love no one, and I hate no one. I am the one who bestows the fruits of actions. A person receives the reward of his particular mode of approach to Me. The feeling with which a devotee approaches Me determines the kind of reward he is going to get, whether it is the chakra, which is the symbol of death, or a blessing."

The Guru is ever-content within himself, and the bliss that flows within him is absolutely full, it is perfect, and it cannot be increased by any outer factor, by any act on the part of the devotee or disciple, by any act of service, purity, or act of devotion. Because as far as the Guru's own bliss is concerned, it is ever-perfect, it is ever-full, it is ever-complete.

But the particular feeling of satisfaction which arises in the Guru as a result of tapasya on the part of the disciple, as a result of his great inner devotion for the Guru, bestows all powers, all knowledge on the disciple. Those who are able to please the Guru through their selfless devotion or service will attain everything in the world. There will be, in fact, nothing which will be beyond their reach. Therefore, paradoxically speaking, the Guru feels satisfied when he is already satisfied, when he is already fully contented, and he feels angry when he is already beyond anger. You attain what you already have and the peace which comes already exists within you.

Visitor: *During meditation, sweet and noble feelings arise within my heart, but after I get up and begin to attend to things outside, those feelings vanish, in spite of my best efforts to retain them. On the other hand, in spite of my best efforts to control impure or tamasic feelings, they come up and possess my mind. What should I do in order to retain those noble feelings at all times, in every situation?*

Baba: This is a very good question. It's very good to experience sweet and noble feelings during meditation, and you should try to experience them more and more. Take the case of a man from Bombay who goes to a hill resort during summer: he spends some time there and returns to Bombay before the summer in Bombay has ended. After returning to Bombay he will feel worse than when he left, because of the sharp contrast. In the hill resort he was enjoying such nice cool air, and the heat of Bombay now oppresses him twice as much as before. Besides, before going to that mountain resort, he was able to bear the heat by force of habit, but now that his habit has somewhat weakened during his stay in the mountain resort, his power of endurance has also weakened, and he feels much more miserable than if he had never gone to that mountain resort. After returning to Bombay and staying there for a while, he is able to bear the heat as before. But this doesn't mean that the temperature has come down. What has happened is that as a result of staying in Bombay for a little while, he has been able to bear the heat which he was accustomed to previously.

And this is exactly what happens to a meditator. During meditation the mind turns inwards and one is able to dive deeper and deeper, as a result of which one experiences sweet and sweeter and even the sweetest feelings of bliss bubbling up from within; and these feelings are pure and sattvic. And when he comes out of meditation into the outer world, he begins to feel miserable because of the contrast. Whatever you call happiness or joy in the outer world is basically rajasic, and it is because of contrast—the sattvic bliss enjoyed in meditation and the rajasic pleasure enjoyed normally—that one begins to feel miserable. It doesn't mean that one has fallen lower or that one has fallen into a worse state.

While writing my commentary on the *Guru Gita*, I mentioned that a meditator is able to make even his body divine, even in his body he becomes one with the Supreme Being. So while you are meditating, you experience pure bliss inside. The sweetest impulses arise from within and this bliss cannot be experienced from anything in the outer world. What is inner is inner, and what is outer is outer. If you have begun to experience inner bliss, it doesn't mean that you will be able to experience it in the outside world also; that will take time. Let's say the joy or the peace that you experience during the sleep state will not be experienced by you during the waking state. However, if you can get into the same state that you experience during sleep, while awake, you will be able to experience some of that joy. This inner nectar, this pure bliss which arises from within, begins to spill through all the seven constituents of the body. You should learn to drink more and more of this inner nectar. And the more you drink this nectar, the more will it permeate all the seven constituents. And there will come a time when your entire body will be saturated with the nectar of inner bliss. Then your body will become divine, and you will enjoy the same bliss even after coming out of meditation, in spite of moving and acting in the outer world. In that state your experience of bliss will never be interrupted, will never be broken.

The Guru's body is described as divine, as consciousness, and that is true. In fact, the body of each one of us is fully conscious, but we realise it only when as a result of daily regular meditation this inner nectar begins to spread through all the different parts of our body. After it saturates all the different parts of the body, the body in its totality realises its divinity. It is in this context that Tukaram Maharaj says, talking about the body, not the mind, "It is the body of a devotee which becomes one with the Lord, which becomes fully divine."

April 10, 1972

Visitor: *Why do we worship Shiva and Krishna separately when the Lord, the Supreme Being, is one and the same?*
Baba: The Lord is one, there is no doubt about it, but the devotees are many, and the different modes of worship are taken recourse to by different devotees; the Lord doesn't need different ways of worship. The author of the *Shiva Mahimna Stotra* says, while addressing the Lord, "Though Thou art one, yet devotees worship You in different ways, depending on their temperament and taste." In fact, the way in which you worship the Lord depends entirely on your own inclination, or the character of your own mind. As far as the Lord is concerned, He has nothing to do with it. Take for example, the case of a Jain monk who happens to see somebody killing an animal: he would be so shocked that he would probably go on a fast for two days. Then on the other hand, take the case of that tribal chief called Kanapa, who had taken a pledge that he would first offer to the Lord whatever he got to eat. Then he would kill an animal, and offer it first to his deity and then partake of it. Obviously, what you are doing depends on your own inclination, not on what God has commanded.

Then there is a sect of yogis who prepare a special thing called roti which is like a chapati, but which is much larger and much thicker, and it has rich ingredients. They add so many dried fruits to it and they fry it in ghee, and as a result, it can last for a long period. They say that they are cooking it to offer it to the Lord, but what happens is that they need it when they go out for a long journey, and they keep pieces in their pockets, and whenever they feel hungry, they can eat them. So the kind of prasad that they are offering to the Lord depends on their needs and inclinations.

Therefore, the way you worship the Lord depends on your own inclination. If a saint finds peace through a certain method, he begins to recommend it to his followers and that is how different sects come into existence. However, the true nature of worship is entirely different. Jnaneshwar Maharaj while describing worship, says that true worship means becoming absolutely still, doing nothing. Meditation means that you yourself become all, become everything. And true offering to the Lord is the state of equanimity, the state which is completely free of any sense of distinction, the state of profound peace. My Guru used to drink coffee, and he invited me also a couple of times to have coffee with him. And even now if you go to the Samadhi early in the morning you will find a few cups of coffee sitting on the Samadhi. People still offer coffee to the Samadhi thinking that it will go to Baba. If somebody were to ask them why they were doing it, they would say that this is how they like to worship their deity. These different modes of worship are nothing but different ways to satisfy your own mind, to soothe it. Because as far as the Lord is concerned, He is completely full in Himself, He is beyond all worship. You can worship Him truly only when you yourself become divine, when you become one with Him. While worshipping the Lord, when you become completely absorbed in the act of worship, that is the highest worship. The Lord describes true worship in the 13th chapter of the *Gita*. He says, "He is My true worshipper who is able to see all the different things of the world—favourable or unfavourable, agreeable or disagreeable—as one, as Me manifested in all these different things."

Mahadeviji: *Is it a sin, or does one incur sin while killing the flies and other insects which one may find crawling in the kitchen?*
Baba: Even if you were not to kill them, they would die very soon by themselves. And if you kill them, then you are doing something for their own good, sort of. But if you do not kill them, then they will kill many of you first, and then die. Therefore, to make sure that your eating place is free from all germs and insects and flies is quite proper, because that would take care of your health.

Ron: *When I experience light during meditation, my body usually feels very heavy and remains so for a while after the meditation. Why is this?*
Baba: There is a certain process in yoga called kumbhak, retention of breath, and if you were to hold your breath, the body would become very heavy. If I were to hold my breath

in a certain way, and sit on the elephant, the elephant would find me so heavy, he would perhaps collapse. When during meditation, the prana becomes still and steady, the body begins to feel heavy, and that is a very good sign. That feeling of heaviness vanishes in course of time. For a certain length of time, all the different constituents of the body, the body fluids and the limbs which are constantly active, become still, and it is as a result of that that you find heaviness in the body. What is happening to you is quite in order. That shows that you are experiencing stillness during meditation.

Elizabeth: *Although you have blessed me with much peace of mind and joy since I arrived here, my concentration is still very poor. I try to be patient, knowing that you will bless me with meditation one day, but how can I love my inner Self if I don't have any contact with it? Is it that I have so many impurities that prevent this?*
Baba: It is not merely impurities which prevent it; a part of your mind must be diverted towards home. Just a tiny little? So you can concentrate on only one thing. You can either concentrate on what is happening here, or in England. Continue to keep on honouring yourself through meditation and you will certainly get it one day. Everyone should try to get beyond the mind and get deeper into the Self during meditation. You will certainly find peace. True peace cannot be had so easily. It is not so cheap that you can buy it for practically nothing. You have to make a very earnest effort to get it. However, this is true: he who has a simple, uncrooked heart, and who is able to turn his mind inwards without difficulty will find peace very soon. Do you feel angry every now and then? Just as anger comes again and again, so peace will come again and again, because peace is allied to anger.

Dan K: *After waking up, I have a great deal of difficulty stilling my mind down to meditate. I am flooded with impressions, wave upon wave of memories, dream images and uneasiness. Also with these impressions comes a sense of sadness and futility. What should I do?*
Baba: Regardless of what is happening you should persist

in meditation. All kinds of thoughts and feelings will keep on passing through the mind for a long time. If your mind were to remain completely empty, then what would be the need of meditation? It is because the mind continues to wander that one feels the need of meditation. Otherwise, meditation would be utterly pointless. You should not dwell upon the thoughts, impressions, memories and feelings which flood the mind, because it is not to focus your attention on them that you are sitting for meditation.

You should first decide: what is the object of meditation? What is the purpose of meditation? First we must understand very clearly without the least bit of confusion what exactly meditation is, how we should meditate and what we should meditate on. Are we going to focus the mind on one particular object during meditation, or are we going to use our mental energies in fighting with all the different thoughts and feelings and images which keep pouring into the mind? You have to decide whether you are going to concentrate on the thoughts which arise in the mind, or on the nature of the mind, or on the Lord Himself? If you have to meditate on the Lord, then you shouldn't bother about these thoughts and feelings and images which come up in the mind. If you try to drive them away from the mind, it is just like a person trying to remove everything on the way from his room to the meditation hall here. One's effort to empty the mind of thoughts is just like the effort to remove everything from the roadside. Then what would happen if that person, after coming into the meditation room, began to be distracted by all the different things lying there, by the photos of Baba, the cushions, and the other meditators? He would probably want to shove all those out also. He would like the pictures to be removed, he would like all the cushions to go, and he wouldn't like to have any other meditators around either. If, instead of bothering about all those externals, a person were to come straight from his room to the meditation hall, remaining absorbed in himself all the time, thinking of his own Self every moment, and then sit down and again turn his attention inside, he would not be at all bothered by those outer objects.

So now we have to decide what is the true object of meditation. Is it the mind or the intellect or the ego or the inner Self? Therefore, sit calmly for meditation and let whatever thoughts arise in the mind, arise. Let new worlds come into being within you, and let them pass out of existence. You should only try to be aware of the one who is witnessing all these thoughts. You should ask yourself, "Who is seeing all these thoughts coming into the mind?" You should meditate on the inner Being who constantly keeps awake and watches what is happening in the mind all the time, who witnesses all the thoughts, memories and images which spring up in the mind, who tells you whether you are able to meditate or not, and who, when you pass into a state of deep meditation, remains conscious and watches even that state. Try to meditate on that Self who is continually witnessing, who is continually wakeful. This Being, though dwelling within the mind, keeps on watching all that happens in the mind without becoming one with it even for a moment. And this Being is without attributes, without form, and He is the constant witness of the universes which are springing into existence in your own mind. So meditate on That. Do not meditate on ordinary thoughts and memories which distract the mind. You have to be aware during meditation of the inner Self, of God, of the Supreme Being, not of the ordinary contents of the mind.

There are so many visitors coming to the Ashram, and what do they come here to see? They should know what the most important thing in the Ashram is, whether it is the gatekeeper, or certain trees, or the elephant or the gardens, or Baba's statue in the temple. Similarly, while meditating, we should first decide what is the true, the supreme object of meditation. All the time different thoughts arise and subside in the mind and this process has no significance. Once you begin to be aware of the conscious Self, then the contents of the mind will lose their importance for you. Therefore, you should not attach any importance to your thoughts. Leave them aside.

Carol: *I feel witness-consciousness growing. What can I do to stay centred in this consciousness? How does it relate to discrimination?*
Baba: The only way to stay centred in witness-consciousness is to stay as a witness. You should continually remain

a witness to what is happening inside, and you will remain centred in that consciousness. In your ordinary life, sometimes it happens that even when you are participating in different things you feel that you are different from all those things. Similarly, to remain aware of the inner witness is what is called discrimination, or true knowledge. If you have achieved discrimination, then even witness-consciousness would not be necessary. If through discrimination and knowledge you were to understand that you, the real you, the inner Self is the constant witness—witnessing whatever you are doing, whether you are bathing, sweeping the floors, eating, or meditating—then you wouldn't have to practise witness-consciousness. If you have understood that the inner Self is aware of what is happening in meditation all the time, then even meditation would not be necessary. It is the Lord Himself who is the inner witness. This witness is completely pure and never gets tainted by anything. To understand this, to be aware of this, is discrimination.

Roderick: *For months I have been nagged by thoughts of home and my continued education. Now that I am idle because of this illness, it is worse. Please advise me as to the best thing to do.*
Baba: You must realise that it is the very nature of the mind to keep thinking constantly. At present you are thinking about your home and education, and if you were not thinking about your home or education, your mind would be thinking about something else. It may start thinking about the future, or it may begin to make plans, obliterating olds ones and making new ones all the time. The mind has to think about one thing or another. If you wish to continue your education, then you can go back home and finish it, because education has great importance. After you recover from your present illness, go back to your country and finish your education. It is quite natural for you to remember your home and your country where you spent such a long period of time, and to which you must have become strongly attached in the process. It is for this reason that the sages and seers ask you to think of the Lord, so that at a later stage, thoughts of Him may arise in the mind spontaneously again and again. Just as you are now recollecting your old streets,

your old home, or your school, similarly, when you go back you will recollect what you are doing here now. You will recollect chanting, swadhyaya and meditation. That is why I ask you to undertake all these practices with love and with reverence, so that their memory may spring up in the mind again and again when you are not here.

Kedarnath: *On which side of the vision of the Blue Pearl, or the experience of turiya, does Gopi-consciousness lie? This side or the other side?*
Baba: It is the experience of the Blue Pearl which constitutes the true Gopi-consciousness, because it is that experience which is the goal of this consciousness. It involves becoming one with what you are thinking about. The Gopis used to become completely absorbed in the ultimate truth, which lies even beyond the Blue Pearl. The Gopis were fully aware of the existence of the Supreme Being, the Being who is without form, without qualities, the constant witness. You should not think that the Gopis were ordinary women, or people who didn't have much intelligence, or who got attracted towards worship of the form in an unintelligent manner, through lack of discrimination. It is the vision in which you see the Blue Pearl exploding, and the blue light spreading all around which is the goal of the Gopi-consciousness. It is this Blue Pearl which assumes the form of Krishna or Shiva or Rama or Nityananda. There is nothing sectarian about this light, because this light is pure Existence, and that is neither with form nor formless. The Gopis were intensely drawn towards the personal form which this pure light assumes. The Gopis wanted to see the pure blue existence in the personal form. A long time ago I copied down a verse describing the state of the Gopis in a most beautiful manner. Gopi-consciousness was a very high state of consciousness, because they were aware of the pure blue light. They could see Krishna whenever they wanted within that blue light. So mighty is the power of the blue light that it can become not only one Krishna, but a thousand Krishnas.

Pratibha: *I want to become so completely absorbed in devotion to the Guru that I begin to feel that whatever I do arises* *from inspiration from the Guru. But in such a moment my mind tells me that I have possessed this kind of urge right from my birth, and such a noble urge was present in my mind even before meeting my Gurudeva. So how should I resolve this feeling within me?*

Baba: The second part of your statement is nothing but an egotistical illusion which has been produced by your silly education; it doesn't go with the first part. Otherwise, the first part will have to be dismissed as an illusion. Therefore, you should realise that it is an illusion on your part to think that you had all this since your birth. You should understand that the contact with the Guru is based on a relationship with him which has lasted through countless births. Some past relationship has to be at the back of even an ordinary contact with some other person. You may be coming to the Ashram now, or you may be seeing your Guru only now for the first time, but the fact is that your contact with him is very old. You should become so immersed in your devotion to the Guru that there should be absolutely no room left for the sense of 'I'. So to feel on the one hand that it is the Guru that is doing everything, and then in the next breath to feel that this is your innate tendency, these two things don't go together. Why don't you submerge your ego, your sense of 'I', in your devotion to the Guru?

The fact is that the Guru has been with his disciple throughout many births, and to be aware of this fact is to be aware of a great truth. So the Guru and the disciple have a very strong relationship with each other, lasting through many lives. It is only as a result of this that all the disciples of the Guru feel drawn towards him at one time or another, regardless of the different countries or the different races or the different religions they may have been born in. To an ordinary person, India is divided into different parts, such as Gujarat, Maharashtra, Kannada, Punjab and so on. But to the sun, India is one. If you were to ask the sun, "Where is Gujarat?" the sun would not be able to answer, because the sun is not conscious of these distinctions. So for God, the division of the world into different countries such as America, Australia, India, Africa and so on is not at all valid. To the Lord the world is one, and whenever there is a need, He makes sure that certain people get together in a certain place at a certain time. The entire earth belongs to us, and this sense of distinction is a mere illusion. In your practical life you do need these divisions, but as far as higher awareness is concerned, that should be free of any sense of distinction or difference. When you are attending to your practical affairs, you should be guided by practical considerations.

Therefore, if you have surrendered yourself completely to the Guru, then the question of the sense of 'I' existing even in a small degree would not arise. It is only when you do not surrender fully that 'I' remains with you.

April 12, 1972

Craig Hughes: *I have great respect for you, and my devotion to you appears to be increasing. I say 'appears', because my ego and worldly thoughts seem as strong as ever. Is it false and selfish to want to be more and more devoted so that I may achieve some degree of Self-realisation?*
Baba: It's very good that you have great respect for me, and that your devotion to me is increasing. And it should continue to increase; you shouldn't stop half-way. This constant increase is the only way of insuring continuous growth. Take the case of the Ganges which arises as a tiny trickle in the mountains: as it comes down towards the plains, it begins to swell, and it swells bigger and bigger until it reaches the ocean. The result is that it finally becomes one with the ocean. After the Ganges has become one with the ocean, it doesn't maintain its separate identity any longer. And that is exactly what should happen in your case, also. Your devotion should continue to increase until you lose your sense of 'I'. It is only when the Ganges loses its separate existence that it becomes the ocean. As long as it retains its separate existence, it is only a river. A poet-saint says that he alone truly lives, who obliterates his consciousness of the

world, and his sense of self, and becomes one with Brahman. Such a one becomes immortal from being merely mortal.

It is not at all selfish on your part to want to be more devoted; it is a very valid desire. I wonder who would call it selfishness? Even if it is selfish, it is selfishness of a different sort; it is a noble or sublime selfishness, very different from ordinary selfishness which seeks sense gratification, pleasure, and the satisfaction of its own tummy, and is not interested in anything else. Such a desire can never be called selfish. It is a true spiritual urge. To merge oneself in the Lord is the most natural thing for one to do. Once somebody asked a question of me, and he said that he had put this question to many others, and had not gotten a satisfactory answer. The question was, "Why is it that all the rivers rush towards the ocean?" I said, "Look, it's from the ocean that vapours arise, and these vapours become clouds and clouds turn into rain, and as a result of rain a river comes into existence. So it is quite natural for the river to rush towards the sea, because the sea is its very source. The sea is the place from which it has sprung, and to which it owes its existence, so there could be nothing more natural for a river than rushing towards the sea and losing its identity in the sea."

The drop which we call the embodied soul has emerged from the ocean, the limitless ocean of the Supreme Being, or God, and it is quite natural for this drop to feel an intense yearning to become one with its source, to become one with this limitless ocean of consciousness. This alone is the most natural dharma. All other obligations and duties are adharma. They are not natural dharma. There are so many different dharmas, and forms of duties. They don't have much importance; they are at best secondary. The most important dharma, the most important duty, which is also the most natural for man, is to want to become one with the source, with the Being from whom he has emerged. And this has been sanctioned by all the scriptures.

Ron: *For the last few weeks I have been chanting Guru Om during most of my meditation. Last week I increased my meditation to two and a half to three hours a day. But since*

Monday I have been getting headaches. Am I doing something wrong? Or is this pressure necessary as the mind is strengthened?
Baba: First you should be sure whether you are getting a headache or it is just pressure which is building up in the head. (Pressure.) You should use the correct word. You cannot call pressure a headache. Pressure is a good sign, while a headache is not a good sign. A headache is an ailment which comes from other causes. Now it is summer time and you should reduce the period of meditation to one hour, or at the most one and a half hours. And you should increase japa. What you feel as pressure is nothing but a sensation which accompanies stillness of mind. If you were to run your finger over the back of your hand at great speed, you would not feel any weight on the hand. But if you were to slow the movement down, you would feel some pressure, some weight. And if you were to just hold it stationary, the weight would be the greatest. This is exactly what happens with the mind also. In our ordinary condition the mind moves at such great speed that we do not feel its movement at all. But during meditation it begins to slow down, and as it slows down, we begin to feel pressure in the head. This is a good sign.

Kalyani: *You said that one who honours food will be honoured by food, while one who does not will always be begging. Does this also hold true for money? If I have been extravagant and careless in my financial dealings in the past, how will this affect my future? What should be the proper attitude of a sadhak towards money or the lack of it?*
Baba: One who spends extravagantly will not take long in turning into a beggar. Otherwise, to get more money you will have to resort to all kinds of dealings, even improper dealings. The Vedantic viewpoint, or the viewpoint of a meditator, should be that the universe is full of Chiti, the universe is nothing but Chiti. And it is foolish to look upon things as being different from one another. To look upon money, bananas, mangoes, and other things as being food, clothes, money, and so on, is a very ordinary viewpoint. It is the viewpoint of ignorance.

Money must be spent with great care, with great respect, systematically, properly, discreetly. If you insult something, you will be insulted back; that is the inexorable law of God. You should not regard a piece of cloth as a mass of threads. It is God Himself who is appearing in the form of threads. And the same God is appearing in your form. Therefore, you should consider everything to be divine, to be full of God, and having this viewpoint, you should spend money. You should have proper reverence for everything. You may spend as much as is necessary, regardless of the amount involved, but you must not spend indiscriminately. So much work is done to prepare food and to produce food. So is it proper on our part to slight food? Then, you work so hard for money. One undertakes different practices such as yajna, japa and tapa and it is as a result of these meritorious deeds performed over a long period of time that one comes into wealth. And when this is the case, would it be proper to waste the same money foolishly, or to spend the same money indiscriminately?

There is an abundance of food here, yet if you were to waste two chapatis, I would become so angry that people would think that I was the worst miser on the surface of the earth. But that only shows how much respect, how much reverence I have for food.

I'll tell you a story. There was a great, very rich millionaire in Madras, and he was very rich. He was so rich that when his firm was wound up, the property and money were divided into 3,500 equal parts. People said that his income amounted to more than a million dollars a week, and they also said that he owned all the banks in the neighbouring countries, such as Singapore, Burma, and other places. Once, Shankaracharya of Kamakshi Pitha had to build up a monastery, and for that he needed money. Somebody suggested that they approach this millionaire. They expected a handsome donation from him, and they said others would also donate, and with that money they would be able to build up the math. A group of people went to him to ask for a donation. They got there about 2 or 3 p.m., and when they reached his store they found to their utter surprise that the millionaire himself was clad in a simple lungi bending down picking each little grain of wheat that had fallen down on the floor.

That is exactly what my attitude is. If I happen to go to the kitchen and see five grains of dal on the floor, I'll call the cook and ask him how come those five grains are being wasted.

Shankaracharya was a member of this group, and when they reached the store they asked where the millionaire was. They could not believe the man crouching on the floor collecting those little grains could be the millionaire himself, and when they were told, "Yes, it is he," they spoke in a very rude tone, "Could that fellow be he?" Then they were introduced to the millionaire, and the millionaire treated them with respect. He took them to his seat and asked them respectfully what had brought them there. They said, "We are intending to raise a large math. For that we shall be needing about a million rupees, and you should also make your donation."

He called his secretary and asked him to issue a check for a million rupees right there. This flabbergasted Shankaracharya, because Shankaracharya in the beginning had thought that this fellow, who was so particular about every single grain that had fallen on the floor, would not like to give them any money. Then the millionaire said, "It is because I have treated wealth with respect, with such reverence, that today I am in a position to donate a million rupees."

Even now that family is quite prosperous; one of that family was a devotee of my Guru.

Therefore, money must be honoured, it must not be slighted. Otherwise, Lakshmi, the Goddess of wealth, will curse you and leave you in a miserable plight. And once She has pronounced her curse, whatever you may do, you will not be able to regain the wealth that you have lost. Similarly, if food becomes angry on being slighted by you, it leaves you, and it will never come back, no matter how hard you try. Usually we find people praying to the Lord, "Lord, give us wealth, give us factories, give us horses, give us elephants, give us this, give us that." So whatever possession we have is a gift of God, and it must be treated as a gift of

God. If we dishonour it, if we treat it irreverently, then we are treating God with irreverence.

We must spend our money carefully, and we must be sure that we put it to good uses. This applies to everything. If you have spent your money extravagantly and carelessly in the past, it is only destitution which awaits you in the future. We should have respect for money, being aware of the fact that somebody has worked very hard for it, and moreover, it is the gift of God. You should see how all the articles given to me as offerings are treated here, what respect and reverence and care is lavished on them. You can see how all the different articles the devotees bring are kept in the Ashram. They look as though they were articles of worship. They will, of course, be given away some day to people who are worthy, but that doesn't mean that they should be neglected now.

You should produce as much food as you can and feed as many people as you can, but you have no right to throw food away. Earn as much money as you can, but utilise it in a noble manner. You should give your money away liberally, to make as many people as happy as you can. It is stupid to waste your money on horse racing, drinking, nightclubs, or luxuries and pleasure-seeking.

Therefore, everything should be honoured, and whatever you have should be looked upon as your own merit. The clothes which you are wearing should not be treated as mere clothes. It is your past merit which is covering your body in the form of clothes.

Bill: *Should I do asanas in the morning, or should I spend that time in meditation? And if I should do asanas, which ones, and should I do them before or after meditating?*
Baba: What time do you get up? If you sit for a long time in a meditative posture, then you get the benefits of all the different postures. So spend your time in meditation. If you feel the need of asanas, then you can practise a few asanas, say about five or six, and then sit for meditation.

Kedarnath: *These days after meditating for fifteen or twenty minutes I feel acute pain between my eyebrows. It*

feels as though somebody were thrashing me severely, and my head also becomes heavy. Because of these things I have to sleep, even though I don't want to sleep. Is it proper for me to sleep?
Baba: For a month or two, until the rainy season, you should not meditate. Instead of meditating, do japa, or remember the Lord. Increase the repetition of the mantra. As a result of the processes which are taking place in your case, a great event, known as bindu bheda, or piercing of the ocular chakra, will take place in course of time. The eyes will begin to revolve. Let them revolve. You should spend more time in japa.

Draupadi: *Many seekers here have specialised in meditating during swadhyaya. Some of them even sit on one side to perform kriyas. Does it mean that the Shakti is against swadhyaya? Or is it pleased with those who meditate instead of doing swadhyaya, but displeased with those who do swadhyaya devotedly?*
Baba: Shakti is a great lover of music and song. Have you listened to the hymn to Goddess Chandi? That hymn has been sung by me in a particular manner, and in a particular rhythm. Shakti is greatly pleased with music, so much so that Saraswati is always holding her sitar in her hand. And I wonder if she ever sleeps.

Swadhyaya can go on even while you are doing kriyas. If as a result of kriyas you have to stop chanting, then it means that there is something wrong with your kriyas; they are very inferior kriyas, and there isn't much meaning in them.

It is swadhyaya which has the power of activating kriyas. How does one get into the heightened state? Does one get into a heightened state through chanting, or does it come itself? Those who have to stop chanting in order to do kriyas are absolutely dry and joyless people, incapable of experiencing any rasa. When instead of chanting they begin to move their hands, they seem to be saying, "You are neither here nor there, neither inside or outside, you are nowhere." If the kriyas were really joyful then you could combine them with swadhyaya. You would chant, and along with that you would be experiencing delicious currents of joy shooting through your body.

You should understand exactly what swadhyaya is, what the nature of the sound is. Swadhyaya is nothing but worship of the Supreme Being as nada or sound. Those who stop chanting become alienated from nada Brahman, or Brahman appearing as sound, and become engaged instead in dry, joyless kriyas. If you were to chant along with the kriyas, you would enjoy the kriyas much more. In fact, the bliss that you would feel would be so intense and so sweet that you wouldn't even be able to imagine them. You must have heard how I used to chant *Narayana, Narayana*; that was the result of a certain kriya going on within. Also, during the Saptah sometimes people become so excited that instead of chanting they become more interested in dancing; the tempo is quickened so much that the rhythm player even breaks the rhythm, and the other musical instruments are broken, and what is worth doing, namely chanting, is neglected and something secondary, dancing, or merely jumping around is preferred.

Sound has more importance. Before swadhyaya there is time for meditation, and you meditate during that time. So what's the point of meditating in swadhyaya? Meditating during swadhyaya is just like going to the kitchen and falling asleep there. Then the kitchen is not being used as a kitchen, but as a bedroom. The kitchen is not a bedroom, and when you are in the kitchen, you should be eating— along with kriyas, if they are taking place. Similarly, during the time of swadhyaya you should be chanting along with the kriyas. Those people who are not chanting are only depriving themselves of the opportunity of purifying their organ of speech, their tongue. And purification of speech is a great siddhi. Whatever words you utter come to be true. This siddhi, however, can only be acquired by those who chant with devotion, remain silent after swadhyaya, and speak only if necessary. Then your voice becomes exceedingly sweet as a result of swadhyaya, and your tongue becomes completely purified. We are defiling our tongue all the time by forcing it to taste all kinds of foods.

Shakti can never be against swadhyaya for the simple

reason that swadhyaya is undertaken to worship Shakti. You may look at any picture of Shakti, and you will find her holding some musical instrument in her hand. Shakti is so interested in music and in chanting that if Tansen and Narada were to sing to the accompaniment of the tambouras, then Vishnu Himself would beat the rhythm on the mridung, and Brahma would play the cymbals.

I am happy about one thing, and that is that it is mostly Indian girls who seem to prefer meditation to swadhyaya. The number of foreign girls who prefer meditation seems to be very small compared to them. The foreigners are quite intelligent, and they follow scrupulously what they are told to do, and that is why they make quick progress.

Shakti is not a jealous washerwoman who would be displeased with those who are doing swadhyaya. Only those people who join an ashram just to spend their days without any purpose neglect swadhyaya. And those who have come to the Ashram with a definite purpose, with a serious purpose, would do everything in a proper manner, and follow the Ashram discipline fully. You find all kinds of characters getting into the Ashram, characters who are frivolous, flippant, and have no interest in sadhana. And these people after coming to the Ashram—if it is a girl she starts looking for a boy, and if it is a boy, he starts looking for a girl—and they become interested in detestable pleasure-seeking. They are not at all worthy of living in an ashram. This morning I went for the darshan of the Goddess Vajreshwari, and as I reached the temple, I was surrounded by eighty policemen. I am not a criminal. They surrounded me because of their love for me. I asked them, "Why have all of you come?"

They said, "We have to come here in full force, because all kinds of characters come to attend such fairs."

Similarly, all kinds of characters get into an ashram. There are some who come here only to kill time, because they have nothing else to do. There are others who come here as sincere, earnest seekers, who have much interest in spiritual attainment. There are some who are very keen on instantaneous enlightenment, and there are others who seem to have infinite patience, and who won't mind getting a thing when it comes, however long the time lag may be.

April 14, 1972

Visitor: *What is the importance of wearing rudraksha beads, and who is qualified to wear these beads according to the scriptures? Are these beads a sign of beauty?*
Baba: Rudraksha are not a small sign of beauty, they are a most important symbol of beauty. Just as in worldly life the beauty aids which you use are cosmetics, different ornaments, cremes and powders, in spiritual life, it is your rudraksha mala which is the best beauty aid. In ancient times, the ways in which one beautified himself were also useful for the body. But today, unfortunately, the ways of adornment are merely for fashion and have no use for the body or for other aspects of one's being. There was a time when people wore silk and pure cotton. These materials have great qualities; they are very good for the body. But today, people wear artificial silk or things made of synthetics, and these are not at all good for the body; they create all kinds of troubles, and they affect the skin very badly. Whatever was recommended by the rishis was good for the body, good for the people in different ways, and it also enhanced beauty.

Take another custom: for instance, here our women used to wear gold ornaments. Gold not only adorns the body, but it also has great medicinal value, because gold destroys all kinds of diseases. When our women used to wear a lot of gold, they would not fall prey to diseases so easily. But today, now that they have stopped wearing gold, they have to resort to ointments and bandages much too frequently.

Rudraksha beads not only adorn the person, but they also are very useful in spiritual life. Moreover, rudraksha beads destroy germs, and they keep the blood pressure normal. Rudraksha beads free us from so many other troubles. It is essential for spiritual seekers to wear rudraksha beads because they are extremely useful. They insulate a seeker from all misfortunes and calamities. Besides, it is also the question of following the example of great people, and that is what the Lord emphasises in the *Bhagavad Gita*. There was a time when Mahatma Gandhi wore a plain and simple cap, and all his followers started wearing that kind of cap. It was Lord Shankara, right in the beginning of time, who was the first to wear rudraksha beads, and after Shankara, all the spiritual seekers started wearing them. Rudraksha beads keep the body pure all the time. There are different ways of keeping the body pure, say touching the body in different places with the repetition of mantras, which is called nyasa, and washing it a number of times. But these ways cannot keep the body pure even for twenty-four hours. But if you are wearing rudraksha beads, they keep the body pure at all times, and you do not have to resort to other practices.

All those who have faith and devotion are qualified to wear rudraksha beads. There is no other special qualification required for wearing them. Women are as qualified to wear them as men. Rudraksha beads have been honoured from time immemorial. They are mentioned in the *Upanishads* and also in the *Vedas*. If I were to put it concisely, I would say that rudraksha beads are Rudra Himself, Lord Shiva Himself.

Mahadev Prasad: *What is the significance of saints producing miracles? Do these miracles help people in any way to attain spiritual bliss?*
Baba: I have come across many miracle-mongers in the course of my life. Only the other day one of them was here. His name is Narielwala Baba (the Baba with the coconut). If you ask him a question, he breaks a coconut and produces a printed answer from it. But none of those people could help me attain peace, in spite of the fact that I knew them intimately. I don't know exactly what is behind these miracles, even though I have met so many who perform them. From the right viewpoint, the universe is the most amazing miracle.

I am surprised that people attach so much importance to artificial, fake miracles, and that they neglect the most natural miracles. I wonder whether it is the nature of man to neglect what is of importance to him. The universe itself is full of amazing miracles. Take the case of birds who fly in the sky and who can float in the sky for hours and hours. Isn't that a most natural miracle? Yet there are people who go after a sadhu who can levitate just about an inch. Isn't it surprising that people should neglect this most natural miracle of birds that fly in the air, and pay so much attention to a sadhu who can levitate just about an inch?

Take the case of fish or other aquatic creatures. The fish spend their entire life in water; they procreate in water, they live in water with their entire families, with their little babies. Yet people neglect this phenomenon which is natural. But if there is a yogi who can sit on the water for about half an hour, you find millions going after him. Isn't that a surprise?

If one were to meditate, one would see most natural miracles within his own being. But unfortunately, people do not want to see inner miracles; they are only interested in seeing phony outer miracles and all kinds of spectacular displays. It is a matter of great sorrow that man has become so accustomed to ignorance, that he doesn't mind falling into it deeper than ever before. In his worldly life he remains forgetful, and even in spiritual life he doesn't abandon that tendency.

A new miracle, fresh from the oven, is occurring in Vajreshwari. Shall I tell you about it? A sadhu has come to Vajreshwari with ten young dogs, and he has put them in a tent. If Mr. Yande were to go there, and if his watch were to be taken by Mr. Marwar and if Mr. Marwar were to go inside that tent, then the dog would take the watch from his pocket and give it back to Mr. Yande. If that sadhu himself were to perform the same miracle what would be so special about it, when even a dog can do it? You can go yourself and see the miracles performed by these dogs. If you make four people stand before these dogs, and if you were to ask one who has eaten more, and who has eaten less, they would be able to point them out. Those dogs are performing most wonderful other miraculous feats; I have described one or two, and I do not want to spend too much time on it, because once you get entangled in miracles, its a hopeless entanglement.

No great saint has ever performed miracles. People have followed great saints being aware of their spiritual greatness. However, we must make a distinction between the miracles which happen during natural course in the lives of great saints, and the miracles which are stagey, showy, which are performed for display. What's the use of the things which are materialised? They are the very things which we find around us in our everyday life, so what's the point of making them by magic? Finally, one gets sick of all these stagey miracles, and one has to resort to a most natural method. Whatever miracles a saint may perform, they are of no use to him personally. He still has to wash his body in ordinary water, the same water which other mortals wash their bodies with; he has to wear the clothes made of the same material as that of others, he has to eat food and drink water to live like others. So what is the use of these miracles?

The other day there was a man who came here from Bombay. He foretells the future, and he told me that his son had run away, and he asked me to tell him when he would return. Then I asked him, "Look, you used to charge Rs. 100/- from a person to answer this about his future, and now that your son has run away, you have come rushing to me to find out when he will come back, so what were you telling those other people?"

Performing miracles is also an addiction, and some people indulge in them because of their craving for personal glory. Different people are driven by different cravings, cravings for status, honour, wealth and titles, and these people are only interested in having large crowds of followers around them, and that is why they indulge in miracles. And that is all there is to it.

Dayavati Khanna: *What is the significance of the sacred thread and the tuft of hair on the head?*
Baba: The sacred thread ceremony is based on certain very important things connected with life, so when the sacred thread is worn, mantras are chanted and thus the wearer is influenced by the power of those mantras. Among the sannyasis there is a sect of those who carry a staff, and they believe that once a member of their sect takes a staff he becomes Narayan Himself, because his staff is the symbol of the supreme Lord. Such a sannyasi would wash his staff every day, regarding it as Narayan, and this way the staff reminds him of the Lord.

Similarly, one who is wearing the sacred thread according to scriptural instructions would also be washing the sacred thread, and this way he would keep himself aware of certain things. The tuft of hair is respected very much, and for rituals it is very important. A devout Muslim would wear a beard; similarly, a devout Hindu would wear the tuft of hair on the head. It also has a part to play in rituals.

Janardan Trivedi: *The repetition of the Name is called japa yajna, and chanting of the Name is called the yoga of sankirtan or devotional sankirtan. What is the difference between the two? Does chanting of the divine Name form an independent spiritual discipline by itself? The scriptures say that one who chants a divine Name is delivered from all sins immediately, regardless of whether he has knowledge and devotion or faith before he begins to chant the divine Name, because all these qualities come up themselves during the course of chanting. What is your view?*
Baba: You must first be sure what the scriptures say. Don't the scriptures say that these qualities come to the person who continually chants the divine Name, and would you be able to continually chant the divine Name without faith or devotion? So even for chanting the divine Name, faith is required. And if you do not have faith in it, why should you be chanting the divine Name all the time? However, chanting is a yoga in its own right, and yoga and yajna are in fact, synonymous, having the same meaning. The difference between Japa Yoga and nam sankirtan is that while japa is practised in solitude, and silently, the Name can be chanted either by oneself or with other people. Chanting which is done with great devotion, with great love is considered to be the most sublime method, the best method: If one has full faith in God, and one becomes intoxicated while chanting the divine Name, so much so that he begins to dance, then one discovers the nectar which is in the Name. In the olden days, devotees used to chant the divine Name with great fervour, and in the course of chanting the divine Name, they would not care for propriety or decorum. They would begin to dance with abandon, and this way not only would they purify themselves, but also all others. One who is practising japa makes only himself clean and pure and blissful,

but one who is chanting the divine Name purifies and cleanses all the people who listen to the sound of the chant— and not only all the people, but also all the other living things including plants and creepers, germs and insects and ants. All of them within the radius of the sound of the divine Name get purified. It is quite natural for man to begin to dance when he is feeling fully contented. This is exactly what happens during chanting. Chanting releases so much bliss inside that one becomes intoxicated and begins to dance. While doing japa you have to make an effort to keep the mind focused on the mantra, and then you have to follow certain rules. But in chanting there are no rules to be followed, and concentration of mind comes in the most natural manner. The ears begin to hear the sound of the chant, and the tongue begins to sing the divine Name, and all other organs become engaged in executing different gestures and dancing. Besides, through chanting, it is much easier to feel inner joy, inner ecstasy. Chanting intoxicates one much sooner than japa. Tukaram Maharaj, while describing the power of chanting, says in one of his verses that by the force of the divine chant he will make a knower of Brahman, who is talking about Brahman all the time, leave his knowledge aside and begin to chant. He will compel a yogi who is lost in the bliss of samadhi to come out of samadhi and even lose interest in the bliss of samadhi, and participate in the divine chant, and then he will compel a ritualist to give up his rituals and wear anklets on his feet and begin to chant and dance in sheer abandon. And he would also compel a sadhu who has extraordinary powers to forget all about his powers and to wear beads and join the throng of the chanters of the divine Name. The scriptures say that chanting is dear to the Lord also. Very shortly we are going to have sankirtan here and you can test the veracity of what I am saying through your own experience, through chanting and dancing.

Charles: *When I close my eyes I see an aggregate of little blue and red squares. What does this mean, and how should I behave towards them?*
Baba: In such a time, the seeker should only continue to see these things and also wait for what is going to come next. It must be red and blue lights which appear in the form of

squares. You should continue to gaze at these squares. Do these squares also shine (No.) It's a good experience. Continue to watch these squares. Other visions will also come. It's very good to see these inner lights.

Ron: *A number of times last fall, and once last week, usually while meditating, I felt pressure in my forehead and a small circle pushed into my forehead. What does this mean? If it happens again should I bring my concentration to this area and chant the mantra?*
Baba: Is it a circle or a ring? Is it a circle of light? (Just pressure, no colours.) That indicates that some kriya is taking place in the nerve channels. The prana is being stabilised. You should not do anything when this happens again, because you didn't do anything in particular to bring it about, so when it occurs again, you should stay absolutely calm. When you say a circle one would take it to mean a certain thing. What must be happening is that the prana must be getting accumulated inside the head. Does that happen? (I'm not sure.)

Olivier: *When at your side I find traces of the universe in myself. I feel an understanding of the sun, sky and stars, but not of the moon. Her language is strange to me, all her movements, phases seem to me beautiful and as subtle as the Guru. Sometimes I feel restless and uneasy before her. Please speak about the inner meaning of the moon.*
Baba: You say you have understood the sun, so in course of time you will also understand the moon. Why should you be in such a hurry? The nature of the moon is quite opposite to that of the sun. The moon bestows the experience of coolness within, and that is all that there is to it. You feel restless because you do not understand the moon. In fact, the moon is the presiding deity of the mind, so it is the deity of restlessness. The moon is also the deity of coolness and sometimes you get a vision of it in the sahasrar. But you should not get preoccupied with the moon. You should try to see what lies beyond that. You should try to see what is beyond the moon, the moon which shines in the sahasrar. It is very good that you are acquiring an understanding of all these outer spheres, the sun and the stars. Whatever

there is in the external universe, is also within man, and in meditation you will be able to see all these things within yourself. It is for this reason that I say again and again that inner miracles are far more interesting, far more valuable than external miracles; and you should try to see the inner miracles. Don't you think it is a great miracle to be able to see the inner moon? There is a moon in the outer universe, but the inner moon is far more fascinating. You are meditating very well, and you should advance further.

Bramachari Anantram: *To constantly hear the sound of the pranava, the sound of Om, to have visions of lights, to have the experience of the upward movement of prana, are these possible only after Kundalini awakening, or can they come without this awakening also? Can the Kundalini which is once awakened go to sleep again for some reason, and if that happens how can you explain it?*
Baba: To be able to constantly listen to the inner chant of Om, to have visions of lights, these experiences can come only after Kundalini awakening. They are, in fact, gifts of Her grace and they cannot come without such awakening. When the letters and the different sounds and letters composing pranava come into friction against one another, lights arise.

After Kundalini awakening, the prana is bound to rise upwards, and as a result of this, the prana and apana become equalised. The two become one in the sushumna and then the distinction between prana and apana vanishes. It is only then that supreme bliss arises. As long as prana and apana do not become one, or do not become steady, then bliss does not come.

These experiences cannot come without the awakening of the Kundalini. Kundalini, once awakened, will never go to sleep again; and if She goes to sleep again, that shows that the seeker must be guilty of a very great blunder, or he must have been slighting the Guru. If a seeker while living in the Guru's abode begins to do things which are improper, if he begins to pursue a vicious course, then the Kundalini can go to sleep again. Not only that: the Kundalini can even create a mental imbalance in such a person. While the Kundalini is getting awakened, if the seeker begins to follow improper or vicious courses, then that awakening is interrupted and the Kundalini goes to sleep again. Then what happens is that in the course of the awakening of the Kundalini, the disciple seems to become cleverer than the Guru, and then he leaves the Guru and sets himself up as a Guru in his own right. Such a one has not even become a full disciple, and he now claims to be a Guru, and as a result of that, Kundalini would throw him into a hopeless situation. There were quite a few people in Ganeshpuri whose brains were adversely affected and who suffered in other ways.

After the Kundalini awakening, one should remain fully vigilant. If the Kundalini is pleased, then She takes you to heaven, but if She becomes displeased, She can also throw you into hell. So, therefore, one should treat Kundalini with great reverence. The Kundalini can stop working if a seeker does not follow the discipline which is indispensable, or if the seeker slights the Guru and begins to follow a vicious course secretly. However, one has to be very discriminating in this matter, because sometimes after the Kundalini has finished working on the gross body, and begins to work on the subtle body, it appears as though the Kundalini has stopped working all together. So one should be very clear in his mind as to what exactly is happening. If one turns into a Guru and begins to award his grace on different people and begins to awaken their Kundalini, then whatever Shakti he received from his Guru is lost. It's just like a man borrowing Rs. 200/- from one man and lending Rs. 225/- to another. What will he be left with?

April 17, 1972

Bramachari Anantram: *In the scriptures on Jnana Yoga, we do not find any descriptions of the Kundalini. Does a person who is practising sadhana according to the disci-*

plines of Jnana Yoga, and who attains full knowledge as a result of that, attain Kundalini awakening or not, and is it possible to attain knowledge of God or supreme liberation without Kundalini awakening?

Baba: In Jnana Yoga, also, the final initiation is given by the Guru. That initiation itself is the awakening of the Kundalini. The familiar verse which occurs in the *Upanishads* describes the effects of such an initiation. It says, "As a result of such an initiation all the doubts of the mind are dispelled, all the sins are destroyed and a vision of God is had within." If that were not the case, there are so many professors of philosophy or great scholars, and you can go to them and ask them how much supreme bliss they have gotten from their knowledge of philosophy. In Vedanta, also, initiation is of vital significance as it is in other disciplines.

Larry: *How does a seeker know if he has become urdhvareta? What happens to the seminal fluid before and after this state?*

Baba: One is able to see and feel in meditation that the seminal fluid which was previously flowing downwards has now started flowing upwards towards the heart. And after one becomes an urdhvareta, an inner kriya takes place, the name of which is vajroli, and the seminal fluid which was previously flowing downwards and being ejected outwards, now rises to the sahasrar. Then even if such a one is with women, his seminal fluid does not flow downwards. This is the surest mark of urdhvareta. In meditation when this fluid is actually rising from the sex organs towards the sahasrar, one is able to feel the movement. It is only after this that a yogi experiences great bliss. The seeker comes to perceive during meditation that his seminal fluid is rising towards the heart. Anyone in whose case this process is taking place would be able to perceive it.

Mahadev: *Is it possible to make equal spiritual progress under a Siddha who leaves the spiritual discipline up to the individual, as it would be in a disciplined environment such as this Ashram?*

Baba: What do you understand by sadhana? What else is sadhana if not discipline? Discipline is not just ordinary exercises that you do when you get up in the morning. What is discipline after all? Getting up early and going to bed early, eating regularly and so on is all a part of yoga. The discipline here also includes meditation; and to consolidate or increase meditation we have chanting of the divine Name. So all these different things are interrelated and they help each other; they are all different aspects of yoga. If somebody were to understand by food only bread or chapatis, what would you consider chutney or other dishes to be, if not food? Just as the word food includes so many dishes and preparations, similarly, sadhana also has so many different aspects, and discipline is one of them.

Whoever the Siddha may be, the important question is: how has he attained Siddhahood? Siddhahood is the result of a long period of sadhana. A seeker may be living with a Siddha, yet he will not become a Siddha automatically. He will remain a seeker. Being with a Siddha does not mean that you have already achieved Siddhahood. You have to attain Siddhahood through sadhana. After you have attained Siddhahood, after your journey is over, then you would be under no compulsion to follow discipline. You do not have to give up sadhana then; it drops away by itself when the goal is attained.

Wherever you may be, you will have to follow a certain daily routine, you cannot escape it. If you were not to follow any routine you would become lazy and lousy. What special freedom can you enjoy with a Siddha who leaves the discipline up to you? Every seeker has to sit in a certain position —no Siddha can exonerate you from that. And everyone has to eat—no Siddha can free you from the need of food. So I don't understand what you mean by freedom and what kind of freedom you could enjoy with a Siddha who leaves the discipline up to you.

If a Siddha has left the question of discipline entirely to the will of the seeker and if the seeker concerned does not follow any discipline, then what can the Siddha do for him? It is quite natural for everyone not to be disciplined, to be irregular in food and sleep and other matters. Everyone feels like disobeying discipline every now and then. There are people who would not mind missing lunch in the hope of having a sumptuous dinner. Isn't it better to eat a regular lunch than to overfill your stomach at dinner? And how much better it is to get up early and go to bed early than to keep late nights, to stay awake until two or three a.m. and remain asleep during the day. Even if this question has been left to the individual, the individual cannot afford to remain lying down all the time—he will get up some time. He will sit in meditation for some time. Isn't it better to sit in a proper position? And whether or not discipline is being insisted upon, you are going to eat once or twice a day. Isn't it much better to eat regularly at one place than to keep your pockets filled with all kinds of trash and keep on munching at all hours?

If a Siddha does not have an ashram, then his students may have to spend their days going from one tree to another, moving constantly. But if there is a Siddha who has a regular ashram, isn't it much better to stay in that ashram? And if you are staying there, shouldn't you keep it clean and orderly?

All I can say is that where discipline is not insisted upon you become licentious. You go on eating and sleeping all the time. If this is your idea of divine Siddhahood, then there's nothing more to say. However, after the Siddha has taught all the discipline that is necessary, after he has perfected his students, then he can leave this question entirely to their will.

Whoever you may be, wherever you may be, even if you are in Vaikuntha, you will have to sleep, eat, wash yourself and attend to many other things. Don't think that Vaikuntha is full of dirty people. Gods, in fact, are very neat and clean and they probably bathe at least two or three times a day. Even if you enjoy the grace of a Siddha you have to do regular sadhana. There is no escape from it. Nobody should think that the grace of a Siddha will uplift you even if you are spending your time loafing around.

And what kind of Siddha tells visitors they can do whatever they want, eat whatever they want, sleep whenever they want, while he insists on strict discipline for his disciples? The other day a controversy came up around a certain political figure of our country. He has sent his children to

America for higher studies and in his public speeches he has been telling everyone that you don't need too much by way of education. What's the point of that kind of Siddhahood, when you tell one thing to people but practise something quite different?

I have seen some students of Siddhas, who even after having been with a Siddha, feel the need of attending minor courses on meditation with ordinary teachers. I wonder what kind of students they are and what kinds of Siddhas they go to if they feel the need for such courses even after having been with a Siddha. Such so-called seekers go to Siddhas and live their life in their own self-willed way and then after some time they begin to complain that they have not gotten anything. They begin to feel restless and then they feel the need of going to other teachers for other things. If you have received the grace of a Siddha, you get beyond the pull of all these different forces, beyond the pull of different methods. You feel fully contented remaining with the Siddha whose grace you are enjoying. You get completely free of the greed of having to buy everything from every shop. A Siddha is a perfect being, so his grace is perfect, his realisations are perfect and the way given by him is also perfect. So anyone who obeys such a Siddha and enjoys his grace will himself become perfect.

Pratibha: *In answer to a question of mine you said that the relationship between the Guru and a disciple continues through a number of births. In this birth, you are our Guru, and we are the disciples, but I wonder what must have been the nature of the relationship in past lives. You perfected your sadhana in this birth and became a Guru. Were you also a Guru in your past lives? Were we disciples? And what is going to be our relationship to you in future births, because you are not going to be reborn?*
Baba: It's true that the relationship between the Guru and his disciple continues through a number of births, and you can find it out from meditation. Increase your meditation and in meditation some time you will be able to see your relationship with your Guru through the past seven lives. If you are following all the rules of the discipline most faithfully, and if you are meditating with utmost care, and if you

are able to penetrate to subtler and still subtler levels, you will be able to see your past lives, and you will be able to see the movie depicting your past seven lives.

It's not at all certain that I am going to come again. If God were to ordain that somebody else should sit in my place, what would you do then? There is no need of my being reborn, because God has so many others that He can use. Once you have been blessed with grace, then it is Shakti Herself who will take you further and further, and you do not need the physical presence of the Guru that much. Even after a Guru leaves his physical form, he stays in a subtle individual form for a very long time. Take the case of Bara Baba, Baba Nityananda. It does not take him even a moment to appear in his individual form from Siddhaloka. In fact, this is something which you should find out through meditation. This isn't a matter for a question and answer session. There are many places to which when I go I recollect things connected with past lives, and I feel very extraordinary vibrations. You should meditate and find out the truth yourself. In any case, what is past is past, and your concern should be strictly with the present.

The fact that disciples are able to stay with the Guru for such a long time, and they have so much love and respect for each other, shows that this relationship has deep roots in the past. Here so many people from different places have been staying together for such a long time. They have all been eating together and living together happily. Would it be possible without there having been a relationship in past births? The visitors who come to the Ashram, in fact, feel amazed when they look at you. They begin to wonder how it is that so much love prevails in the Ashram, and people live here in such harmony, and work together and are so earnest and full of devotion. They are full of admiration for you. We have been together for such a long time. Each one of you does his work, and after finishing work, each one sits in his own place and does his own sadhana. So this relationship has continued through many births. Before coming into this world, all of us were together in some place. Then even though we have been born in different countries, and we have been brought up in different ways, yet in certain moments we travel to the place from where we all came.

According to divine dispensation, we have all come together once again. You should find out the nature of the relationship through meditation.

April 19, 1972

Vatsala Amma: A close relative of mine is a good and God-fearing man, but he doesn't believe in Gurus. Is it possible for me to do something to make him change his mind?
Baba: How do you know he is God-fearing? (He believes in God.) It's not enough just to take the name of God or to express disgust for certain things. Anybody who is entirely God-fearing would be following all the injunctions of the scriptures. A truly God-fearing person is he who follows the discipline laid down by God and who knows that this discipline is in the best interest of everyone; and if it is not followed, it will only harm him. He who thus understands the divine law, who abides by it, and who is scared of violating it, does not have to believe in the Guru. It is enough for him to believe in God; that would be good enough.

A God-fearing person obviously believes in God, and he also accepts the divine law. And he will also have to believe in the Guru. In the *Srimad Bhagavat Purana*, the Lord Himself says, "*Srutis, Smritis,* the *Vedas* and other scriptures contain My commandments, and anyone who violates them cannot be My devotee, and he cannot be considered to be a Vaishnavite either." So a God-fearing person would accept the divine commandments and the divine law and follow them. Therefore, if there were a person who remained calm and feared God, even that much would be enough for him.

Bramachari Anantram: Through the practice of yoga the three bodies, gross, subtle and causal which are the crea-

tions of the sattva, raja and tamo guna are completely purified. As a result of this purification, the seeker obtains knowledge, power and wealth. Does knowledge constitute the highest goal of life, or is life fulfilled only when all these three things are obtained in the right manner? Are power and wealth obstacles on the path of God-realisation, or are they conducive to it? To obtain all these three and yet remain detached from them, would you say that is the highest state?

Baba: A very important question has been raised: whether through the practice of yoga one gets knowledge or wealth and splendour. Yoga gives man knowledge, not wealth and splendour. There is no doubt that it releases all the Shakti of the atman. If there is a yogi who has attained fullness of knowledge, and whose inner Shakti has been totally released, would he depend on wealth and splendour?

This question is self-contradictory. We have to see exactly what it is that impels a yogi to undertake the practice of yoga. Is he undertaking the practice of yoga for external wealth and glory, for achieving the seat of the lord of heaven, Indra, or he is practising yoga after getting disillusioned with all these external things? Is he in quest of something subtle, something invisible? Yoga can give a person full knowledge, and it can also totally release the power of the soul. But yoga is not a kind of factory where glory or wealth are manufactured.

However, this is true: that great saints have a most wonderful destiny, and it is as a result of destiny that you find some of them being utterly poor, and others being surrounded by wealth. It shouldn't surprise anyone if I were to receive hats from Indians, but every month I receive at least half a dozen hats from America also. What do you ascribe that to: yogic Shakti, or destiny?

Two great yogic saints of Maharashtra were contemporaries, Nigudi Rang Nath and Ramdas. The Samadhi of Rang Nath is situated in Jalana. Though Ramdas was the Guru of the king, he lived a most simple life. His only possessions were a loincloth and his yogic stick. He would beg his food from several different families every day. Rang Nath, on the contrary, was most lavish. He would wear gold ornaments right from his wrist to his elbows and he would also wear gold ornaments around his waist. He would change clothes at least three times a day, and his dresses were quite magnificent, royal in splendour. And he would ride at least three different mounts a day: first an elephant, then a horse, and finally a palanquin. Both of them were equally great Siddhas, and they had equal power. Ramdas was a royal Guru, he was the Guru of Shivaji, who was the king at that time. But Ramdas's destiny was different.

So wealth is a gift of destiny. Some yogis can get full knowledge and full Shakti, but not wealth. And as far as wealth is concerned, it is possessed by very ordinary persons. Wealth can be acquired very easily if you are a shrewd businessman.

The destiny of a yogi is most wonderful. One may have a very large ashram which is full of wealth, where there is an abundance of everything, while another may be completely poor, even a beggar. But that doesn't mean that there is any difference between their inner states; they have attained the same realisation. Bhartruhari describes the different conditions of different yogis which are the result of the strange ways of destiny. Some saints are so poor that they don't even have a dwelling to rest in, so they lie under a tree or a bridge, and the earth is their bed, and their pillow is their own arm. Others live in royal splendour.

The ways in which different yogis act are also different. A yogi after the final realisation attains divinity, and as a result of this divinity, he attracts different people to himself. And these different people, while gathering around him, also make donations or contributions, and that is how wealth piles up around him.

Wealth does not have much significance. It comes very easily. It is, however, true that everyone feels drawn towards a genuine yogi. The scriptures say, "He controls the one under whose control everything is." In other words, for him who controls God, who controls everything, wealth is very, very ordinary. I am reminded of a verse from Tulsidas in this context which has great meaning and significance. It's a verse which one should think about again and again. Tulsidas says, "No one can equal the yogi or saint in whose heart Rama Himself is manifested. All eight siddhis and nine riddhis are drawing water or are dancing attendance on a yogi. All these riddhis and siddhis remain around a yogi by the power of the divine Name, or by the power of the Name of Rama. Once a sage has realised Rama, he has everything."

There was a great yogini in Maharashtra called Bahinabai, and she says in a verse, "You should continually meditate on the Lord and not worry about anything else. You should meditate with the faith, 'I am Brahman', 'I am the Lord', 'I am Hara'. Once you are able to realise the Lord then riddhis and siddhis will draw water for you."

So if you find wealth around a yogi, it shouldn't surprise you at all, because wealth is something very, very ordinary for a yogi. If one has achieved perfection in yoga, then he has achieved everything. Everybody is drawn towards purity, towards divinity, towards true holiness, true greatness. So it is no wonder that wealth should also be drawn towards such a one.

Visitor: *What is the difference between the jnana sadhana of continual remembrance of one's own nature and the sadhana of devotional love?*
Baba: It is only the two terms which are different. The content is the same. Remembrance of one's true nature and devotional love are only two different phrases; they refer to the same state. Bhakti is only another name for intense love for the inner Self. Continual remembrance of one's own nature is devotion. So to become perfectly interested in the inner Self is the true nature of devotion. Continual remembrance of the inner Self is the highest kind of devotion. Therefore, the two are one, and there is no difference between the two. One who has supreme love for the Lord will find the same love bubbling up in his own inner being. On the other hand, one who is continually remembering the inner Self will finally become one with the Lord. While one is remembering the inner Self, one is presumably aware of the truth that the inner Self is higher than Brahma, Vishnu or Shiva, higher than all beings or creatures or things. Similarly, the attitude of a bhakta is that he is aware that the Lord is the inner Self of all, that the Lord is the Supreme Being and that is why he loves Him with utmost devotion. So the two are one.

Jon: *Please tell me how to become and stay healthy using understanding, will, directing Shakti, mantra, meditation or other methods besides medicine and diet.*
Baba: To stay healthy you should be regular in your diet, and not make friends with the palate. Eat only to live, do not live to eat. Consider food to be medicine, and take it in a measured quantity. That is how you can stay healthy. If you eat a small amount you will never contract any ailment. People contract ailments only because they eat too much, not too little. Keep your senses calm, and do not allow them to become restless. Only he whose senses become disturbed and troubled falls prey to all kinds of diseases. But he who has completely mastered his senses, who has established full control over all his senses, will remain free from all diseases.

Just as after getting fatigued as a result of a day's work, you go to sleep and wake up refreshed the next morning, similarly, when your mind becomes tired, you should empty it of all thoughts and thus provide it with much needed rest. That is how you can strengthen your mind. The best state is not to think about anything at all. But if you have to think, think only about the atman, or the Lord. Don't think about anything else. When you are in Ganeshpuri, Bombay ceases to exist completely. Similarly, for a seeker, everything else but the Self and the Lord ceases to exist. Do not tax your mind by thinking too much. Keep it calm. It is not good to take medicine continually. There is such a thing as getting addicted to medicine. Just as one gets addicted to a morning cup of tea, similarly, one gets addicted to medicine. You find such a one taking medicine every day, religiously, throughout his life. You should eat only as much as your body can digest, and do not try to emulate the glorious example set by your neighbours.

Kalyani: *Could you please explain how the mind and the inner being are affected by the offering of food to the Lord, and the attitude with which it is eaten?*
Baba: Bahinabai was a great saint, and she used to live in Pandharpur. I read a great deal of her poetry, because I have been very fond of reading poetry, and through the poems of different saints, I have been able to understand

many things. She says in one of her verses, "Attitude has so much power that it will bring you the desired fruit." That is exactly what the *Upanishads* also say: that the Lord exists neither in a holy place nor in stone, He is present in our own attitude. God is present in our own attitude and feeling, and it is our feeling or attitude which manifests God in stone. So if we have feeling for the statue of our Guru, then we will see our Guru in it. Otherwise it will be mere stone. Feeling or attitude has tremendous power. While describing the importance of bhava, which can be translated as feeling or attitude or thought, the Lord says in the *Gita*, "It is by the power of My thought that all these different worlds are being held in position."

So it would be quite natural for the heart to be strongly affected by the attitude with which one is eating. If one eats, having offered his food to the Lord with a feeling of deep devotion, then the food, after going inside, turns into divine nectar and spreads through all the nerves and parts of the body. If you eat food after offering it to the Lord, your heart is filled with divine emotion.

In our Ashram we do not spice our food too strongly. The food here owes its taste to the good and noble deeds being performed by the seekers here, to the continuous chanting of the divine Name, to the atmosphere of this place. Therefore, a seeker who is interested in living a life of calm and peace, should offer whatever he does to the Lord with deep devotion. If there is a man whose heart is not pure, who has no faith in God, who has no devotion, in what way is he better than an ox or an elephant or a donkey? Even elephants, donkeys and horses eat. If a man also eats, that certainly does not make him great or constitute his uniqueness. Therefore, it is absolutely essential for man to always remain pure and feel deep devotion to the Lord. One should always pursue peace and heaven, not restlessness, agitation, and hell. Thank you for such a nice question.

* * * *

Man is a most noble creature, but what constitutes nobility? To be worthy of his unique nobility, man must think and act in a way which will distinguish him from other creatures, from animals and beasts. It is a matter of great joy that the Lord Himself is actually holding His sport within the heart of man all the time. So when this is the truth, when the Lord Himself is holding His sport in his heart all the time, how should man behave? One should think pure and noble thoughts. One's life should be disciplined so that joy and contentment arise from his heart. You cannot find peace in external things and possessions. The titles which the government may award you, or your wealth, or your status, the food that you eat, or the comforts that you may enjoy or the battery of washermen who may be washing your clothes, cannot give you any peace. Man's human life is not like the life of other creatures, animals, birds and beasts, who after being born, live out their brief existence in eating, sleeping and indulging in sex. Man is certainly different from all these creatures.

Remember that if any part of the body becomes damaged, if any sense organ becomes weak, it is very difficult to repair it; it is very difficult to regain its original strength. Therefore, you should be very vigilant about your body. You must keep it very pure, you must keep it strong. And for that it is essential that you eat and drink regularly, sleep regularly, not talk unnecessarily, only when necessary, and during the remaining period remain silent and calm, and thus keep your mind pure and strong. If your mind is distraught, intensely disturbed or troubled all the time, no matter how much medicine you take, you cannot become healthy. Medicine only suppresses disease, and thus aggravates it in the long run. It doesn't remove a disease. Remember that health and sickness come from the mind, not from your environment; they are not things which depend on external factors. So, therefore, learn to keep your mind pure, clean, strong, and free from thoughts all the time. The more your mind gets agitated, the more adversely the body is affected, and that is what we call disease. Disease is not something which is born outside. Disease is only a reflection of a certain mental condition. Disease is not like food which is grown in fields; there are no external breeding centers of disease. Therefore, keep your mind calm.

If you wish to do good to your own Self, then you must learn to keep your mind still and free from thoughts. If you do not know how to do good, improve, uplift your own Self, what can you do for others? What can you do for the world?

Therefore, look into your own Self all the time. Think of your own Self, remain aware of your own Self continuously and become aware of your own divinity. The worst tendency which man has is to keep looking at other's faults all the time, and to ignore his own. One should be continually asking oneself, "What have I learned, what have I gained, and what have I lost? How much of my life has been spent fruitlessly, and how much of it still remains to be lived? What exactly is my condition?" Forget about others for the time being. Find out how much you danced as a result of pure inner contentment, as a result of happiness arising from your own depths, of deep joy bubbling up from your own soul. If a neighbour happens to treat you to a cup of tea and a few snacks, you thank him. If on the contrary, there is somebody who happens to abuse you, you get enraged and feel like shooting him. That is what the ordinary human condition is. But you should try to see how many times you have thanked yourself for being virtuous, for being good, and how many times you have abused yourself for being wicked, for being vicious. It is very easy to abuse others, to feel jealous of others, to complain against others. But one's concern should be with oneself. I wonder how many times you have been angry with yourself, how many times you have felt disgust with yourself for being what you are.

In the *Mahabharata* there is a dialogue between Lord Krishna and Duryodhana in which Duryodhana says to the Lord, "Lord, I will never accept that happiness and sorrow are things which are caused by others, because this is entirely false." It's futile egoism which makes one say, "I did that, I do that, I'll do this, I'll do that, I'll achieve this, I'll achieve that." The truth is that man's own actions bring him happiness or sorrow, and there is no escape from the fruit or rewards, whether good or bad, of one's actions. Therefore, let your actions be pure. Create your own paradise and learn to dwell in it joyfully.

It is unfortunate that man does not want to do anything himself, that he does not want to work on himself; he always wants something from another. But that does not serve any purpose for us. There is a nectar of love which is surging within. Learn to drink that, because that nectar is very highly intoxicating. Do not go after the filthy intoxicating drinks or what people consider to be nectars which are sold in the market. You do not know what filthy things the manufacturers put in the different liquors. Stop depending on them for intoxication. Learn to become intoxicated within yourself. There is a nectar of pure being flowing inside. Drink that. Mansoor Mastana says, "Keep drinking the wine of the love of God. If you drink that wine, your intoxication will be pure and you will not lie in a gutter emitting a foul stink, so that you neighbours have to turn their noses away from you in sheer disgust." Mansoor says, "Eat joyfully, with love, with regularity. Do not enfeeble yourself by practising all kinds of fasts, depriving yourself in all sorts of ways. Your heart is full of dirty, stinking, foul filth. Learn to sweep it away with the broom of love of the Lord. If you are really keen on meeting the Lord, on having a vision of Him, keep your mind constantly joined to Him, constantly fastened on Him, continually thinking of Him. That is what true meditation is, and that is what chanting is."

It is in fact a very long poem, and I have shortened it. Mansoor Mastana says, "I tried to find Him outside, in external things, and people, but I could not succeed. Finally I found Him within my own being. That is the true tavern. That is the tavern of the true seeker, the joyful aspirant. Do not wander here and there, reducing yourself to a state of hopelessness and misery. Remember that Rama dwells within everyone and learn to worship the inner Being. Eat well, sleep well, do well, and the fruits that you obtain from these activities will also be good."

April 21, 1972

Girija: I sometimes fall into the role of teacher when talking to others, when they ask for advice. Occasionally I get so inspired that while talking I am even surprised by my insight and great wisdom. I feel great power and often great love. However, I also feel my ego intruding from time to time. Are the wisdom and insight an illusion? Does the presence of ego invalidate what I say? Please advise me how to manage my teaching samskaras.

Baba: There is no harm if one who has learned himself in a proper manner begins to teach others when they approach him for advice. The truth is present as knowledge; so knowledge is present in its fullness in everyone. It's only ego which is a disease and which is not worth anything. The inner Self is without any qualities, it is pure consciousness, and it dwells within everyone in the form of knowledge.

In fact, knowledge is present already in everyone and new knowledge doesn't have to come from outside. It's the supreme teaching of Bhagawan Nityananda that the Supreme Being dwells within everyone in equal fullness, and if we worship Him in a visible form, we must not forget that we are worshipping the inner Self in a visible form. We should not think that the Self dwells outside. External worship is not true worship. It is only the worship of the inner Self which is true worship. He made me give up all forms of external worship and directed me to inner worship. If I am indulging in external worship, it is because of a certain old addiction of mine. It's because I am addicted to my love for the Guru; it is not something which he taught me. If he were still in his physical form, he would have felt very angry with me for worshipping him like that. Because he was a believer only in the inner Self.

It is very good that you feel such power, and so inspired, and that knowledge comes bubbling up from inside. That is what should happen with everyone, in fact. Otherwise, what is the point of your coming to Ganeshpuri and staying here? If you do not gain access to the vibrations of your own Self, what is the use of your being here? If Nityananda Bhagawan were to ask me what I did, what should I tell him? However, this should not swell one with pride; it should not make one arrogant or conceited, or inflate a person with a sense of self-importance or superiority. This must not cause you to look down upon others. You must always be aware that this inner inspiration is meant for serving the purposes of righteousness, of ethics, and it will lead you to liberation.

Malti: *How is it that some people, in spite of living for a long time in an Ashram which is diviner than the divinest, indulge in absolutely corrupt actions, actions which can only spring from a vitiated mind?*

Baba: This question used to be raised quite frequently in the time of Nityananda Baba also. He was asked many times, "Baba, how is it that even though you are an absolutely pure being, some of the people around you behave in a certain way? How do you explain this?"

And Baba would always say, "A crow will be a crow even if he is in heaven. A crow will not stop feeding himself on shit, a crow will not change, even if he is in heaven. He can't help being what he is."

No matter how great an ashram may be, no matter how divine, if a person living there is an utterly low, vicious character, what can the ashram do for him? If there is anyone who even while living in a pure ashram indulges in foul deeds, well you can take it for certain that such a one is a hellish insect, and even though he is living in a pure ashram, he is only looking for a corner to indulge in vicious deeds.

Without mentioning any names, I will tell you something which happened yesterday. I asked Desai to talk to certain people here, to tell them that if they felt certain uncontrollable urges, they could go to Bombay. They are householders, and they can satisfy their urges. But the answer which one of the married people gave was that he has come to the Ashram because he is sick of those urges, because he is absolutely fed up; he has had too much of it in his life. And when that answer was reported to me, it pleased me very much; it gave me very great happiness. And I have no words to thank such people.

So what can the Ashram do for a person who is basically a depraved, vicious character? In this context I am reminded of a verse from Tulsidas. Tulsidas says, "Catch hold of a donkey and take it, not to a mere ashram, but directly to heaven itself, and even there the donkey will only be looking for filth to wallow in. If you were to adorn a monkey with the finest ornaments, he will show no respect for those ornaments; he will only play with them and break them in the process."

A person who is wicked and depraved, whether he is in an ashram or in heaven itself, will always be looking for hell, because he feels comfortable only in hell. To manage the fair which occured in Vajreshwari only a few days ago, a large number of policemen had come. In fact, 150 had come. And I went there, and they all received me. I asked them why they had come in such full force. "What is the need of so many policemen even in a religious fair?" I asked.

Their reply was, "Many pickpockets come to such fairs. They come not out of devotion for the Goddess, they come only to pick pockets. In fact, in such a fair it is very easy to pick pockets. So the Goddess is a Goddess only for devotees. She is not a Goddess to pickpockets or thieves. Therefore, we are here not to look after the devotees of the Goddess but to look after the devotees of the pockets." So there is a kind of person who will be true to his own degraded self, regardless of where he is.

Bill: *I often experience that I do just the opposite of what I want and intend to do, that a resolve in the mind for greater self-control leads in behavioural fact to greater self-indulgence. Why do I have this fickleness of mind? And how may I overcome it and find the strength to ensure that my acts are true to my ideals?*

Baba: This is what happens with a mind of a particular kind. Besides, during the period of sadhana many obstacles come up, and nobody should be under the illusion that sadhana is a bed of roses, or that one can reach the goal without the least difficulty. If you read the difficulties which many of the saints came across during the course of their sadhana, it may scare you. There are two causes: one is the life which a seeker lived before coming to the Ashram, and the other is the obstacles which come up during the course of sadhana. And there are only two ways out of it: one is to obey the Guru most faithfully, and the other is to abide by the Ashram dharma with as much fidelity as one is capable of. Otherwise, the mind is a most difficult, a most formidable enemy, and a seeker has to fight with it for a long time. A seeker has to engage himself in fighting with the mind, with nothing else. It is for this reason that I tell you again and again not to be led by your own impulses. You should not do whatever comes to your mind. You should abide by the scriptures, you should abide by the Guru's word. The truth is that everyone is great, everyone is sublime, everyone has infinite power in him. It is only the mind which has reduced you to your present state. It is only the mind which reduces strength to weakness. It is only the mind which is the root of all evils. And because the mind is constantly changing its tactics—sometimes it appears in the garb of a friend, at other times it threatens like a formidable enemy, it thinks all kinds of thoughts, it entertains all kinds of fancies, it harbours all kinds of intentions—there is no enemy worse than the mind. An enemy who is standing with a dagger in his hand, about to cut your head off, is nothing to be afraid of. But while confronted with your mind, you have to respect its evil propensities.

It's the mind which is responsible for all the wretchedness and misery which we are entrapped in. But for the mind, all of us are great. If we could rise above the mind, we would realise our inherent essential greatness this very moment. The fact is that God dwells within, and the mind pushes a seeker from one corner of the world to another in search of God. There is no individual in the world who has not been put into a wretched condition by the mind.

It is only after one receives the boundless grace of a great Guru that one is able to move towards God easily, and is able to experience deep peace, not being troubled by the mind so much. So God, too, reveals Himself only when the mind becomes pure. God doesn't seem to want to reveal Himself when the mind is impure. Therefore you should keep praying to the mind constantly. You should implore your own mind for its blessings on you, for inner peace.

Pratibha: *Is one born a saint, or can one attain saintliness by effort?*
Baba: Saints are born and saintliness can also be attained by effort. There are saints who were born saints, and there are other saints who become saints through their effort. The truth about those saints who appear to us to have been born saints, is that they have practised devotion through countless births. Some of the great saints who rose to the highest heights were able to do so because they had the enormous

merit of many past lives behind them. Women saints such as Muktabai, Mirabai, Janabai, belong to this class. Janabai was a very special kind of saint. The Lord Himself would come and ply the grinding wheel with her like an ordinary person, so you can imagine how much merit she must have earned through a number of births. Or take the case of Surdas who was blind. He would be led from one place to another by the Lord Himself, who held his stick, so you can imagine how great his devotion must have been.

So there are saints who are born as saints, as a result of the meritorious deeds they performed through countless lifetimes, and then there are others who by coming into contact with such a saint achieve great heights of saintliness during the same birth. To live in the company of saints, to spend your time in constant contact with them, is of utmost importance. I am not speaking of those who are spending their days in the company of a saint. In an ashram, it is much easier to spend your days, because here you get everything at a proper time. It is, in fact, easier to spend your days in an ashram than it is in your home. I am referring to those who live with a saint with true aspiration, with genuine devotion to him. What matters is to translate the teachings of the saint into action, to undergo a total self-transformation. What is of importance is to live in the company of a saint with an open heart, with sincere aspiration and deep devotion. Mere physical company is not enough.

The true meaning of satsang is to live with a saint, and to transform yourself completely. We should know how to live in the company of great saints. We should be aware of the state which a saint is established in, the mission of his life. Mere physical company would not serve much purpose. There are many people who get this privilege, and yet nothing happens. Take the case of the town of Alandi, the population of which must be quite large. I wonder how many true followers of Jnaneshwar are there. Take the case of Ganeshpuri which has so many people. Out of so many, how many are Nityananda's true followers? We will have to ask the same question with regard to Shree Gurudev Ashram. There are so many people living here, yet how many of them are true inner followers of Muktananda? So one becomes a saint through the company of a saint, by following the example of saints. By living with them we also become saintly.

* * * *

I thank everyone for having listened so well. Now the Saptah is close at hand, and all of you should get a lot of rest, because the Saptah must be celebrated with great zest. During the Saptah, nectar should be flowing within you, and you should undergo some genuine inner change. The earth should feel gratified and the Lord should be pleased by the Saptah.

I am very happy that the seekers here are very good. If you are able to get through the test of discipline, it means that you have some strength. Do not let your inner heart remain petty, bound to a separate identity, keep it full of God. Consider yourself to be highly worthy, great. But do not look down on others. There is no yoga or austerity or any other method which is higher than the right attitude to one's Self. You may be anywhere, yet if your heart remains small and petty, you will not be able to achieve anything. Always think about what you truly are. Make your heart very large. Feel, be aware that "Nothing else exists besides me." To worship one's own Self joyfully, blissfully—is there any tapasya greater than this?

April 24, 1972

Kedarnath: *Is it proper to meditate at noon and in the afternoon? Is it good for health and what effect does it have on the brain? How much should we meditate and at what times should we meditate in summer?*
Baba: In summer you should meditate only in the morning, not at noon or in the afternoon. In this season you should neither meditate too much nor should you perform too many asanas. Those who are eating in restaurants must be very careful. They should not take too much fried stuff,

because if you eat something fried it causes excessive thirst. Water is against fire, and if you drink too much water, the gastric fire will lose its intensity. And that causes excessive bile in the system. And that causes diarrhea and vomiting and other troubles. You should eat very carefully and meditate a little and do just a few asanas. It's much better to read in the afternoon. The present heat is very unusual. I haven't seen anything like it in the past twelve years. Last year we didn't have such heat around this time. These disturbances might be the result of the nuclear tests.

Kedarnath: *During the period of sadhana almost everyone gets constipated and has a lot of gas in the abdomen which causes a lot of trouble many times, particularly during swadhyaya sessions. What should be done to control this excessive wind in the system?*
Baba: You should ask somebody to get you about a half-kilo of haritaki. Even if a kilo were brought, it would be all right, because this is a yogic herb and yogis must eat it. I took it for a long time and I use it. Everybody should keep one of these things. It's like a nut. Part of it should be chewed before going to bed. Those who use haritaki regularly derive immense benefit from it; their bowel movements are regulated and the excess wind is expelled from the system. This herb also helps with the upward flow of the seminal fluid. The mind also becomes stronger. It is very good for students in particular. There was a time in our country when mothers used to give their children pieces of this herb before they went to bed, and it always did them a lot of good. Those who use this herb regularly will never have wet dreams.

There was a great physician in ancient times called Dhanvantari, and by means of his art he hid himself somewhere for some time. When people could not find him, they became very disturbed and they began to ask each other, "Now that Dhanvantari is no longer with us, what shall we do? Who will take care of us?"

When the people were expressing their grief and their regret, this herb appeared and said, "Don't worry, I'll do all that Dhanvantari did for you. So if he doesn't come back, you shouldn't worry. I'll serve as an effective substitute."

I'll ask somebody to bring it from Bombay and we will distribute one nut to each. You can keep it in your pocket and take just a little bit before going to bed. It's a great blood purifier, it regulates the bowel movements, expels the waste matter from the body, helps in the upward flow of semen, and it also has other good qualities.

Girija: Can we schedule more sessions of singing the divine Name? For example, continuously from the end of Guru Gita in the morning until evening arati?
Baba: In fact, I have been thinking about it for a long time. The first ashram I was in at Hubli had this continuous 24-hour chant every day, *Om namah Shivaya.* And I have been thinking about introducing it here, also. But there are certain needs which have to be met. Don't think that I am interested in the expansion of the material side of the Ashram, or in worldly activities. There are lots of other people who are interested in them. You find most Indians, particularly the political leaders in the country, people who are holding positions of authority, being concerned with improving society in various ways, or with welfare projects. Well, I am one of the very few who are interested in the invisible inner spiritual work.

Be quiet for a while. It is very hot now. We are going to have the 14-day continuous chant very soon; and that is why I have asked people to get more rest—so they are in proper shape for the Saptah.

I can assure you that in the end you will get nectar only from the divine Name. There is so much nectar flowing from the divine Name, so much power in the divine Name, that Janabai used to ply her grinding wheel while chanting the divine Name and became so completely absorbed in it, that the Lord Himself wanted to hear her chant the divine Name and He would come down and sit with her and work with her and listen to her singing.

I have a mind to introduce continuous chanting into Ashram life. We will put seekers in different batches and those batches will chant for different hours. Besides that, seekers will also do a little Ashram work. But I can't say when exactly it will begin. Take the case of the greatest saints; they gave up everything. And after having given up everything, even after having perfected their sadhana, they finally took to the divine Name. What joy, what sweetness flowed from the divine Name into their hearts. There is a sect in this country, followers of a great saint called Dadu. The disciples of Dadu were highly learned people, in Vedanta and other scriptures. But Dadu says in one of his songs, "Dadu, give up all other company and continually repeat the divine Name, continually remember the Lord."

You can realise the power of a word from one simple fact. If somebody uses an ordinary foul word for you, it affects you immediately. It sets you boiling, it fills you with wrath. So it is no wonder if the divine sound releases pure nectar inside. Therefore, in Ashram life, the Name is going to be given a lot more emphasis. It is for this reason that we are going to have a 14-day chant instead of a 7-day chant.

The forthcoming yajna is being held so that our Ashram will become very strong, so that everyone coming here may have his inner Shakti awakened, so that the Ashram may become saturated with the powerful vibrations. We are going to hold the forthcoming chant with great love and great reverence.

So, for the moment, you should be quiet about a daily continuous chant, because it is very hot. If it were cold, like on Shivaratri, we would have started the continuous chant already. You should be totally dedicated to the Name. You should talk less and practise the divine Name all the time. Remember that all realisations flow from the divine Name. All powers of yoga can be gained from the divine Name.

Rajendra: *To live with you for a long time, to have love for you, to feel closeness, but not to have any real interest in the divine Name, or in swadhyaya, how do you explain this?*
Baba: It cannot happen. And if it happens, it is a serious obstacle. I don't mind devotees living away from me, but they must have interest in the divine Name. Those people who have no interest in the divine Name should consider it a very serious obstacle. Such people are not aware of the value of the Name. I wonder what such people do during swadhyaya. I do not let them stay with me during that time. Even if you were to sit silently, withdrawing your attention from everything else, that, too would be good. Just as in the

rainy season, if you happen to stay outside you will become wet by a shower of rain, in the same way, if you are attending a session of swadhyaya no matter what condition you are in, you are bound to be affected by the vibrations of the holy text, by the sound of the Name. I still like to listen to it sitting here. In spite of everything, I listen very carefully, particularly to find out how all of you carry out swadhyaya. If I feel that somebody sitting, particularly in the front row, has passed into samadhi, I go to the hall window and peer into the window to see exactly who it is. Samadhi is very insignificant compared to chanting and swadhyaya. Chanting has so much rasa, so much nectar in it that it forces even yogis out of samadhi.

I am quite conscious of the fact that many people here are doing swadhyaya not because they are interested in it, but because they are scared of me. If you were to do swadhyaya for your own Self, instead of doing it out of fear of me, you would be able to enjoy its true nectar. It's very strange. In fact, it's a vital question: when the divine Name has so much power, why doesn't man repeat it, why doesn't man drown himself in it? Tukaram Maharaj says that the divine Name is the simplest and easiest means. The divine Name is purest nectar itself. But to enjoy this pure nectar which is so easily available, one needs to have intelligence. Stupid persons cannot enjoy this nectar. Swadhyaya should be done with great reverence. I wonder at the obtuseness of those people who are not able to understand that when it is so very difficult to get rid of those impressions of the brief company of some unwanted character—and these impressions in fact sometimes get so deeply implanted in the heart that they keep on harrassing a person from time to time until his last breath—there is no reason why swadhyaya should not form equally strong impressions inside, which will release pure love.

Rana: *Do you and your Ashram exist in some other loka or not? I have seen you many times in meditation. Is what I see a hallucination, or a true vision?*
Baba: What you see is an illusion, and it is also true. Your experiences will be reliable only when you begin to see the entire universe as emanating from Chiti. And as it ema-

nates from Chiti it is not different from Chiti. In fact, it is Chiti Herself. It is Chiti who has created innumerable worlds, who has Herself become innumerable people and who has Herself become innumerable ashrams. Muktananda is only one of Her creations. Chiti has countless ashrams in different worlds. And if I am one with Chiti, I can also have any number of ashrams in different worlds. But there must by many other yogis like me, and many other ashrams like this Ashram.

You can understand it from an example. Take the case of an ambassador coming from America. He is not the only ambassador in the world. There are many other ambassadors also. Similarly, in this world, which is full of Chiti, there are countless people. In fact, so many that you can't keep track of their numbers. When real knowledge arises, you begin to see everything as a form of your own Self. Ordinary knowledge or awareness, according to which this particular child is my baby, or this particular house is my house, while another child is somebody else's baby and another house belongs to somebody else, is not true knowledge. It is only worldly knowledge. But scriptural knowledge, or the knowledge embodied in the scriptures is entirely different.

Jnaneshwar Maharaj talks about this right knowledge, true knowledge. He describes the attitude of a saint who has achieved such true knowledge. In his commentary on the ninth chapter of the *Gita*, Jnaneshwar Maharaj says, "The person whom we call jnani, the knowing person, the person who has achieved true wisdom, becomes aware that this universe is mine. In fact, I have become this universe. It is I who have become all these countless movable and immovable and animate and inanimate creatures." Lord Krishna says to Arjuna in the *Gita*, "O, Arjuna, it's only when a yogi, a saint, a great souled person comes to realise that all these countless beings and things which appear to be diverse, which appear to be different from each other, in reality emanate from Me, arise in Me, exist in Me, are sustained in Me and finally merge in Me, can he be said to have achieved true knowledge."

From this viewpoint, from this true spiritual standpoint, all the ashrams, whether in this world or other worlds including the present Ashram are mine. But from an ordinary standpoint, the worldly view point, even this Ashram does not belong to me. This Ashram belongs to the Trustees, and I am only one of the people staying here. I am here to serve the people and I am just a guest.

Kedarnath: *Is it possible for different students of Siddha Yoga to have experiences which are entirely different from one another, and different from the ones described in Chitshakti Vilas? And can these experiences follow a different sequence than those mentioned therein? If it is possible, how do you explain this difference?*
Baba: The experiences of the red, white, black and blue lights cannot be different for different people. They are the same experiences, because these lights represent the different bodies. They cannot appear in different forms for different seekers. The gross body may have several colours, it may be fair, dark, black, or yellow, but as far as the inner bodies are concerned, their colours are fixed. For instance, the subtle body is white. It can't be any other colour. Different seekers can see different lights, but those differences are due to impurities of their minds.

Malti: *Is it possible to love two Gurus at the same time? For instance, before coming to the Ashram, somebody has had a Guru and after coming to this Ashram he comes to have a different Guru. Can the two go together, and is it possible to have loving devotion for both of them?*
Baba: It is only a harlot who can love two Gurus at one time. A true seeker, a true disciple cannot love two Gurus at one time. If he can, he lacks loyalty. These days, things have changed. For instance, you find a woman having one husband and a boyfriend besides, and maybe a second boyfriend also. But that doesn't apply to the Guru. You can have only one Guru. However, you can have several teachers until you meet your real Guru. There are people who accept the statue of a certain Parsee gentleman in Bombay as their Guru, and they worship that statue as their Guru. But if one of these persons happens to meet his real Guru, would it be proper for him to continue to worship that statue even then? If before coming here you had a teacher who

was imperfect, it is all right. But if you have a perfect Guru now, then it doesn't make any sense to worship two at one time.

First we should understand whether devotion is exclusive or promiscuous. Your devotion to a person will bring fruit only if you are absolutely loyal to him. Sundardas says that promiscuous devotion cannot command any respect, and a person guilty of such devotion cannot have any realisation. He cannot, in fact, go any distance on the spiritual path. If your mind is full of true devotion, it will become fully absorbed in the object of devotion. Then how are you going to divert a part of it to somebody else? It is only that mind which has not yet become fully absorbed, which has not yet experienced absolute single-minded devotion to one deity, or one Guru, or one particular divine image, which can scatter itself among different Gurus, and can pursue different disciplines at one time. It is only because of such promiscuity that a seeker is not able to make much progress, because promiscuous devotion is temporary devotion. Jnaneshwar Maharaj, in his commentary on the *Gita*, has commented on non-promiscuous devotion very beautifully.

A true seeker has only one mind, and that mind is fully given over to the object of devotion. From where will he get another mind to give to some other object or some other Guru? Anyone who claims that he can pursue several different disciplines at one time, that he can worship several Gurus at one time, is only deluding himself. It is just like a person having his two feet in two different boats and thus succeeding in going only to the bottom of the sea. He can get fully into neither of the boats and he only falls into the middle. Why should a seeker have such a mentality? There are many politicians who keep changing their affiliations and finally they are disowned by every group and they fall into a very bad condition.

It is only when the mind becomes fully enveloped by the object of its single-minded devotion that it will be able to receive all the qualities of the object of its devotion. Jnaneshwar Maharaj says, "If you want to serve God, you must not have any room in your mind for promiscuity. Your mind must become single-pointed, absolutely loyal."

Visitor: *Is it not an exaggeration to say that if the divine Name were to be chanted even by mistake, even without devotion and faith, under compulsion, without any feeling, all the sins of countless births would be destroyed?*

Baba: The divine Name has limitless power. Tulsidas says that if you were to repeat the divine Name, whether with devotion or without, whether willingly or unwillingly, whether wakefully or slothfully, it is going to work, it is going to yield its full fruit. Because the divine Name has divine power.

I would like you to believe this, not only from the testimony of the scriptures, from saints or yogis, I would like you to turn to your own daily life and see how the different activities of your daily life are being conducted. It is words which have the greatest power, even in daily life. Now the space ship sent to the moon has not yet returned, but today's paper says that they have sent a message saying that they are coming back with a ton of moon soil. People are eagerly awaiting them. This message has come through words; this expectation has been aroused through the use of certain sounds. Therefore, the power of the Name is quite real. Forget good words for the moment. Everyone has had the experience of bad words, especially when they are used against you. I have read many scriptures on the power of the Name, yet I find the testimony of everyday life much more convincing than what the scriptures say. You find a person saying, "Such and such fellow used such and such words for me, and since then I have not been able to rest." Now that person was not shot with a bullet, nor was a hand grenade thrown at him. No explosion took place and yet he feels an actual fire burning within him. And if I tell such a person, "Forget about it, be at peace," he says, "How can I forget about it, how can I be at peace?"

Such is the power of a certain sound or a certain word. There was a great woman saint who wrote many songs on the power of the Name. She says in one of her songs, "What is the use of practising yoga, what is the use of Sankhya philosophy if you are not practising the divine Name? How can any desire or hope be fulfilled if you are alienated from the divine Name?"

So the Name should be repeated with great reverence.

Maharashtra, the state which all of you are living in at present, has produced very great saints, saints with divine powers. And most of them attained their high states only by the power of the Name. All that is said about the power of the divine Name cannot be an exaggeration. When just one word of abuse can have such an effect, there is no reason to believe that the divine Name will not have any effect. It is enough to use it only once. You may not even repeat it. Yet the fire kindled by it keeps burning. The Name is true. There is no exaggeration in all that is said about its glory. It is a matter of great regret that in spite of the fact that the Name has such power, man does not feel drawn to it, man does not repeat it. In the *Mahabharata*, one seer says, "Isn't it a matter of great surprise that though the divine Name has such great power, it can grant you the desired fruit at any time, man does not like to repeat it?" Man does not like to chant it with love in spite of the fact that it is so easy. Once during the course of my sadhana, I contracted a very terrible headache. It was so acute that I could not even sleep. At that time, I went to Pandharpur. Many great saints come to Pandharpur and give discourses on the power and the glory of the divine Name. And these saints are very highly realised. So I happened to listen to a few discourses and immediately after that I bought a tamboura and I still have it with me here. I began to sing the divine Name to the accompaniment of that instrument and in a short time I got rid of my terrible headache, and I began to enjoy sleep once again. Not only that, after that, I could put so many people suffering from insomnia to sleep.

One should repeat the Name continuously from within, because repetition of the name grants great siddhis. The sects following great saints, such as Nanak, Kabir, Dadu and Tulsi, are founded on the divine Name. We also revere the divine Name very much here. It is for this reason that we are holding a 14-day chant this year instead of a 7-day chant. Through the Name, great nectar is released. Man should repeat it from within.

Pratibha: *When we were told to give questions about the divine Name, my heart went to the name of Gurudeva, instead of to God's Name. Please tell me, what exactly is the* *meaning of the three elements of your name, Swami Muktananda Paramahansa? Why does the name of a sannyasi have 'ananda' as its suffix? Is there such a custom for sannyasinis also?*

Baba: The true name of Gurudeva is the word Gurudeva itself. It is for this reason that I give the mantra *Guru Om* at the time of initiation, and I ask people to repeat that mantra. This mantra, *Guru Om,* is considered to be the prince of all mantras. It is not Muktananda which is the name of Gurudeva.

The suffix 'ananda' which is added to the name of a sannyasi refers to his true nature. Sannyasa is taken, not for wandering from one holy centre to another, not for observing fasts, sannyasa is taken for experiencing true inner bliss, for experiencing one's own true nature, for an earnest seeking after the Supreme Being. I also receive many sannyasis here and some of them tell me, "Swamiji, could you tell me a suitable place where I could go and perform tapas, or austerities?"

And I ask them, "What is the need of austerities after sannyasa has been taken?" And they are not able to give any reply.

What we generally find is that people take sannyasa without knowing what the purpose of sannyasa is, or what the duty of a sannyasi is. 'Ananda' is added to the name of a sannyasi because a true sannyasi, not a false one, belongs to the family of supreme bliss. The first name is given to a sannyasi by the Guru who gives him sannyasa. That name depends on the quality or worth of a seeker. I was intensely fond of reading hymns on the theme of jivanmukti, that is liberation in this body. I would also read books on this subject, and whenever I talked, I talked with great passion on this theme. It was for this reason that I was given this name, Mukta—Mukta means jivanmukta.

The name of a sannyasini, too, would have 'ananda' as the final element, because sannyasa does not recognise the distinction of sexes. This distinction is a mere physical distinction. Man and woman are not at all different from one another from the point of view of the inner Self. Sannyasa does not recognise the distinction between man and woman, because sannyasa transcends sex. The only object of sannyasa is the attainment of the true Self, the realisation of the true nature which is beyond sex.

It was only the other day that a sannyasini came here. Her name was Premananda, and she stayed here for a number of days. You must have seen her.

The inner Self is beyond the distinction of name and form, because the Self is the same in all. It is only the body which has a certain form and a certain name. A name which is given to the body comes from a source outside the body; it doesn't belong to the body inherently. You find girls quite fond of changing their names many times, not boys so much. As long as a girl is at her parent's place, she has one name. But after she goes to her in-law's she adopts a different name. The person doesn't change, the person remains the same. Nor do her form or nature change. 'Ananda' is added to the name of every sannyasi whether man or woman.

Amrita: *There are certain seekers who during swadhyaya make an effort to meditate or fall asleep, but there are others who while chanting the divine text become immersed in inner samadhi. Then they are not in the position to chant on the gross level. All this happens under the influence of Shakti, so how far is it proper to blame them for their silence on the gross level?*
Baba: The most vital rules of the game of swadhyaya is that everyone should chant and anyone who violates this rule is to blame. In my part of the country, Karnatak, worship of Shiva is held. That particular form of worship is not true worship of Shiva, it is fake worship, that is worship of sheer sloth. You find most of those wretched worshippers locking themselves up inside the shrines. They have, of course, applied vibhuti, but all they do is sleep. They come out after two or three years and look quite intoxicated.

The cool morning air seems to be particularly suitable for the samadhi of sleep, and in the name of samadhi you find people dozing off. It may be partly samadhi, but it is certainly partly sleep. Samadhi should not be an escape from a certain effort; it should be a genuine experience.

If there is anyone who really gets immersed in true samadhi, he can't be blamed. Nobody can say anything about him. And if anybody says anything against him, he should bear it cheerfully.

You should meditate before swadhyaya, and your meditation should be so intense that you get the deepest experiences before coming to swadhyaya. One gets into this state because one gets intensely fascinated by the *Guru Gita* and the sound of the mantras. If devotion were less, perhaps this kind of thing would not happen. But then you must remember that there can be only one or two genuine Majanus. The entire city should not be full of Majanus. If every person were to become a Majanu, the king would become bankrupt.

Tukaram Maharaj would frequently pass into the state in which he had no control over his tongue. Those people who understood him admired him saying, "What a wonderful state to be in. " But then there was only one genuine Tukaram and there are hundreds of imitation Tukarams. When those fakes realised that it was very easy to gain distinction and honour, they all began to imitate Tukaram. This happened during the time of Shivaji. Shivaji soon discovered that the divine Name had become a joke.

Inner samadhi should not become a joke. If all of you were to pass into samadhi during swadhyaya, that samadhi would lose its value. So at the time of Tukaram, thousands of people began to chant or pretend that they had lost control over their tongue. The king thought of a clever device and he issued a royal proclamation saying that on the 16th day of the month, all those singing the divine Name would be hanged. All these devotees threw their malas away and they also wiped off the holy marks from their foreheads. They ran away from there. There was only Tukaram sticking to his guns and chanting *Viththale*.

One finds that during the *Guru Gita* many people fall asleep. It is also seen that there are quite a few people who sleep right until *Guru Gita* time and when they hear the bell for *Guru Gita*, they get up, splash water on their eyes and rush down. And the moment they pick up their books, they pass into samadhi. Shouldn't they feel ashamed of themselves? Why are they here? These people are getting tired only by sitting and eating; it is not because they are working hard, not because they have done anything worthwhile.

Even older people stay awake. It is only younger people to whom the recitation seems to be such a drag. And even if no one were to point it out to you, you should at least have some self-respect and you should feel ashamed of that kind of fake samadhi. One should have a sense of shame, one should at least notice what others are doing, and one should also take note of the attitude of people who are much older in age.

However, I agree that as a result of swadhyaya one gets intoxicated; and that intoxication is bound to come; there is no method to conquer it. Swadhyaya is a form of tapasya and you should all keep alert and wakeful as far as possible. If during swadhyaya you insult it, then in course of time swadhyaya will make you deluded. What happens to people who only make a pretense of devotion? Would they go to heaven or hell? Bad actions will bear corresponding fruit, and even if he is a yogi, how can he escape? There were many such pretenders around my Guru. Finally many of them became mental cases and quite a few became so disturbed that even begging could not help them. You should be continually aware of the fact that it is only the fruits of your karma which you are eating. It is not I who am going to award the fruits of your actions to you; it is your own inner Self who will give the fruits of your actions to you.

So if a certain devotional intoxication comes, that is all right. And if you have risen above the senses, nothing can be done about it. About two years ago there was a person here who had mastered the art of passing into samadhi right at the time of *Gita*; every day he would be found going into samadhi right at that time. That was creating a problem for everyone, so one day I happened to say, "Look, he is a fake character, he is a pretender, he is just pretending to be in samadhi," and the moment he heard this, he flared up. The next day I showed him my stick telling him that he was only making a pretense of meditation to avoid the *Gita*, and he left.

If you pass into a genuine state of devotional frenzy, that can not be controlled.

GLOSSARY

Adharma: unrighteousness, dereliction of duty (see dharma).
Ajapa japa: automatic repetition of the mantra from within.
Ajna chakra: two-petalled lotus between the eyebrows; the seat of the Guru.
Akasha: subtle inner space.
Alandi: place of Jnaneshwar Maharaj's samadhi shrine.
Allopathy: Western medicine.
Amma: mother; also the name of one of Baba's foremost disciples living at the Ashram for the past 13 years.
Antahkarana: literally the "inner psychic instrument"; in yogic thought it has four parts: manas (thinking mind); chitta (subconscious); ahankara (ego); buddhi (intellect).
Arati: waving of lights and/or fragrant incense to an idol or a saint; a ritual of worship.
Arjuna: a great warrior, the disciple of Lord Krishna. The teachings given by Lord Krishna to Arjuna constitute the Bhagavad Gita (see Bhagavad Gita).
Asana: posture; seat; exercise.
Ashram: the abode of a Guru or saint; a spiritual community similar to a monastery.
Atman: soul; inner Self.
Avadhoot: a great mystic-renunciate who has risen above body-consciousness, all duality and conventional standards.
Avatar: God in human form; one perfect from birth.
Avidya: ignorance.
Ayurveda: the ancient Indian science of medicine and surgery.
Baba: term of affection for a saint or a father.
Bandha: a Hatha Yoga practice; a muscular lock.
Bhagavad Gita: the most important Hindu scripture, a portion of the Mahabharata in which Lord Krishna instructs Arjuna in the secrets of God, universe and Self, and of the different forms of Yoga.
Bhagavat: see Shrimad Bhagavat Purana.
Bhakta: a devotee; a follower of the path of love.
Bhakti: devotion and love for God.
Bhastrika: a breathing exercise; form of pranayama.
Bhrikuti: place between the eyebrows.

Black light: see four bodies.

Blue light: see four bodies.

Blue Pearl: (neel bindu); the abode of the inner Self, a vision of which comes in the higher stages of meditation.

Blue Person: exists within the Blue Pearl; He is the Lord who grants the final beatific vision.

Brahmajnani: literally a "knower of Brahman"; a realised soul.

Brahman: the Absolute.

Brahmin: priest (see caste).

Buddha: Siddhartha or Gautama, the founder of Buddhism. He lived in Northern India in the 15th century B.C.

Caste: ancient Indian society was organised into four varnas, divisions or castes for efficient performance of various functions: Brahmins (scholars, priests and preceptors), Kshatriyas (rulers and warriors), Vaishyas (business and agricultural classes), Shudras (menial workers). Later, caste degenerated into hereditary privileges, social snobbery and exploitation. Modern India is doing her best to get rid of this stigma.

Causal body: see four bodies.

Chakra: a subtle centre of energy in the body.

Chandraloka: the subtle world of the moon.

Chapati: a kind of thin pancake made from wheat flour; Indian bread.

Chiti: Chitshakti; Kundalini; Mahamaya; Parashakti; Shakti; divine conscious energy; dynamic aspect of Godhead; referred to as a goddess.

Chitshakti Vilas: literally, "the play of consciousness"; Baba's spiritual autobiography, also published under the title Guru and Play of Consciousness in the United States.

Darshan: seeing a saint or a sacred idol, which bestows blessings.

Desai: Gopal Desai, General Secretary of Shree Gurudev Ashram.

Dharma: righteousness; duty; morality; religion.

Dhyan: meditation.

Dronacharya: the archer, teacher of both the Pandavas and the Kauravas in the Mahabharata; finally took the side of the Kauravas.

Durga: a name of the Divine Mother meaning "hard to conquer". She is a fighting goddess holding weapons in Her several hands and riding a lion.

Duryodhana: eldest son of Dhritarashtra in the Mahabharata and leader of the Kauravas against the Pandavas.

Ego: (ahankara) the factor of individuation; the consciousness of separation; (yoga's goal is to destroy the ego-sense).

Eklavya: a tribal boy who, on being rejected by the great royal teacher Dronacharya for being of low caste, mastered the skill of archery by practising before a clay image of Dronacharya with deep devotion and dedication. He surpassed even the best princely students, including Arjuna. He is cited as an example of an ideal disciple. His story occurs in the Mahabharata.

Eknath Maharaj: a great 16th century poet-saint of Maharashtra. He combined perfect spirituality with life as a householder.

Eknathi Bhagavat: Eknath's commentary on the 11th chapter of the Shrimad Bhagavat Purana.

Four Bodies: the four bodies are contained in the physical body. There is the physical body, the subtle body, the causal body and the supracausal. The four bodies correspond to the four states: when one is awake he is in the physical body; during dreams he is in the subtle body; during deep sleep he is in the causal body, and during meditation he is in the supracausal body. They also correspond to the four lights seen in meditation: red light—physical body; white light—subtle body; black light—causal body; blue light—supracausal body.

Four states: the four states of consciousness: waking (jagrat), dream (swapna), deep sleep (sushupti), and transcendental (turiya).

Fourth state: the turiya state, beyond waking, dream and deep sleep; the transcendental state (see also turiya).

Gita: see Bhagavad Gita.

God-realisation: the final goal of yoga. The realisation that "God dwells within you as you"; enlightenment.

Gopala: the young Lord Krishna.

Gross body: see four bodies.

Gunas: the three basic qualities of nature: sattva—light, balance, harmony, purity; rajas—activity, passion; tamas—inertia, ignorance, darkness.

Guru: a spiritual Master who has attained oneness with God and who leads his disciples from darkness to light, from bondage to liberation. He is God in a human form. His physical body is not a mere material form, but is the very light of consciousness. For this reason, its worship is the same as the worship of God. To a disciple there is nothing more sacred than it. The Guru's feet are especially holy as they send out divine vibrations. By touching them a disciple feels supremely blessed.

Gurubhava: love for the Guru; identification with the Guru.

Guru Gita: a Sanskrit text chanted each morning at the Ashram. It is found in the Skanda Purana, and in it Lord Shiva expounds the mysteries of the Sadguru to his consort Parvati.

Gurukrupa: Guru's grace.

Guru Om: a mantra for meditation on the Guru.

Guru paduka: the sandals worn or once worn by the Guru; worship is performed to them, and they are objects of the highest veneration.

Guruseva: service to the Guru.

Hare Rama Hare Krishna: a powerful mantra used in the week-long, 24-hours-a-day chanting at the Ashram during festivals.

Hari: a name of Lord Vishnu meaning, "The one who removes miseries and sorrows and delivers one from sins."

Hari Om: a mantra of Lord Hari.

Hatha Yoga: a yogic discipline which involves gaining a mastery over the body and its functions through postures, breathing exercises and other means.

Heart chakra, heart lotus: the fourth or anahat chakra; seat of love and the emotions.

Heena: an Indian perfume (favoured by Baba).

Hinduism: the Vedic religion of India. It is based on the direct revelations of ancient seers.

Illusion: maya; the veil of ignorance.

Impersonal aspect: see nirguna.

Initiation: acceptance of a disciple by the Guru usually by transmitting a mantra; the awakening of the disciple by Shaktipat diksha.

Inner universe: the subtle interior realms which can be seen in meditation.

Japa: repetition of a divine Name or mantra.

Jnaneshwar Maharaj: a great saint of Maharashtra (13th century) whose brilliant commentary on the Gita, written before he was twenty, Jnaneshwari, is one of Baba's favourite books.

Jnana: knowledge.

Jnani: an enlightened person; a seeker on the path of knowledge.

Jyota se jyota: an Ashram chant which asks the Guru to light the disciple's lamp of knowledge from his own.

Kabir: a great poet-saint of medieval India.

Kailas: Mount Kailas, a mountain in the Himalayas of Tibet; the abode of Shiva.

Kalas: attributes; also the golden dome on the Ashram.

Kali Yuga: the present age; the age of moral and spiritual decadence.

Kannada: a language of south India, Baba's native tongue.

Karma: action, force or effect of one's accumulated past actions.

Karma Yoga: selfless action performed as service to the Lord.

Khir: an Indian sweet, made usually from milk, sugar and rice, drunk hot.

King Janaka: the king of Videha who appears in the Ramayana and the Mahabharata. He is the father of Sita and a fully enlightened sage as well as a powerful king.

Krishna: the central figure in the Indian epic, the Mahabharata, of which the Bhagavad Gita forms one chapter. He is considered the most complete incarnation of God; the Lord who attracts irresistibly.

Kriyas: yogic movements or processes.

Kum-kum: coloured powder used in putting auspicious mark on forehead; made from turmeric.

Kundalini Yoga: the yoga which attempts to awaken the latent serpent power.

Laddu: an Indian sweet in the shape of a ball.

Lila: play or sport.

Lingam, Shivalingam: oval-shaped symbol of Lord Shiva, made of stone, metal or clay.

Lotus feet: the feet of the Guru or the Lord; the highest objects of worship and refuge.

Lotus posture: padmasana; the ideal posture for meditation.

Lungi: common dress for men in India; cloth worn tied at the waist, resembling a long skirt.

Mahabharata: the Hindu epic, in which Lord Krishna is the main figure and from which the Bhagavad Gita comes.

Maharashtra: a state in west India in which the Ashram is located; it has been the home of many great saints.

Mahasamadhi: literally "the great samadhi"—a yogi's conscious exit from the body at death.

Maha Yoga: see Siddha Yoga.

Majanu: hero of a story who fell in love with the Princess Laila, and whose love and devotion for her became legendary.

Mala: a string of beads used for japa.

Malpura: a sweet fried pancake.

Mantra: sacred words or sounds invested with the power to transform the individual who repeats them: Name of God.

Mantra Yoga: the form of yoga that uses the repetition of mantras (japa) as its means.

Mind: see antahkarana.

Moksha: liberation, freedom from ego-sense; the goal of yoga (see also God-realisation).

Mudra: a pose, posture, gesture.

Nada: divine inner music or sound.

Nirguna: without attributes; the formless aspect of God (see also saguna).

Nirvikalpa, Nirvikalpa Samadhi: mentation-free samadhi.

Ojas: strength; the sexual fluid is converted into ojas in the course of yoga when continence is practised.

Om: the primal sound; the Word from which the entire cosmos emanates. It encompasses all sounds, words and languages, all things and all creatures. It is the innermost essence of all mantras.

Om namah Shivaya: a mantra meaning, "Om, I bow to Shiva."

Pandharpur: a sacred place of pilgrimage in Maharashtra State with a famous image of Lord Viththal.

Patanjali: a great yogi of the 5th century B.C.; the author of the Yogasutras, the classical work on the eight-fold yoga.

Pitruloka: the world of ancestors.

Prana: the vital force of the body and the universe which makes everything move.

Pranayama: control of prana; breathing exercise.

Prarabdha: accumulated past karma which determines the present birth.

Prasad: food that has been offered to God or the Guru and is then distributed to the devotees, sanctified; a gift from the Guru.

Puranas: mythological and historical stories; part of the Hindu scriptures.

Purusha: person; the Lord.

Rajas: the guna of activity (see also gunas).

Rama: an incarnation of God; the central character in the Indian epic the Ramayana; the Supreme Lord who pervades all beings and all things within and without.

Ramakrishna Paramahansa: a great saint of Bengal (died 1886), the Guru of Swami Vivekananda.

Ramayana: see Rama.

Raslila: the mystical play of Krishna with the Gopis (milkmaids) of Vrindavan; the external dance or love-sport of the Lord with individual souls.

Ravana: the chief enemy of Rama in the Ramayana.

Red light: see four bodies.

Rudra: the destructive aspect of Lord Shiva.

Rudraksha beads: prayer beads made from seeds of a tree sacred to Lord Shiva.

Sadguru: the true Guru (see also Guru).

Sadgurunath Maharaj-ki Jaya: victory to the Sadguru.

Sadhaka: seeker.

Sadhana: spiritual discipline.

Sadhu: an ascetic.

Saffron light: a golden halo mingled with saffron that surrounds the Blue Pearl.

Saguna: having attributes; the personal aspect of God (see also nirguna).

Sahasrar: the thousand-petalled lotus in the brain, located at the crown of the head; the seat of Shiva.

Sai Baba: the great saint of Shirdi in Maharashtra (died 1918). He is very well-known and revered in India.

Samadhi: a state of meditative union with the Absolute.

Samsara: the world of change, mutability and death; the world of becoming.

Samskaras: past impressions.

Samyama: the three-fold technique of inner yoga, comprising dharana, dhyan and samadhi, by means of which the innermost nature of anything can be directly perceived, or the direct knowledge of the universe gained.

Sannyasa: formal vow of renunciation.

Sannyasi: a swami or monk; one who has taken formal vows of renunciation.

Satsang: a meeting of devotees to hear scriptures, chant or sit in the presence of the Guru; the company of saints and devotees.

Sattva: the guna of purity (see gunas).

Seera: an Indian pudding made of wheat, ghee and sugar; like a thicker sweeter breakfast cereal.

Seminal fluid: the power in the semen that is used in yoga for spiritual purposes; for this reason continence is helpful for yoga.

72,000 nerves: the network of subtle nerves or nadis which serves as a channel for the flow of prana.

Shakti: force, energy; the divine or cosmic energy which projects, maintains and dissolves the universe; Chiti Kundalini, Kundalini, Chiti; spouse of Shiva.

Shaktipat: transmission of spiritual power (Shakti) from Guru to disciple; spiritual awakening by grace.

Shiva: the Supreme Lord who is transcendent as well as immanent; one of the Hindu trinity, representing God as the destroyer.

Shivalingam: see lingam.

Shiva Mahimna Stotra: a Sanskrit hymn honouring Shiva, that is chanted nightly at the Ashram.

Shivaratri: night sacred to Lord Shiva.

Shivasutras: a text Lord Shiva Himself gave to the sage Vasuguptacharya to perpetuate the non-dual philosophy. Baba is very fond of the Sutras and has been writing commentaries on them.

Shivo'ham; Shivah-aham: I am Shiva. A mantra.

Shrimad Bhagavat Purana: a Hindu scripture containing the life of Lord Krishna and the famous story of the Gopis.

Shrikhand: a much-loved Indian sweet resembling a thick, sweet yoghurt.

Siddha: perfected one; one who has attained oneness with God.

Siddhasan: the perfect posture: a type of posture good for meditation.

Siddhaloka: the world of the Siddhas. An actual world like our world, though more subtle and entirely different in character.

Siddha Yoga, Siddha Mahayoga: the yoga which is received by the grace of a Siddha, a perfectly realised Master. It is called 'Maha', great, because it includes all other forms of yoga—devotion, knowledge, action, mantra, posture and respiratory movements. As the Guru's grace begins to work within a disciple, all these forms of yoga are unfolded within him spontaneously.

Siddhis: supernatural powers.

So'ham: a mantra: sah (That) plus aham (I), "That am I."

Subtle body: see four bodies.

Sushumna: the central and the most important of all the 72,000 nerve channels. It extends from the base chakra to the sahasrar, containing the different chakras. When the prana constantly flows through it one becomes enlightened.

Swadharma: the personal dharma or duty of an individual, the law of one's own nature.

Swadhyaya: study of Self; specifically, study of scriptures; chanting; repetition of a divine Name.

Swarga: heaven.

Tali: a metal plate.

Tamas: the guna of darkness (see gunas).

Tamboura: a stringed instrument.

Tandra, Tandraloka: the state of high consciousness, only a little beyond that of sleep, in which one sees invisible things and comprehends incomprehensible mysteries.

Tantra: the esoteric, gnostic teachings of Hinduism and Buddhism that bring great powers and finally God-realisation.

Tapasya: penance; austere or ascetic practice; prolonged self-denial or self-mortification; spiritual endeavour.

Third body: see four bodies.

Tonga: two-wheeled horse-drawn carriage.

Turiya: the fourth state, beyond waking, dream and deep sleep, the transcendental state; also called Turya.

Upanishads: literally "sitting near"; the knowledge transmitted by the great ancient seers to their disciples sitting near them. This knowledge is contained in works called Upanishads which form the end portion of the Vedas.

Vaikuntha: the abode of Lord Vishnu.

Vedanta: non-dual philosophy of the Upanishads.

Vedas: the basic revealed scriptures of the Hindus, four in number: the Rig, Sama, Yajur and Atharva Vedas.

Veena: stringed instrument.

Venkappa: one of Baba's oldest devotees, living at the Ashram.

Vibhuti: sacred ash permeated by mantras which is worn on the forehead and the body by Lord Shiva and his devotees.

Vishnu: the Supreme Lord; one of the Hindu trinity, representing God as the sustainer.

Waking state: see four states.

White light: see four bodies.

Witness-consciousness: remaining an uninvolved witness of

events; the Supreme Shiva who witnesses the play of the universe but is unmoved.

Yajna: ritualistic sacrifice; any work done in the spirit of surrender to the Lord.

Yama: the god of death.

Yoga: union with God or the inner Self; a method of achieving this union; integration of personality; severance of contact with suffering; the attainment of everlasting bliss.

Yogasutras: see Patanjali.

Yoga Vasishtha: a great work of non-dual philosophy in which seer Vasishtha, a son of the Creator, instructs Lord Rama.

INDEX

Ahalya Bai 59
Airavat 158
Ajapa japa 44, 227
Ajna chakra 57
Akbar 107
Alandi 33, 352
Amma 21, 57, 68, 96, 100
Anger 53, 106, 181, 206, 214
Animals 224
Antahkarana 29, 265
Anxiety 176
Arati 72, 100, 198
Arjuna 29, 36, 80, 112, 152, 169, 170, 214, 358
Asanas 72, 105, 299, 321
Ashram 5, 6, 7, 8, 15, 22, 25, 26, 27, 37, 39, 49, 70, 100, 106, 167, 171, 219, 222, 262, 279, 294, 298, 349, 355, 357
Attachment 93
Austerities (see also tapasya) 29
Avidya 267
Ayurveda 120, 291
Bahinabai 103, 271, 342
Bali 4, 11
Bandha 187
Bathing 185
Begging 10, 11, 269
Bhagavad Gita 2, 21, 29, 43, 112, 152, 162, 170, 182, 187, 242, 265, 309, 358
Bharadwaj 240
Bharat 4
Bhartruhari 277
Bhastrika 72, 144
Bhima 257
Bhrikuti 58
Blame 62
Blue light 24, 330
Blue Pearl 24, 116, 129, 142, 158, 163, 314
Body 16, 105, 263, 264, 281
Brahmadeva 121
Brahman 194
Brahmin 10
Breakfast 37
Buddha 62
Calesthenics 299
Cancer 263
Celibacy 39, 60, 69, 91, 197
Changdev Pasashthi 157
Changing Gurus 270
Chanting 84, 91, 111, 225, 329, 355, 356, 361
Charak 200, 291
Cheese 37
Children 288
Chinmudra 212
Chitshakti Vilas (Guru) 41, 88, 278, 300, 359
Christians 268
Clothes 83
Concentration 57
Constipation 354
Crowds 4
Dadu 356, 362
Darshan 68
Debt 3, 10, 11

Depression 176
Desai (Gopal) 6, 25, 26, 27, 189, 62
Desai (J.) 233
Desire 20, 21, 138, 156, 250
Destiny 17, 277, 340
Detachment 214
Devaki 140
Devidas 31
Devotion 1, 9, 16, 17, 24, 25, 97, 125, 129, 131, 227, 228, 314, 316, 342, 359
Dhanvantari 354
Dharma 49
Diabetes 263
Diet 96, 187, 200, 212, 217, 250, 343
Diksha 130
Disciple 1, 8, 9, 51, 76, 88, 116, 125, 130, 161, 203, 218
Discipline 5, 7, 8, 49, 168, 188, 222, 232, 262, 270, 288, 334
Discrimination 11, 43, 105
Disease 263
Dishonour 61
Divine Name (see chanting, japa, mantra, swadhyaya)
Draupadi 81
Dreams 75, 224, 251
Dronacharya 125
Durga, hymn to 62
Duryodhana 16, 346
Duty 3, 18, 24, 25
Ego 36, 115, 142, 181, 347
Ekadasi 23, 31, 77, 96, 283
Eklavya 125
Eknath Maharaj 1, 22, 23, 24, 107, 197, 274
Elephant 158

Epilepsy 263
Evolution 28
Eye sight 20
Faith 9, 293
Fasting 96
Fault-finding 279
Fierceness 203
Formless 24
Four levels of sound 85
Freedom 14, 15, 169
Ganapati 123, 158
Ganesh 158
Ganges 23
Garlic 37, 120
Gas 37, 354
Gentleness 205
Ginger 37
Gita (see Bhagavad Gita)
Gopis 25, 160, 183, 229, 253, 274, 314
Gora 23, 31, 41, 169
Govinda Singh 1
Grace 16, 17, 82, 113, 160
Greed 225
Guru (see also Sadguru) 1, 2, 9, 11, 12, 13, 21, 22, 23, 24, 29-36, 38, 46, 51, 67, 71, 74, 76, 79, 88, 92, 97, 99, 103, 108, 111, 117, 122, 125, 126, 128, 130, 131, 139, 143, 144, 146, 160, 161, 177, 180, 194, 196, 198, 203, 248, 249, 255, 280, 304, 339, 359
Guru (Chitshakti Vilas) 41, 46, 66, 146
Gurubhava 1, 22, 99, 194, 198, 253
Guru-disciple relationship 1, 76, 88, 119, 161, 203, 219, 248, 249, 272, 314, 337

Guru Gita 8, 21, 22, 24, 29, 72, 97, 100, 109, 157, 198, 218, 246, 307, 365
Guru Om 22, 44, 72, 100, 146, 148, 194, 215
Guru's feet 212, 219, 240, 256
Guruseva (see also work) 1, 29, 42, 61, 68, 178
Hanuman 220
Happiness 15, 16
Hardwar 23
Haritaki 354
Hastamalaka 17
Hatha Yoga 110, 238
Heat 213
Hinduism 268
Homosexuality 197
Hypnotism 171
Ice cream 37
Ida 201
Illness 72, 200, 281, 344
Immortality 109
Independence 14, 15
Indra 158
Initiation 17
Inner Guru (voice) 9
Insects 224, 309
Insecurity 14
Insult 61
Janabai 31, 169, 352
Janaka 19, 152, 197, 246, 248
Janardan Swami 22
Japa 9, 19, 20, 44, 91, 102, 142, 173, 227, 241, 263, 329
Jealousy 225
Jesus 210
Jews 40
Jiva 194
Jivanmukta 243

Jnaneshwar Maharaj 2, 17, 32, 154, 157, 170, 181, 187, 218, 308, 352, 358, 360
Jnaneshwari 2
Kabir 17, 44, 62, 78, 122, 156, 161, 166, 169, 175, 218, 226, 256, 362
Kailas 112
Kakabhushandi 240
Kali Yuga 134, 150
Kalyan 221
Kamsa 140
Kanupatra 23, 263
Karma 11, 16, 17, 40, 45, 263, 277, 318, 346
Kashi 23
King Parikshit 134, 150
Knowledge 16, 17, 157, 251, 281, 340, 342, 348
Krishna 16, 29, 36, 80, 99, 140, 152, 183, 210, 229, 242, 346, 358
Krishnasuta 42, 61
Kriyas 53, 66, 100, 104, 120, 122, 145, 146, 173, 182, 289
Kumbhak 145, 170, 182, 309
Kundalini, awakening 13, 14, 44, 53, 75, 121, 123, 128, 144, 173, 238, 250, 332, 333
Kunti 29
Lakshmana 11
Lemon 120
Liberation 67, 128, 271, 275
Love 14, 15, 16, 113, 148, 342
Lust 225
Madhur bhava 25, 26, 27
Madhyama 85
Mahabharata 1, 16, 28, 29, 346, 362
Maha Kali 63

379

Maha Lakshmi 63, 158, 320
Maha Saraswati 63
Mahatma Gandhi 28
Mala (japa) 121, 325
Mansoor Mastana 347
Mantra 44, 54, 63, 72, 94, 102, 103, 114, 130, 142, 145, 146, 148, 159, 161, 174, 175, 211, 214, 227, 289
Massage 191
Meditation 8, 9, 19, 37, 43, 57, 68, 72, 85, 91, 92, 93, 98, 102, 110, 111, 120, 126, 130, 131, 144, 158, 159, 163, 170, 171, 173, 174, 224, 239, 250, 252, 289, 299, 301, 306, 310, 317, 331, 353
Mental worship (manas puja) 256, 271, 296
Milk 37, 120
Mind 29, 30, 86, 106, 113, 177, 178, 187, 190, 192, 251, 258, 291, 313, 343, 350
Mirabai 4, 134, 184, 352
Miracles 326
Modesty 201
Money 319
Moon 331
Mudras 212
Muktabai 352
Music 20, 21
Nada 21, 155
Namdev 30, 41
Nanak Dev 1, 2, 362
Narada 17
Narasimha 204
Navel chakra 238
Nityananda 11, 56, 68, 72, 180, 210, 213, 218, 255, 260, 276, 309, 348, 349, 352

Nivrittinath 218
Nudity 201
Obedience 11, 12, 77, 156
Obstacles 73, 79
Om namah Shivaya 72, 94, 144, 215, 355
Om namo Narayanaya 94
One-pointed devotion 97, 206, 359
Onions 37, 120
Pain 43, 173, 191, 264
Panchabhavas 99
Pandavas 257
Pandharpur 30, 169, 283, 362
Para 85
Parents 3, 4, 14, 15, 18
Pashyanti 85
Patanjali 259
Personal chores 83
Pilgrimages 22, 23
Pingala 201
Pleasure 20, 264
Posture 37
Prahlada 4, 204
Praise 62, 115
Prana 17, 18, 128
Pranayama 17, 18, 72, 287
Prarabdha 17, 45
Prasad 68
Pratyabhijnahridayam 191
Prayer 174, 176
Prayer, to Guru 79, 160
Pride 41
Punishment 205
Purification 226, 239
Purunderdas 247
Rama 4, 11, 134, 152, 164, 220
Ramakrishna 99, 148

Ramananda 161
Ramayana 240
Ram Tirth 17, 21, 114, 264
Raslila 229
Reading 140
Reason 43, 147
Reincarnation 40
Renunciation 10, 11, 186
Rest 213
Reward 205
Rice 45
Rituals 72, 131, 134, 212, 271, 289
Rudra 203
Rudraksha 59, 65, 325
Sacred thread 328
Sadguru (see also Guru) 8, 24, 113, 239, 243, 246
Sadhana 55, 108, 112, 166, 223, 232, 275, 279
Sahasrar 45, 57, 155
Saints 31, 68, 181, 276, 351
Samadhi 8, 110, 164, 193, 365
Samartha Ramdas 221, 285, 340
Sandhya 201
Sanskrit 21
Sannyas 104, 363
Saptah 133, 353, 355
Satchidananda Saraswati 14
Satsang 68, 352
Sat Yuga 150
Satyaloka 258
Sauta 23, 31, 169
Science of the Soul 66
Seeker 9, 186, 279
Self-control 28, 138, 214, 350
Self-deception 240
Self-effort 16, 152, 220, 351

Self-restraint 28, 232
Semen (seminal fluid) 39, 45, 69, 91, 197, 237, 334
Sena 23, 31, 169
Sense pleasures 20, 21
Sex 164, 301
Shakti 9, 20, 45, 63, 86, 104, 108, 145, 182, 185, 206, 217, 283
Shaktipat 20, 45, 75, 108, 122, 129, 217
Shaligram 59
Shankaracharya 17
Shanmukhi mudra 287
Sheshnag 208
Shiva 19, 242, 244
Shivaji 221
Shivalingam 34, 58, 258
Shiva Mahimna Stotra 101
Shivaratri 100
Shivasutras 43
Shrikhand 23
Shrimad Bhagavat Purana 49, 140, 161, 169, 229
Shuka 137, 197, 246
Siddha 23, 75, 103, 122, 125, 334
Siddhaloka 75, 123
Sita 11
Sleep 54, 57, 224, 291
Snoring 56
Society 24, 25, 27, 28, 268
So'ham 102, 194, 229
Solitude 167
Speech-4 levels 85
Spiritual practices (see also sadhana) 3, 27, 28, 97, 196
Sri Ramakrishna, Gospel of 99
Sthita prajna 244
Suffering 28, 29, 59, 65

Sugar 37, 45
Sunderdas 36, 107
Surrender 71, 79, 93, 105, 131, 152, 160, 193, 206, 248, 315, 316
Surdas 352
Sushumna 56, 201, 250
Swadhyaya 8, 91, 286, 322, 356, 364
Tact 205
Tamas 213
Tandra 8, 43
Tapasya 10, 11, 207, 232, 254, 264
Tests 11, 12, 13, 116
Thought 251
Throat 241
Tratak 287
Tukaram Maharaj 23, 80, 90, 111, 226, 239, 264, 283, 307, 365
Tulsi 65
Tulsidas 4, 17, 229, 349, 361
Turiya 244
Uddhava 197
Understanding 207, 251, 290
Upanishads 86, 169, 179, 182, 344
Urdhvareta 197, 237, 246, 334
Vaikheri 85
Vaikuntha 112, 134
Vairagya 214
Vajreshwari Temple 63, 324

Vasishtha 207
Vasudeva 140
Vedanta 1, 136, 194, 277, 304
Venkappa 15, 143, 233, 262
Vibhishan 4
Viraha 229
Visobha Kechar 33
Vishnu 65, 203
Vishnu Sahasranam 8, 22, 100
Vishvamitra 207
Visions 102
Viththale 90, 365
Vivekananda 17
Vyasa 19, 139

Wankhede S. K. 6
Will 105, 178, 350
Witness-consciousness 10, 138, 236, 251, 312
Wooden sandals 212
Work 11, 205, 275, 292
Worship 46, 131, 256, 271, 292, 308

Yajna 93, 295
Yajnavalkya 152, 248
Yande (Pratap) 6, 327
Yeola 106, 167
Yoga Sutras 259
Yoga Vasishtha 190
Yogi 17, 18
Yudhishthira 16

Zipruanna 180, 218